The *Fort Mackinac* lurched in pr... ...orehouse lost his footing. The sodden deck was treacherous and he fell backwards, his head striking an eye-bolt in the poop-deck as the ship bucked upwards with a sickening jar. Blood flowed across the dark, wet planking and, in an instinctive reflex to help the stricken man, Dunbar let go of the wheel.

Instantly he knew the gravity of his error, for not only was poor Moorehouse dead, but the wheel, no longer subject to the restraint of Dunbar's strength, took charge and spun under the impetus of the rudder below. Although Dunbar was back at his post within three seconds of being seduced by compassion, the *Fort Mackinac* was rapidly slewing to starboard and began to broach-to, falling into the trough of the sea where the weight of the wind once more fell unmercifully upon her beam and pressed her even further over to port.

As she heeled, the deck trembled faintly from a further shift of the cargo below.

Also by Richard Woodman

In the Nathaniel Drinkwater series

AN EYE OF THE FLEET
A KING'S CUTTER
A BRIG OF WAR
THE BOMB VESSEL
THE CORVETTE
1805
BALTIC MISSION
IN DISTANT WATERS
A PRIVATE REVENGE
UNDER FALSE COLOURS
THE FLYING SQUADRON
BENEATH THE AURORA
THE SHADOW OF THE EAGLE
EBB TIDE

WAGER
ENDANGERED SPECIES
THE DARKENING SEA
WATERFRONT

UNDER SAIL

Richard Woodman

WARNER BOOKS

A *Warner* Book

First published in Great Britain in 1998
by Little, Brown and Company
This edition published by Warner Books in 1999

A CIP catalogue record for this book
is available from the British Library.

ISBN 0 7515 1646 5

Typeset by Palimpsest Book Production Limited,
Polmont, Stirlingshire
Printed and bound in Great Britain by
Mackays of Chatham plc, Chatham, Kent

Warner Books
A Division of
Little, Brown and Company (UK)
Brettenham House
Lancaster Place
London WC2E 7EN

UNDER SAIL

PART ONE

Home Waters

Suffolk, London and Tyneside, 1908

CHAPTER ONE

The Alien

'Damnation!'

The first large raindrops fell on the stretched paper and blotched the drying wash. James Dunbar glared at the painting for a moment. His seaman's instinct had been suppressed by his concentration on the view before him and his despairing attempt to fix it on the sheet of paper. He gave one final irritated glare at the landscape.

From the top of the low hill the ground fell away into a wide, shallow valley. The River Clay wound through this, unseen beneath the canopy of trees until, half a mile to the eastward where the landscape changed abruptly, it emerged into a wild, bleak delta of tidal saltings. Beyond the salt-marsh huddled the clapboard hamlet of Clayton Wick, an uncertain cluster of fishermen's dwellings, erected rather than built upon the shingle strand that briefly confined the river between black staithings, before releasing it into the sea.

Clayton Wick, with its small fleet of fishing smacks, was Dunbar's first spiritual home, and he was momentarily distracted by the masts of two smacks, which were etched black against the gleam of the North Sea beyond.

His actual home, the village of Clayton Dobbs, lay

3

below him. The square, grey stone tower of the parish church, of which his father was rector, rose conspicuously from the trees, whose leaves were already turning red-gold at the fall of the year. Most spectacular were the twin lines of chestnuts marking the avenue up to Clayton Hall. The tiled portion of the hall showed a deeper red where the roof was partly visible, if you knew where to look.

The raindrops were now drumming on his stretched paper and he looked down as his watercolour dissolved. Then his easel, with its burden of the board, blew over in a sudden gust of wind. Dunbar swore again and looked round; behind him the countryside was blotted out by the advancing squall, which spread a grey curtain down from a dark and roiling cloud. Hurriedly he packed away his paints and easel. His work was despicable and the rain had saved him the trouble of destroying it himself. The attempted landscape was abandoned. Gathering up his kit he took to his heels, just as the wind-lashed downpour began in earnest.

By the time he reached the unmetalled road he was cursing his distraction. Had he not been so engrossed in his painting, he would have noticed the abrupt chill in the air and the first stirrings of the wind that was already gusting strongly. Ahead of him the sky was still clear. It was almost as if the landscape had mocked his inability to capture it on his heavy cartridge paper, and the weather was now chastising him for his presumption.

By the gate where the cattle habitually waited to be called in for milking, the muddy hoofprints were already full of water and the rain had quickly turned the area into a slippery mire. Fortunately there were no cattle about, but he slithered precariously, burdened as he was with paintbox, easel and board. Struggling through the gate, he scraped the worst of the mud off his boots on the tussocky grass lining the track that ran between

4

Clayton Hall and Home Farm. The rain hissed down with a malevolence to which he resigned himself; he was going to get soaked. Tucking his gear under both arms, he hunched his shoulders and trudged off towards the rectory. Metaphorically and literally, the day was a complete wash-out.

'Or perhaps I am,' he muttered bitterly, thinking of the disastrous failure digging into his right armpit. He had been seduced into attempting landscapes by a brief success down at Clayton Wick. It had been beginner's luck, of course. The steely washes of the sea and the gleaming mud of half-tide had spread across the paper from the heavy sable brush with a deceptive ease. He had laid the sky down with little trouble, receiving as his reward that quickening of feeling which he had found so addictive in Mexico and had enjoyed several times since.

With a drier brush, the firm, dark tones of the smacks' hulls, the slate-grey of their topsides and the black gun-wales went on as though from a practised hand. So too did the lighter strokes delineating masts and topmasts, and the fine down-swipes of halliard and stay. The curls of purple-shadowed burnt sienna showed along the booms where the furled mainsails lay, with a squiggle forward to show the collapsed and idle jibs. It had all been too damned easy. And unrepeatable, as the evidence under his arm testified, even before the weather decided to put in its own modifications. So preoccupied was Dunbar with these morose and dispiriting thoughts, and such was the sibilant, wind-driven noise of the rain and the tossing of the hedgerows, that he did not hear the approach of the trap, even though the horse came on at a smart canter and its hooves struck the flints embedded in the track. It was upon him with a rush; he turned with a start, the rain lashing his face, and the board with the despoiled painting slipped from under his arm and fell in the mud.

He bent to retrieve it while the snorting bay pawed the air and glared down at him, its great bony forehead vertical as it fought the tug of rein on bit, the whites of its eyes indignant at his presence in the centre of the track. He drew awkwardly aside, saw the ripple of the reins and heard a woman's voice shout 'Yup!' The bay threw up its head, struck a spark from a flint and the trap jerked forward.

A yellow and black wheel spun past. He blew the rain from his nose, blinked and looked up at the driver. Under her tied-down hat the woman was as wet as himself. As the trap accelerated past him their eyes met and he recognised her at once.

'Damnation!'

For a moment he stood stock-still in the road looking after the wobbling trap, then he saw it stop and the young woman turned to look back.

'Is that you, Mr Dunbar?'

'Yes,' he called back, unmoving and suddenly encumbered by all his silly artistic lumber.

'Well, come on then, hurry up!'

He walked forward, opened the little door in the trap's rear and threw his gear in, scrambling after it to seat himself opposite her as she whipped up the bay again.

'I didn't recognise you,' she said, turning towards him. 'I had heard you were in London, taking examinations or something.'

She watched the road again and her elegant profile stood out against the blur of the hedge behind. She was dressed in a dark grey habit, with cream silk at her throat and a hat held down by a black ribbon. The wide, down-turned brim channelled rain like a gutter down her back but failed to conceal the rich profusion of her auburn hair.

'I've been back a few days,' Dunbar said, 'I'm waiting for my examination results.'

'Oh,' she said, turning and looking at him with a smile. 'What on earth are you doing out in this weather? Is that a picture?'

He looked at the messy blotches on the drawing board beside him. 'It was an attempt at a landscape,' he said ruefully, 'but it wasn't very good, even before the rain had a go at it.'

She cocked her head on one side, looking critically at the ruined painting, and pulled the corners of her mouth down. 'I don't know; it might pass muster as a master-work by a Fauve.'

'Might it,' Dunbar said. 'I'm afraid I don't know much about art as such.' He felt slightly at a loss at this admission. He wanted to ask what a Fauve was, but felt inhibited. Julia Ravenham might be said to have little to her name beyond her looks, but the fact that she was Colonel Scrope-Davies's niece set her higher in the world than James Dunbar, son of a rather down-at-heel rector, and a merchant seaman to boot. He rather wished she had left him fulminating in her wake; it would have better suited his dismal mood of failure. His present circumstance of being beholden to her for this lift was irksome enough, without the added annoyance of being patronised by the cool and confident young woman and exposed as an ignoramus.

'But I hear you can paint,' she said, looking directly at him again. She had a beautiful face and he felt the prickle of attraction stir in him.

'How the dickens did you know that I daubed?'

'Oh,' Julia said off-handedly, 'Jenny told me . . .'

'Ah . . .' He nodded, 'She would.'

He thought for a moment of Jenny Broom, who had for years lived in the rectory as housekeeper and maid to the Reverend and Mrs Dunbar and their family of three sons. Jenny had been the first focus of Dunbar's adolescent lust and, on his return from his first voyage to sea, had frustrated him by marrying Alfred Slater, bachelor of his father's parish, that of St Nicholas, Clayton Dobbs in the County of Suffolk. Her departure, though only for the purposes of cooking Slater his meals and sleeping with him in his cottage, had seemed like a desertion, even though Dunbar himself no longer quite regarded the rectory as home.

The rain and wind buffeted the trap, adding to the jolting of the unmade road, discouraging conversation. They were descending into the village and had passed into the shelter of the trees before she turned again, looking at him curiously.

'D'you remember coming to dinner? Years ago . . . You had just completed your first voyage to sea, I think. I remember,' she added smiling, 'you were brick-red and the colonel called you a *rooinek*.'

'I remember that,' he replied, smiling. The colonel's remark had seemed disparaging at the time.

'You were annoyed.'

'How on earth did you know?' he asked in astonishment. 'Did I show it?'

'Oh yes. I remember that very well. But I think you were wrong. The colonel was being wistful, not harsh. He was thinking of Hugh. I dare say you reminded him of Hugh.'

Dunbar recalled the colonel's son, Hugh Scrope-Davies, who had died in South Africa at the age of twenty-two as a subaltern. He had been leading his men across the Tugela River to engage the Boers on the far side. The assault had been a disaster and now he was another dead hero commemorated in wall-mounted marble in St Nicholas's Church. 'I never thought of that,' Dunbar confessed. 'How selfish of me.'

He found her looking at him again, a cool, appraising look, and he felt awkward under her scrutiny.

'That was a long time ago,' he said to terminate the

silence as the trap curved round towards the church and splashed through a large puddle, lurching as it did so.

'And you've been all over the world since then.' It was part statement, part question.

He nodded, possessed of a sudden desire to tell her things about himself, but the candid intimacy of the ride was almost over and the church swung into sight, with the rectory beyond.

'And what have you done in the interim?' he asked suddenly as she gathered up the reins to halt the bay.

Without turning her head, she pulled the corners of her mouth down. 'Not very much . . .'

He sensed an evasion. 'Well, I know you haven't been here in Clayton all the time.'

'No . . .'

'Where then?' he persisted as the trap drew to a standstill and the rain fell from the leaves of the overhanging chestnuts as they swayed and soughed in the gale.

She shrugged and turned towards him. 'Oh, London for the most part,' she said, waiting for him to dismount. He was suddenly pained by the air of dismissal and jumped to the ground, taking his easel, paintbox and board with him.

'Well, thank you for the ride,' he said, looking up at her, trying to gauge her attitude.

'Bye,' she said abruptly and flicked the reins along the bay's steaming flanks with a sharp 'Yup!'

He watched her go with that small, sad regret that is sometimes the beginning of love.

Dunbar spent the next two days mooning morosely about the village, driven from the rectory by his own restlessness, unable to pick up either pencil or paints after the failure of his landscape and, though he did not acknowledge it, the distraction of meeting Julia Ravenham again.

The weather continued blustery and in tune with his own mood. The gale abated, then renewed itself with a vicious, sudden fury that stripped the glory of autumn from the tall chestnuts, swiftly reducing the rich foliage to a mulch and drifting it up against hedgerows and fences. The countryside was abruptly changed and wintry vistas opened up, where only a few days earlier there had been thick and ruddy vegetation.

'Blustery ole day, Master James,' remarked an elderly man leading a pair of heavy draft-horses into the smithy yard, just as Dunbar was passing. He could not recall the villager's name, but agreed. 'They ole 'daws doan like it, neither,' added the man, nodding up at the church tower where half a dozen cawing jackdaws flapped against the gale.

The old man swung the horses round and grinned toothlessly. 'Bet you'm glad you ain't at sea then.'

'Yes.' Dunbar smiled back, staring for a moment at the steaming horses and the interior of the smithy, from which Jaybez Elson emerged wearing his leather apron. The smith nodded at the old man and Dunbar, before smacking the nearer horse on the flank and running his broad, stub-fingered hand down the hind leg until the horse lifted his hoof and both blacksmith and customer turned their attention to the job in hand.

Dunbar walked on, trying to remember the old man's name. His progress was aimless. He thought of walking the two miles to Clayton Wick, but the road round the salt-marsh was tedious and exposed in this weather, and there was rain on the wind again. He dismissed the idea; the smacks lying alongside the rudimentary quay would only disturb him. The desire to be back at sea, always running strong in him when he had to live under his father's roof, was not as uncomplicated as it had been. Julia Ravenham had seen to that.

Yet he could scarcely walk up to the Hall and ask to see

her. The sooner he was out of the village and back where he belonged, the better. Besides he had plans, and he had yet to broach the matter with his father, with whom he guessed the idea would find no favour. It all hinged upon whether or not he had passed his examination. He decided it was better to hold his peace until he knew for certain.

Making up his mind, he swung abruptly aside and crossed the road to the post office, entering it amid the tinkle of the bell and the first swirl of rain.

'Mornin' Master James,' the post-mistress's bright eyes peeped at him over her half-moon glasses. Mrs Coxford's vivacity was the last remnant of her youthful attraction. Her first husband had followed the squire's son Hugh into the Tugela River, where the Boers had coiled barbed-wire obstructions. Ensnared, the dismounted yeomanry had been picked off by enemy marksmen with their German Mausers. The widow had mourned for several years before marrying an older widower, John Coxford, who missed a woman's help about his home and business. She now ran the post office with energetic enthusiasm.

'I know you're waiting for a letter, but I'm afraid,' she shook her head in a smiling gesture of shared and sympathetic regret, 'it hasn't arrived. I would have sent it up as soon as it did, you know.'

'Of course, Mrs Coxford, I know you would.'

'Ah, but you're impatient, I understand.'

'It's rather important.' Dunbar hesitated, feeling foolish. 'I'm sorry to have bothered you.'

'It's no bother. There's nothing worse than waiting for news.' A pained, yet somehow small look of unhappiness swept across her face and Dunbar's eye was caught by it. He recalled her bereavement and the air of tragedy that lent something to her face. His abstraction left him momentarily speechless, so that a silence grew between them as she waited for his retreat, feeling his gaze lingering on her.

'Is there something else?'

Mrs Coxford's enquiry was terminated by the intrusive jingle of the door-bell as another customer came in. He shook his head. 'No, thank you. Thanks very much.'

'I'll let you know . . .' and she turned towards her new customer. Dunbar could hardly wait to get home.

The rectory, it seemed to him, had subtly changed since he had come home after his first voyage to sea. He saw it now as an outsider, a different perspective from the intimacy of childhood. So much of that first voyage's experiences in the SS *Kohinoor* had changed him that any reversion to the past was impossible. Yet he had suffered the first agonies and humiliations of adolescent lust and had come close to having his first true sexual encounter under the rectory's hallowed roof. But that unfortunate incident, which had involved Jenny Broom, had now faded in his memory. Dunbar's bruising encounter with unrequited passion and his subsequent initiation into the delights of physical love had taken place in the unlikely surroundings of a Mexican bordello.

In distant Puerto San Martin, a copper port on the bleak shores of the Sea of Cortez, the euphemistically named Hotel Paradiso had given him more than a mere acquaintance with the world of the *demi-monde*. His sincere but fatuous love had been spectacularly repudiated by the beautiful Conchita, and though he had been saved from despair by the tender affection of an older beauty, Señora Dolores Garcia, it had been his encounter with the mysterious owner of the Hotel Paradiso that had unlocked a greater potential in the young *caballero*.

Disfigured, dishonoured and yet the dominatrix of Puerto San Martin, Richenda Hawkshawe sat in her darkened attic and unburdened herself to her young fellow-countryman. As a young woman she had been travelling home from Australia aboard the *Macassar*, a sailing ship in whose lazaretto lay gold from the Ballarat fields. The crew had taken over the vessel and her family had been destroyed in the horrific mutiny. The young Miss Hawkshawe had been spared, but the ordeal of survival had compelled her to endure greater terror and humiliation. All these facts she laid before the hapless and innocent Dunbar.

For James Dunbar, the event was deeply affecting. It was also profoundly catalytic; the strange acquaintance played on his imagination, and in his subconscious response he was transformed from a competent, enthusiastic and amateur dabbler with sketching pencil and watercolours, who had recorded the *cordilleras* of the Magellan Strait and sketches of seabirds and dolphins, to a man with a passionate desire to express the wonder of things through the medium of paint. Yet it was no representation of the horrors of mutiny that inspired him in that moment of self-revelation. Through Richenda Hawkshawe he had become the lover of the brothel's madame. In his portrait of Dolores Garcia, Dunbar had produced something approaching a tiro work of art.

It had thus been deeply depressing to find that he could not revive that spark of creativity in the landscape surrounding Clayton Dobbs. It had been his first attempt at anything more than an idle sketch for some time, such had been the preoccupations of his studies and the pressure of his examinations. But now he hurried home and made straight for his room, avoiding interrogation by his father, whose habit it was to break from sacerdotal studies to enjoy his 'elevenses'.

There had been something undeniable about Mrs Coxford's face and the fall of light upon it, something at once reminiscent of Dolores Garcia, and yet so very different. It had been a long time since Dunbar had felt the urgent, unavoidable prompting of inspiration. He picked

13

up a soft pencil and, before the image had faded utterly, dashed it down, trying to capture the vivid *chiaroscuro* and the slash of light across her glasses. The crude spontaneity of the drawing pleased him and he forbore from over-working it. He propped the sketching block up and contemplated his work. It pleased him sufficiently to give him a twinge of modest satisfaction; perhaps he had not, after all, lost that curious inner quickening that he had found in the darkened upstairs room of the Hotel Paradiso; perhaps it was not entirely attributable to the strong sexual impulse and the erotic relationship he had had with the beautiful Dolores. On the other hand, perhaps it was.

The thought disturbed him. There was no erotic emanation from Mrs Coxford. It had simply been the fall of light and something in her face that, in the dingy post office, had caught his eye with the brilliance of a revealed icon. It was in the nature of such things to catch Dunbar's imagination.

Somewhere in the house a door banged in the wind, and he heard his father's voice. The morning office had been read, the priestly thoughts assembled and an intellectual high water reached; it was time for elevenses. There would be tea in the kitchen, and probably some of Jenny's biscuits. He abandoned his train of thought. The drawing existed and he could leave it for a moment. Hugging his sense of achievement, he ran downstairs to the kitchen.

It was a large, stone-flagged room dominated by an enormous cast-iron range, which gleamed with blacking and rambled along one wall. Pots, pans, skillets, knives, whisks and all the paraphernalia of the culinary art adorned its burnished rails. Along one wall ran a wide, low window, which looked out upon an untidy, formal garden. The kitchen had never quite been Jenny's preserve, for Mrs Dunbar was of a practical, no-nonsense turn

14

of mind, willing to share the household's burdens with her helpmeet. As the rector's wife, Anne Dunbar happily occupied the middle ground of social life, combining a pragmatic outlook with an ability to hold her own in both wings of society. A rare and cheerful woman, she was proud in her own self-contained way. Handsome and energetic, her blonde hair fading to silver, she never meddled in the affairs of others, yet had a happy knack of turning up at the door of a sick parishioner with the very thing the household lacked, whether it was meat or merely sympathy. She was a listener rather than a gossip and received all manner of confidences, most of which she kept to herself, and had thereby earned a measure of respect among the villagers. If people felt the need to comment, they generally contrasted her favourably with her husband.

The Reverend Dunbar was as well-motivated as his wife, but, while he possessed great presence, he lacked her common touch. As a young man he had been moved by ritual, and through the forms of the liturgy had come to a reconciliation of the physical and spiritual, which imbued him thoroughly. He was a large and imposing man, dark of visage, black of hair, and with an assiduously shaved but heavy beard that gave his features a bluish cast. He wore his frock of office with authority, and the simple bronze cross that hung upon his broad chest bespoke a man of plain and candid faith.

His personal struggle, long reconciled, had left him with an intellectual bent and the deep satisfactions of the inner life. He cared passionately about his flock, but he lacked imagination, and his wholehearted faith elevated his opinions to that of the high Tory. He was at once compassionate towards those less favoured than himself and conventional to the point of intransigence. Though he had few faults as a priest and his coldness as a shepherd was more perceived than real, it did not exempt him from a reciprocal suspicion on the part of his parishioners. This suspicion, in turn, fed his sense of remoteness and of being misunderstood. His greatest acts of charity were, in any case, mostly concealed. He had once done the Scrope-Davies family a service and arranged for Hugh's bastard child to be discreetly adopted by a family in Ipswich. The child's young mother he had quietly taken into service in his own home. Jenny Broom's secret was scarcely recollected even by those most closely associated with it. Hugh had paid the supreme sacrifice, and Jenny had earned her respectability through the expiation of hard work. Girls got into trouble; it was in the nature of things. The rector did what he could and in such matters he had the full support of his wife.

Dunbar's parents were not therefore ill-matched, nor did they fail in their combined ministry, for Mrs Dunbar was no less devout than her husband. Both were motivated by a strong sense of duty and both came from families secure amid the minor gentry, whose sense of worth came from the rightness of their opinions more than their fortunes. Firm in their devotion to God, the King and the episcopal structure of the Church of England, the Dunbars knew also that amid the certainties of imperial might there still resided the eternal bedevilments of poverty, ignorance and disease. Both believed, with unshakeable faith, that the gradual improvement of mankind under the banner of Christ was ineluctable; both saw themselves as soldiers of the Redeemer, alongside whose watchwords of faith, hope and charity lay the galvanizing command 'Forward'.

They had three children. James, their first-born, had been followed by twins, David and Michael, whose blond good looks were inevitably considered angelic. Both twins had proved studious and seemed destined for solid careers, probably in the Church herself. But it was James, like his father, always a little wayward, never quite conforming, who had proved the most troublesome of their offspring.

James himself had always felt different, as though he stood slightly to one side of life in and around the rectory and its neighbouring church. Whereas he had inherited his good looks from his father and his quiet self-containment from his mother, his boyish imagination had been fed by a quite different source. It had been nurtured by the great red ensign that hung in his father's church to commemorate an admiral, whose marble memorial nestled on the wall behind its folds. The drapes of the huge flag hung like a torrent of blood from the clerestory. Its scarlet folds seemed to enshroud great events that lay beyond the tranquillity of the church. The paradox of its impropriety within the consecrated walls struck him emotionally long before he understood or questioned it intellectually. In short, it had turned Dunbar's mind towards the sea, and as a boy, following an outbreak of temper from his provoked father, he had run off to join Skipper Hopton's smack the *Eliza Maude*, sailing away into the North Sea without a thought for his parents. He had returned home a week later to a thrashing from his father on account, he was told, of the anxiety he had caused his mother.

In the end his father had reluctantly abandoned his attempt to turn James into a hoplite of Christ. Through the good offices and influence of Colonel Scrope-Davies, Dunbar had been bound apprentice to the South Wales Steam Navigation Company, and in the autumn of 1904 he had joined the SS *Kohinoor*.

On Dunbar's return from his first voyage, his father had not been entirely displeased with his son. There had been jests about the prodigal's return by which, Dunbar suspected with some misgivings, his father hinted at a fall from grace. It was unclear to Dunbar whether this was a measure of his father's apprehension or his father's perception. As for himself, although he had become

17

a sinner, his conscience was untroubled by his affair with the voluptuous Dolores Garcia, though other events surrounding that extraordinary and exhilarating intimacy were far more complex.

For the returning Dunbar, events in Puerto San Martin might well have occurred to another person, except for the lingering dynamic of artistic pretension that Señora Garcia had unwittingly stirred in him. This had endured all the subsequent voyages he had made aboard the *Kohinoor*, the *Orloff* and the *Star of the South*, resulting in some canvases and a folio of drawings, few of which, however, showed the promise of his first portrait.

Whatever the Reverend Dunbar's private suspicions, his eldest son seemed a more settled and self-confident young man than the boy apprentice he had seen off on the filthy dockside at Swansea four years earlier. Today, when he looked up as his son entered the kitchen, he might almost have been persuaded that his offspring was a credit to him.

Dunbar glanced round the kitchen and smiled; the scene had all the charm of familiar routine. The rector was in his shirt sleeves, sitting at the wide table, a cup of tea in one hand and a large, home-made biscuit in the other; his wife, also at ease, sat with her cup of tea, while Jenny laboured at the range, having just refilled the huge black kettle and put it back on the hob.

'Tea, James?' his mother asked, her hand already on the handle of the pot.

'Yes, please.' He sat and reached out for a biscuit as his cup was filled. The kitchen was hot, warm enough to induce a somnolent state after the cold outside. Jenny turned from the range and wiped her hands. Marriage had altered her, made her more matronly and less comely. She smiled at him.

'I heard you spoke to Father this morning, Master James.'

'Your father . . . ?' James frowned. Apart from the family she had married into, Jenny had no living blood relations.

'I met him on my way back from the bakery; he was at Jaybez Elson's.'

'Of course!' James remembered the old man with the ploughing team. 'Your father-in-law. I knew I ought to know the old fellow's name. How stupid of me, it was Mr Slater.'

'Fancy you forgetting that,' said his mother with a hint of reprobation in her voice. She would have regarded it as a dereliction of duty, Dunbar thought.

'I haven't seen him for a long time,' Dunbar said, excusing himself, irritated at the awkward guilt that his mother's tone had awakened in him. He felt like a child again.

'I hope Mr Slater didn't notice,' his father added.

'Bless you, sir, old Tom wouldn't mind, not a bit of it.' Jenny shot Dunbar an understanding glance and he responded with a small smile. Dunbar rallied under the combined onslaught of his parents.

'I'm sure Mr Slater didn't notice,' he said, sipping his tea, 'I was perfectly respectful to him. I just couldn't place him for a moment. It vexed me, but I have been away for some time.'

It seemed so trivial a matter, until it occurred to him that his parents' vision was limited by the parish bounds. His own horizons seemed limitless by comparison, and the thought stirred in him an unbearable restlessness.

'We have received an invitation to the Hall,' his father said portentously, 'for dinner tomorrow evening.'

'Oh . . .' Dunbar thought of Julia.

'You are included.'

'Am I?'

'You owe the colonel a lot.'

'I owe the colonel for a pair of binoculars.'

19

'He found you a position . . .'

'You paid a premium for me, Father. The colonel is a charming gentleman, but it cost him little effort to find me an apprentice's berth in a company in which his family has some interest and, as you well know, he had no use for his son's binoculars . . .'

'James!' his mother broke in, her voice shocked by his impropriety. Those who made the supreme sacrifice should be held in eternal esteem, it seemed. He thought of death, of Richenda Hawkshawe and the terrorised passengers of the *Macassar*; thought too of the beautiful whore Conchita dying in his arms. The momentary abstraction saved the situation.

'Mother, I don't think I owe any great obligation to Colonel Scrope-Davies,' Dunbar said, smiling, 'though I'm perfectly happy to acknowledge my debt to you and Father. Do you wish me to reimburse you the expense of my premium?'

'Good heavens no, boy!' his father said in an outraged tone, shooting an embarrassed look at Jenny, who had had the good sense to be industriously skinning the rabbits that would go into tonight's pie.

'Come then, Father, what's the point of being angry?'

His father glared at him, darted a look at his wife, rose abruptly and left the kitchen.

'You go too far, James.'

'Oh, for heaven's sake, Mother, all this arises out of my forgetting the name of Jenny's father-in-law. It's not exactly a crime.' He looked at the cook's back; Jenny's concentration was palpable.

'I don't know why you can't get on with your father.'

Dunbar remained silent. Apart from his improper allusion to the colonel's dead son, whose binoculars he had been given, he knew that he had touched his father's most exposed nerves. The Reverend Dunbar was a snob, holding the belief that each man's estate

20

was ordained by God. The rector was also piqued by his own penury which, while he was immeasurably better off than most of the inhabitants of Clayton Dobbs, was irksome whenever he moved out of the village. He was also exceedingly irritated by the incompatibility of these two notions; it was the paradox upon which Dunbar had trampled, rendering his father speechless and sending him back to the gloomy recesses of his book-lined study.

Anne Dunbar sighed. 'You ought to make more of an effort, James . . .'

Dunbar finished his biscuit and rose from the table. 'Don't fret, Mother. I shan't be under your feet for much longer.' He smiled, concealing his annoyance. 'I just hope that I've passed my examinations.'

'Of course you have.' Anne Dunbar reached out and patted her son's hand.

'I'm sorry I forgot Tom Slater's name, Jenny,' Dunbar said as he left the room.

'Oh dear,' sighed his mother after he had gone, 'what are we to do with him?'

'He's all right, missus,' Jenny said, with the liberty of long-standing servitude. There was more she could have said, but she held her tongue and dismembered the second rabbit with more energy than the task warranted.

Dunbar hesitated outside his father's study. After a moment's consideration he knocked on the door.

'Come in.'

The rector was standing at the window, staring outside, where the tossing trees attested to the continuing vigour of the gale. He swung round and Dunbar could see that he had expected his wife. There was an instant of awkward silence, then both spoke at once, before his father gave ground, sat himself down behind his huge desk with its litter of ecclesiastical papers and waved his son to a seat. Dunbar occupied one of two worn, upright chairs intended for petitioning parishioners.

'Look, Father, I meant no offence and am sorry if I have caused you any.'

'It was improper of you to allude to money in front of the servants.'

The use of the plural, subservient noun for poor Jenny irritated Dunbar. As far as he was concerned, the insensitivity lay with his father, but he forbore to comment further. It was clear that their points of view were completely irreconcilable.

'Father, I appreciate what you are saying and don't wish to take issue with you. All I want to point out is that we are different people. I respect you for all that you believe in and stand for, but my own experiences . . .' He faltered, then resumed as the rector remained forbiddingly silent, 'Well, they are bound to drive us apart to some extent.' He felt that his exposition was lame and incomplete. It withered under the rector's frowning gaze.

'Nothing about faith ever changes, my boy. We were always different people, but you were brought up in a Christian household, and my faith is your faith . . .'

'Father, I forgot an old man's name . . .'

'James, you move in a world so very different from ours here at Clayton. These experiences of which you speak, they are like to be the temptations of the devil . . .'

'For heaven's sake, Father, whatever happened to those who go down to the sea in ships and see the wonders of the Lord?'

The rector suddenly leaned forward. 'I do not want you to become an apostate, James. We have achieved so much in this country, and at such a cost. You think that we dwell in a rural backwater here in Suffolk, but I am aware that there are dangerous notions abroad in the world, which threaten our very existence, not just as a nation, but as soldiers under the banner of Christ.'

'Have they not always been there?' Dunbar responded quickly. 'A constant threat which we have to fight with equal, opposing constancy? I recall hearing the story of a mutiny aboard a ship not so many years ago, in which the most terrible things happened.'

'That is my point, James! My point exactly! We must be eternally vigilant. Our souls are forever besieged by evil, whether here in Clayton or on board your ship, wherever that may be.'

James smiled. 'You mean she is not always on the deep, confronting the wonders of the Lord?'

His father overlooked the touch of blasphemy and took the olive branch. 'I am glad you see my point, James.' The rector stood and held out his hand. The gesture, well meant, struck Dunbar as curiously laughable. 'I believe Julia is staying at the Hall,' his father added. 'D'you recollect her? Dinner should not be too irksome, even for a revolutionary like you!'

'Yes, I do remember her,' James remarked drily, taking his father's outstretched hand. As he left the study the rector turned to the window again.

Dunbar did not know whether to be annoyed at being branded a revolutionary or merely amused at his father's extraordinary misperception. The remark that dinner should not be too 'irksome' was a plea for him to conform and not to disgrace the rector by some indiscretion in front of their social superiors. It was almost pitiable, but perhaps he should feel nothing, for at least the rector's unburdening had restored his equanimity.

Dunbar had always accommodated his father's beliefs, he realised. It was a small enough price to pay, though it made him feel increasingly alien in the family home and smacked somewhat of moral cowardice. Yet it was the imposition of this conciliatory self-denial that had driven him in upon himself and which now threatened to burst outwards with the energy of creative ambition.

CHAPTER TWO

The Amateur

'You have not yet had the results of your examinations?' Julia asked over the top of her claret glass.

'No. But I should think it may well be in Monday's post. I know I have passed my orals and if I have messed up the written papers, well, I'll simply have to sit them again next month.'

'And then what?'

Dunbar looked at his father, who was in eager conversation with Colonel Scrope-Davies and Mrs Cross, a large, well-formed and pleasant lady whose husband owned land adjacent to the colonel's. Mr Cross sat opposite Dunbar and was paying court to his mother, who, Dunbar thought awkwardly, was rather enjoying the experience. Cross was as large and handsome as his wife, and they were a popular and successful pair. Two other couples graced the table: the Bretts, of whom the husband practised as a solicitor in Ipswich; and the Morrisons, who also farmed and hunted, and whose land lay to the west of the colonel's.

Dunbar turned back to Julia. The auburn hair was piled on top of her head and her slender neck was girdled with pearls, *à l'Alexandra*. He thought her exquisitely beautiful and her frank gaze so disconcerted him that he hesitated a moment before replying.

'Well, I shall go back to sea . . .'

'And we shall lose your company.' She pulled the corners of her mouth down in a moue of mock regret.

He shrugged and smiled ruefully. 'Alas, Jack has to make his way in the world . . .'

'Alas,' she broke in quickly, 'so does Jill.'

'Well then, we both have our crosses to bear,' he riposted as they smiled at each other, 'but I have a mind to make mine a little unorthodox.'

'How so?' she asked, sipping her wine again.

'I intend shipping in a sailing ship. It's a rather odd notion and I'm not quite certain whether it will do my career much good, but I think if I do not do it now, I shall regret it later.'

'Didn't you run off in one of those little fishing boats from Wick?'

'That was a long time ago,' Dunbar grinned. 'I'm surprised you know about it.'

'I remember the fuss it caused.'

'I had no idea . . .'

'I also remember thinking what a romantic thing to do. I don't think I would now, though.'

Dunbar smiled, flattered, but relieved of a reply by the maid removing his cleared plate and Julia looking up to confront the colonel's eye. 'Excuse me,' she whispered and rose with a susurration of silk.

'Ladies, I think we shall leave the gentlemen to their cigars.' Whereupon the rustle grew, as the ladies rose and the gentlemen were prompted into the convention of standing while the ladies withdrew.

Cross subsided beside Dunbar with a groan. 'Damned rheumatics,' he grumbled good-naturedly. 'They tell me you don't get 'em from sea-water, James, is that true?'

'I'm no expert, sir, but the old boys down at Clayton Wick all seem to have arthritic hands.'

'Ah yes, but they're fishermen, getting their hands wet

and cold all year. You chaps in steamers don't do that sort of thing nowadays, do you? I hear you've been off in hot climes enjoying yourself.'

'James has been all over the world,' put in his father unnecessarily.

'They say travel broadens the mind,' added Colonel Scrope-Davies, 'but I never found it did anything more than make one damned uncomfortable.'

The obligatory laughter that followed their host's witticism also greeted the circulation of the humidor and the decanter, in which Dunbar senior hid his discomfiture. Mercifully the conversation veered away from James, as the subject of foxes came up. In a few moments the rector had forgotten the snub that the colonel had unconsciously delivered and was able to contribute fully, for he had a passion for the hunt that James had always found incomprehensible until, seeing his father in such animated debate, he realised from whom he had inherited his own impetuosity. The revelation came as a shock, yet like all such simple things, its truth struck him with the force of the obvious. It struck him too that since the characteristic took such different forms in the two of them, it would always serve to separate rather than unite them.

Dunbar had no obvious contribution to make to the chat of intimates, and instead he played a game with the smoke of his cigar, thinking of Julia until the blessed moment came when they rose and joined the ladies.

There was, as far as Dunbar was concerned, one small mercy about dinner at Clayton Hall. The obligatory after-dinner entertainments were reduced to cards. The colonel refused to have the grand piano played, his late son having been an impressive player with a fine baritone voice. Since his bereavement, the colonel had insisted that the piano remained closed, though a man came out from Woodbridge once a year to keep it in tune.

'Just because I don't want to hear it doesn't mean that someone might not want to tinkle on the damned thing when I'm gone,' he had once said to Julia with a meaningful glance. 'Waste not, want not, I say, m'dear.'

None of the Hall's guests ever referred to the ebony monster, which served as an overweight stand for a variety of photographs. The Bretts and Crosses made a four for bridge, as did the Dunbars and Morrisons. Colonel Scrope-Davies personally disliked card games, although he was content for others to enjoy the pleasure, liking the laughter in the otherwise empty old house. As was his wont, he settled himself with a book of military history.

As uninterested in cards as her guardian, Julia sat on the large sofa and indicated that Dunbar should join her. They sat at opposite ends, their arms extended along its back so that their hands overlapped, but did not touch.

'So, you will shortly be back at sea,' Julia said, picking up the conversation where it had been left off.

'Yes, but tell me what you will be doing?'

'Me? Oh,' Julia shrugged, her bare shoulders glowing in the lamplight, 'I shall stay down here until the end of the month, return to London until Christmas and then, well, who knows?' She smiled again. 'And you'll be heaven knows where.'

'I shall miss you at Christmas, wherever I am,' he said, emboldened by the port. 'It's a rotten time to be at sea. Very unromantic, I can assure you.'

'I remember missing *you* at Christmas . . .'

'Missing me?' Dunbar frowned, suddenly troubled by an old recollection. 'When?'

'Oh, I don't know. Six or seven years ago. It had snowed, I recall . . .'

'You came to the rectory and took the twins out for a walk,' he interrupted. 'I saw you.'

'You wouldn't talk to me.'

'You wouldn't talk to me!'

Their mutual indignation turned suddenly to laughter as they discovered something stronger, drawing a glance or two from the bridge players, two of whom noticed the first touching of their fingers along the back of the sofa.

'How odd that we should both remember—'

'James,' Julia broke in, 'will you show me your paintings?'

'My paintings?'

'Yes. Is there something so very extraordinary in my asking? Paintings are, after all, to be looked at.'

'Well, a professional's perhaps. I'm just an amateur.'

She was giving him a funny, cock-eyed look. 'James, the distinction between amateur,' she drawled the word disparagingly, 'and professional is nowhere more blurred than among artists. Most, apart from the fashionable portrait-painters, make little money. Do let me see them. Please?'

'You seem to know a lot about the subject.'

'And you, I recollect, said you know nothing. Well?' She hesitated.

'What are Fauves? I think that was the word you used the other day?'

'They are a number of artists who caused a scandal in Paris a few years ago with their wildly colourful paintings. Their technique appeared deceptively simple and their name was coined by an art critic, a man named Louis Vauxcelles. He saw an exhibition of their work at the Independant's Salon of 1906, in the middle of which was a classical bronze. "Ah!" exclaimed Vauxcelles, *"Donatello parmi les Fauves!"*, meaning "a Donatello sculpture among the wild beasts", and the deprecating remark stuck, much as Monet's painting called "Impression, Sunrise" gave a name to the so-called Impressionists.'

'And do you admire these wild beasts?'

Julia shrugged. 'Some of their work is powerful and I can admire it without liking it, or coveting it. More important, their work is full of energy and life, just as the work of the Impressionists was twenty years ago. I do like Albert Marquet's work – no-one paints water quite like him – and I like the work of Maurice de Vlaminck. He is self-taught, an amateur like yourself.'

'I assume you have seen all these artists' work?'

'No, not all. But I have seen some of them.'

'In Paris?'

'Yes. But they no longer exhibit together; they were not a "school", just a group of like-minded men who worked together and inspired each other.' She paused a moment, then added, 'I should perhaps say that I was being facetious when I remarked that your soggy painting resembled a Fauve work.'

'It didn't?' He was smiling.

'No,' she smiled back, 'I'm afraid not.'

'Afraid? I should have been rather disappointed if all I had to do was hold some rather badly laid-down washes out in the rain to produce even an amateur painting.' He chuckled. 'Actually, it was awful. If I had stood there for a month of Sundays it would have been awful. I'm no artist, Julia, just a jack who thinks he'd like to mess about with a box of colours.'

'I'd still like to see your work. Drawings as well.'

'I'd be flattered.' He thought of the painting of Dolores Garcia. It was his best work, but he did not have to show it to her, and perhaps when she had seen the rest, her interest would fade. Her interest in his artistic achievements, that is. Looking at her, he rather hoped he might be able to secure a more permanent place in her regard than mere curiosity in his drawing and painting.

'You must name the place and time, but the sooner, the better.'

'You are most persistent,' he hedged. The thought of

her coming to the rectory and being obliged to show his work under his father's roof was unsettling, but there was no alternative. Besides, it was Sunday tomorrow, the day when his father was most preoccupied, and Dunbar craved greater intimacy with Julia Ravenham.

'Tomorrow?'

'Tomorrow.'

He had stacked the canvases in the unused room that had once been occupied by Jenny Broom, and at the door of which he had long ago come closest to making sexual advances towards her. He had lost his nerve, of course, and had grown old enough to laugh at his adolescent discomfiture. Stacking his work against the end wall, Jenny's stripped bed and the washstand at which she had been standing that summer evening stood as solemn monuments to the end of his childhood. It had been a moment of transition; somehow such moments were always charted as humiliations.

Julia walked from matins with his mother and himself, accepting the invitation to come to lunch, which in the rectory was always eaten at three o'clock on a Sunday. The day was grey and cold; the air still after the disruption of the gales. The change of season had been sudden, dramatic, and they commented upon it as they shuffled through the still half-green leaves, which caught in the tussocky grass of the churchyard's remote corner where a break in the wall led through to the rectory's unkempt garden.

Dunbar was vaguely excited, aware that tongues would wag as the village noted Miss Julia in his company, and it seemed that his mother's mood, lifted by the solicitations of Mr Henry Cross, were not immune to some silly speculation.

'I wish James to show me his work, Mrs Dunbar,' Julia

had explained as she joined them in the church porch and, once in the house and divested of hat and coat, she had dealt firmly with the anxious propriety in Anne Dunbar's expression.

'I have been to Paris, Mrs Dunbar, quite on my own, and I am certain James offers no threat to me.'

The forwardness of this remark so stunned Mrs Dunbar that she was rendered speechless for the moment or two it took Dunbar to lead Julia upstairs. She retreated, one ear cocked, to her kitchen. Here she was alone, for Jenny Broom, now that she was married, attended the rectory on a Sunday only up to the time of matins and, having put the joint of beef into the oven to roast, went home to her husband. Basting the sizzling shoulder, Anne Dunbar began reassessing a future linked with Miss Ravenham.

In the freezing attic, Julia regretted removing her coat, with a noticeable shudder.

'I'm so sorry,' Dunbar said. 'Please use the counterpane from the bed. Wrap it about you.'

'I'll sit on the bed and you can hold them up for me to see. No, place them on the chair. I shall pretend I am a one-woman Academy hanging committee.'

Dunbar began with the finished paintings, taking each one and placing it on the rickety, upright chair with its rush seat that was depressed from the imprint of Jenny's buttocks. He looked up at Julia who, under the patchwork counterpane, bore a Romany air. Her face was almost expressionless as she stared at the first canvas. He looked down at it. The heavy impasto of the oils had gathered dust from the attic's mote-laden atmosphere. It was an oil painting of Mr Rayner, mate of the *Kohinoor*, lately made Captain Rayner, master of the *Pitt*.

Julia studied the work for a few moments then said, her voice so flat that Dunbar could detect nothing from its tone, 'Next.' There followed a series of oil studies – he could not bring himself to call them portraits – of men with whom he had sailed. The ancient Sudanese Number One greaser of the *Orloff*, whose sons were *askaris* in Kitchener's army; a Chinese steward on the same ship, whose moon face was startlingly handsome and who stared from the coarse canvas with the composure of a Ming emperor and bore no trace in his mien of the servitor; the bronze features of a Malay boatman and the creased, careworn visage of a Chinese 'sew-sew' woman from Singapore.

Dunbar could not determine whether Julia regarded these works with disdain or approval. His own heartbeat, raised at first in anticipation of he knew not quite what reaction, gradually subsided. Julia looked at each painting just long enough for him to think it might be with approval and then asked, almost snappishly it seemed at times, for the next to be shown to her.

The brick-red faces of Dunbar's European shipmates were paraded before her and then he moved on to some paintings of ships. These profiles she spent far less time on, lingering a little longer when he showed her scenes on board, little vignettes of men at work stripping down derricks, chipping and painting, the white bulkheads behind their muscular bodies spotted with bright patches of red lead-primer.

'That's all,' he said when he had finished.

'What about drawings and sketches?'

'You don't want to see . . .'

'I do.'

Now her tone was undoubtedly imperative. He sensed a shift of mood, an intensity to which he reacted with a quickening heartbeat. He dared not ask her, yet he felt her interest like a palpable touch, arousing, direct.

The drawings lay in an old tarpaulin chart portfolio, which he drew out from under the bed and laid beside her. He began to unlace it, but her own fingers were already at work. She began to turn the pencil sketches and the rough watercolours. There were a great number of them, some drawn on sheets of worn sugar paper, even a torn-open paper bag, but most on cartridge paper or grubby, well-used chart paper, whose obverse bore the neat cartographical representations of coral-girt lagoons, dotted sand-bars or the vastnesses of the ocean, scribed with the isopleths of equal magnetic variation.

Julia riffled rapidly through the drawings, every now and then pulling one aside and laying it upon the exposed blanket with a swift decisiveness.

'What's this?' She broke the silence between them, looking directly at him for the first time. In her hands she held up a large chart. One side bore the carefully etched shoreline, contours and isobaths of Hong Kong, showing the Kowloon peninsula and the archipelago stretching across the mouth of the Pearl River to Macao. On the reverse sprawled a vigorously delineated group of struggling figures. Limbs were ambiguous with alternative positions, almost nothing was exactly defined and it looked, in the dull attic light, as if the struggle were still in progress, all indistinct, like a waterfront brawl half-seen down an alleyway at twilight.

'Oh, it's an idea I had for a formal painting . . .'

'A figurative painting,' she said in unconscious correction, 'like a Jacques Louis David. Tell me about it, it's very dramatic.'

'Oh, it was just an idea.'

'Don't hedge, James. There's a figure here, a half-naked woman, and there seems to be a fight. What is it, your idea of the rape of the Sabine women?'

He hesitated only a moment longer. If anything was to have meaning, if this acute woman was to occupy some part in his life, there seemed little point in hiding his past. Besides, this was the place where his libidinous self had again tried to emerge. On that occasion shame and guilt had overwhelmed him, but now he felt none of that constraint. On the contrary, the act was pre-ordained to happen under his father's sanctified roof and Julia, he sensed, half-understood his exposure.

'She,' he pointed to the sketched-in figure of the girl, 'was a hostage to the man who is restraining her. He has his arm about her neck . . .'

'And something at her throat – a knife by the look of it.'

'Yes. The would-be rescuer there,' he pointed to a man lunging forward, 'has a sword-stick.'

'And who are these?' Julia pointed to a small group in what looked like a doorway.

'Oh, they are also trying to intervene.'

Julia was silent for a moment, then she said, 'This isn't the Sabine women. This isn't figurative. This is from life, isn't it? You were there . . .' She looked up at him, her eyes wide.

He sighed, nodding. 'The girl's throat was cut. She was a whore . . .'

'And you?' Julia's eyes were staring at him.

Dunbar pointed at the swordsman.

'You are the man with the sword?' Her voice was thick with wonder. 'I had no idea.' As their eyes met, he felt that early sensation of inferiority evaporate. 'What did you do?'

'I stabbed the murderer and . . .'

'And?'

'I was scarred for my trouble.'

'No wonder you wanted to paint the scene.'

Dunbar shook his head. 'No, I didn't. I thought I did. I did this drawing too long after the event to make much sense of it. I gave it up. As I think you can tell, I have no real liking for such subjects; besides, I have no sense of composition. I simply could not get the group to tell the story and look right. I suppose there's a name for my predicament but, well, it doesn't matter now.'

'Where did all this happen?'

'In Mexico. Perhaps I'll tell you all about it one day. It's not important. I just happened to get involved.'

'With a sword?'

'It was a sword-stick. The woman who ran the hotel enlisted my help to stop the brawl. She lent me the stick. Tell me,' he asked, changing the subject, 'why did you put these aside?' He indicated the pile of selected drawings and watercolours.

'They are good enough to exhibit as works in their own right.'

'*Exhibit*?'

'Yes, James. Your work is mixed, I grant you, but some of it is good, very good. You have, I think, what might be called a natural and original talent.' She paused a moment and then added, 'Yours would be considered, and without reproof, a naïve talent.'

He remained silent for a moment then asked, 'Forgive me, Julia, but how do you make such a judgement? Flattering though I assume it is, I mean, how . . . ?' he faltered awkwardly.

'How do I know anything about painting or drawing?' He nodded. 'Well, while you have been playing the cavalier in your Mexican bordello, I have spent time in London and Paris studying art. How else would a helpless country girl know about Les Fauves?'

'But I don't understand . . .'

'Not now, James. We have plenty of time. Come and see me in London before you go to sea again. But first show me your best work. What about the painting of the Spanish woman?'

'Spanish woman?' he frowned.

'That is what Jenny Broom called her, but I suppose she was Mexican.'

'How the devil did Jenny know about that?'

'Never mind. She isn't here. Do show me.'

Dunbar had hidden the portrait of Dolores Garcia under an old curtain, away from casually prying eyes. Clearly he had been unable to combat the more purposeful espionage of Jenny Broom. Where once he had spied on her, she had turned the tables on him with a singularly poetic justice, informing Julia of the painting. Oddly, he found he did not mind, as though that strand of fate that bound them was not yet cut.

He held up the coarse old canvas, which had once been a hatch tarpaulin and was now tensioned by a crude stretcher. Outside it had clouded over and the attic grew dark. Although he half-hoped that this providential gloom would mask the picture from Julia, he watched her face with a breathless anticipation as she scrutinised the proffered canvas.

This time she betrayed her reaction with a whisper of pure admiration and a shake of her head.

'This isn't daubing, James,' Julia said vehemently, 'this is painting!'

The moment passed and was terminated by the tinkle of the bell summoning them downstairs for the Sunday lunch of roast meat. In a sense he was glad there had been no time for more elaboration; he would have spoiled the perfection of her approval by his gauche questions, but his head buzzed with them. Her easy acceptance of the site of Conchita's murder, the remarks about London and Paris and her implicit hints of another life caused him to ruminate for most of the dull, rustic meal, which so contrasted with the stiff formality of the previous evening.

Fortunately his mother kept the conversation going, though it was some time before the preoccupied Dunbar, just then realising that he had not shown Julia the sketch of Mrs Coxford, which he had left in his bedroom, woke to the fact that Mrs Dunbar was probing Julia for some indication of how she spent her time. Clearly the young woman was adept at evasion, quite used to giving away only as much as she wished to.

'The colonel told me you occupy rooms in Chelsea.'

'Actually, they are in Pimlico and are rented by a distant relative who rarely uses them. It is most convenient.'

'And have you business which takes you up to town quite a lot?'

'I like to spend time in London. There's so much to see and do, as I'm sure you'd agree,' Julia remarked dismissively with a sweet smile. And Anne Dunbar found herself agreeing, though she had no idea what a young and single woman found to do in town that was not improper. No more had her husband who, under the circumstances, possessed the weight of both parental and clerical suspicion.

'What do you do, my dear?' he asked with a practised bluntness, which could unnerve young countrymen who came to put up premature banns.

'Why, Rector,' Julia trotted on, still smiling, 'I occasionally occupy myself on my uncle's business. You know how he so hates London and,' she half-turned to James Dunbar, as though to offer him the courtesy of an apology on the colonel's behalf, 'although he still retains some considerable investment in the Navigation Company, he is not himself much interested in its day-to-day affairs.'

'So he allows you to, er, act for him, does he?' The air was stiff with the rector's disapproval, not merely of Miss Ravenham's youth, but of her sex.

'Do you have an interest in the Company yourself?' Mrs Dunbar put in, seeking to turn her husband's blundering into the acquisition of intelligence that might, under certain circumstances, effect a change of heart.

'Oh no. I have no head for such matters. It's just that my uncle prefers some matters to be transacted personally, rather than solely by letter. He thinks,' and here Julia gave the Reverend Dunbar a cool, appraising stare, 'he thinks one can better judge a man by the way he reacts, rather than by what he writes. Moreover,' she smiled again, turning to Mrs Dunbar, 'sometimes a woman is better placed to decide such matters.'

'If you mean feminine intuition,' riposted the rector, 'I'm not certain I'd care to base my decisions on it, especially by proxy.'

'Julia clearly has an ability that the colonel appreciates, my dear,' Anne Dunbar soothed.

'Oh, it's quite all right, Mrs Dunbar,' Julia added brightly, 'I quite understand. I have to admit it's most unusual, but,' she shrugged with a charming air of fatal resignation, 'neither the colonel nor I have anyone else and we must make a virtue of necessity.'

Dunbar concealed his smile with difficulty. That Julia had ended her intriguing explanation, which begged more questions than it answered, on a note of certain virtue was masterly.

'They must think I am some kind of whore, like your Mexican whatever-her-name-was,' she said, kicking the leaves aside as Dunbar escorted her home in the early autumn twilight.

'You live on the edge of convention, Julia. It frightens them; they like their certainties, buried down here, delightful though it is.'

'Who was the woman, James?'

'The little whore? Her name was Conchita.'

'No, no, the Mexican woman.'

'Her name was Dolores Garcia and she ran the bordello in a town called Puerto San Martin. The place was actually owned by an Englishwoman who was, ironically, the daughter of a churchman. She lost her family in a particularly nasty mutiny and was badly disfigured as a consequence. She had chosen to make her life . . .'

'On the edge of convention?' Julia put in.

'Yes. Very much on the edge, and I say "chosen" but destiny or fate, or God Almighty, actually did the choosing.'

'And how did you come to meet these two women?'

'It is a long and complicated story. Let us just say that I had been sent by the master of the ship . . .'

'The *Kohinoor*?'

'Yes.'

'That would have been Captain Steele.'

'Yes, that's correct. The old woman owned most of Puerto San Martin, I think, not just the bordello.'

'And did you paint her?'

'Good Lord, no; she would never have consented. Besides, she had been badly wounded by a knife and, poor soul, was not pretty, though I dare say she had once been comely enough.' He paused for a moment and felt Julia slip her arm through his, then he went on, 'She was subject to vague wanderings of the mind and took me at first for her brother, or a reincarnation of him. Apparently the boy had been killed in the mutiny, along with her mother, father and most of the other passengers of the ship in which they were all returning from Australia.'

'Gold?'

'Yes. The result of the diggings at Ballarat. It was all a long time ago.'

'Curious that you were caught up in its aftermath.'

'Yes, it was. I suppose all acts have consequences, and those following acts of violence last longest. Something like the atmosphere that is said to exist in a room where someone has been murdered.'

'Don't,' Julia said with a shiver. 'And Dolores Garcia sat for you?' she asked, swiftly changing the subject.

'No, she sat for old Miss Hawkshawe. It was she who commissioned the portrait.'

'How did she know you could paint?'

'She saw me doing some drawing. I wasn't very good.'

'But you are, James, you are.' She pulled away from him and stopped, so that he was forced to face her. They were halfway along the avenue of chestnuts and the tops of the trees gave out a soft roar as the wind rose again. The fallen leaves laid a rustling carpet about their feet. Julia's face glowed in the half-light. He was about to bend and kiss her when she said, 'You absolutely *must* come and see me before you sail again.'

'In Pimlico?' he asked wryly.

'Yes. And it is between ourselves; a secret.'

'Of course.'

'Your parents are good people, but they wouldn't understand all this chatter about bordellos, would they?'

'No,' he laughed, 'and I have to confess it has me slightly mystified.' Tantalisingly, Julia merely grinned and they resumed their interrupted progress towards the Hall.

They walked on in silence to the end of the avenue. As the drive opened out, the full façade of Clayton Hall confronted them, rising into the night sky, a black mass pierced with feeble lights in two windows. Julia stopped and cocked her head contemplatively to one side. 'Just think,' she said, 'this place once supported three generations of the Scrope-Davies family. Now there's only the old colonel.'

'And you.'

'No. I'm not really family. D'you remember Hugh, the colonel's son?'

'Yes, vaguely.'

'I do,' she said wistfully, 'he was always very sweet to me, but it's his ghost I fear.'

'The colonel's refusal to have the piano played after dinner is all very well, but a bit morbid,' Dunbar agreed.

'And I don't think Hugh would have approved,' Julia added, 'but there we are.'

'The colonel gave me Hugh's field glasses when I first went to sea.'

'That was kind of him. D'you still have them?'

Dunbar nodded. 'Yes. You'd have thought he would have wanted to keep such a memento, wouldn't you? I mean, it's more comprehensible than not being able to sing for our supper.'

'No. I understand the old boy. A pair of binoculars gathering mould in a leather case is, in a way, the greater morbidity. Besides, they're useful and the colonel, as an old soldier, wouldn't approve of waste. On the other hand, not having any music acts as a constant reminder, not just to the colonel, but to all those of us present. Anyway, if you don't want the glasses, give them to me.'

'I use them actually.'

'Well then, that's marvellous.' They walked on, the gravel crunching under their feet. 'I suppose when the colonel dies, the place will be sold.'

'Won't that be up to you?'

'Oh no. Don't believe all that tosh they speak about in the village. I'm not the Scrope-Davies heiress. Why d'you think I work in London?'

'I'm not quite certain what you do in London. Or Paris, for that matter, though I think you turned my mother's probing very skilfully.'

Julia laughed. 'Oh, I'm mercilessly cruel. What I said was absolutely true, but it was only part of the story. Anyway, I have no reason to conceal anything from you, James.' She slipped her arm in his again as they fell under the chill shadow of the house, which rose into the darkening sky.

'You're very sweet, Julia, and . . .'

She stopped again and put a finger to his lips. 'No speeches, James. Not yet. Just come and see me in London. Promise?'

He seized her by the upper arms and pressed her in a brotherly fashion, then, leaning forward, he kissed her lightly on the cheek. 'I promise.'

'I *might*,' she said with slow emphasis, pulling away from him and backing towards the front door, 'only *might*, you understand, but I might let you paint *my* portrait, so bring your paintbox. Your oils, not your watercolours.'

CHAPTER THREE

The Aesthete

The following morning the post brought Dunbar the news that he had successfully passed his Certificate of Competency as Second Mate of a 'foreign-going steam ship'. The news, spread about the breakfast table, was accompanied by parental congratulation and the inevitable paternal enquiry as to what his intentions were.

'Colonel Scrope-Davies assured me,' his father said, 'that a position with the South Wales Steam Navigation Company was open to you and that, if you successively passed the examinations for First Mate and Master, a command would be highly probable before you are thirty.'

'*Captain* James Dunbar,' his mother said smiling, and Dunbar felt more than a hint of veiled social ambition running through his parents' minds, as though that title would elevate him a little, and perhaps place him in a strong position to aspire to the hand of Julia Ravenham. The attachment to Julia was not without its attractions – indeed, he had slept badly on account of the beautiful young woman – but he had his own plans and they were as uncertain and illogical as ever, based on a wayward desire to adventure a little in the world before beginning the slow and plodding path of a career officer.

In the four years of his apprenticeship, the dull tedium

of tramping about the globe had offered him little incentive to join the Steeles and the Rayners, worthy and steady shipmasters though they undoubtedly were.

'Well, boy?' his father prompted, prising him out of his abstraction.

'Well, Father, it is very good of the colonel, but I have a mind to widen my experience a little.'

'You're not thinking of going on one of these Arctic expeditions, are you?' his mother asked anxiously, her hand flying to her throat in apprehension.

'They're *Ant*arctic, Anne,' his father corrected.

'It doesn't much matter, does it,' the rector's wife replied sharply, 'both are dangerous and cold!'

'It has nothing to do with the poles, Mother,' Dunbar broke in quickly, sensing that this tartness was a small manifestation, like the visible portion of an iceberg, he thought with casual aptness, of some discord on his account. 'I simply don't want to confine my experience to tramp ships, or be entirely beholden to the colonel.'

'Now that, my boy, is foolish talk. The world—'

'Is a big place, and I would like to command something a little better than a South Wales tramp. I need a master's certificate to get a berth as a fourth officer in a decent liner company.'

'You mean P and O?' his mother asked, relieved that he was not intending to go south with either Commander Shackleton or Captain Scott.

Dunbar shrugged. 'Well perhaps. Or British India, Blue Funnel, or Royal Mail; oh, there are lots of them. But it's quite a complicated business and I would first like the experience of a voyage under sail . . .'

'A *sailing* ship? Whatever for?' his father asked sharply. 'Surely the future lies in steam?'

'That is precisely why I want the experience in sail. Most of the big companies train their people in sail because of the grounding it gives them. I would only make one voyage.'

'But not as an officer?' The rector frowned.

Dunbar shook his head. 'No, but that would not affect my chances later on and it does not worry me.'

'It worries me, my boy!'

'Oh, Father, don't be so old-fashioned. There is nothing wrong with shipping out as a seaman.'

'How can you possibly say that, the morning you receive your qualification as an officer?'

'Simply because it is what I wish to do!'

Both men were sitting upright as Anne Dunbar sought to soothe them, and they were on the brink of a row when a knock at the kitchen door produced a sudden silence.

'Come in,' Mrs Dunbar called and the latch lifted with a click to reveal the face of a small boy who peered round the door.

'I've a note here for Mr James Dunbar,' he said, holding out an envelope. 'I were pertic'lerly to ask for Mr James,' he said importantly. Dunbar recognised the stable lad from Clayton Hall and fished in his pocket for a threepenny bit, exchanging it for the rather crumpled envelope. He tore it open as the door clicked behind the departing boy. There was a further short silence as the rector and his wife swapped troubled glances. Dunbar looked up from the short note at his parents' expectant faces.

'It's from Julia. She's gone up to town this morning.'

'Oh, what a shame,' Mrs Dunbar remarked, her expression one of relief.

'And I,' added Dunbar, rising from the table, 'must go and find a ship.'

He left the kitchen to the disapproving rustle of the rector opening his morning newspaper.

*   *   *

Dunbar arrived in London twenty-four hours after Julia. Leaving Liverpool Street Station, he walked directly to Leadenhall Street and within two hours had secured a berth on a four-masted barque belonging to Bullard, Crowe and Company. Their agents, in St Mary Axe, had offered him a choice of three ships: the *Fort Mackinac*, which had just arrived in the Tyne to dry-dock before loading coal for Australia; the *Fort Frontenac*, which was due to sail in three days' time from Birkenhead for San Francisco; and the *Fort George*, which would arrive in the Clyde from Belfast 'within a fortnight'.

He had chosen the *Fort Mackinac*, then caught an omnibus bound for Westminster and from there walked to Pimlico. A pale yellow sunset presaged a cold night and threw the skyline of chimney pots into sharp silhouette. He had exactly ten days before he need join the *Fort Mackinac* and had given himself a week in London, if Julia would live up to the intimation in her note. To this end he had brought his 'paintbox'.

After a single enquiry in a baker's shop, he found the address that Julia had sent him by way of the stable lad. His knock was answered, not by Julia, but by a tall, slim young man in a dark frock-coat, who removed a pipe from his mouth before holding out a welcoming hand and remarking, 'Ah, you must be James. Julia asked me to keep an eye open for you. Come in, come in. My name is Dacre, Icarus Dacre; here, let me help.'

'It's quite all right.' Dunbar refused the offer and lugged his suitcase into the small hall, then followed the long-haired Dacre into the living room. The immediate impression was of stale air and cluttered untidiness. The room was dominated by a large, battered sofa covered with a heavy drape over which was flung a man's cape, presumably Dacre's, an abandoned newspaper, also presumably Dacre's, and a brilliant silk scarf, which Dunbar decided was not Dacre's.

Two time-ravaged upright chairs were similarly encumbered. A fur wrap was discarded on one and a small pile of books lay upon the other. An occasional table stood in the centre of the room on an antique Indian rug, of rich but stained appearance. It too was laden with the debris of indolent activity – an empty bottle and some dirty glasses had escaped the confines of a silver salver. A small dining table was covered with oddities: a small maquette, some drawings that escaped from a tatty folio, some tubes of paint, a jar of brushes and two small tin containers of oil. A large oil lamp, with a cut-glass reservoir and a tall, fluted chimney, and a hammer and nails all lay upon a velvet cloth that had seen better days.

In the corner of the room, beyond the small table and its quartet of tall-backed upright chairs, a heavy curtain was looped across the room, suspended from the picture rail. For a moment Dunbar was reminded of the screen that he had once been told all well-to-do houses originally had in their dining rooms, behind which a less-than-discreet easement took place.

The cluttered nature of the room was further enhanced by two tall, laden bookcases, which not only bore books standing vertically, but others stuffed above them, lying horizontal, like so many drunks desperate for shelter. These bookcases stood either side of a tall cast-iron fireplace, in the grate of which newspaper and sticks had been laid, though little attention had been taken to clear the ash and debris from the previous fire. Above the fireplace, the overmantel bore a withered flower in one of three tall and unmatching vases, two neglected brass candlesticks, both of which bore the stumps of candles, a stopped clock and a variety of notes and opened envelopes. Above this haphazard evidence of a disorganised life hung a large, startling watercolour representation of an odalisque. Beyond the near-naked woman, the pale but vigorous figures of Arab horsemen caracoled their mounts in the purple shadow of a minaret.

Used to the genteel, vaguely intellectual disorder of the rectory, Dunbar felt almost at home, except that it surprised him that the cool and rather haughty Julia should live in such a state, while his ordered seaman's mind saw a lack of husbandry bordering on the squalid. But then, contemplating the presence of Mr Dacre, he wondered if Julia did indeed live here.

'I'm sorry the place is untidy,' Dacre apologised. 'It's my fault. I promised Julia that I would ensure we had removed the worst of last night's debauch before you arrived,' he gestured at the wine bottle, 'but we weren't certain what time you would turn up.'

Dacre swept cloak, scarf and newspaper to one side and sat down on the sofa, waving Dunbar to the other end and clapping his hands. Feeling rather like the proverbial bad penny, Dunbar sat down just as an elderly woman in a plain grey dress and white apron appeared.

'Tea, Mrs Stevens, if you please. You do take tea?' Dacre asked with sudden solicitude.

'Yes. Thank you.'

There was a moment's silence as Dacre appraised Dunbar and the latter cast yet another glance round the room, fixing his gaze on the large and refulgent painting.

'Don't tell me,' said Dacre, 'you are wondering about this place, Julia, me and the debauchery, are you not?'

Dunbar turned back to his quizzer. 'Something of the sort.'

'Julia tells me you paint,' Dacre said, infuriatingly, transferring his attention to the odalisque.

'Yes, a little.'

'That is one of Ketlar's. You'll meet him later. I expect Julia will invite him to dinner. That's why she inveigled me to engage Mrs Stevens. I think she wished to make an impression on you, or something.'

'I see,' Dunbar replied awkwardly.

'I can see that you don't,' Dacre laughed amiably, 'but all will become clear in the fullness of time. I suppose we are rather an odd lot. It's a pity Maureen won't be joining us, but then she so seldom does and I rather think Julia has contrived to have her out of town just now; Maureen is rather a self-effacing type and so confoundedly quiet that one wouldn't notice she was in the room, if she wasn't so lovely. Julia tells me you have an eye for beautiful women.'

Dunbar flushed. He was accustomed to a brutal frankness among seafaring men, but this open, direct manner was something new to him, though he knew now where Julia had picked it up. 'No more than any man,' he hedged.

'Julia says you are inspired as a painter of them.'

'Julia, it seems, has a great deal to say about me.'

'She's very fond of you, Dunbar. I think she regards you as her discovery.'

'Discovery?' Dunbar frowned.

'As an artist,' Dacre said, a faint air of exasperation in his voice. 'Julia is always making discoveries.' Dunbar was rescued from his discomfiture by the arrival of Mrs Stevens and the tea.

'Are *you* an artist?' he asked Dacre as he stirred his tea.

'I am, of sorts,' Dacre said enigmatically. He leaned back with his teacup and saucer, crossed his legs and stared into a middle distance of his own imagining. This deliberation, Dunbar concluded, was designed to confer great importance upon his pronouncements. 'I am a poet and a critic.'

'A published critic, or merely one of those persons with an opinion for every occasion?' Dunbar's lack of reticence surprised even himself.

Dacre turned and focused his glance upon Dunbar.

49

'*Touché*: "a word, like an arrow, cannot be recalled".'
Dacre's glance was arch. 'You are truly Julia's *enfant terrible*.'

'I am scarcely anyone's *enfant*, Dacre,' Dunbar retorted, 'let alone Julia's. I meant no offence, but since we are referring to Julia and her relationships, what exactly is yours?'

'Mine? You mean *vis-à-vis* Julia?' and, seeing Dunbar's nod, Dacre explained. 'We are friends, Dunbar, simply friends. I have known Julia since she first came to town and we have a number of acquaintances in common. I have already mentioned Ketlar and Maureen; there are a few others – another German, though a Jew, Rollo Münck; and Eric Retyn, who might be anything but claims he comes from a long line of Cornish warlocks, which wouldn't surprise me in the least. *Nous sommes les habitués de l'atelier de* Seymour Conrad Strachan, of whom you have doubtless heard.'

'I'm afraid not.' Dunbar's denial of this particular knowledge, in contrast with his ignorance before Julia of Les Fauves, filled him with delight. He was beginning to dislike Dacre, and wondered what it was that Julia saw in him. There was an ease in Dacre's demeanour that bespoke a complete and easy familiarity with Julia's rooms; they were clearly intimates, perhaps even lovers, Dunbar reluctantly realised with a pang of pain. Dacre's definition of 'friendship' might be elastic.

'Oh.' Dacre paused, as though deciding to make an effort, then went on, 'Well, Julia will almost certainly introduce you to Conrad Strachan. We all admire him as a great painter. Ketlar,' Dacre returned his now empty cup to the tray and gestured at the odalisque above the fireplace, 'seeks to emulate him, but Ketlar is a German with his eye, regrettably, on the main chance. He might inherit Strachan's mantle, I suppose, if we aren't soon at war with his countrymen, but then,' Dacre added drolly, 'he could become court-painter to the Hohenzollerns, I suppose.'

'And Strachan?' Dunbar prompted, quite unimpressed by Dacre's discursion.

'Ah, I see I command your interest,' Dacre smiled aloofly. 'No, Strachan is not court-painter, but he is considered, by those who ought to know, the finest portrait painter in London.'

'By "those who ought to know" I assume you mean those who have a great deal of money to spend on such things.'

'I mean the most beautiful women in London, or at least their menfolk.'

Dunbar barked a short laugh. 'Ah well, it will be interesting to meet him.'

'Should you not like to paint the most beautiful, and wealthy, women in London?'

'I have not always found that the two things go together.'

'Don't tell me you are a cynic?'

'I think of myself more as a realist. Besides, I prefer to paint, how shall I put it without offending your sensibilities—'

'Which means, my dear Dunbar,' said Dacre, suddenly sitting up and leaning forward with a broad grin on his superior features, 'that you have every intention of offending them, but do, pray, go on. What do you prefer painting?'

'Well,' resumed Dunbar, aware that Dacre's charming interruption had robbed him of his advantage, 'more ordinary people.'

'Oh,' said Dacre dismissively, 'that is only because you have not had the opportunity to do otherwise. Anyway, that should suit the admirable Maureen very well. She, I am almost persuaded, thinks of herself as quite ordinary. She is very far from that, of course, she is *extra*ordinary.'

'And who is she?'

'Maureen?' Dacre nodded at the odalisque. 'Well, that is Maureen as a matter of fact.'

'She is a Moor, or a Moroccan?'

'No, no, she is a model. This is technically her flat, I believe.' An odd relief filled Dunbar, as though detaching Julia from the untidy mess of his surroundings, and with it a curiosity about the girl who posed as the harem-woman.

Further discussion was cut short by the rasp of a key in the door. Dacre rose to his feet and turned to meet Julia as she entered the room. 'And here,' announced Dacre quite superfluously, holding out his arms, 'is Julia.'

Despite Dacre's inference that they would eat in, they dined out in a small exotic restaurant, which Dunbar thought was run by Hungarian gypsies, who turned out to be Montenegrins. On their way out, Dunbar discovered that Dacre also owned the exotically hued silk scarf, which gleamed at his throat in the gas lamps and the glare of the passing cabs' lights.

A brace of braised fowl swam in a stew of vegetables and spices washed down with copious quantities of cheap but drinkable red wine. Julia, looking as lovely as when Dunbar had dined with her at the Hall, was clearly at home amid the bohemian riff-raff of which the group was composed. But the mood of intimacy they had established only the previous Sunday in the rectory attic seemed to have vanished, as remote and insubstantial as the rectory itself.

Nevertheless, Dunbar found the company convivial and welcoming. It was only in the comparatively few moments when they forgot his newness and relapsed into the asides and obliquities of old intimates that he felt isolated enough to regard Julia's distance as mildly dismissive, when contrasted with her obvious affection for the three young men who surrounded her as courtiers. He felt a prickly unease and sensed that her worldliness, so charming in the rustic surroundings of Clayton Dobbs, owed its disquieting origin to her loudly laughing companions.

Ernst Ketlar proved to be a bearded German with a face so hawk-like as to suggest one of the Arab horsemen in the background of his own painting. He wore a short serge jacket like Dunbar's own, and had about him the air of a prosperous and hard-working artisan; Rollo Münck, on the other hand, looked less Semitic, though Dunbar recalled Dacre's assertion that Münck was Jewish. He was a quieter man, more reflective in his demeanour than either Ketlar or Dacre. From the occasional remark he made, Münck seemed to be deferred to even by Dacre, and Dunbar felt oddly attracted by him.

'I am told you paint portraits, James,' Münck said kindly, his accent barely discernible.

Dunbar made a dismissive gesture. 'I am just an amateur . . .'

'Who has more than an amateur's talent, we are given to understand,' Dacre added, breaking in presumptuously with a meaningful nod in Münck's direction.

'You are not to tease James,' Julia interrupted. 'He has yet to realise what he is capable of. I hope that, before he goes to sea again, we shall provide evidence of his talent.'

'Ach, you are a sailor, yes?' Ketlar asked enthusiastically, 'I haf been a yachtsman myself, at Kiel.'

'I'm afraid I have only served in steam ships.'

'But now James is making a voyage under sail, to study and paint sailing ships and their sailors,' Julia explained.

'Rather a contrast with beautiful women,' put in Dacre.

'I shall leave them to Herr Ketlar,' Dunbar inclined his

head gracefully and Dacre raised an almost complimentary eyebrow.

'Well, well. But tell us, why do you paint at all?'

Dunbar hesitated, unable to think of a glib answer and hoping to avoid the question, but they were all looking at him in some anticipation. He might claim to be an amateur, but he was not sure that he wanted to appear a gauche rustic and, while he did not care a fig for Dacre's opinion, he wished for some reason to earn the good opinion of the two Germans.

'Well, I paint because . . . because there are certain impulses which, when I see something,' he thought of the light on Mrs Coxford's face and how he had forgotten to show Julia that hurried drawing, 'moves me with an irresistible compulsion. I suppose I am an amateur because I cannot simply set to and paint *anything*. I need to feel that compulsion.'

'And beautiful women give you that compulsion?' Münck asked seriously.

'Yes; but they do not have to be beautiful, and men's faces can inspire me too.'

'So you will be quite at home with your sailors,' Dacre sneered.

Dunbar shrugged, refusing to be drawn. 'Seafaring is my job. I have a living to earn. Do you have a living to earn, Dacre?'

'You have a wicked tongue,' he replied, apparently unoffended. 'Ernst here,' he went on, 'aspires to paint the ultimate female nude, don't you, Ernst?'

Ketlar shrugged. '*Ja*, of course. It is my ambition to complete the work of Botticelli. You know Botticelli, James?'

'Yes. "The Birth of Venus" and "Primavera"; but what do you mean by complete Botticelli's work?'

'Until Sandro Botticelli,' Münck explained quietly, 'only the male body was painted nude. It expressed

54

muscular power and action. But Botticelli painted his Venus unclothed and Ernst wishes to paint a female nude of such quality as to be unsurpassable.'

'That is a very grand aspiration,' Dunbar said.

'Of course,' replied Ketlar, modestly casting down his eyes, 'I shall fail, but if I did not attempt it, my life would be worthless.'

'If your Kaiser goes to war, it will be worthless anyway,' Dacre added, lighting a cigar with a flourish.

'Stop that!' Julia commanded. 'Politics are not to be spoken of. I thought we had all agreed upon that!'

Dacre shrugged. 'Paint away, Ernst. Perhaps I shall award you my personal *palme d'or* and write your name in history as the legitimate heir to the little barrel himself.' Here Dacre waved his cigar so that the blue smoke formed the letters *B O T T I* and hung for a breathless moment in the heavy air.

'Well, James,' Julia asked after a moment's awkward silence, leaning forward on one slightly tipsy elbow and staring at him over her glass, 'what do you think of my *beaux*?'

Dunbar smiled. 'You are a greater enigma than ever, Julia, and as for your *beaux*, well . . .' He paused and looked round the trio of young men. They were all a little drunk and looking at him expectantly. 'They seem a perfectly contemptible set of fellows, but I guess I shall grow to like them.'

There was another short silence, then Dacre leaned forward and said smiling, 'What? Even me?'

'Even you, Dacre.'

'Call me Icarus.'

'I can't. It's too ludicrous.'

'They liked you, my dear. Your joke at Icky's expense was masterly.'

'Icky!' Dunbar snorted. There was a cultivated air about Dacre that Dunbar took for falsity. 'Is Icarus his real name?'

'Yes, I believe so. He considers himself a wit, a poet and an aesthete, but there is little that's original in him. No, the man to watch is Münck. And Eric Retyn, though he could not join us tonight. He's similar to you. Anyway, Münck liked you.'

'I think I liked him,' Dunbar replied, as Julia's hand slipped under his arm and he felt her body pressed against his as they walked back towards her rooms. With a wonderful sense of happiness, Dunbar realised their intimacy had reasserted itself. It was as though Julia could not reveal herself in the company of her friends, but now that they were alone they had taken up not merely where they had left off outside Clayton Hall, but where Julia had half-promised.

'Julia,' he said laughing, 'I must find somewhere to stay tonight.'

'Why? Don't you want to stay with me?'

'With you in your rooms?'

'Yes, of course. That's what we decided, isn't it?'

'Is it?'

'Of course it is.'

'And what of Dacre? And the others?'

'Do you think I am a whore?'

'Of course not.'

'But?'

Dunbar stopped and swung her towards him. 'You know I think you are very beautiful, Julia. Any man would. On Sunday, in the attic, I thought we were close.'

'We are close.' Her breath was warm on his face and he bent to kiss her. She yielded easily, at once gratifying and irritating him. After a long moment she drew back. 'Tomorrow you are going to paint me.'

'But . . .'

Julia laughed and walked on. 'No buts, James, I didn't ask you to London just to flirt with you. You are going to paint me and on Friday we are going to see Strachan.' She paused, letting the information sink in. 'There,' she added, 'now you know. I have everything you need.'

And it was only later that Dunbar realised that she had made no enquiry as to how long he could stay and what his plans were. Julia Ravenham did not concern herself with such details.

He woke to a cold dawn, his body uncomfortably twisted on the long sofa. Getting up, he raised the blinds and opened the curtains. The sudden light exposed the tawdriness of the room. Dust and stains lay on the table tops, while the rucked furnishings and disorder were cheated by the daylight of their romantic association with more elevated preoccupations. Bohemianism was revealed as dissolution, abstraction as laziness. Dunbar wandered into the small kitchen and put on a kettle, then returned to the sofa to locate his trousers. He was fastening his belt when Julia emerged from the bedroom that she apparently shared with the absent Maureen. Her hair was coiled in an untidy knot and she wore a kimono of yellow silk.

'You can't paint in them,' she said after wishing him a 'good morning', indicating his dark serge trousers. 'D'you have something less formal? If not, there are some workman's overalls in the oak chest behind the curtain. They're Ernst's, but he won't mind.'

After a breakfast of coffee and toast, which seemed to be the extent of Julia's larder, she went through into the living room. She paused briefly at the door.

'Leave the table. Mrs Stevens will clear away. You brought your paints?'

'Yes, but I have not replenished them. I'm afraid some

of the tubes are almost exhausted. I certainly don't have sufficient for a large work and I have no canvas.'

'You will find an easel and some paints and brushes behind the curtain and I have a new canvas for you . . .'

'You have thought of everything,' he called after her. He drained his coffee and stood up. 'I can't imagine why you are doing all this.'

'Because I want you to be a success,' she called.

'Why? I'm a seaman.'

'You're an artist too. I'll be ten minutes.'

The door of her bedroom shut again and Dunbar went in search of Ketlar's breeches and the paints. Behind the curtain was an Aladdin's cave. A low oak chest contained not only a pair of workman's overalls, but what looked like theatrical props. Here lay the origins of the odalisque: a pair of curly-toed slippers in tooled, scarlet Morocco leather, a square of pale-green silk veil, a headband adorned with brass coins and a murderous and dully gleaming Arab *miquelet*.

Dunbar changed his trousers. Next to the chest stood a tall and battered collector's cabinet. Its top bore a number of bottles and tin-plate containers of oil, a stone jar holding a multitude of brushes, three palette knives and a short mahlstick, while its drawers yielded a copious supply of paints. Faced with so many tubes, twisted and squeezed by familiar use, Dunbar hesitated. Ernst's trousers were more easily purloined than his materials. The half-used tubes with their dull silver barrels and gaily coloured labels looked like the exhausted corpses of soldiers, victims of Ernst's energetic rapacity as a craftsman. Dunbar felt a vague disquiet at using another man's property. Then he quelled his conscience, deciding not to over-reach himself. He selected only those colours that he habitually used and lifted the large palette which, scraped clean, stood on edge between cabinet and chest.

Dragging the tall easel out into the centre of the room,

he squeezed his selection of colours into small, oleaginous hillocks, fitted and filled the double dipper with linseed oil and turpentine, and chose three brushes from the plentiful collection in the stone pot atop the cabinet.

He was about to call out to Julia and ask where the canvas was when he caught sight of the brown paper rectangle dropped behind the sofa. The sight of it brought him down to earth with a bump. The slight headache of a latent hangover had numbed him; it was only now that the import of his morning bore down upon him. He was to paint Julia. Not only that, but he was to paint her under orders. In effect this was his first commission, a portrait done to order. After his manifesto the previous evening, and his claim that he could paint only when inspired, he felt a sudden spurt of anger at Julia for her presumption.

How the hell could he pretend to paint her? She had assented to his embraces and kisses the previous night, but when he had ventured a hand upon her soft breasts, she had stopped their love-making at that charged moment.

He had not resented this. On the contrary, it came as something of a relief to know that it took more than the most casual seduction to gain her full compliance. Perhaps she was not the promiscuous young woman he half-hoped, half-feared she might be. And something odd had held him back, claiming him despite the prompting of the wine. In his mind's eye, he had caught sight of Dolores Garcia.

Now, as he lugged the large canvas over the sofa, he recalled perfectly the pleasure not of Garcia's bed, but of painting her. Could he recapture that quickening of the spirit that seemed to have lent an enchantment to his hand? Could he enjoy again that sense of almost rapturous inspiration, which had moved him almost as much as the sensation of entering the secret recesses of Dolores Garcia herself?

He felt a brief, biting pang of regret for something that was irrecoverable; he had painted Dolores as a lover, in the sad, sweet afterglow of post-coital *tristesse*. But this was no more than a commission and Julia, for all her apparent worldliness, could never offer the same sense of encompassment, of elevation that Dolores had bequeathed him. He was a fool to think such moments could be repeated.

He dashed aside the emotion; the canvas was a long rectangle, Julia's choice – a reclining or a standing figure? He tried to divine her mind with a quickening of excitement just as she emerged from her bedroom. She appeared unchanged; her hair was still coiled above her head and she still wore the yellow kimono. She walked back into the kitchen and returned with two glasses, a corkscrew and a bottle of wine. She put the glasses down on the table and handed Dunbar the corkscrew and bottle.

'Be a dear, James,' she commanded, then turned to the easel and, while Dunbar uncorked the wine and filled the glasses, she pulled the easel across the carpet. 'With so little space, you'll find the best light like this,' she explained. Then, taking her glass, she stood before him and looked up into his eyes. She had painted her face, he noticed, and her eyes were beautiful.

'You shall be a success, James. You are a better painter than Ernst; you have something I cannot quite define and I do not know how I know, except that I do know.' Her voice was low and he knew she was excited. He bent to kiss her, but she turned her face aside. 'No. Not yet. Last night you wanted to sleep with me and I wanted to sleep with you, but,' she paused to sip her wine, 'but this morning matters between us would have seemed, I don't know,' she looked about her, searching for a simile, 'as seedy as this room.' She drew away. 'Now, I am not a very good model, so I shall make the pose easy to break. Ernst wants to paint the ultimate,' she uttered the adjective with a droll emphasis and pulled a face that made him smile, 'the ultimate portrait of a nude woman. Let us see what you can do. No preliminary sketches, no careful working up a studied portrait. Just paint me as I am, in an unguarded moment. Ernst will try too hard and make a mess. Did you find the charcoal?'

'Yes. Are you going to recline or stand, or what?'

'Stand,' Julia said, pouring a second glass of wine. 'Don't use linseed oil. There's some of Robertson's medium on the cabinet there. Use that, it dries quicker, it's made up of copal varnish, white wax and poppy oil; very wicked stuff, but Rollo swears by it.'

Dunbar located the tin bottle and carefully exchanged the media. When he turned round Julia had finished her wine and had drawn an upright chair in front of the easel.

'Don't look for a moment,' she said, almost diffidently. Dunbar secured the canvas, its longer axis vertically in the clamps, and laid palette and brushes ready beside him. Then, his heart hammering in anticipation, he took a stick of charcoal and peered round the edge of the intimidating white surface.

Julia stood naked, facing him as though before a mirror, her weight borne predominantly on her left leg. She had drawn a hair brush from her discarded kimono and had paused in the act of drawing it backwards through her hair. Dunbar stared at her for a moment. Her breathing was heavy with the effort of calming herself and it occurred to him that she was not only nervous, but extraordinarily brave. Then his eye fell on the inclining of her pelvis and the line cut by the jutting of her left hip against the dark curtain, and the edge of her leg as it carried most of her body-weight.

Without thinking, in long, sweeping strokes of the velvet-black charcoal, he began to draw.

CHAPTER FOUR

The Artist's Model

Dunbar struggled with the painting for four hours, breaking the pose every twenty minutes or so. To his surprise, Julia put up with her ordeal with a marvellous patience that bordered on an uncharacteristic and inexplicable docility. By the early afternoon, however, he was in despair and it was clear to Julia, who in the breaks never looked at the canvas, but swiftly wrapped herself in her yellow kimono and walked up and down, or padded through into the kitchen to make tea, that matters were not going well.

They were about to start work again when she said, 'James, I didn't suppose it would be easy, but if you'd rather not go on, I'd understand.'

'No, no,' he protested with an edge in his voice, taking up palette and brushes and glaring at the canvas. 'I'm damned if I'm giving up.'

'If you're sure.' The concern and kindness in her voice made him look up, see her as Julia rather than the evasive image that mocked his inadequacy as a painter. He supposed it had been a foolish conceit that he could recapture that excitement he had once felt; such inspiration was surely like lost love – a regret to be mourned at leisure. What he had first felt was no more than an emotional echo of that original *frisson*, combined with the headiness of concupiscence. Julia's detached posing was clear evidence that she had done this sort of thing before, presumably for the shadowy Strachan; moreover, her professional quiescence was self-effacing. It was as though in her silent stillness her human presence shrank and his artistic endeavour increased in proportion, so that it gradually filled the room with its gloomy despair. Now her sudden concern transformed her and he knew in an instant what was wrong.

'The pose! It's the damned pose! Keep staring at me like that, Julia! Brush your hair at the side of your head.' The twist in her neck was anatomically more difficult, but it made the pose more dynamic, and her wide eyes showed not a Julia glimpsed voyeuristically at ease, but a Julia startled by what might have been a deliberate, but could equally have been an unintentional, intrusion.

'Got it,' he crowed, and kept her there for forty long, painful minutes before he remembered his manners and allowed her to relax.

'God, James,' she said in the throes of agony as the blood slowly found its way back into her prickling extremities, 'you are a terrible taskmaster.'

'Forgive me, Julia. D'you want to see?' he asked in a vain attempt to conciliate her.

'No. When you have finished it; will that be today?'

He looked at the canvas. 'You want to show it to Strachan, don't you?' She nodded, rubbing the nape of her neck. 'That's a tall order,' he said. 'I think you're the harder taskmaster.'

'Perhaps.'

'Well, it'll take some time to dry.'

'I have some special separators,' she broke in, 'you stick them at intervals round the painting and a board covers the wet surface.'

'I can see I'm to have no remission.'

'No.'

'Well, the light will be gone in an hour and since this is not going to be submitted to the Royal Academy, why don't we have another look at it tomorrow?'

'I have arranged to call upon Strachan on Friday.'

He looked at her incredulously. 'You have engineered this entire thing!'

'Of course. I believe in you, James, as an artist.'

'And as a man?'

She drew the kimono around her, shaking her head. 'There is time enough to discuss those other aspects of our friendship,' she said coolly. 'It is friendship that is important at the moment. I hope you agree.'

He grinned. From a totally supine creature, she had re-emerged as Julia the intriguer, quietly manipulative. He shook his head.

'You're a wonderful girl, Julia. I'm ready when you are.'

'Wonderful woman, James,' she riposted, shedding the kimono and for a moment standing before him with a naked imperiousness that he found devastating. 'You shouldn't ask me my opinion of you as a man and then refer to me as a girl. It's offensive.'

But he was not listening. She had resumed the pose and he was working again.

The studio of Seymour Conrad Strachan was illuminated by a large, north-facing window. The window consisted of three tall panes of glass set in leads of an art nouveau design. The entire atelier had been built in this modern style and was airily light. A tall fireplace boasted an elaborate design of interlocking lotuses, which spreadeagled a lively fire.

The room was almost bare, a single picture hanging above the fireplace, a finely executed study of an elderly woman's face. It appeared unfinished, the clothing fading

64

to some broad brushstrokes, which gave way to mere sketched lines at the extremities of the pose. At the far end of the room a raised dais stood behind the master's easel. Beyond this what struck Dunbar as the obligatory curtain partially hid the props of the artist's trade – two chairs, a white box and some odds and ends similar to those in Julia's flat, which, including the portrait over the fire, seemed now to be in emulation of this room, even down to the tall-boy of paints and equipment against the wall to the left of the easel. Also against the wall stood a large canvas, its wooden stretcher and wedges, making a crude, almost medieval artefact in this clinical room. Dunbar accurately guessed it to be a work in progress, for the wooden floor was stained with coloured paints about the easel, while otherwise it was polished and, at the opposite end, a square of Persian carpet bore a pair of small settees and an occasional table. Gingerly, Dunbar leaned his half-dry painting with its covering canvas against the wall.

Strachan's housekeeper had shown them into the studio with a friendly curtsy at Julia. Here at least, exterior appearances confirmed Julia's status as a lady.

'Mr Strachan will be back in a moment, Miss Ravenham. He likes to . . .'

'I know, Mrs Hardie; the post.'

'Of course.'

'Is he married?' Dunbar asked, looking round after the housekeeper had gone.

'No. Mrs Hardie keeps house for him.'

'And you model for him too?'

'Me?' Julia turned, a look of surprise on her face. 'Whatever made you think that?'

'Mrs, er . . .'

'Mrs Hardie knew me, is that what you mean? Implying I'm what, exactly?'

She faced him, suddenly angered, but Dunbar was

65

quick to react. 'Julia, I implied nothing!' The vehement sincerity in his tone reassured her.

'I . . . I'm sorry, it's just . . .'

'Just what?'

'Just that it's easy to make judgements.'

'Julia, for heaven's sake, believe me, I'm the last person to make judgements. I simply assumed you had posed for Mr Strachan. I didn't imply there was anything in such an act, any more than there was anything in posing for me.'

But his conciliation was ill-judged, provoking Julia even further.

'D'you think I take my clothes off for anyone? I suppose if you think I model for Strachan, you also think I model for Rollo and Ernst?'

'Julia,' Dunbar said with increasing exasperation, 'I don't know who you model for.'

'Damn it, James!' she hissed, 'I model for you! For you!'

It took a moment for the truth to dawn on him. Whatever Julia's connections with Rollo Münck and Ernst Ketlar, and they were clearly not entirely innocent – at least not as innocence was understood in Clayton Dobbs – she was not the happy-time girl he had been in danger of taking her for. To be truthful, she was an enigma, and she seemed to be saying something more profound, something that revealed more of herself than he had had the wit to grasp, something that would make her less of a mystery, if he could only fathom it.

'You mean I am the first person you have modelled for?'

'Yes, you damned fool!'

He sighed, taken aback by the privilege. 'Julia, I . . . I don't quite know what to say.'

It all made sense to him now: her reticence after they had entered the flat after dinner with Münck and

Ketlar, the passion in their kisses and her slow, but firm withdrawal from his caresses.

He stepped towards her, pleading. 'Forgive me, Julia. I was insensible of the honour you were doing me . . . What can I say?'

Julia sniffed, her triumph complete. 'You could try "thank you",' she replied.

'Of course. My sincere thanks. But do put me out of my misery; what is your relationship with Strachan?'

But his curiosity was to remain for the time being unsatisfied, for just then the door swung open and a tall, cloaked figure swept into the studio.

'Julia, my dear!'

Strachan extended both hands to take Julia's, over which he bent, assiduously kissing her fingertips with a familiar and obvious delight. Dunbar noticed, with a pang of pure envy, the glow of pleasure in Julia's eyes. Straightening up, Strachan held onto her hands, leaned back and gave her an appraising glance.

'As lovely as ever, my dear,' he declared, then let her go and, unfastening the chain of his cloak, removed it with an artful flourish and sent it like a black wing over the nearer settee. 'And this is the young man you spoke of, eh?' Strachan strode forward, extended his right fist and gave Dunbar a firm handshake.

'James Dunbar, sir. Honoured to make your acquaintance.'

'Conrad Strachan.'

Still holding Dunbar's hand, Strachan now stared at him. 'Strong features, Julia, strong features; better proportions than your tame Goth, Ketlar . . .'

Dunbar blushed under the forthright scrutiny. Strachan's piercing grey eyes were deep-set under bushy eyebrows and his long face was framed in a dense beard. The dome of his head was almost bald, except for a few long locks of hair that swept across his pate. But a luxuriant fringe joined his beard, grew over his ears and curled over the collar of his morning-coat. At the temples it was grey and his beard bore a pronounced streak of silver at the chin, so that he put Dunbar in mind of a fierce, yet oddly benign badger.

'Ah, he's English; your Goth wouldn't colour up like that.' Strachan let go of Dunbar's hand and smiled. 'But can you paint? It isn't your appearance that's important, it's your work. D'you know this young beauty has been singing your praises, eh? Wrote to me from Suffolk with the news that she'd discovered some rustic genius!'

'Hardly genius, sir, and hardly rustic, if you'll forgive the contradiction.'

'Of course; and it's Con to friends. I take it you'll be a friend, James?'

'Of course, sir . . . I beg your pardon, Con.'

'That's better. Now,' he turned to a side table against the wall and picked up a decanter. 'Sherry?'

There was an energy about the man that showed in his every movement and although he was tall and well built, he was far from clumsy. Dunbar caught Julia's eye and it was clear that she blossomed in the presence of Strachan, for she smiled with delight and Dunbar knew that their petty differences of a few moments earlier were forgotten.

'Sit down, the pair of you,' Strachan commanded, turning with two glasses full of *oloroso*, 'and drink your respective healths.'

'And you?' Dunbar enquired.

'Never touch the stuff, but I know you young people can do little without the fruit of the grape.' Strachan smiled and, having given them each a glass, sat down and leaned forward, his legs splayed, his elbows on his knees.

'Well now, let us see; tell me about painting. And spare me the modesty.'

'Well, there's not a great deal to tell.'

'James.' Julia sounded a warning note not to waste the opportunity.

'I always quite enjoyed drawing, but I was given some oil paints when I was in Mexico . . .'

'Mexico! And what the devil were you doing in Mexico? Ah, I recall, you are a sailor of some sort. Then who, in Hades' name gave you oil paints in Mexico?'

Dunbar laughed. 'It does sound improbable, I suppose, but the ship's second mate had some. He used to paint flowers, quite well, I remember, but no-one wanted them, poor man. Anyway, he discovered I had some small ability and gave me his paints.'

'And what did you do with this fortuitous gift? Paint ships, or men in *sombreros*?'

'Well, neither . . .'

'James. Con knows about the portrait.'

'Do tell me yourself,' Strachan said.

'I became involved with a woman – it's a complicated story, and not quite what you might think – but I painted the portrait of a woman named Dolores Garcia.'

'Have you brought it to show me?'

'No, I'm afraid not.'

'Pity. Is that all?'

'Yes, I suppose so.' Dunbar looked at Julia, aware that he had somehow fallen short of expectation.

'And were you in love with this woman when you painted her portrait?'

'Well, I, er . . .'

'Of course he was, Con. She was beautiful; stunning. A really voluptuous creature. You can tell from the picture.'

'Ahhh.' The monosyllable of satisfaction escaped Strachan and his eyes switched back from Julia to Dunbar.

'And this was a work of inspiration?'

'I suppose so.'

'You know it was, James,' Julia put in.

'He's an Englishman, my dear. Born with reticence stuck in his craw. Art, my dear James, is about forsaking your inhibitions. What the layman calls inspiration – an insipid word by more than alliterative comparison – is really the irrepressible explosion of emotion; your emotion, in response to what moves you, but I think you understand this, eh?'

Dunbar felt the sherry uncoil in his belly. 'Yes. I was asked to paint the picture for another woman, an older friend of Señora Garcia.'

'The older woman was her lover, Con. James fell for the younger in a brothel.'

'A brothel! My word, we have a bohemian at least!'

'It's a much more complicated story than that,' Dunbar protested.

'I'm sure,' Strachan observed drily, 'and as long as you didn't catch syphilis, it was doubtless an experience of some interest.'

'This all happened some years ago,' replied Dunbar, blushing furiously, 'all I'm claiming is that while of course I didn't learn to paint—'

'Perhaps you did,' broke in Strachan, suddenly standing up. 'Of course, one never stops learning to paint, and I'm sure you learned little technically, but if you understood the *meaning* of painting, that amounts to a great deal.' Strachan had crossed the room and turned back to his young visitors, leaning elegantly on one elbow against the overmantel of the fireplace. 'What do you make of this?' He jerked his head, indicating with a minimum of effort the half-completed painting of the elderly woman behind him.

'I imagine it is probably your mother,' James said without hesitation.

'Why do you say that?' Strachan asked quickly. 'Does it look like yours?'

'No, of course not,' replied Dunbar uncertainly. 'I suppose I guessed.'

'No, no, no, that won't do at all. You think you guessed, but in fact you came to an instinctive conclusion from evidence presented to you and registered in your mind. Now, what did you notice about the painting?'

'Well, the woman is elderly . . .'

'Go on.'

'The picture is incomplete. I mean, you have concentrated on the features alone . . .' Dunbar felt an awkward reticence fade into complete foolishness.

'Come on, come on. What do you deduce from these things?'

Dunbar shot a look at Julia. The intensity of her expression urged him on. He swallowed hard, momentarily embarrassed. 'Well, from its incomplete state I imagine it was not a commission. You painted it for yourself, so the face was what mattered. Perhaps too,' he went on, warming to an encouraging nod from Strachan, 'you didn't want to finish it, as though to do so might in some way affect some covenant with fate.' A smile radiated across Strachan's face, which for an instant Dunbar thought might be ridicule, but he was filled with his own rhetoric now and determined to risk Strachan's scorn. 'I cannot imagine a relationship other than that between a mother and son that would be so easily explained. Furthermore, though I have to admit I am more acquainted with your reputation than with your work, there is a freedom of style, an energy which, I submit, might not be found in your more formal, commissioned work. I may, of course, be quite wrong, but I don't think so.' Dunbar stopped and looked from the portrait to Strachan. He shrugged. 'That is all.'

'Well, young man, that's damned perceptive, though I hope that you are wrong in respect of the energy I put into my paintings. A picture is dead without energy.

Perhaps you've discovered how the composition will confer energy. More so than the mere application of paint. There are some French gentlemen who'd argue the point, but then the point of art is largely argument. As an artist, you hold up a painted mirror to society and it points its ridiculed finger back and squeaks, "That ain't me!" Ridiculous. 'Tis but the "power gi'e us, tae see ourselves as others see us"!

'Of all the canvases I have ever painted,' Strachan said, turning to look up at the portrait for the first time, 'this is the most important. D'you know why? Not because it was of my mother, but because in painting my mother I took a risk, and because it was the first canvas that I executed from the gut. There is a piece of me in that picture.' Strachan stabbed his chest as he uttered the personal pronoun and his eyes flashed with wildness or emotion.

'I understand that,' Dunbar replied quietly, unaccountably moved, so that he felt the faint prickle of tears in his eyes.

'Yes,' said Strachan in a low voice, 'I thought you might.' He cleared his throat. 'Now, James, since you have failed to bring me Dolores Garcia, perhaps you would be kind enough to show me what you have brought.'

Dunbar rose and crossed to the double canvas. 'Put it up on the easel,' Strachan instructed, placing his right palm across his eyes.

'It isn't quite finished, I'm afraid,' Dunbar apologised as he bore his work nervously across the expanse of the studio floor. He sensed Julia's agitation and suddenly realised her embarrassment. If Strachan had never seen her naked, his change of her pose had removed all traces of anonymity. The enormity of her gift struck him, a gift far greater than a more carnal availability of her body. 'And I don't mean in the way that your mother's portrait isn't quite finished,' Dunbar mumbled as he pulled the protective blank canvas off the still partially sticky painting.

72

'No painting is ever finished, James,' Strachan remarked, his hand still obscuring his vision, 'it is merely abandoned.'

The remark struck Dunbar as he hoisted up the full-length portrait of the naked Julia and stepped back. He had certainly abandoned his landscape of the estuary of the Clay. He dared not look at Julia, but he was aware that she had risen to her feet in a reflex of apprehension. Instead, he forced himself to face Strachan as the artist lowered his hand.

They had returned to Pimlico in almost total silence. Strachan had courteously ushered them out some twenty minutes before the Countess of Linlithgow arrived for a sitting. It was her portrait that faced the wall adjacent to Strachan's easel. Not even the artist's remark that he would see Julia 'at the usual time on Monday' intrigued Dunbar enough to provoke a single comment, beyond those necessary to convey the reviewed painting on the homeward-bound omnibus.

It was only as they descended from the omnibus and a light drizzle prompted them to hurry, whereupon Dunbar stumbled awkwardly, that he resentfully remarked, 'I should have thrown the damned thing in the Thames.'

'Don't be a dog in the manger, James,' Julia responded tartly.

'I feel most sorry for you,' he blundered on. 'Having been so wonderful, you must feel it a humiliating waste of time.'

'Don't be stupid,' Julia sniffed.

'I don't know how you can be so damned philosophical.'

'Perhaps because I am more philosophical.'

'And I thought it was going so well.'

'Perhaps it did go well.'

'How can you possibly say that?'

'As well as you had a right to expect.'

'I had a right to expect! Damn it, Julia,' he puffed, trying to keep up with her as passers-by gave them curious glances, 'the meeting with Strachan was your idea – a good one on the face of it, I'll admit – but your idea and one from which you must have had some expectations.' She bustled on, ignoring him. He was irked and added, 'You might be a philosopher, but you aren't a philanthropist.'

She stopped and rounded on him with such suddenness that he cannoned into her. 'For God's sake, stop dripping, James. Just stop; we'll talk about it when we get indoors. Just watch what you're doing with it, that's all.' Then she turned and walked on.

Having struggled up the stairs in her wake, he caught up with her on the landing as she fished in her handbag for the key.

'Look here, Julia, I meant no offence. It was a good idea.'

'Don't be so patronising.' She paused and put a hand on his arm. 'Look, did you really think Con was going to hail you like the Messiah?'

'No, but I thought you did,' he riposted with a rueful smile.

'Of course not. Now let's get inside and put the kettle on.'

He followed her into the hall and through into the main room. After the uncluttered elegance of Strachan's studio, the quality of the room's neglect outweighed its emulation. Adding to the generally louche air, Dacre lounged on the sofa.

'Icky, what are you doing here?' Julia's tone was testy.

'Ah Julia . . . and Dunbar, what an unexpected pleasure.' Dacre made a half-hearted attempt to rise, then waved an airy hand and subsided again.

74

'Try and conceal your hypocrisy, Icky. You knew perfectly well that James would be with me.'

'Ah. You've been to see Con Strachan. I had forgotten, Julia. Upon my honour I had,' he added, seeing the look of stark disbelief in her eyes. 'I had, upon my word as an Indian scout. What can I do to make amends?'

'Put the kettle on,' Julia quickly retorted.

Dacre rose with an exaggerated effort. 'Oh, by the way, in answer to your question as to why I'm here, I brought Maureen back.'

'*What*?' Julia's irritation fuelled the single querying syllable. She shot a quick look at Dunbar, who intercepted it as being vaguely hostile, as if the presence of Maureen or himself was inopportune.

'Look,' he offered hurriedly, 'it's probably time for me to pack my traps.'

'No, no, my dear fellow,' Dacre soothed, 'we're all dining out tonight. Anyway, I want to see this masterpiece for myself.'

'Where is she?' Julia asked sharply.

'Oh, powdering her nose,' Dacre said dismissively. 'Whatever's the matter, Julia? She simply summoned me from the station, asked me if I could pick her up from Paddington.'

'Yes, yes, of course,' Julia brushed the explanation aside and threw Dunbar a falsely reassuring smile. 'I'm sorry,' she turned to Dacre, 'it's just a bit of a surprise, that's all. The kettle . . .'

'Of course.' He pulled a conspiratorial face at Dunbar and remarked, 'I do want to see it,' before disappearing to fill the kettle.

Dunbar had stood the double canvas against the wall and helped Julia off with her coat. 'I'm sorry. Sorry about today and sorry about all that,' she said, her voice low as they stood close together.

'What is "all that" about?'

'Oh, nothing really. I hadn't expected Maureen back. Not while you were here, anyway.'

'If my presence compromises you, I'll go,' he offered, 'you've done enough on my behalf.'

'No, no,' she patted his arm, 'it's quite all right, really it is.'

'Who is Maureen?'

'She's a model. A real model, you know.'

'Oh, I see.'

'Kettle's on.' Dacre bounced back into the room. 'Now do let me see this painting of yours.' Dunbar hesitated and Dacre added, 'Look, I know it's of Julia, and if she's favoured you by taking off her clothes, she isn't the first naked woman I've seen.'

'It would be the first time you've seen me,' snapped Julia.

'All cats are grey at night,' Dacre retorted.

'Except the toms . . .'

'Look, is this a private dispute?' Dunbar put in with a false chuckle. 'If you don't want me to show it . . . I mean, I've already offered to throw it—'

'No, no,' Julia stopped him saying any more, 'show it to him. I'll make the tea. Only, Icarus . . .'

'Yes, milady?'

'Your honest opinion.' And she turned away while Dunbar and Dacre exchanged glances.

'Didn't Strachan like it?'

'Should he have done?' asked Dunbar, taking off the protective board for the second time that day.

'Why is it that when I ask a simple question, one question is always answered with another?'

'Why shouldn't it be?'

'Because it hardly advances the cause of human amity, does it?'

'There you are,' Dunbar retorted, though whether he referred to Dacre's final interrogative, or to the suddenly exposed painting, was not clear to Dacre, who gave a long whistle.

'My word, Dunbar, what a damnable eyeful . . .' Dacre cradled his chin in his hand and stared long and hard at the nude. Then he went to the table and lit the large oil lamp, for the afternoon had grown prematurely dark as the drizzle intensified into a steady downpour.

Dacre continued to study the painting, with Dunbar looking silently on as Julia returned with a tray and, at almost exactly the same moment, another woman entered the room.

She was of middle height, but willow slender, which, in her light grey dress seen in the umbral recesses of the room, made her look taller than she was. Her face had a sculpted quality that gave it a dark elegance. Her eyes seemed coal-black, intense under the dark arches of her brows, while her mouth was well shaped. Dunbar's eyes flicked to the Moorish odalisque above the fireplace and he thought he had never seen anyone so arrestingly beautiful since the little Mexican whore Conchita. He had fallen head over heels in unrequited love with her years earlier. He was less impetuous now, but he could not help the thunder of his heart as he inclined his head, half-thinking her to be the countess escaped from Strachan's studio.

But the strange young woman was not looking at him, she was staring at the painting illuminated in the gloom of the wet autumn afternoon by Dacre holding the lamp. Fascinated, Dunbar watched the newcomer's face crossed by a momentary frown, which faded to a smile. He was smitten by that simple lateral elongation of Maureen's mouth, half-choked by the surge of emotion that the apparition had caused in him.

'That's Julia,' the young woman said, advancing into the room as Julia set the tray down with a clatter.

'Ah, Maureen,' Dacre said, turning with a kindly smile,

'meet the artist, James Dunbar.' Dacre gestured at Dunbar and then at the woman in grey. 'Dunbar, may I introduce you to Miss Maureen Fletcher.'

'It is an honour,' Dunbar said, inclining his head for the second time. She dropped him a curtsy with a shy smile that Dunbar found entrancing, then she gazed at the painting again.

'It's very good, Mr Dunbar.'

'James, please; but I'm afraid Conrad Strachan didn't think much of it.'

'What did Con say about it?' Dacre asked.

'Never mind Strachan,' Julia put in as she poured the tea with an irritated tinkle, 'what do you think, Icarus?'

'Me? Well . . .'

'Go on,' prompted Dunbar, still gazing at Maureen and happier now than he had been since leaving Strachan, secure in the knowledge that this lovely creature thought it passed muster as a work of something approaching art.

'Well, it is bold and the brushwork is vigorous . . . most energetic. I mean, I can see why Julia thought Con might like your work; his own has a similar quality.' Dacre paused, then added, 'There is some problem here,' pointing at the lower left leg, 'and perhaps here,' he extended his hand to wave it vaguely in the vicinity of the left collar bone and the adjacent shoulder. 'I should not call it a masterpiece,' he said reflectively, 'but I would put it at better than a tiro work.' Dacre, no longer facetious, turned to Dunbar with a genuine interest. 'You have not, I think, had much experience or practice with anatomical study, is that not so?'

'Very good, Icky,' said Julia handing out the tea. 'You might almost have been at Strachan's . . .'

'You mean that is what Con said?' There was a gleam of anticipatory delight in Dacre's eyes.

'He was not as charitable as you, though,' Dunbar added.

'What did he say, then?' Dacre persisted.

'That it was anatomically inept.'

'That's not true, James,' Julia interrupted. 'He was highly critical of the feet and the left shoulder. You could hardly expect him to be little other than specific, but he intended to help you. You're being unreasonable. Besides, you should not take it as damning. Bonnard can't do feet and no-one holds that against him.'

'Who the devil is Bonnard?' Dunbar asked, trying to sound off-handedly amusing.

'One of Julia's French acquaintances,' explained Dacre.

'I've never met him, but I have seen his work in Paris,' she said.

'Well, never mind about Bonnard. I have seen worse and heard it praised.' Maureen's accent had a country burr to it, reminding Dunbar of his native Suffolk.

'Thank you,' he said, acknowledging her compliment.

'Well, if you have all finished admiring James's work, there is some tea here.'

'But what,' persisted Dacre, accepting a cup from Julia and seating himself next to her with a delicate withdrawal of his trouser legs, 'what did Con actually say?'

'He said,' Julia explained, 'that Dunbar's work showed promise, but that he was academically weak in anatomy, that he should lose no opportunity to study it from the masters, should draw the plaster casts and attend every life-drawing class he could . . .'

'In other words, he should give up his career as a sailor and enrol as a student at the Academy, or one of the other London schools.'

'He even went so far as to suggest the Slade, promising a recommendation,' went on Julia.

'Ahhh, so it's the horns of the dilemma,' Dacre smiled at Dunbar. 'You are, as it were, on the very cusp of a decision.'

'How good an artist is Strachan?' Dunbar asked suddenly. 'I mean, I know him to be a society portraitist with a glittering reputation, but . . .'

'He paints the rich and famous,' said Dacre, 'in such a way that they can see just how rich and famous they really are. He confronts them with the arrogance of their success. They are seduced by their own pride. And *love* it.'

'But is that art?'

'It's income, my dear fellow, income; infinitely more important for the well-being of the body. Forget all ideas of posterity. If posterity wants you, she'll have you, but it will avail you little because you'll be dead.'

'But income is the very point. I don't have any income other than what I earn, so artistic pretensions are out of the question.'

'You will go back to sea?' asked Dacre, in disbelief.

'Of course. I shall have to,' and Dunbar shot a miserable glance at Maureen, who had remained quiet throughout the exchange.

'I think that would be a waste,' said Julia in a tone of quiet determination, 'because Con was far from dismissive.'

'Oh, I think you are right,' Dacre confirmed. 'You would be wasted as a sailor.'

It suddenly occurred to Dunbar that while Julia's motives were obscure, her intention was not. For some reason, she had brought him to London and posed naked before him in order to enable him to be taken seriously as an artist. Suddenly his stupidity in not understanding this seemed obtuse; not merely insulting to Julia, but cavalier in the extreme. It was as though he was backing out of a commitment, made worse by the lengths to which she had gone to help him.

The realisation struck him like a blow and was all the more confused by the presence of Maureen. She was clearly not the intellectual equal of the others, for she quite obviously took little part in these discussions. Dunbar had already detected the long-standing dialogue, of which the events of the last few days were but a part, between Julia, the independent woman, and Dacre, the aesthetic exquisite.

In this instant, Dunbar felt guilt in respect of Julia, shame in front of Maureen and, for himself, the sense of being compromised. A wave of miserable humiliation swept over him and he stood up. 'I'm sorry, Julia. I had no idea where all this was leading. I think I have made a fool of myself. I must go . . .'

'Dunbar, for God's sake sit down,' Dacre commanded.

Dunbar shook his head. 'I mean no disrespect, but this is no affair of yours, Dacre.'

'You don't have to go,' protested Julia, 'please . . .'

'I do,' he said.

'Look, Dunbar, we can discuss this over dinner. I've got old Stevens brewing something for us all in my rooms. The moment I knew Maureen was on her way back it occurred to me that it would be enjoyable to meet Münck and Ketlar again.

Dunbar capitulated out of good manners, a desire to try and apologise to Julia, and the forlorn hope that he might amend the impression he must have made on Maureen.

'You're just a bit depressed,' said Dacre soothingly, pouring oil on troubled waters. 'It's a big decision to have to make.'

Dunbar held his tongue; he was grateful to them all, but he could not make his life in their midst. He recalled the moment when, as a boy, he had pushed open the door of Jenny Broom's room and caught her washing herself. It was when she looked up that he had felt the compulsion to run. He felt something similar now. Maureen's beauty was as intimidating, in its own way, as the desire in Jenny's eyes had been. He had never realised Jenny's need, but his own fear of rejection

81

drove him from Maureen at the very moment he fell in love.

But falling in love, he had learned in the Mexican brothel, was a self-centred flirtation with one's own dreams, better eviscerated in uncomplicated lust. No, he must forget all this nonsense; must resist the silly impulse to daub, just as an alcoholic must resist the temptation to drink. He was better off at sea, away from these odd, yet seductively charming companions. He did not, could not, belong with them.

He did his best to sustain his part in the evening's conversation, but Julia flirted outrageously with Dacre and Ketlar, and Münck in his gentle way made something of a fuss of Maureen, so they subconsciously rejected him, even as they sought to make him welcome.

Only in Julia's rooms in the small hours did she finally turn to him. 'I suppose I knew you wouldn't wish to stay,' she said dejectedly.

'Did you really want me to?'

She shrugged. She was more than a little drunk and her eyes swam with tears. 'It would have made some meaning of my life.'

'Julia, I am truly sorry. I had no idea.'

'No, there was no point in saying anything. I just thought . . . It doesn't matter.'

'But why did you do it? Just because you thought I had some small talent?'

'I thought perhaps you had a great talent, you stupid fool. I see now, I made a mistake.' She smiled and looked at Maureen, who was smoothing her dress before retiring to the bedroom.

'Goodnight,' she said, and Dunbar looked up at her, marvelling at her beauty. Then she was gone.

'Who is she?' he asked, the tactless question out of his mouth before he could stop himself.

'I told you,' Julia said sharply, 'a model; an impecunious young woman who makes a living by standing naked in front of men who wish to paint her.'

'Julia, I'm sorry. Let me rip the canvas off the stretcher and burn it.'

'No! Don't you dare! Leave it here, for me.' Her vehemence astonished him and he relinquished the troublesome thing without protest.

'You bought the canvas: it is yours.' And with that Julia withdrew, privately acknowledging that her mistake was not in bringing Dunbar to London, but in not insisting that he brought with him the portrait of Dolores Garcia.

Dunbar watched her go, then flung himself on the sofa. He slept fitfully and badly. By the first gleam of dawn he was fully awake. Turning, he stared at the painting. The tall, pale nude, almost colourless in the twilight, seemed to emerge from the shadows, gathering solidity as if in confirmation of his ability to paint form. He looked at the awkwardness about the shoulder. He recalled struggling with it two days earlier; as for the feet, Strachan was correct, he had no knowledge of the bone structure beneath the skin, a knowledge that would have made his task easier.

He had to admit it was his own equivocation that had turned Julia's endeavour to abject failure, for Strachan's criticism was valid and perhaps Dunbar's own talent not entirely contemptible. But he knew he must go, leaving the riddle of Julia's intent unsatisfied, leaving the beauty of Maureen to others and leaving Strachan's encouragement to wither. Quietly he gathered up his few belongings and slipped out into the street.

CHAPTER FIVE

The Able-Seaman

The four-masted barque *Fort Mackinac* lay alongside, her yards cockbilled at untidy angles, braced clear of the hatches, which lay between the three deckhouses along her main deck. Dunbar could see heads bobbing about the outboard after boat on the skids at the break of the poop.

He lowered his bags and looked down at her from the quay. The ice, lying in the puddles, crunched under his feet and the burden of his baggage. The young flood tide flowed in from the North Sea and sent the filthy water of the River Tyne back upstream. Slow whorls of scum and dunnage turned slowly under the barque's counter. The once silver bellies of three dead fish gleamed dully under the grey overcast of the sky and turned lazily with a large, sodden paper bag, to drift slowly along the quay wall. The *Fort Mackinac*'s exposed boot-topping and topsides gleamed with fresh paint, proclaiming her newly out of the graving dock, while the liberal dressing of dust miring her decks with a wet, frosty slime, indicated that she had just completed loading coal. Dunbar raised his eyes up the steel masts. Above the new paint on her hull, the barque had a raffish appearance; Bullard, Crowe and Company were clearly among the parsimonious majority of British ship-owners. Rime frosted the stout steel stays and he wondered how he would cope off Cape Stiff, climbing out along the foot-ropes to secure an upper topsail of grade-zero canvas. He felt fear touch him, felt trapped by the foolishness of pride now that the romance had evaporated in the face of reality. He had stepped from an effete world inhabited by exiled Germans and dubious Englishmen, not to mention a curious, misanthropic Scotsman who seemed to be sycophantically regarded as a genius, into the chillingly cold reality of a riverside winter's day and the lonely moment of joining a ship. It was a descent into hell: physically and spiritually. The four-masted barque *Fort Mackinac* looked as bleak as Dunbar's own future.

He bent, gathered up his kit and made for the precipitously sloping gangway, to slip and slither down it to the foot of the port poop-ladder. He arrived on deck just as the hands emerged from behind a deckhouse, where they had been securing the starboard boat on the skids that arched over the after-end of the main deck.

'Well, look what we have here.' A tall, rangy man of about thirty adjusted his woollen hat and pitched a dog-end over the ship's side. Behind him, their breath making little clouds of vapour in the cold air, followed a few sailors, who peered at their new shipmate. An older man with a cast in his eye and an accent that Dunbar could not place held out his hand.

'New sailor, huh? Okay, my name is Sails. Ze bosun is ashore and the ship signs on this afternoon. Stow your gear in the fo'c's'le. You,' he gestured at the tall, rangy man, 'show him.'

The man made a resentful face then jerked his head and asked, 'What's your name?'

'Dunbar. James . . . Jim Dunbar.'

'I'm Grant.' His guide led the way forward, leaving Dunbar to hump his kit and wonder whether Grant was the fellow's Christian name or surname. As they went forward, leaving the after-hatch and boat skids behind them, Grant pointed out the barque's main features. 'After-deckhouse is the half-deck, but there's no sign of any apprentices yet. Mizen-mast and main hatch.' As they passed the pinrails around the huge steel column and the intervening hatch, Dunbar thought briefly of his own time as an apprentice and wondered if the *Fort Mackinac* would carry any trainee officers. 'Midships house,' Grant went on, striking the white-painted steel bulkhead in passing as they walked beneath the shadow of a second set of boat skids. The midships house was much longer than the boxy half-deck. 'Galley, chippy's shop and the bosun and chippy's cabins, donkey boiler and steam winch.' He led on past another opened hatch giving access into *Fort Mackinac*'s cavernous interior. Dunbar's nostrils were assailed by the sharp, dangerous stink of steam coal and he caught sight of the dull gleam of the black diamonds below.

'None of Jarvis's patent brace winches on this bare bastard,' Grant confided over his shoulder. 'This,' he thumped the side of the forward house, opened a teak door and, clambering over the high sea-step, vanished inside, 'is the "fo'c'sle",' he continued as Dunbar followed him into a gloomy space, dark after the brilliant winter sunlight. 'This is where we will all live in utter fucking harmony for two fucking years.'

It was not the forecastle, of course, it was technically the seamen's house, but the usage of sea-life transferred the historic noun to the modern improvement of accommodating the barque's seamen in a deckhouse, rather than under the actual forecastle itself.

'Port watch, port side; starboard watch, starboard side. Very civilised. Watches to be chosen when we sail. Just dump your gear and pick a bunk. Got a donkey's breakfast?'

'No. I shall have to go ashore.'

'Well, she signs on at noon.' Grant pulled a ready-rolled cigarette out of a tin, stuck it in his mouth and lit it, peering at Dunbar through the smoke as the new seaman laid his kit on the boards of a vacant bunk. Dunbar had forgotten about a palliasse to sleep on, the 'donkey's breakfast' of Grant's argot.

'You a proper seaman?' Grant asked suspiciously, catching sight of Dunbar's wooden paintbox. 'What was your last ship?'

'Oh, the *Orloff*. I've been in steam for a bit,' Dunbar answered with casual evasion.

'Never heard of her.' Grant dismissed the intelligence, clearly considering steam ships of no importance. 'You look like a fucking artist.'

Dunbar grinned. 'Actually, you might as well know, I was a fucking apprentice, but . . .' he shrugged and let the remark tail off; it did not do to reveal all one's personal secrets at once.

'Failed yer fucking ticket, eh?'

'Well, not exactly.'

'Got a woman and failed to sit for it, eh?' Grant grinned and spat out a small piece of tobacco. 'Always a woman at the bottom of everything. I wouldn't be here myself if there wasn't a woman . . .'

'Where's the best place to get a donkey's breakfast?'

'Up in Shields. We can get a drink, come on.'

'I don't want a drink.'

'Everybody wants a drink before signing on. This bunch are only working-by because they got paid extra. Bloody bastard's red with rust below. Just out of dock and the owner too tight to pay the dockies to paint her hold ceilings. Be our first job, you see if it ain't, once we dig the fucking coal out in Port Lincoln.' Grant turned in disgust and stomped out on deck, leaving Dunbar to a moment's repentance for his folly in initiating this mad enterprise. Then he followed the tall, rangy sailor and set off ashore in search of a bed.

They signed on in the comparative comfort of the saloon below the poop, crowding into the officers' quarters for the dull, bureaucratic ceremony. The master and mate of the *Fort Mackinac* sat at the table, staring from one face to the next as the men assembled. Some were clearly ill at ease, while others lounged with an almost palpable insolence. On behalf of the Board of Trade, the shipping master droned through the articles of agreement, stipulating the rate of pay against each rank and rating, and the scale of provisions, the quantity of pounds and pints the master must supply, which were the minimum necessary to keep their bodies and souls together during the forthcoming voyage.

Looking about him, Dunbar suffered another pang at what he had forsaken by choosing the spartan forecastle. When the shipping master had completed his ritual litany, the master opened the articles of agreement by signing them first, followed by the mate. Dunbar contrived to hang back and was the last of the deckhands to sign the document that would bind them all as a ship's company for two years. As the line of men shuffled forward in response to the mate's summons, Dunbar contrived to keep his new certificate of competence concealed, thinking the *Fort Mackinac*'s commander and the Board of Trade's shipping master, whose role was to oversee the ceremony on behalf of the regulating authority, would understand his reticence. In this he was mistaken. The mate called him forward.

'Dunbar, James, to be rated able-seaman,' the mate intoned, matching the list of names that the company had posted north from London. 'Papers, Dunbar.'

The mate held his hand out and looked up. Dunbar

handed his certificate over. As an apprentice he had no previous discharge papers and had to submit his certificate in evidence of having completed his indentures.

'What the dickens is that?' asked the master, whose name Dunbar had quickly read on the articles was Crawhall. Dunbar felt himself scrutinised by a pair of chillingly pale blue eyes. He was also aware of the men leaving the saloon ahead of him turning out of curiosity at the Old Man's loudly uttered question.

'Second mate's ticket, sir,' said the mate.

There was a moment's silence, then Crawhall asked, 'How old are you?'

'Twenty, sir,' Dunbar answered. 'I have just passed for second mate, but it's a steam ticket, sir.'

'You want the experience in sail, eh?'

'Yes, sir,' replied Dunbar, relieved that his point of view was understood.

'We've got a damned pilot-in-the-making here, Mr Mate,' Crawhall said in his loud voice.

'So it would seem, sir. That could be most unfortunate.'

'Are you a fo'c'sle lawyer?' Crawhall asked, turning back to the blushing Dunbar.

'No, sir. And I've no intention of becoming a pilot, sir,' Dunbar said. 'I've served my time, sir, but I had a notion to try a voyage in sail.'

'Had a notion? Had a notion! D'you hear that, mister? The young puppy had a notion! Well, my notional buckaroo, there's seaman's work aboard this ship. There's no room for a rust-chipping make-weight who thinks the ability to take an azimuth makes him a proper seaman.'

'I've sailed in North Sea smacks, sir, stood my watch and hauled nets when there was ice on the rail.'

'Have you by God?' There was a dangerous gleam in Crawhall's eye and Dunbar met the master's gaze and submitted himself to further scrutiny. He felt cowed by the man, but he stood his ground.

'D'you want him or not, Captain?' the shipping master interrupted. 'He can rate as an able-seaman and in time he might make you a third officer.'

'There's no wages for a third mate and he's had no experience,' Crawhall declared, 'and I'd rather not give him ideas.'

'I've applied for an AB's berth, sir. I'll be quite content with that.'

'Well, I'm damned glad to hear that!' Crawhall said sarcastically, sitting back, pulling a ready-filled pipe from his pocket and tamping down its contents. 'Very well, sign him on.'

Dunbar bent and added his signature under the column of variously ascribed identities, each set against a name penned neatly by the mate, alongside which was the man's rating. He noted three crosses, and a painfully juvenile hand beside Grant's name. The formalities of the signing-on concluded, Dunbar was about to follow the rest of the seamen on deck when Crawhall stopped him.

'Dunbar.'

'Sir?'

'Keep out of the half-deck. You're not an apprentice any more. You've just agreed to be an able-seaman: don't forget it.'

Crawhall jerked his head in dismissal and Dunbar scrambled up the saloon companionway and emerged on the poop, where the rest of the seamen were milling.

'So you *did* get your ticket.' Grant's tone was hostile. Though but an hour earlier he and Dunbar had stood side-by-side in a pub in North Shields, he had clearly drunk more than the pint of mild that Dunbar had stood him for his help in purchasing a palliasse.

'Well,' said Dunbar, smiling in conciliation, 'it doesn't amount to much; it's a steam ticket.' He turned to the men behind Grant. 'Anyone sailed with the Old Man before? He seems to have taken a dislike to me.'

'Aye. He's up through the hawse-pipe himself and hates 'prentice boys, but he's right enough.' The speaker was a middle-aged man, and an older able-seaman standing alongside added, 'If it's experience in sail you want, young man, you'll not be disappointed. Father's a driver; made his reputation in the *Erl King* after she was bought by Tricker 'n' Cox . . .'

'The *Erl King*? She was a tea-clipper, wasn't she?' Dunbar asked.

'Aye, one of the best . . .'

'Some say *the* best.'

'Well,' put in Grant, 'this'n ain't no bloody tea-clipper.'

'She ain't no wall-sided wind-jammer, neither.'

'Don't talk crap. One dreaming bugger's enough. This hooker's a Clyde four-poster, so stow your gab about tea-clippers.'

'You can git the speed out of a Clyde-built barque if'n you drive her, mark my words. Over a passage there ain't so much diff'rence, an' you can stow three times the lading. Tea-clippers was fucking yachts, an' no good for nothin' else but tea.'

'Aye, get a man like Charlie Crawhall up 'ere on the poop an' he'll drive this bugger like a Yankee hell-ship . . .'

The talk drifted off the personality of James Dunbar, quondam apprentice, to the familiar ground of old ships and former shipmates. After a few moments, however, with the cook and steward added to their company by the due process of signs manual, the bosun appeared and turned them to.

'You'll find yer hexperience wiv a chippin 'ammer a great hadvantage, for all their fucking ranting o' tops'ls and buntlines,' an old sailor said to Dunbar, as they went forward to the lamp-room in search of caustic soda with which to soojee the bulkheads and rid the *Fort Mackinac* of the dirt of the coal-staithes.

The next two days were spent in the limbo that precedes a ship sailing for a voyage in deep water. There was plenty of work to be done preparing the ship for sea. The yards, still braced diagonally across the ship, were trimmed to the horizontal. Dunbar's first experience aloft came with the hoisting and bending of the sails. These long, obdurate rolls of hard canvas, whose bolt ropes comprised up to three-quarter-inch-thick steel wire, and which were accoutred with steel earings, thimbles, cringles and spectacle plates, were laboriously hoisted aloft to their appropriate yard. They were then stretched yard-arm to yard-arm by their earings, and stopped off along their heads by the rovings that secured them to the steel rods known as jackstays, which extended the length of the yards. With the ship still wanting a few men, this arduous task, undertaken by a handful of able- and ordinary seaman and so-called 'boys', took them two days. The appearance of these monstrous rolls of fabric were at odd variance with the accepted concept of a ship under a pile of billowing canvas. Their unforgiving nature was not entirely foreign to Dunbar, whose experience in smacks such as the *Eliza Maude*, sailing out of Clayton Wick, had at least familiarised him with the feel of wet, wind-filled heavy-grade flax canvas. For Dunbar the difference lay in the matter of scale: *Fort Mackinac*'s mainsail was roughly the size of Colonel Scrope-Davies's tennis court.

The tugs came for them just before daylight the following morning when the last items of cargo were delivered by dray. These, some cases of personal effects and, of all things, a grand piano were swung aboard and stowed below. The hatch tarpaulins were pulled taut and secured by the carpenter with bars and wedges. Dunbar was assigned to help with this task, common to both steam and sailing ships, while the more experienced able-seamen were aloft squaring the yards. He did not resent the discrimination, glad to prove his energy and ability at once, rather than be shown up aloft at the very outset. There would be time enough to learn the ropes thoroughly; in the meantime he kept his eyes and ears open and his mouth shut.

In addition to his companions in the forecastle, the four brass-bound apprentices arrived with their trunks. Fresh-faced and wearing reefer uniforms, their appearance struck Dunbar with a nostalgic envy. The oldest was almost Dunbar's own age, the youngest a bare sixteen, a first-tripper with all the gauche bravado of the breed. Nevertheless the youngster beat Dunbar into the rigging, being sent by Mr Snelling, the mate, up and down all four masts before breakfast the day before they sailed.

Now, as in response to the pilot's whistled signals, the tugs drew the *Fort Mackinac* off the berth, Dunbar found himself handling the after-lines on the poop, coiling the mooring ropes away and tending the after-tug's hawser. As the barque swung head to sea, the pilot advised Crawhall to let the after-tug go.

'She's all reet now, Cap'n. You can let the head tug take her.'

'Aye, aye.' Crawhall turned aft. 'Very well, Mr Wilson, let go the after-tug.'

Wilson, the young second mate, nodded to Dunbar and the other men on the poop. 'Stand-by the tug's hawser!' He went aft just as the pilot blew a series of short blasts on his whistle and the tug's screw race under her counter eased. The hawser dipped into a slackening curve. 'Leggo!'

The men aboard the *Fort Mackinac* took the weight and Dunbar threw the spliced eye off the high bitts, eased it through the after-lead and let it drop into the murky water of the Tyne with a splash.

'Farewell, bonny Shields,' someone remarked.

'Aye, an' good riddance,' added another.

'That'll do, men,' Wilson ordered, not wanting his after-gang to draw down displeasure from the master and pilot, who were standing just forward of the helmsman. At the wheel stood the senior apprentice, assisted by the most junior.

'Steady now,' ordered the pilot as the barque's spike bowsprit aligned itself with the sulphurous cloud of smoke that betrayed the presence of the forward tug under their bows.

To port the fish quay, backed by the serried and rising ranks of houses and chandleries, stores and net sheds, clustered round the square white tower of the high leading light at North Shields. On the opposite bank the dry-docks gave way to a similar landscape, then the banks fell back, the Black Midden Rocks showed briefly to the north as the swell rolled in through the piers, and the statue of Tyneside's great naval hero, Cuthbert Collingwood, surrounded by his granite cannon, stared stonily out above their mast-heads. Then the *Fort Mackinac* was past the twin towers of the Tyne Piers lighthouses and quite suddenly at sea. Ahead of them, through the tug's smoke, the grey North Sea extended to the distant horizon.

Despite the long, low swell, there was little wind and the tug, her paddles thrashing and her hawser rising and dipping with the intermittent strain, towed them through a dozen assorted vessels off the Tyne Piers, to steady on a southward course.

What little wind there was came out of the north-east, so all hands were called to set the topsails and Dunbar found himself scrambling aloft once more, hanging back-down as he negotiated the main lower futtock shrouds. On the main upper topsail yard he and another seaman, whom he had heard called Bill and who seemed to be an old hand, each moved out from the parrel, edging towards a yard-arm, casting off the gaskets. As soon as the clews were let go, the chain sheets rattled as the lower corners of the sail were hauled down to the extremities of the lower topsail yard below, and then the halliards took the weight of the yard and sail, hoisting them until the sail was spread. Soon all six topsails were filling with a northerly breeze just strong enough to overcome the ship's own wind, caused by the speed of her towing.

Having set minimal sail to assist the tug, Captain Crawhall called the hands aft. He stood at the break of the poop flanked by his two officers.

'Well, men, we're outward bound and will take the tug until we make some offing or get a wind. We're bound for Australia. I'm a fair man, but I'll stand no nonsense, so those of you who don't know the ropes, make it your business to find out.' And with this short speech, which Dunbar felt was aimed at himself, the master turned to the two mates. 'Choose your watches,' he concluded gruffly.

The mates began to call out the men's names, just as the teams for football had been called out at school. Dunbar found himself in the second mate's watch which, as befitted Mr Wilson's junior status, remained on deck while the mate's watch drifted off below.

To occupy the watch, the men were ordered to set the top-gallants. The *Fort Mackinac*, although built by Russell's yard on the Clyde, possessed what was colloquially known as the 'English-rig'. Her sail plan consisted of single deep top-gallants above her double topsails, and these were surmounted by royals. This elegant configuration was enhanced by her line of 'painted gun-ports' along her hull. Above the dull red of her anti-fouled boot-topping, the barque's topsides were in three bands. The lower and deepest was painted in French grey and terminated in a narrow black ribband. The upper part of the hull, from the rail downwards, consisted of two bands, the upper of black, the lower intermittently of white, for it was broken up by the black rectangles of artificial 'gun-ports'. This traditional form of decoration was reminiscent of the days when merchant ships bore cannon. Four-masted barques possessing 'painted ports and royal yards' were thus regarded as old-fashioned and, with their deep top-gallants and royals, were considered much harder work than the bald-headed rig, which consisted of double top-gallants and no royals.

Mast by mast, Mr Wilson's men went aloft, cast loose the top-gallants, sheeted them home and hoisted the yards. The light wind made the task straightforward, a small mercy for which Dunbar was profoundly grateful. The fact that the watch was doing the work unaided, without much shouting of orders, meant that it proceeded slowly, allowing the novices both to understand what was going on and cope with the unfamiliar environment of the barque's yards.

After a few moments of terror, Dunbar felt increasingly at ease as he lay over the heavy steel yards, his feet braced against the foot-ropes, which swung out alarmingly near the horizontal behind him as he cast off the gaskets.

'All right?' the man alongside him asked. It was the same man with whom he had worked aloft earlier.

'Fine, thanks.'

'You wait till you're taking sail in and it's full of wind,' said his new friend encouragingly, 'and it's torn from your bloody fingers.'

Dunbar managed a grin, swallowed the bile that rose unbidden in his throat and struggled on. 'What's your name?' he asked through gritted teeth.

'Bill,' came the reply, 'Bill Andrews.'

'I wish I could say I was pleased to meet you, but right now I'm having second thoughts about signing on.'

Andrews laughed. 'Make the best of it. Old Crawlie's a bastard for getting wind. There doesn't look like much now, but it's out of the north and I'll bet my pay-off there'll be half a gale before nightfall.'

Dunbar looked astern. A few white wave-caps tumbled in their wake, but the sea was sullenly grey, almost as leaden, it seemed, as the monotonous coastline that lay on their starboard quarter. 'D'you think so?'

'For sure,' said Andrews finally, sliding in towards the shrouds and the way below. 'Come on, don't let the after-guard know you're nervous.'

'I'm not nervous,' Dunbar jested feebly, 'I'm terrified.'

Andrews grinned. About twenty-six or -seven, his lean body seemed at home aloft and his accent was difficult to place, genteel enough to arouse Dunbar's curiosity as to his origin. Andrews, Dunbar mused as he descended, keeping his mind off how far below him the deck actually was, might almost be the son of a vicar himself.

An hour later Dunbar found himself clambering aloft again to overhaul the buntlines and stop them with rope yarns from chafing the foreside of the sails and inhibiting them in their efforts to pull. His increase in confidence gave him the latitude to notice the canvas below him, stretching and tautening with the steady increase in the wind's speed. From the fore top-gallant he looked down on the tug ahead. Her sulphurous funnel gases were blowing forward and the hawser dipped slackly between them: *Fort Mackinac* was over-running her.

At that moment he saw a flurry of activity on the tug's tiny bridge wing, watched a figure emerge, look astern and reach up a hand to the whistle lanyard. Puffs of white steam billowed into the air, and a second later the warning hoots of the steam-whistle rent the air, to be followed by Crawhall's imperious bellow from the poop. Dunbar tumbled down on deck to help let go the tug. The hawser was thrown off the forecastle bitts and hauled in by the two men who had made a sudden appearance on the tug's open after-deck. Having recovered her line, the tug's helm was put over and she slewed to starboard and tore down the barque's side with a valedictory wave from her skipper on his tiny bridge. The bright colours of her funnel and upper works gleamed dully beneath the overcast sky for a few minutes, then she quickly faded to an insubstantial spot astern, as grey as the land, indicated only by the smudge of her smoke.

When eight bells were rung and Dunbar had eaten his dinner of fresh beef stew and dumplings, he went below. Most of the watch took to their bunks, though few were tired, all having had the previous night in bed. A few dropped off to sleep through the habitual practice of seamen to store up rest against the hours when they would be denied any; others read, mostly copies of recent, if tatty newspapers. Andrews, Dunbar noted, lay reading a book. As for himself, he had been too long ashore, in the comfortable routine of shore life, to doze off, yet he did not want to read. There would be time enough for that later. Instead he lay and thought of that last night in London.

They had all met for dinner at Dacre's suite in Chelsea.

Grander than Julia's rooms, Dacre's establishment declared him a man of private income. An antique bronze male nude graced one corner of the elegant dining room. Upon one wall hung a classical landscape of ruins under a molten sunset. In the corner of the painting a voluptuous young woman was being carried off by a vigorous young man. She gave the impression of semi-compliance in this act of putative violation.

'It's a rather good copy of a lost Poussin rape,' Dacre had said, handing Dunbar a glass.

'The alleged act,' added a heavily bearded and heavily built man in a thick Cornish accent, who had been introduced to Dunbar as Eric Retyn, 'seems to consist more of the youth exhausting himself by running off with the swooning maid. I always think it's difficult to understand why the desired consummation cannot take place on the spot, since there isn't another soul in sight and all this masculine activity will be prejudicial to its eventual outcome.'

'It's a metaphor for universal guilt,' Dacre had explained. 'The act must be carried out unseen; the violation must be private.'

'She doesn't look as though she's going to put up too much of a fight,' offered Dunbar, frowning, 'but if it's an abduction . . .'

'Oh, James, you disappoint me,' Dacre had said, smiling with mock disapproval. 'I had thought a seaman would not have stooped to a euphemism. It's a rape!'

'It's what passed for a rape,' Retyn had said. 'The thing was painted for clientele who would not have been too happy to have had the real thing depicted in detail on the wall of their withdrawing room.'

'Well, of course that's why it forms only a part of the composition.'

'Then it's a commercial product,' Dunbar said.

'Of course,' Retyn had replied, looking at Dunbar with

a certain interest for the first time. 'Did you think it was a work of art?'

'I am not sure.' Dunbar had shaken his head. 'I wondered why anyone should want to paint such a thing other than to please a patron and earn his daily bread.'

'Quite so, but Icarus likes it because it is worth far more money than the artist received for it. Or so he says. It was painted, he claims, by Balbaricci.'

'I'm sorry, I've never heard of him.'

'Nor has anyone else,' Retyn had said drily, 'though Icarus has some fantastical notion that he was a man to rival Poussin and Claude Lorraine, a great original Italian talent.'

Dacre, who had turned aside to provide drinks for Ketlar and Münck, swung back with a wicked gleam in his eye. 'Oh, but you are wrong, Eric. Your own charlatanry perverts your perception.' Retyn had laughed this insult off. It was clear that he and Dacre were sparring partners of long standing.

'Icarus thinks me a charlatan,' he had explained to Dunbar, 'because I have abandoned the rules and conventions that have shackled artists for centuries. You've met the great Conrad Strachan, I gather. As a craftsman, the man is a genius; as an artist he stands in line with Balbaricci as a conventional drone.'

'And his opinion?' Dunbar had asked.

'What, Strachan's, of your own work?' Dunbar nodded and Retyn asked, 'Did you feel what he told you was correct?'

Dunbar had thought for a moment. 'Well, I suppose in a technical sense it was, but . . .'

'But what?' Retyn had prompted impatiently.

'Well, I thought it was unjustified.'

'Why should you think that?'

The buzz of conversation in the room had fallen silent in one of those pregnant pauses that occur from time to time when company is assembled. Dunbar had become conscious of Ketlar and Münck, of Julia and the dark and beautiful Maureen, all waiting for him to reply.

'Well,' he had said flushing, 'I didn't think . . . I don't think he . . . I don't know.'

'Come on, man,' Retyn had nudged, sweat pouring down his coarse face as though he agonised over Dunbar's reply. 'What didn't you think?'

'That he quite understood . . .'

Dunbar had had no time to finish, for Retyn had roared a triumphant bellow and shoved his bulk through the company to seize Julia's hand and kiss it.

'Julia, you are a witch and you are right.' Retyn turned on Dunbar and raised his glass. 'My friends, I give you James Dunbar. An original!'

They had toasted him inexplicably and Julia had flushed with evident pleasure.

'I'm sorry, I don't understand . . .'

'Eric is a boor,' Dacre had attempted to explain, but Retyn had crossed the room again.

'My friend, do not listen to Icarus. His wings inevitably melt when he nears anything approaching the sun. I've seen your damned painting and I liked it.'

'For what *that's* worth,' Dacre had interjected.

Retyn had ignored the snub. 'It was not a work of genius, but by God I *felt* something.'

'And by implication,' Münck had put in, 'your work has integrity.'

'And you have promise!' Retyn had roared enthusiastically.

'Have you seen the painting, Rollo?' Dunbar had asked Münck. Münck shook his head. 'No, but I would trust Eric's opinion more than Conrad's.'

'That is because you do not wish to discourage me,' Dunbar had grinned.

'No, it is because I value Retyn's opinion. Conrad is a

highly accomplished portraitist, but success has corrupted his talent. His work is technically superb in all respects, but he is, how do you say – locked into, is it not? Yes, locked into the cage of success. He cannot break away from earning money; he is a slave not to art, but to money. Perhaps,' Münck had turned to Julia, 'Julia should not have taken you to him. Why did you do it, Julia?' he had asked in his gentle voice.

'Because,' Julia had said, speaking for the first time, 'Conrad was the only person I knew of sufficient stature to persuade James to take up a career in portraiture.'

'And why did you want to do that?' Ketlar had asked.

'Because like you, Ernst,' she had looked at each of them in turn, 'like you all, in your different ways, I think art is the most important thing there is.' She had turned to Dunbar and faced him squarely. 'And I thought I had discovered in James a talent worth nurturing.'

A short silence had followed. Dunbar had felt an intense embarrassment, not in the grandiloquence of Julia's assertion, but in the extent to which he had failed her.

'That is not quite true,' Retyn had said, breaking the momentary hiatus, 'love and food are more important than art.'

'But only just,' Dacre had jested quickly.

'So, Icarus, we agree on something! And here is Mrs Stevens like an angel, on cue as ever.'

Lying in his bunk, Dunbar could make no more of the evening in retrospect than he had at the time. The vapourings of the languid Dacre and the support of the opinionated Retyn faded; he better recalled the curiously introverted expression of Julia, whose manner that night had been withdrawn. He knew that he had unwittingly hurt her, but that he had been betrayed by his own ignorance.

How could he be an artist if he did not feel like one? He was no aesthete like Dacre, nor an artist of the modern school as Retyn was alleged to be, though Dunbar had seen nothing of the large Cornishman's work. And yet the thought of having disappointed Julia brought out in him a complex reaction of wounded pride, inadequacy and foolish pretension; and though the harsh and uncomplicated world of the four-masted barque *Fort Mackinac* seemed a somehow more honest, comprehensible and suitable environment in which he, James Dunbar, was infinitely more at home, he yearned still to do something with paint and canvas.

It was incomprehensible to him, until into his mind's eye swam the vision of loveliness that he knew only as Maureen Fletcher.

PART TWO

Deep-Water

At Sea, 1908–12

CHAPTER SIX

The Apprentice

Most of the life of a seaman, no matter what his station or ship, is monotonous. This monotony is interspersed with occasional enlivening events – an argument that might lead to a fight perhaps, the trailing of lines and the capture of fish to supplement the meagre and wearisome diet. Even the passing of another ship could rate as noteworthy. Aboard a sailing ship the relationship between her crew and the elements was more intimate than that aboard a steam ship, moved under the remorseless impetus of her own power, which was slowed only for self-preservation in the worst of weather. Both steam and sail, however, afforded the common experience of toil, much of which was sheer drudgery.

The scaling of rust in steel ships was a labour that supplanted the former tedious task of pumping, so prevalent in wooden sailing vessels. Scaling consisted of chipping and scraping, then coating the deoxidised surface with concoctions of boiled linseed oil and red-lead paint, according to the personal theories of the vessel's mate. Opinion varied as to the best methodology of preparation prior to the application of several coats of undercoat, over which hard gloss put the finishing touch. Such work filled the days of seamen on steam ships, but it was not all they did. There were the decks to scrub every day, the cargo-handling gear, consisting of derrick runners, guys and topping lifts in flexible steel-wire rope, to be overhauled along with all the associated gin blocks, pulley sheaves, leads, shackles and cargo hooks. On long passages between ports the engineers would emerge on deck and cosset the steam winches, which nestled at the corners of every hatch and, linked with the derricks and their wires, hauled slings of cargo in and out of a ship's holds in port. The standards to which all these duties were undertaken depended upon the resources made available to the ship's officers, the type of trade in which the ship was employed, and the diligence and competence of her crew.

Thus a cargo liner would appear smarter than a tramp-ship, and a passenger liner would outshine them all, rivalling even a flagship of the Royal Navy in the gleaming of her brasswork, the whiteness of her scandalised teak decks and the uniformity of her well-dressed crew as she glided in and out of the world's ports, the post-horn pendant of the Royal Mail at her foremasthead and perhaps the blue ensign at her stern, indicating that a high proportion of her company were naval reservists.

James Dunbar had been used to occupying the lower echelons of this mercantile hierarchy. As an apprentice bound to a single company, he had sailed on vessels owned by the South Wales Steam Navigation Company. These were all underwritten at Lloyds, registered in Cardiff and flew the red ensign. The *Kohinoor*, *Orloff*, *Star of the South* and *Pitt* had been tramp-ships, named after famous gems in honour of the black diamonds they habitually carried on their voyages outward from the United Kingdom. Thereafter, until fortune in the form of a cargo carried at a favourable rate, or a telegram from their owners ordering them to do so, they 'tramped' the globe in search of homogeneous cargoes. Their only respite was submission to the occasional survey and dry-docking, dictated by the rules of Lloyds of London to maintain the hull and machinery in an insurable and usable condition.

The economics behind sailing vessels were very little different. They too tramped, soliciting for homogeneous cargoes, with the disadvantage that they could voyage successfully only in the regions of the globe where the great winds were predictable and strong. On the other hand they required smaller crews, and while they might carry a donkey steam engine to power capstans and winches, management of this auxiliary machinery was entrusted to a single 'donkey-man'. There was no need for qualified engineers, nor the firemen who tended boilers, nor the greasers and wipers who looked after the steam reciprocating engines, the shafts and bearings and the increasing additional plant, such as electric generators, freezing plant and pumps, which were appearing in the most modern steam ships.

The needs of a world whose oceans had remained comparatively tranquil for a hundred years after the defeat of Napoleon were served by a multitude of ships. Thus the slim profits accruing to ship-owning kept seamen's wages depressed. So slim were these margins of profit that a considerable number of sailing vessels continued to exist parallel with steam ships and, moreover, to develop. But, dislodged from their position as the world's general carrier, big four-masted barques like the *Fort Mackinac* remained viable only so long as they plied their trade in the regions of the great winds.

These encircled the globe predictably from a westerly direction between the latitudes of forty and fifty degrees south, interrupted only by the southern promontory of the Americas, Cape Horn. In the northern hemisphere the continents obstructed this natural flow of surface air, so a sailing ship bound from the industrial heartlands of either Europe or North America had to sail south, the whole length of the Atlantic. In so doing she must necessarily pass through the windless 'horse' latitudes near the equator, which lay between the wind systems of the two hemispheres.

Here, Dunbar learned, the heavy canvas that he and his colleagues had so laboriously hoisted aloft in the Tyne had to come down for overhaul and repair, ready for the long passage round South Africa and eastwards to Australia in the higher latitudes of the so-called 'Roaring Forties'. In its place older, worn and patched sails were sent aloft, to answer the swinging of the yards as the watches sweated tirelessly on the braces to make the ship answer every zephyr, respond to every approaching cat's-paw of wind spotted by the officer of the watch.

This tortuous period followed a hard-running month as the barque had beat her way down through the English Channel, then, on Christmas Day, had rounded Ushant, trimmed her yards to the starboard tack and headed south. Crawhall had certainly proved a driver. Both Mr Snelling, the stocky mate, and Mr Wilson, the younger but no less competent second mate, had supported the master with equal determination. The *Fort Mackinac* had furled her cross jack and stowed her upper staysails and royals, but she had not yet shortened down to topsails, and the crew had done little more than haul a double-reef into the deep top-gallants. Not that this should convey the impression that her people had had an easy time of it. The beating to windward out of the English Channel was hard and demanding work. The ship, heeled either to port or starboard, was wet and bitterly cold. Her long main deck was almost constantly sluiced by sea-water, and the men clung to the lifelines as they struggled to haul the braces and heave the fore and main tacks down to weather cathead and chess-tree respectively. It was drier up on the poop struggling with the wheel, or on the top-gallant forecastle, where Dunbar found himself with the carpenter handling the headsail sheets as the barque went about. Nevertheless spray whipped across all decks as the *Fort Mackinac* bucked through the wind, then laid down on the new tack and, while narrow catwalks extended fore and aft along the roofs of the deckhouses, the seamen's work kept them largely in the barque's consistently inundated waist.

And when the men finally went wearily below at the end of their stint on deck, their accommodation was mildewed and damp, surroundings robbed only of their bleak misery by the extremity of exhaustion. The possibility of 'all hands' being called persuaded most of them not to undress beyond the removal of their oilskins and sou'wester hats. Indeed, most even kept their sea-boots on, for the struggle back into them when half-dopey with fatigue and sleep was too much of an effort and took too long.

On a steam ship the monotony of the day was interspersed with meals. On a liner these meals assumed an importance far beyond the matter of mere sustenance. On a hard-driven lime-juice barque they rarely achieved even that dignity. Before the fresh provisions that had enriched their first stew had run out, the gales and consequent sea conditions frequently swept the galley with water. This drove in through the doors, so that boots for the cook were as necessary as boots for the able-seamen. Meals were therefore reduced to simple fare: porridge, beans, curried salt beef or pork with rice, a meat stew called 'wet hash' made from tinned meatballs, tinned sausages, pea soup, stockfish and the dry hash called lobscouse; macaroni and pancakes, garnished variously, served as main or second courses; while stewed fruit and suet puddings provided regular sweets. In fine weather, bread would be baked and tinned, salted butter and jam made a treat of this, to be enjoyed with a pint of hot sweet tea in the off-duty dog-watches that divided the afternoon between four and eight o'clock. And each watch was compulsorily issued with a strong, undiluted essence of lime juice, that partially effective anti-scorbutic, which gave British ships and British seamen their enduring nickname.

But there were moments, rare enough to be truly appreciated, when the unremitting labour eased and they slipped for a while into the balm of a less troubled routine. As the barque drove south, the sun rose higher every noon and the hostility of the northern latitudes gave way to the steady trade winds. During the week they ran through the north-east trades, the drier air enabled them to air their accommodation, clothes and bedding and to enjoy the brief respite of the dog-watches.

As the *Fort Mackinac* reeled along in the trades under every stitch of canvas that her plain rig permitted, it was hardly necessary to start a sheet or trim a brace. The watch on deck relieved the wheel and lookout, and wielded their chipping hammers in a desultory manner. Occasionally either Mr Snelling or Mr Wilson would urge them to 'put some ginger' into their efforts, but this seemed more for form's sake than for expediting the removal of scale.

Even Captain Charles Crawhall wore a more cheerful countenance and would be seen, it was rumoured by the helmsmen, in almost idle conversation with the officer of the watch. He would ensconce himself at the weather break of the poop, where a notch in the teak cap-rail was formed by the right-angle at the top of the poop ladder, would take out a short-stemmed pipe and fire it up with the use of copious lucifer matches. But idle conversation or not, Crawlie's eyes never left roving over his ship, spotting a too-taut buntline chafing his precious sails. On such an occasion he would send an apprentice aloft to overhaul and 'stop' the buntline, for chafe was a great enemy of sail cloth and indeed was the reason why sail-changing was necessary for the light winds and calms of the tropical belt.

Another of Crawhall's favourite tricks was to observe from his vantage point the members of the watch at work on deck. He took a particular interest in the maintenance of the barque's sails. This the watch carried out sitting in a line along the lee scuppers, some on low wooden stools, but most on the deck itself, with one of the heavy-weather suit of sails stretched fore and aft over their collective legs. Under the direction of the old sailmaker, a Swede who had once been married to a Scots lassie, the men carefully overhauled each of the sails. They replaced stitching along worn seams, sewed patches, herringboned small tears where a flogging wire had snagged the canvas, or worked new cringles into the bolt ropes, a job that was hard on the hands. Old 'Sails' would issue each man with a palm and needle, along with a block of beeswax and a spindle of yarn. The yarn was rubbed along the beeswax to draw off a coating of the wax, which acted as both preservative and catalyst, making the constant passing and repassing of the thread somewhat easier. It was an invariable rule that the gauge of stitches was eight or ten to the needle-length. Crawhall could spot a diversion from this, it was said, the entire length of the main deck.

Dunbar, inured to the utter tedium of rust chipping, found himself 'promoted' to sail tending. Fortunately even tramp steam ships bore canvas awnings and boat covers, the repairing of which was usually given to the apprentices, so the conventions of simple sewing were known to him and he acquitted himself well enough, though not without trial. Bent over the almost rigid zero-grade canvas of the fore lower topsail, the last sail that would ever be borne on a windjammer in the most extreme of conditions, he was aware of an attentive Sails bending over him.

'Goot, goot, zat is ver' goot,' the sailmaker said, poking at the work with a bent and brown forefinger, its nail blackened and cracked, so that it rasped audibly, despite the constant harping of the wind and the incessant low, hissing roar of the sea as the *Fort Mackinac* made her eleven knots towards the Cape of Good Hope.

'Let me see, Sails!' a voice commanded, and both Dunbar and the petty officer started and looked up. On the catwalk above them Captain Crawhall, his pipe clamped between his teeth, a plain peaked cap on his head and his windburned cheeks a-bristle with his old-fashioned mutton-chop whiskers, stared down in judgement upon them.

Dunbar endured the scrutiny with a beating heart and then Crawhall removed the pipe and nodded. 'Very well, but mind you keep them ten to the needle, Dunbar. No more from you.'

Crawhall turned aft and Dunbar felt the sailmaker's hand on his shoulder. 'Goot,' he said again with a chuckle. 'He like you.'

Despite this praise, spiced as it was with a quasi-warning that Crawhall still nursed suspicions about him and required a high standard by way of reparation for his effrontery, Dunbar came to hate those sails in the scuppers. He had lost his fear of being aloft, largely because there were tricks and easements in the matter, as in most things. One never went aloft other than by way of the windward rigging with the wind blowing one against the shrouds and rat-lines. And when the *Fort Mackinac* was laid over in a strong wind, this climb was at a less steep angle than the first induction alongside. Negotiating the futtocks over the tops was similarly less of a terrifying experience than when the ship was bolt upright.

As for laying out on a yard, Dunbar had learned a certain cunning in finding his personal equilibrium so that, while his feet were standing on the foot-rope, he could lay over the yard with his colleagues, their feet riding up with the foot-rope to near the horizontal without the sensation of being in imminent danger of pitching forward over the yard and down onto the deck below. At first he had experienced a heart-stopping fear as others suddenly whipped up the foot-rope, so that his feet came up unbidden to the horizontal with the majority, but soon the men worked in closer unison, so that each leaned down to drag up the sail in conformity with his neighbours. Such teamwork, fallen into with the logic of ease, along with the ancient dictum of 'one hand for the ship, one hand for oneself' gradually soothed his terrors. This therapy was aided by the awful effects of fatigue. Instinct made one cling on, fatigue numbed the imagination; it also made one careless.

Whenever possible, Crawhall only called all hands at eight bells, every four hours when the watches changed, but young men require continuous sleep for several hours and the punishing regime of four hours on deck and four below, broken as it was by eating, meant that sleep was precious. Dunbar learned how to get out of bed, don boots, oilskins and hat without ever thinking about it, and how to be halfway up the lower rigging in response to a call for all hands before truly realising where he was or what he was doing. In recollection, such events shunted one into the other, so that he could never quite remember things sequentially. Instead he had vivid memories of isolated struggles with the terrifying, living entity that wind-filled canvas became, and recalled problems working knots in or out of gaskets, of having a whole sail torn from their hands just at a critical moment, and of losing a fingernail in a searing pain that produced the foulest language of which he was capable.

But this now lay behind them and for a while they could enjoy the north-east trades, which in turn were a pleasant preparation for the arduous workings of the ship through the horse latitudes and the calms of the equatorial belt. It was then that Dunbar's shipmates emerged as individuals, with private lives of their own, for sporadic and often interrupted conversations now gave way to longer discussions as they lazed their short leisure away, or occupied their hands with the scrimshaw and decorative ropework that formed the traditional pastimes of their calling. Others read and, in their quietude, gave Dunbar his new subjects. He began with furtive pencil sketches, but only once drew scorn. Predictably this came from the rangy Grant, but Dunbar's subject, Bill Andrews, asking to see 'what sort of a hash' had been made of his likeness, was agreeably surprised and asked Dunbar to finish it. Having done so, the drawing was submitted to all the occupants of the 'forecastle' for approval, after which he did not lack subjects. Even the wretched Grant was moved to sit, and thus Dunbar's abilities were revived and encouraged by the simple tolerance of his shipmates. This pattern of occupying the dogs continued through the doldrums where, as they passed over the equator into the southern hemisphere, a brief rite of passage was undergone. They had caught their first shark and its fin had been nailed to the bowsprit end by the most junior apprentice. This initiation was, however, to be followed by the ritual humiliation of crossing the line.

The anarchic ceremony was enacted shortly after the beginning of the first dog-watch, with Neptune, played by the bosun, accompanied by his hideously ugly wife – scarcely recognisable as the sometime sailmaker of the *Fort Mackinac*. Various courtiers accompanied King Neptune, emerging mysteriously from the paint-locker under the forecastle, their rope yarn wigs, wood and cardboard crowns, mitres, fins and implements of office or terror crudely constructed and painted. Able-seaman Grant was the barber, and for twenty minutes the junior apprentices, boys and ordinary seamen were terrorised

116

through the rigging until finally captured, stripped to their underwear and brought before Neptune, who ordered them to be purged, shrived, shaved and dunked. The cook, who played in this game the role of doctor, the soubriquet by which he was commonly known, administered a draught of his own prescription. After this disgusting brew had been forced down the throats of the initiates, they were compelled to confess their sins before the priest. Dunbar had been cast in this office, for Andrews, in the only confidential betrayal he ever made, had let it be known that Dunbar came from an ecclesiastical family. Having extorted the reasonably accurate admission that they all masturbated, Dunbar blasphemously blessed them with episcopal dignity and they moved on to the barber. Grant was savage in this office, literally cropping the boys' skulls with a none-too-sharp pair of scissors, though Crawhall, invigilating with his officers from the poop, stopped him scraping them with a deck knife, for fear of blood poisoning.

Finally the initiates were 'seduced' by the mermaids, the remainder of the able-seamen, variously attired in travesties of wig, breasts and finny tails, who threw the wretches into the temporary bath made by a top-gallant suspended amidships and filled with sea-water. Having tossed their victims in, these gentle sirens leaped in after them and proceeded to half-drown them in their enthusiasm. Such was the vigour of their assault that this too was finally stopped by Crawhall, who summoned each in turn to the poop.

Several of them could hardly manage to stagger up the ladder, so breathless and exhausted were they by their ordeal, but each received his certificate from the *Fort Mackinac*'s master, who quietly asked if they were all right, and then they went back among their quondam terrorisers to grins and back-slaps that put relieved smiles upon their young faces. It was a short and frivolous interlude, but it marked the boys' welcome into the rigorous and largely bleak world of the seaman, and for all its crude and superficial horror, it had in it a generosity of acceptance by the older men. As long as a lad endured his humiliation without complaint, he would never again be the butt of jokes aimed at his inexperience, and the occasion had in its contrived silliness a stoic element: preparation for what lay in the future.

Eventually they picked up the south-east trades on the far side of the equator. By this time Dunbar had revealed his oil paints and had executed a fine likeness of Bill Andrews, who sat patiently for him, as though understanding why Dunbar was compelled to work thus in his off-duty hours. Ironically, the necessity of leaving Andrews's portrait to dry allowed it to be seen by one of the apprentices, who, coming from a landed family in Pembrokeshire, fancied a portrait of himself with the ship in the background.

'I doubt,' the young man said confidently, 'whether I shall stay at sea. I think Papa thought it a good idea that I should see the world for a while before I took an interest in the estate, but I would so like a memento of this voyage.'

And so Dunbar painted Alan Moorehouse, who hung the finished canvas, itself a scrap of old number one from a ruined fore-royal, stretched by Chippy upon a frame made of planed-up dunnage, in the half-deck, where it was in turn seen by Mr Snelling. The mate had been inspecting the apprentices' accommodation and took the news of this embellishment aft, where he mentioned it to the master over dinner that day. Captain Crawhall therefore saw it for himself on his Sunday inspection and, after ruminating for a couple of days, ordered Dunbar to lay aft.

'I understand you do a bit of daubing, Dunbar?' Crawhall asked, standing in his customary position at the windward break of the poop. His pipe wobbled up and down in the corner of his mouth as he spoke.

'A little, sir, yes.'

Crawhall removed the pipe and waved it airily about, encompassing the entire main deck of the barque before him. 'Have you done any daubing about the decks?'

'You mean have I drawn or painted any scenes on deck, sir?'

'Yes,' Crawhall answered curtly, shoving the short-stemmed pipe back in his mouth. 'What else would I mean?'

'Well, I've done a few sketches of deck fittings, and young Moorehouse wanted the ship in the background of his picture. I'm not certain that I quite understand what you want, sir.'

Crawhall took the pipe out of his mouth again, 'I'd be prepared to pay you for a good picture,' and here the captain paused, fixed Dunbar with his cold, blue eyes and stabbed the chewed and discoloured pipe-stem at his face, 'a good picture, mind you. A portrait. Paint me up here,' he jerked his head backwards, 'with the poop astern of me and two men at the wheel. Behind them I want a big comber. D'you understand?'

Dunbar nodded. 'I think so, sir. Would you mind if I made a few sketches first? Perhaps did some drawings, and then you could decide which you liked best.'

Crawhall considered the matter for a moment or two and then agreed. 'Very well.'

'If the weather allows, I'll try and complete the painting before we reach Australia.'

'Well, we'll see about that.' Crawhall nodded dismissal and Dunbar turned forward.

So, as the *Fort Mackinac* stretched down towards the Cape of Good Hope and exchanged the blue skies of the South Atlantic for the grey overcast of the Southern Ocean, Dunbar crouched in the after-starboard lifeboat, or clung in the lower rigging, filling half a dozen pieces of chart paper with boldly drawn sketches, all broadly similar in content, but each subtly different in viewpoint. Then he sent word aft by way of the steward to say that he was ready for Captain Crawhall to make his choice.

He was pleased with his work, not only because it stretched him intellectually after the mind-numbing physical effort, which was all that was really required of him as a mere able-seaman, but also because it would be a truly figurative painting, such as he had tried once before with the death of Conchita, which he had shown to Julia Ravenham. Or had he? That Sunday in the rectory attic seemed so far removed in time and distance that he doubted it had ever happened, or that there were such sentient beings as Icarus Dacre, Rollo Münck, Ernst Ketlar or Eric Retyn anywhere on the face of this vast planet, which consisted only of a heaving grey sea. Julia too had almost gone, withdrawn as it were into an ever-fading image, like the curious coloured shapes seen when one rubs one's eyes, which seem to have endurance, but which finally vanish. As for the likes of Seymour Conrad Strachan, Dunbar cared not a fig, for the satisfaction of drawing and painting again, independent of all their alleged intellectual baggage, was simple, pure delight. Strachan's existence had become irrelevant to him.

Only the mysterious Maureen remained to haunt him, but even she, so imperfectly known and half-glimpsed, was more a product of his imagination than of any reality.

Crawhall sent the drawings back without consulting the artist. *This one*, he had scrawled in pencil over a heavily worked sketch which showed him in his oilskins, pipe in mouth, with the poop and wheel, the boom end and the clew of the spanker all behind him. It was not his best composition, Dunbar realised, but he could see its attraction for a man who occupied the centre of the little world that was the hurrying barque *Fort Mackinac*.

By mid-February they had passed some 400 miles to the southward of Cape Agulhas and, with the yards squared, the royals and crossjack furled, the three top-gallants hard reefed, ran their easting down towards Australia, 3,000 miles ahead, dead to leeward. The great combers of the Southern Ocean roared up astern and sometimes threatened to break over the poop, but it was high summer and things were not as bad as Dunbar had feared. He took a high pride in fisting the canvas when they reefed the top-gallants, and felt the pure exhilaration of youthful endeavour, of physical fitness, his lungs full of clean air, the view of the heaving sea from the upper yards quite magnificent and the rigging holding no fears that his lean and fit young body could not master. Occasionally the *Fort Mackinac* would run in among a school of whales, and various species of dolphins were frequently to be found gambolling under their bows, nudging upwards towards the decorated spike of the aptly named 'dolphin-striker', which stabbed downwards with the scend of the barque and led the guying bobstays down to the stem, tugging downwards against the upward lift of the fully drawing jibs. Their constant companions were the little pied petrels they knew as Cape pigeons and the lordly, gliding albatrosses, which seemed to gain from the rushing wind a power and endurance exceeding that of their great wingspan.

For a week the *Fort Mackinac* ran thus, reeling the knots off and ploughing her white wake through the grey ocean. Although the conditions were ideal for the heavily sparred barque, her crew were troubled by the deep cuts that opened across the palms of their hands, and by the salt-water sores that formed on their wrists where the cuffs of their oilskins chafed. The constant tugging on ropes and hauling on the kicking wheel gave their flesh no respite to repair itself and, without exception, all the seamen suffered agonies from these twin, related causes. Periodically they would see Crawhall and the mates taking solar observations – black, flapping figures, poised against the pitch, heave and scend of the ship as they held their brass sextants to their eyes and patiently brought the sun down to the horizon with the artistry of practice in order to calculate their position.

Then, in the space of one forenoon, their luck ran out. The roar of the wind dropped dramatically and by noon it was almost calm, an oily preternatural calm that had Crawhall edgily pacing the poop, refusing to let the eager Wilson send his men aloft to loose the royals.

'No, no, Mr Wilson. In this calm they'll do us little good and I don't like the look of things . . . It *smells* wrong,' Crawhall added with a frown, taking his pipe from his mouth, always an indication of serious emphasis. 'D'you follow?'

Wilson gave a non-committal grunt, but Dunbar, at the wheel by himself, observed the exchange and knew that the Old Man was right. Before he could check himself, he knew what it meant and instinctively gave voice to the thought. 'Ice!' he announced, with such conviction that both Crawhall and Wilson turned round to look at him.

'What's that?' the master demanded.

'Nothing, sir . . . I just thought the smell, mightn't it be ice, sir?'

Dunbar flushed at his presumption. But Crawhall did not swear at him, or tell him to mind his own damned business. Instead the master spun round to stare about them. 'By God, you're right!' Crawhall peered to the southward and, following his gaze, Dunbar saw it at the same moment. A faint muzziness lay upon the sea, what Skipper Hopton would have called a 'haar', a sea-mist, no more than perhaps four or five miles away. Crawhall turned on Wilson. 'Clew up that mains'l, Mr Wilson, and haul all aft on the port side, starboard tack there, d'you hear! Starboard tack! Then get the t'gallants off her!'

Crawhall stumped aft and up on the grating, on the opposite side of the wheel to Dunbar. 'By God,' Crawhall muttered, 'I've only seen this happen once before!'

It came on them slowly at first, a sudden slight but noticeable drop in temperature, which almost instantly beaded the steel stays with moisture and darkened the deck with dew. Then the upper yards became slightly indistinct and the smell of an old iceberg, for such it was, grew ever stronger in their nostrils. It was not a pungently sharp or offensive smell, just the scent of something different, like the first faint scent of distant land – something vaguely disturbing that woke in them ancient reflexes of apprehension which, in these remote waters, swiftly became fear. Wafted on the fitful wind, the scent dragged wraiths of fog with it. These crowded up from the southward, thickening with every passing moment.

'There, sir! Just abaft the beam!'

The berg loomed low and grey-white, almost like a dead rorqual whale, belly upwards, no more than a quarter of a mile to starboard of them.

'Growler!' Crawhall observed as the low and dangerous berg slipped astern. 'Up helm. Let her pay off a couple of points and ease her round to east-north-east.'

'East-nor'-east, aye, aye, sir.'

The *Fort Mackinac*'s compass turned lazily in its bowl against the reference point of the lubber's line as Dunbar altered course and steadied the ship.

'East-nor'-east it is, sir.'

'Watch her now, son,' Crawhall warned, 'if this is what I think it is . . .' An alarming anxiety was clear in the master's voice.

And then it was upon them. The squall's approach, masked by the mist that condensed out of the comparatively warm air forced upwards as the cold air mass drove like a wedge beneath it, struck like gunshot.

Dunbar's fellow-watchmates had barely ascended the topmast rigging, let alone fisted and stowed the topgallants, when the barque reacted to the onslaught of the wind. The *Fort Mackinac* emerged from the fog at a rush, lay down and drove along with the water pouring over her high port bulwark and sluicing in through her freeing ports. Abruptly the lee scuppers were one seething, white mass of water, in which members of the watch splashed and slithered up to their waists as they fought to slacken the top-gallant sheets and clew up the sails for the reefing parties aloft.

Dunbar was preoccupied struggling with the wheel for a moment as he fought to trim the ship to her course, then Crawhall grabbed the opposite spokes and they tamed the ship between them. Already the piping in the weather rigging had passed the whine of a gale to become the deep, booming roar of a storm-force wind. The intimate presence of the barque's master prompted a question in Dunbar's mind: surely an experienced master like Crawhall had seen this kind of thing more than once before. And then, as though in this moment of extremity, their disparate minds ran in curious parallel, Crawhall spoke through his gritted, pipe-gripping teeth, answering Dunbar's curiosity as though he had asked the question out loud.

'I've only ever seen a damned buster hurling itself out of a fog like that once before, when it took the sticks right out of the old *Blackadder*! Thank God for steel gear aloft.'

But Dunbar was not so sure; such was the great power of the wind that, with immense strength aloft, the barque continued to heel and while the men on deck had succeeded in starting the top-gallant sheets, they had failed to clew the sails up or lower the yards. From aloft there came the sharp crack of viciously flogging canvas.

Meanwhile the lee rail was now permanently under water so that the sea poured over just abreast the foremast and roiled aft the entire length of the main deck, meeting the athwartships bulkhead of the poop like a breakwater. The *Fort Mackinac* developed a wave form alongside her poop and the drag of it almost wrenched the wheel from their hands, as the rudder kicked back through the simply wormed steering gear.

Dunbar winced from the pain of his lacerated hands and thought himself better off than the poor devils ambushed in the rigging, unable to get out and secure the flogging top-gallants for fear of their lives.

'I'm going to lose those damned t'garns'ls,' Crawhall swore and Dunbar looked up from the compass bowl to see that the fog had gone and the mizen-top-gallant had begun to tear along several seams. Two men, Andrews and Grant, clung in the upper topmast rigging, clawing their way aloft, pinned to the shrouds by the sheer weight of wind upon their bodies.

Then Wilson ran aft, his face pallid under the black brim of his sou'wester.

'We must call all hands, sir!'

'Aye!' Crawhall roared his approval just as Snelling emerged on deck, woken from a doze by being thrown from his bunk by the sudden, jarring heel of the ship. His face was white with terror.

'You may drive her, Captain Crawhall, but d'you not hear the cargo?'

'Cargo? What's amiss with the bloody cargo?' Then a brief and almost palpable silence emanated from Crawhall. Even amidst the bedlam of the roaring wind and the flogging sails, as the sea hissed alongside and the rushing ship laboured, her rudder kicking rebelliously back at the twin helmsmen, that instant of her master's incomprehension hung forever in Dunbar's memory.

But the mate had been below decks, away from the elemental screaming and attuned to the internal noises of the barque. He had thus heard the protest of her fabric as something terrible happened to her.

Suddenly, in what was probably less than half a second, though by grasping it Dunbar always afterwards recalled it as a long, protracted period, Crawhall realised the dreadful import of the mate's news and his admonition.

'Up helm, son,' Crawhall ordered, 'let her run off before the wind. Take the helm, mister,' he shouted at Snelling, relinquishing the wheel to the mate, who fought for a footing on the steeply canting deck as Dunbar frantically hauled at the wheel spokes.

Years earlier Skipper Hopton had shown Dunbar how to luff a cutter-rigged smack up into the wind and bring her onto an even keel, her sails a-flutter, robbing the wind and sea of most of their hostility. But in a square-rigged barque one did the opposite, running her off before the wind, so that wind and sea came up from astern and the ship ran away from it, reducing the wind over the deck by the speed of the hurrying ship. More than that, after the hours of calm, the wave-height had dropped and while the shifted wind blew with venomous energy, it was too strong to raise a sea, for no sooner did the sea hump up into a response than the wind tore the crest from it, atomising it and sending it to leeward in a dense spray. This much was in the *Fort Mackinac*'s favour.

But the barque did not come up on an even keel, for, as Snelling had sensed, her cargo of coal had shifted to port. She lolled uncomfortably as those members of the watch below struggled out on deck and waded aft to assist the starboard watch, who were still hauling at the clewlines in an attempt to get the uppermost canvas off the ship.

'Damned foolhardy bugger.' The mate's voice cut through the roaring of wind and sea. 'Drivers always carry sail till something goes wrong and then they learn their bloody lesson too late. He's got more faith in the ship than me, that's for sure.'

Dunbar had no idea whether Snelling was talking to himself or intended anyone else to hear, but all of a sudden the barque's mate could contain himself no longer.

'Hold her steady as you go, damn it. I'll send someone aft to help you.' Then he was gone, following the master forward, leaving Dunbar to struggle with the wheel and keep the *Fort Mackinac* dead before the wind. There was scant shelter at the wheel. The shove of the wind's force caught Dunbar and pushed him forward so that he had to brace himself against the threat of being blown bodily away, while simultaneously fighting the big wheel and trying to keep upright on the canted deck. No-one came to his assistance and the deep cuts in his hands seemed to throb with the roar of the gale, marking the seconds of his isolation with the beat of his frail heart. He struggled thus for some time, unaware of what was going on forward, his eyes fierce upon the compass, well aware of the dangers of looking astern over his shoulder and all the time bracing himself and twisting his body to turn the great, teak wheel through half a revolution and back again. He was pleased at least that he had achieved this partial equilibrium, though each passing spoke drove like fire into his cracked hands.

And then someone approached. It was the apprentice Moorehouse, fighting his way aft stanchion by stanchion against the wind, the young man's face white. His squinting eyes betrayed the hideous sight astern, as the sea was churned to white and the spray drove downwind like gunshot.

'The mate says,' he gasped as he got within earshot, 'that we must lash ourselves.'

127

Dunbar looked around. A coil of rope was stopped off to the taffrail against such an eventuality.

'Get the line then,' he shouted and Moorehouse, blowing spray from his nose, turned and saw the coil, then slid down the listing deck while Dunbar, momentarily distracted, hauled the big barque back from her two-point deviation from her course.

The *Fort Mackinac* lurched in protest and Moorehouse lost his footing. The sodden deck was treacherous and he fell backwards, his head striking an eye-bolt in the poop-deck as the ship bucked upwards with a sickening jar. Blood flowed across the dark, wet planking and, in an instinctive reflex to help the stricken man, Dunbar let go of the wheel. Instantly he knew the gravity of his error, for not only was poor Moorehouse dead, but the wheel, no longer subject to the restraint of Dunbar's strength, took charge and spun under the impetus of the rudder below. Although Dunbar was back at his post within three seconds of being seduced by compassion, the *Fort Mackinac* was rapidly slewing to starboard and began to broach-to, falling into the trough of the sea where the weight of the wind once more fell unmercifully upon her beam and pressed her even further over to port.

As she heeled, the deck trembled faintly from a further shift of the cargo below.

CHAPTER SEVEN

The Accident

The *Fort Mackinac* lay on her beam ends in the hollow troughs of the heaving sea, exposed to the excoriating fury of the relentless wind. The sudden leeward lurch of the four-masted barque had caused every man of her company to fear for his life. The inexperienced felt pure visceral fear, while the more experienced were better able to judge the extremity of their case and the real chances of survival. With the lee yard-arms of the lower yards periodically dipping in the sea, it seemed but a matter of time until the *Fort Mackinac* capsized. She would disappear, to be posted missing at Lloyds in London.

But the trapped energy of the wind in her sails, and the shift of her centre of gravity caused by the lateral movement of her cargo, had found a fragile equilibrium. She had reached that angle of heel beyond which the gale could not push her, and thus her cargo assumed its new angle of repose. The wind was now deflected in a greater measure than it was exerting a capsizing moment.

Such a subtle balance of physical forces was not readily appreciated upon her decks, which were poised almost halfway between the vertical and the horizontal. The whole port side to leeward of the deckhouses was under water, so that the belaying pins situated all along her rail were immersed, while those along the opposite side were difficult to reach. The only mitigation was that the high side of the barque sheltered the clinging seamen from the tearing wind, and the top-gallants had blown away. However, the list made it impossible to lower their stripped yards, a slight amelioration of top weight that would have contributed slightly to returning the ship to nearer the vertical. To achieve this was an overwhelming and obvious necessity, which penetrated even the dimmest consciousness among the men struggling in the stricken ship's waist, and dawned on them in the immediate aftermath of shock.

Captain Crawhall was the first to realise that the situation had stabilised. He had been fighting his way forward to rally the men at the mainmast when the barque broached. As he became aware that the ship had steadied, the natural optimism of those who best wear responsibility asserted itself. It was afterwards said that he appeared to possess an almost demonic energy in his conduct, for he quickly strove to rectify matters; there were those who occasionally even mentioned the word 'heroic', an epithet rarely applied to anyone in the merchant service. But Crawhall was not heroic, he was merely aware that it was his job as master and commander to reverse the situation if it were humanly possible, and the small consolation of realising that the ship was unlikely to heel any further while things remained as they were was simply an opportunity to be seized. Drowning men, it is said, clutch at straws; but not every drowning man had the tenacity of Captain Crawhall. Some tended to give up, to capitulate to fate and shrug their shoulders at the vastness of the task before them, for the captain's words filled even the most optimistic among them with horror.

'Right, men!' they heard him bellow, 'we've no alternative but to get below and shift that bloody cargo back where it belongs. First, though, I want the sails clewed up. Let the buggers blow out, but rise tacks and sheets

130

and clew up! D'you hear there? Rise tacks and sheets and clew up!'

He looked about him and saw the stupefied faces emerging from the trauma of shock. 'God damn you, d'you want to fucking drown? Well, you're not going to drown on my bloody ship!' He approached the nearest man and roared in his face, 'What are you, a sailor or a lubber? Rise tacks and sheets!' He shoved the man violently and carried on bellowing. 'Mr Snelling! Mr Snelling . . . !'

'Here, sir!'

'Port watch forrard! Fore and mainmasts!'

'Aye, aye, sir.'

'Mr Wilson! Mr Wilson! Mr Wilson?'

But no reply was forthcoming from the second mate and, without hesitation, Captain Crawhall took charge of the starboard watch himself, taking them aft to tend the mizen- and jigger-masts. In his mind the priorities were so overwhelmingly straightforward that he thought no further of the missing officer, nor of the fact that Mr Snelling had been last at the wheel. If he considered this point at all, Captain Crawhall thought that Snelling had left his station after they broached and in response to his own summons. Crawhall was not a man for blame while there was work to be done; retrospective reviews could wait until he had the ship under command again.

On the poop James Dunbar stood irresolute, in stark contrast to his commander. He was stunned by the enormity of his guilt and responsibility. For a moment he felt like vomiting and urinating with the terror of reactive fear, as Moorehouse's body lay at his feet. But it was now borne in upon him that the *Fort Mackinac* was not going to turn turtle, that it was his clear duty to make himself useful. He reached for the line that Moorehouse had being making for and lashed the dead apprentice's body to the rail. Then he turned the wheel to put full helm on the ship and slipped the rope becket over a spoke. Finally, he made his way forward.

Captain Crawhall was leading the starboard watch aft to brail up the spanker when they came upon the body of the apprentice lashed by the wheel.

'It's Moorehouse, sir. He struck his head.'

Crawhall stared at Dunbar as though taking a second or two to digest this news; he cast another glance at where the lad's body lay, then his expression hardened.

'Very well. Lay aft, Dunbar, and start the clew outhall.'

Dunbar, half-expecting retribution, ran aft and buried his shame in activity. For two and a half hours they worked about the deck, gradually taking in canvas and to a large extent securing it. The stow was untidy and incomplete, with the lee clews of the courses still flogging their chain sheets into the water alongside, but the ship was eased and the wind, which still raged with ferocious strength, had nevertheless eased a little from that first fierce onslaught. Having achieved this much, Crawhall called the men aft and they assembled under the after-boat skids.

'We'll try and get some hot food prepared,' he began and the cook, who had been struggling among them, nodded.

'Aye, aye, sir.'

Crawhall turned to the steward and ordered an issue of spirits to be made from the saloon store, an announcement that brought wan smiles to the weary faces about the captain.

'Now, men,' Crawhall said, his voice full of the authority of his strong personality, 'we are going to have to get the ship upright. If we give the sea time to build up and the cargo shifts again, we can all say our prayers.' He looked about him, fixing each man with his pale-blue eyes as if daring them to weaken and submit to the private and individual weariness that cold and exertion laid upon them.

132

Dunbar, clinging to the rail at the foot of the starboard poop-ladder, revised his opinion of Captain Crawhall. In his own private desolation of seeing himself as the architect of the ship's plight, wracked with guilt and awaiting exposure, Crawhall's almost matter-of-fact attitude helped him pull himself together. He recalled Snelling's condemnation of Crawhall's driving; Snelling's abandonment of the wheel; and the approach of the wretched Moorehouse, who had only been sent to sea for the experience of making a voyage. Like his fellow-shipmates, Dunbar was touched by the invigoration of Crawhall's apparent optimism. He waited for the captain to go on.

'It's going to be bloody hard work, but I want the covers off the after-hatch here. We'll get access to the hold and then it is simply a matter of shovelling the coal, a hell of a lot of coal, from one side to the other. We'll do it in shifts. Mr Snelling and I will stand the deck watch, the rest of you stay in your watches; this is going to be a long job and we will work two-hour shifts. The starboard watch is to stand easy, to eat as soon as Doc's got some grub ready and then relieve the port watch. Sails, you're to turn-to with the starboard watch. Bosun, you work with the port watch, and the rest of the port watch can turn-to. Get as many shovels as you can, and re-muster here in ten minutes. Has anyone seen Mr Wilson?'

'I think I saw him go over the side, sir.'

Crawhall turned towards the junior apprentice, a lad named Bromley. The young man looked shaken and Crawhall asked, 'Are you certain?'

Bromley nodded. 'Yes, sir. He was at the mizen t'garn clewlines and I saw him washed off his feet. I saw him once and then he was gone.'

There was a moment's silence, then Crawhall glared round at the havering crew. 'What the hell are you all staring at? You've got your orders. Let's get on with it!'

133

And so they set about saving the *Fort Mackinac* and, with the ship, themselves.

The hold of the four-masted barque *Fort Mackinac* was a vast space. Its lower third was one long cavern, which extended from the break of the forecastle to the break of the poop. This cavernous hold contained the bulk of the ship's cargo. The upper third, the 'tween deck, was not full of cargo; there was sufficient spread between the two spaces to load the barque down to her marks and reduce her freeboard to its legal minimum, but it was in the 'tween deck that the greater shift of coal had taken place, despite the erection of timber shifting boards – fore and aft timbers specially built to contain the coal and prevent its lateral shift in sudden heels. They had, under the extreme conditions to which the *Fort Mackinac* had been exposed, proved inadequate.

Coal had shifted to the port side, piling up under the deck above so that one could walk on the bare steel deck to starboard, while the whole port wing, thoughout the length of the 'tween deck, was full of coal. They therefore lifted a corner of the tarpaulin and removed four hatch boards, enabling a rope ladder to be thrown over the coaming into the space below. This was to be not only their sole source of access, but also their sole source of light, for hurricane lanterns would have ignited the gases given off by the coal, which hung in the dust-laden air with a foul stench.

The first man below was Captain Crawhall. He returned to the deck immediately and ordered a windsail rigged to improve the ventilation. While several men went off to roust the windsail out of the sailmaker's shop, Crawhall ordered the first pair of men below to make a start. Two others were left on deck to keep an eye on them. A few minutes later the first pathetic scrapings of shovels against coal were accompanied by the coughing of the unfortunate men below. Half an hour later, provision of the windsail caused a freshening of the air and more men went below. The strong wind that blew into the open maw of the windsail drove a steady blast of cool, fresh air into the 'tween deck and conditions became almost tolerable. Nevertheless, the men had to come up on deck to catch their breath at frequent intervals and the port watch were not sorry to be relieved by the starboard and to scramble along the deck to the galley, to find something hot to eat and pints of tea to wash the grit out of their mouths.

Confronted by the filthy, stinking gloom of the 'tween deck, Dunbar felt touched by a more insidious fear than any he had previously experienced in his life. He quickly learned that a man could be brave in a spontaneous manner when he was suddenly confronted with simple choices. Such moments are perhaps easily imagined, decided as they are by the predispositions of character; but the courage to endure and work in conditions of extreme and dangerous privation requires qualities of a quite different kind. Here a quickly reacting imagination was an enemy, for every second was beset by the realisation that explosion was an ever-present risk, that a shovel could strike a spark off the steel deck and blow them all to kingdom come, while they drew every breath with increasing difficulty in the thick air. Moreover their task was an apparently impossible one. No single shovelful seemed to make the slightest impression upon the great wedge of dusty black nuggets and even half an hour of toil appeared a fruitless waste of energy. To achieve the maximum and fastest reduction of the vessel's list required them to dig out the highest coal and throw it right across the ship, a task that necessitated the diggers working out in the port wing, crouched up under the deckhead and at the lowest point, so that not only were they bent double, but they had to fling the shovel-loads uphill.

The thankless and apparently hopeless nature of the task bore swiftly down upon them, but for Dunbar it had even greater horrors. In one breath-rasping break, as he and Grant stood beneath the after-boat skids at the corner of the exposed hatch, braced against the heel of the barque, while the great wind continued to boom overhead and the sea lipped over the lee rail and ran up and down the lee scuppers, his companion managed to recover his breath long enough to say, 'You let the bloody ship broach! This is all your fault, you bastard!'

Dunbar stared in horror at Grant. The man's lean face was caked in coal dust and drying sweat, his mouth a pink, wet orifice as he waited for Dunbar's response. Guilt overwhelmed Dunbar; what did it matter how Grant knew the truth? It was enough that he knew it, and if Grant knew it, so too would every other man-jack on the ship. Dunbar felt sick and Grant saw defeat in his expression.

'You bloody good-for-nothing, fucking half-bred officer!'

The low, ominous rumble in Grant's voice threatened Dunbar. He knew instinctively that Grant was going to hit him, an instant before the seaman's fist struck him on the side of the skull. Dunbar had not an ounce of fight in him and accepted the blow supinely, as expiation of his guilt. His head spun as he jerked backwards and lost his footing on the wet and canting deck, falling backwards just as Grant too slipped, his equilibrium destroyed by the violence of his own action. As the lights danced in his skull, Dunbar hit the deck, one arm protecting his head from striking the hatch-coaming, but he was spared Grant kicking him, for his assailant fell full-length in the trough of sea-water slopping in the lee scuppers.

Shakily Dunbar rose to his feet and, seeing Grant's plight, took courage. Every time Grant got half to his feet, the lurch of the barque sent a wave first forward and then aft, with such a body of water that the seaman floundered and fell back, never having time to recover his balance and drag himself up the listing deck. As Dunbar's head cleared and he regained his feet, he took pity on Grant. Moving unsteadily to the lifeline and hanging on with his right arm, he extended his left hand to Grant.

'Take hold, you bastard,' he shouted and a moment later dragged the spluttering and sodden Grant up the deck.

'It . . . was . . . still . . . your . . . bloody fault,' Grant gasped, unremitting in his hatred.

'Maybe,' Dunbar snarled, suddenly angry with this intransigent man. 'But what the fuck would you have done if a man had fallen to his death at your feet? Eh? What the fuck would you have done? Told the bugger to get on with dying because some chicken-hearted shithead aloft was too bloody terrified to work his way out along the yard and get canvas off the ship?'

'Why, you . . .'

But Dunbar was too quick; he had turned the tables on Grant, touched some raw nerve in his assailant, and his own anger and guilt fed on itself. Dunbar was not going to surrender the advantage. 'All right, Grant, I know what happened. It's a bastard, but it's the way things happened. Alan Moorehouse is dead and so is Mr Wilson. Snelling left me alone at the wheel and it just happened. I don't need you to tell me I'm a fucking yellow-belly, any more than you need me to preach to you.' Dunbar looked at Grant. The sea-water had failed to wash the ingrained coal dust off him. The able-seaman looked a fright and Dunbar, his left eye half-closed and blood trickling from his nose, laughed in the face of his enemy. 'Christ, you're a sight,' he said.

'So are you,' Grant retorted, wiping his hand across his face. 'I'm no fucking yellow-belly, Dunbar,' he added.

'Nor am I, Grant, and don't you bloody well forget it.' And to stop the partially mollified Grant from renewing the quarrel, Dunbar threw his leg over the coaming. 'Come on. Let's go and shovel shit!'

The succeeding few days passed in a blur of unremitting labour, of exhaustion, of cracking muscles, cramp and headaches due to the foul air below. When the watches changed, men crashed into their bunks fully clothed and filthy with dust and sweat. Sleep was all too short, the meals too hurried and too sparse; their whole lives, it seemed, were encompassed by the stinking darkness, the dust and the rasp of shovel on black lumps of coal, of aching backs and blistered, cracked hands. The coal dust worked into the salt-water sores and splits, clung to their sweaty brows and ran down into their eyes. A butt of fresh water was made available, but even this ceased to assuage their raging thirsts, for within minutes of drinking the liquid was sweated out of them. It was warm in the 'tween deck, so warm at times that old hands feared that water had got below and that the cargo had ignited spontaneously, but mercifully they were spared that added hazard. As it was, conditions were hellish enough and best expressed by Andrews who, in the darkness as the *Fort Mackinac* groaned and creaked, her seams of rivets complaining like a living, aching body, cried out with a strange, plaintive and haunting despair, 'If I ever fucked a woman, I cannot remember it.'

But hardly a man slacked at the task. It was as if they each became a part of something greater than their individual selves. It scarcely seemed possible that each man's pathetic shovelling made the slightest dint upon that great escarpment of coal, and yet each time the watch changed, the men coming below would notice the difference. At first they made no comment, but as time passed the difference not only became more perceptible, but it seemed they would actually succeed if they persisted for long enough, and gradually time and effort brought their reward.

Meanwhile the *Fort Mackinac* drifted to leeward at up to five knots. From time to time they were within sight of small bergs and mist patches closed in upon them. Toiling below, the seamen were oblivious to this, and only Crawhall and Snelling considered the great mystery of their whereabouts. It was the cook who kept the men informed when they slumped over their meals. 'We ain't yet out of the shit,' he would say. It was an understatement in which the faecal noun was capable of several interpretations, according to one's perspective.

It took them four long days and nights of arduous labour to reduce the list sufficiently for Crawhall to order sail set again. By this time the wind had veered back into the west and, by getting the ship before the wind, the upward fling of the coal was considerably lessened. This raised morale and it took only a further three days to restore the *Fort Mackinac* to the vertical. Thereafter the big barque ran downwind as though nothing amiss had occurred.

But while Dunbar mourned the loss of poor Moorehouse, whom they had buried during a brief break in the mindless toil of shovelling almost 1,000 tons of steam coal across the beam of the vessel, Captain Crawhall was considering a more damaging loss to the *Fort Mackinac*, that of her second mate. He was not a man to ponder over past events. His suspicions about how his ship had broached surfaced in a question to Snelling, and the mate confessed that he had left Dunbar alone at the wheel, although he had immediately sent Moorehouse aft to assist. Thus it was Moorehouse's unpredictable fall that had precipitated disaster, for both men knew perfectly well that it was asking the impossible to expect a single man to steer the big barque when she was running hard before a heavy sea.

The question of the unfortunate Wilson's replacement

dominated the discussions of the two men as they handed over the watch, which they were now standing alternately. It was eight o'clock in the evening and would be getting dark within the hour.

'Well, what d'you think o' the situation then, Mister?' Crawhall asked, taking his pipe from his mouth, as this was a matter of gravity. The captain was always willing to ask advice, even when he had no intention of taking it.

'Well, sir,' Snelling replied, 'if Moorehouse was alive, as the senior apprentice, he'd be the fittest to stand a watch as an officer, but his shipmates in the half-deck are still wet back of the ears. On the other hand, if the bosun was a younger man, I'd say he'd make an uncertificated second officer. As it is, well,' the mate shrugged. 'I reckon you're thinking of young Dunbar. He's got a certificate, even if it is only a steam one.' Snelling sighed, 'The sailmaker told me Dunbar had worked like a Trojan shifting that coal.'

Crawhall grunted. 'For once, Mister, I agree with you. At least he'll not let the ship broach, he's learned that lesson, and I'll make certain he calls me if there's any sail handling to be done. Put old Sails in his watch until we reach the coast. The poor old bugger won't like it, but there's nothing much else he can do until then.'

'Aye, very well. And I'll have my lads haul that slack in on the main tack before they go below—'

'No,' broke in the captain, 'leave it. Relieve the wheel and lookout and I'll have young Dunbar aft.'

Eight bells were struck. The helmsmen on the poop and the lookout on the forecastle were relieved by the members of the starboard watch. As he went below, the mate called Dunbar aft by name.

'Sir?' Dunbar responded, fearful that at last retribution had caught up with him.

'The captain wants to see you, Dunbar.' Snelling saw the younger man's eyes flicker upwards to the oilskin-clad figure at the break of the poop, a dark silhouette against the sky. How often had he sketched that stolid body on its short legs, the face inscrutable under the soft brim of the sou'wester hat? Such circumstances had been halcyon compared with now.

'Aye, aye, sir.' Dunbar went aft to report to the master of the *Fort Mackinac*. He clambered halfway up the ladder, then stopped and coughed. 'You sent for me, sir.'

'Ah, Mr Dunbar, come up, come up.' Crawhall drew aside to make room for him. This unusually courteous invitation threw Dunbar into confusion, his heart thumping with apprehension. 'Look forrard, Mr Dunbar,' Crawhall went on, his voice almost soothing in tone, so that Dunbar smelt a trap. 'Come lad, look forrard and tell me if you can see anything wrong with the ship.'

The trap loomed. Dunbar sensed humiliation in store for him and could only guess that Crawhall's intention was to expose him for a fraud, prior to inflicting some horrid punishment for allowing the ship to broach.

'Well?'

'I, er, I . . .'

Some sixth sense warned Dunbar that Crawhall's anticipatory 'Well?' was not a bullying ploy. Crawhall was not goading him, he realised; Crawhall was *testing* him. At least, Dunbar quickly concluded, he would try and play the matter that way and avoid the foolish indecisiveness that threatened to overwhelm him. He stared forward. After the disorder of the previous week, the deck seemed well regulated. All he could see was an untidy bight of the slack main tack.

'The main tack needs recoiling, sir.'

'Well done, Mr Dunbar. I'm making you acting second mate. At least until we reach Australia. You're to refer any change of wind to me, of course. I won't have you hauling braces, but I'm putting old Sails in your watch. D'you understand?'

Dunbar was taken aback. 'Yes, sir. But . . .'

'You know what happens when a running ship broaches.'

'Yes, sir. And, sir, you should know . . .'

'That the mate left you before another man got to the wheel to help. Yes, I know. Moorehouse paid the price.'

'But I . . .'

'You obeyed orders, Mr Dunbar. Continue to do just that. To the letter. I like an officer with initiative, but not too much. Too much initiative is foolhardiness; it's a matter of judgement.'

'Yes, sir.'

'Very well, you may move your dunnage aft in the morning. Now you can take the watch. Keep her before the wind on a course of east by north. If the wind shifts, let me know.'

'Aye, aye, sir. East by north and let you know if the wind shifts.'

Crawhall nodded and turned abruptly away. He paused momentarily, his shrouded face lit by the sunset, which gleamed briefly in a yellow glare between the clouds that gathered on the rim of the world. His pale-blue eyes seemed grey, like a wolf's, Dunbar thought inconsequentially, while the captain's lined face with its pocked and leathery skin seemed carved in bronze.

'Don't forget, Mr Dunbar, any fool can get himself into a mess. It takes something more to get out of one. Now see to that main tack.'

'Aye, aye, sir.' Dunbar raised his voice. 'Grant! Secure that starboard main tack!'

He saw Grant look up. 'Who the fuck . . . ?'

'Mr Dunbar's acting as second mate, Grant.' The captain was beside Dunbar again. 'I'm appointing him and you'll do as you're ordered.'

'You're joking, Captain,' Grant expostulated.

'Don't wait to laugh,' Crawhall shouted grimly back. 'See to that main tack.'

Grant hesitated, then resentfully went forward and Crawhall turned aft again. 'There, Mr Dunbar, they know who you are now. By the way, how did you acquire that black eye?'

'Below, sir, in the 'tween deck,' Dunbar lied. 'Working alongside another man. He poked his elbow right into my face as he took a swing with his shovel. We couldn't see what we were doing.'

'Bad luck.'

'Luckier than Moorehouse.' The words escaped him before he could stop them.

'Don't be talking like that, Mr Dunbar. You're an officer now. Responsibility confers its own perspective.' Then Crawhall was gone and Dunbar was left on the poop with the two helmsmen dark against the last glow of the day and the ghost of apprentice Moorehouse lying in the port scuppers as the *Fort Mackinac* drove into the darkness ahead.

CHAPTER EIGHT

Adelaide and Afterwards

Captain Crawhall had prefixed the title 'mister' to Dunbar's name as a clear indication of his confidence; it was also a clear indication of Dunbar's status. When Dunbar rolled into his bunk that night, it was to the accompaniment of Grant's sarcasm. But the sarcasm was guarded, less explicit now, and it was not long before others in the watch, weary and eager for the balm of sleep, told him to stow his gab. Dunbar kept his own counsel; tomorrow he would move aft, into Wilson's cabin. At least for the time being.

The starbowlines had the morning watch, from four to eight. It was already twilight when Dunbar relieved Snelling and, after they had exchanged the course, discussed the wind and sea conditions and the sail the *Fort Mackinac* was carrying, Snelling asked, 'D'you think you can manage to take stars? The Old Man likes a fix and Wilson regarded it as his speciality.'

Dunbar had been preoccupied with the more practical demands of conning the vessel and had given little thought to having to take a stellar fix at such short notice. He hesitated uncertainly.

'Wilson's sextant's in the charthouse,' Snelling offered helpfully.

'Right,' replied Dunbar, 'I'd better get on with it. Thanks, Mr Snelling, I have the ship.'

The moment the mate had gone below, Dunbar went forward. Just beyond the saloon skylight and immediately abaft the mizen-mast stood the teak charthouse. Dunbar had only ever entered the accommodation beneath the poop to sign on, and so this was only the second time he had been allowed into the charthouse, whence a narrow companionway led below to the officers' accommodation. The charthouse also contained a narrow settee, under which Dunbar recognised the fog-horn, the patent log box and a box containing pyrotechnics. Opposite was a large chart-table, beneath which six wide, shallow drawers contained the barque's comprehensive folios of charts. Let into one end of the chart-table surface, a glass window gave access to the vessel's two chronometers, each in its own gimballed box. A shelf of books hung above the chart-table, containing Norie's *Epitome*, Burdwood's azimuth tables, a nautical almanac, several sailing directions, the manuscript book for the officers' compass-error observations and the vessel's log book. Also above the chart-table were a brass-barrelled clock, an aneroid barometer, an oil lamp and a rack holding dividers, pencils and the parallel rules.

To one side of the charthouse a teak, pigeon-holed locker contained the flags of the international code of signals and a tall rack of shelves fitted for retaining sextant boxes. Dunbar lifted the bottom sextant box out. A paper label was pasted over the wooden cover; it bore the legend *Christopher Wilson*.

Finding some scrap paper in the top chart-drawer, Dunbar gently opened Wilson's sextant box. He thought of Wilson floundering astern of the *Fort Mackinac* as the barque rushed away from him and left him to drown. Imagination conjured up such a vision of desolation that Dunbar could hardly bear to think of it. What a terrible way to die! Dunbar hoped the young officer had been knocked senseless as he went over the side; hoped he had

had his brains beaten out of his skull by the bulwark, the heavy splice of a steel shroud or a rigging screw, rather than be swept astern, to look up and see the white arc of the counter sweeping past. In a few moments the swirl of the wake would subside and all that the doomed man would see, to mock him in his desperation, would be the fading glow of the barque's stern light as she lifted on a swell. Then nothing . . .

Dunbar shuddered and lifted the sextant out of its box. Raising it, he squinted through the tiny optic, which enabled the vernier scale to be read. He saw on the silvered arc underneath the closely engraved intervals marking degrees, minutes and parts thereof, and the maker's name: *Ainsley, Barry Dock*. Pulling the index back to read zero with a sigh, he went on deck.

The daylight was growing fast and the less brilliant stars had already faded. Banks of cloud rolled up astern of them where the night lingered, but apart from isolated patches of cumulus, the sky was relatively clear: Dunbar could not plead the excuse of an overcast sky. He walked forward to the standard compass just beyond the mizen-mast and, with one hand, wrenched the heavy brass cover off to get his bearings and locate a few stars. He found Sirius, low on the horizon to the west, Regulus to the north-west and Canopus to the south-west. Almost overhead, Rigil Kentaurus was close to the Southern Cross, with Spica glimmering above the main yard-arm. Still bright ahead of them, hanging in the lightening eastern sky, mighty Antares rose before the sun. He sighted the red giant through the sextant's telescope and carefully brought the point of light down to the horizon. The hard line was occasionally broken by the intervening crests of the great waves as they ran ahead of the *Fort Mackinac*, but he gently rocked the sextant so that the arc of the reflected image just touched the tangential horizon. When he was satisfied, he began to count the seconds until he reached the charthouse and looked at the chronometers. Having deducted the number of seconds from the time, he noted this, along with the altitude of Antares recorded on the sextant. Then he went and repeated the process with Canopus, Spica and the others, finally walking aft to the two men at the wheel. It was almost full daylight now and the sun's presence could be discerned by the intensifying glow to eastward.

'Morning, *Mister* Dunbar,' said Bill Andrews, with a grin. 'And congratulations.'

'I'm not sure all would agree with you,' Dunbar said, shooting a look at Grant on the port side of the wheel. The able-seaman looked away and spat over the rail.

'They'll get used to it,' replied Andrews pointedly. 'Anyway, you've got the certificate.'

'Only for a fucking steamer,' put in Grant contemptuously, and Dunbar could see from the man's face resentment and dislike still burning within him.

'Well,' cut in Andrews, his eyes on the compass as he moved the wheel a spoke or two, 'at least you can take stars, which is more than most of us.' Andrews looked up just as the upper limb of the sun rose on the starboard bow. 'Course east by north, sir,' he added, accompanying the formal report with a wink.

Dunbar ignored Grant and smiled back. He entered the charthouse and reached for the almanac and Norie's *Epitome* in order to turn the observed altitudes and their times into latitude and longitude. It took him an hour. The truth was, he had never performed the task before; he had learned much of the theory and practice under classroom conditions, but such was the repression of apprentices in the South Wales Steam Navigation Company, and so useful were they to the ships' chief mates, that they were better employed in menial tasks about the ship, being more compliant and less fractious than the hard-bitten seamen in a steamer's forecastle. It crossed

Dunbar's mind in a moment of unhappy abstraction, as he temporarily relinquished his struggle with the haversine tables, that despite his four years of indentured life he was in fact better fitted to be an artist. He turned back to the page before him with a sigh. Eventually, and with a beating heart, he laid his final position on the chart. Dunbar stood back and regarded the small, pencilled spot, a dot some 650-odd miles south-west of Cape Leeuwin at the south-west corner of Australia. He picked up the dividers again and, opening them, stepped off the distance to the entrance to Investigator Strait: a little less than 2,000 miles across the Great Australian Bight. He studied the chart further for a few moments. Their destination, the city of Adelaide, was a small grey area of cross-hatching on the eastern shore of the St Vincent Gulf.

Putting Wilson's sextant away, he went back on deck and gave the watch the news. Then he set to pacing the poop, just forward of the men at the wheel, so that he did not have to engage them in conversation and meet Grant's venomous looks. Bill Andrews, he knew, would understand his self-imposed isolation.

At just after four bells, when it was impossible to stare too long to starboard into the glittering path of dancing light that the risen sun had laid there, Captain Crawhall came on deck. He exchanged a brief grunt with Dunbar's polite greeting.

'That your position on the chart, Mister?'

'Yes, sir.'

'How many stars?'

'Six, sir. Quite a good fix.'

'Was it,' Crawhall replied drily, but it was not a question, more an expression of slightly sarcastic wonder, though Dunbar had not referred to the quality of his own arithmetic, but to the angular spread of the stars he had observed. 'Did you get an amplitude?' Crawhall added.

'No, sir.' Dunbar bit his lip, a victim of paradox. He

had thought about it and then forgotten, in his anxiety to work out the stellar position.

'Why not?'

'I was busy doing my calculations, sir, and I'm afraid I missed the right moment.'

Crawhall grunted with displeasure. Dunbar's short moment of triumph was over. His failure to take a bearing on the rising sun and thus compute the error of the *Fort Mackinac*'s magnetic compasses had clearly failed Captain Crawhall's demanding expectations. 'I was just waiting for the sun to rise a little more before I took an azimuth,' Dunbar offered in reparation.

'Very well,' replied Crawhall, apparently mollified. The result would be the same, though the calculation was a little more complex. Then, having satisfied himself that the wind was holding steady and that the *Fort Mackinac* was under the correct canvas for the conditions, the captain went below to shave and break his fast.

At eight bells, eight o'clock local time, Dunbar was relieved by Snelling, who asked, 'How'd it go?'

'Fine thanks, Mr Snelling.'

'D'you get any stars?'

'Yes. A six-star fix, but I missed an amplitude.'

'Ah. The Old Man know?'

'Yes, he asked me. I got an azimuth, though.'

'Good. Well, go and have something to eat and then you'd better move out of the fo'c'sle and into the second mate's berth.'

'Aye, aye.'

Dunbar made to go forward but Snelling called him back. 'Where're you off to now?'

'Forrard for breakfast.'

'Go and eat in the saloon.'

Dunbar hesitated a moment, then went below through the charthouse. He spared a brief glance at the chart; his pencilled position looked insignificant against the white representation of the vast ocean. As he descended into the saloon, he felt a great loneliness come upon him.

After a breakfast alone, served by a silent and, Dunbar concluded, somewhat paranoically sniffy steward, he went forward to collect his gear. Most of his former watchmates had already turned in, but Grant remained fully dressed and fully resentful. It was clear that Dunbar's earlier attempt to placate the man had failed.

'Ah, here he comes. Only here a dog's watch and too good for us now.'

'Stow it, Grant,' Andrews said from his bunk. Dunbar ignored Grant and as quickly as he could, without betraying unseemly haste, stuffed his few belongings into a bag and gathered up his painting kit.

'Fucking artist!' Grant observed, as though compelled to comment on this unsailorly activity.

Dunbar had decided to leave his palliasse, for Wilson's bunk was provided with a mattress, so he was ready to depart unobtrusively in a matter of minutes. As he turned to leave, he found Grant blocking his path.

'Excuse me,' he said, meeting the seaman's eyes.

'Why? Because you're a fucking officer now?'

'I'm an *acting* officer. In a day or two I'll be back here. Now let me pass . . .'

'You're no fucking good, Dunbar. I can smell bad luck on you; it stinks like death. Wilson and poor Alan . . .'

'Poor Alan be fucked,' said an exasperated Andrews, throwing his legs over the leeboard of his bunk, along with a chorus of protest from the other watch-members who were trying to sleep. 'You never have a good word to say for apprentices, do you, Grant? Why the sudden solicitude for poor Alan, eh? You,' Andrews slid to the deck and loomed up alongside Grant, 'are a heap of shit. Now get out of Mister Dunbar's way!' And Andrews gave Grant a sudden violent shove. 'Get out, Jim!' Andrews said sharply. The other members of the watch peered from their bunks calling for silence, but quite content to be entertained by a brawl.

Grant had fallen sideways with an oath and Dunbar pushed past. 'Thanks, Bill,' he said as he left. Outside on the deck he turned and looked back through the door before closing it. Grant was getting to his feet, torn between responding to his attacker and hurling abuse at Dunbar.

'You'll never make an officer,' he shouted after Dunbar, 'as long as your arse points downwards!'

But Andrews confronted him and called him to order.

'Shut it, Grant, turn in and don't provoke me further.'

'Why, you arse-licking bastard.'

'Oh, fuck you!' And Dunbar saw the flash of Andrews's fist and heard the muffled groan of its recipient, followed by the crash of Grant's body across the mess bench.

'We'll get some kip now,' someone said as Dunbar closed the door, turned aft and made for the poop.

Snelling, Dunbar recollected as he unpacked his belongings and stowed his paints and brushes, had referred to his new accommodation not as 'Wilson's cabin', but as 'the second mate's berth', which of course is what it was, a cabin provided for the barque's junior deck officer. But full as it was with Christopher Wilson's personal effects, it was impossible to dismiss its former occupant. Moreover, in assuming Wilson's rank and duties, it was necessary for Dunbar to appropriate a few items of Wilson's belongings, items that he as a seaman did not possess. He had already determined not to act immaturely and wear anything like the late officer's cap, but the borrowing of Wilson's sextant was followed by the borrowing, if that was the right word, Dunbar thought, of the white shirts and serge trousers in which to appear in the saloon. This was unavoidable, even if he compromised by pulling on a plain blue guernsey, which he had brought for wearing on shore. Sailing ship officers were not hide-bound by the uniformed routines of even steam-tramps like the *Kohinoor*, but they had their own code of respectable attire and Dunbar knew that he was being judged by Crawhall and Snelling, as much as by the disaffected Grant, in the manner in which he handled his sudden metamorphosis.

This judgement was borne in upon him only a few hours later when he appeared on the poop at eight bells. He had eaten hurriedly and alone, aware that his busy morning had not allowed him enough rest and that he had awoken rather late from his cat-nap. Local astronomical noon had occurred with the sun culminating on the vessel's meridian some fifteen minutes beforehand. The captain and the mate had taken their meridian altitudes and calculated the ship's latitude. Snelling had taken an observation of the sun three hours earlier and, by working a running fix, the two men had arrived at a noonday position. As Dunbar climbed into the charthouse to relieve Snelling on the poop, he found Crawhall bent over the chart. Dunbar knew instantly that the master had been plotting the fix and that he could thereby judge the accuracy of Dunbar's earlier stellar position.

'Well, Mr Dunbar . . .'

'Sir?' Dunbar looked apprehensively at the chart, but Crawhall's sight-book, in which he worked out his calculations, was obscuring his own earlier fix.

'Your star sights this morning, Mr Dunbar . . .'

'Sir?' Dunbar repeated, his over-hasty dinner churning uncomfortably in the pit of his stomach.

'You said it was a good fix, I think.'

'I meant, sir, that I had been able to take Spica and Canopus and—'

'Yes, yes, I know what you meant, Mr Dunbar,' Crawhall broke in testily. 'But what I meant was, was it a good fix, a well-observed and properly calculated fix, eh? D'you see the difference?'

'Of course I do, sir,' retorted Dunbar, beginning to bristle. It had not been a good morning, despite the bright promise of the dawn. The unfortunate hostility of Grant and his remarks, which had struck Dunbar with a peculiar aptness, only added to his fatigue and anxiety.

'Very well,' said Crawhall coolly, 'and you would still judge your position as a good one?'

'Well, sir,' Dunbar said cautiously, 'it was done to the best of my ability.'

'If I recollect aright, Mr Dunbar, you have not had your certificate for very long, have you?'

'No, sir,' replied Dunbar, flushing. There was an awful parallel with Grant's accusation.

'Have you ever taken sights before?'

'Only twice, sir, aboard the *Pitt* when I had almost completed my time. The master insisted I took a morning longitude and ran it up to noon.'

'And you've never taken a six-star observation at sea?'

'No, sir.'

'D'you have your workings?'

'Yes, sir.' With a sense of desolate foreboding, Dunbar turned aside and pulled the scraps of paper from the lid of Wilson's sextant box. 'I'm sorry I don't have a sight book, sir.'

'No matter. Wilson had one, you'd better take it over. Let me see now.' Crawhall bent over the columns of figures. Having monitored his vessel's progress across the Southern Ocean, Crawhall knew the approximate values of the figures that Dunbar would have had to lift out of almanac, trigonometrical and traverse tables. He could therefore easily tell if Dunbar had cheated and guessed a position, a not impossible matter with a little basic cunning, and one not unknown to Captain Crawhall.

'Hmm,' ruminated Crawhall, 'well, given that star sights aren't in the second mate's syllabus, you did rather well.' The master pushed the paper back to Dunbar as he looked up and smiled. Then he moved his own sight book aside. It was only when the weight of apprehension slid from him that Dunbar was aware of the stress he had been under. Crawhall was paying him a fulsome compliment. Although it seemed upon the chart that the distance between his own morning position and the master's pencilled mark for noon was insignificant, the relationship was along the intended track of the *Fort Mackinac*, and while navigation such as they practised had much of art in it, it was impossible not to reconcile the two positions each with the other.

'I had my suspicions initially, Mr Dunbar, because it seemed by your observations that we had made remarkable progress. I am always a sceptic in these matters until they are proven. It is of particular importance that we know exactly where we are as we make our landfall.'

'I understand, sir.'

'Good. Well, that's very satisfactory, Mr Dunbar.'

For the next six days Dunbar adapted to his changed circumstances. He was deprived of anything more spectacular than a steady growth in confidence as he took his fixes and worked out his dead-reckoning positions. But that was enough and, thanks to Andrews, who had, for the time being at least, deflected Grant's senseless hostility, Dunbar's morale increased accordingly.

Eventually the *Fort Mackinac* approached Kangaroo Island, which lay in sight on their starboard bow. Ahead of them loomed the blue shadow that would materialise as the Yorke Peninsula, dividing the Spencer and the St Vincent Gulfs. Captain Crawhall laid his course for the Investigator Strait, which lay between Kangaroo Island

and the Yorke Peninsula, and by which the four-masted barque would gain entrance to the St Vincent Gulf and the anchorage off the city of Adelaide. It was to replenish the bunkers of the mail steamers of the Peninsular and Oriental Steam Navigation Company, which called regularly at Adelaide, that the *Fort Mackinac* had hauled her 4,000 tons of best steam coal from the River Tyne.

It was Dunbar's watch as the four-masted barque cleared the inner end of the strait and shaped her course directly towards the still-distant and unseen city. The *Fort Mackinac* had every stitch of sail set to her royals, as the wind was no more than a light breeze. Now it hauled round and it became clear the barque could not reach the roads without tacking. Mindful of Crawhall's order, Dunbar informed the master, who was soon beside him on the poop.

'Very well, Mr Dunbar, you may tack the ship.'

For a second Dunbar hesitated, before acknowledging the order. 'Aye, aye, sir.'

'The wind's light; see if you can manage with the watch.'

Dunbar called the watch to their stations and ordered the crossjack and main course clewed up. Then, while they were occupied in hauling the large sails out of the way, he walked aft. 'Ease her off a touch and keep her full for stays,' he said to the helmsman; it was Grant. The able-seaman stared back.

'Keep her full for stays,' Dunbar repeated, 'd'you hear, Grant?'

'Sure.'

Dunbar, knowing that Grant wanted the petty revenge of refusing a formal acknowledgement to the order, went forward again to the break of the poop. Here Crawhall stood watching and, Dunbar thought uncomfortably, adjudicating, while busying himself with lighting his pipe. The cook and carpenter, whose daywork hours caused them to be unjustly known as the ship's 'idlers', emerged from galley and shop to assist the watch, the former stationed at the fore sheet and the latter up forward to shift the headsail sheets. The rest of the watch, having clewed up the after-two courses, disposed themselves at their bracing stations. A couple of men went to each of the braces of the main and mizen-masts, ready to haul the lower yards, while the boys and ordinary seamen were alert to overhaul the braces of the upper yards, which would come round of their own accord when the topsails were hauled.

'I think they're all ready, Mr Dunbar,' Crawhall said, puffing blue smoke. 'Carry on.' Having said this quietly to Dunbar, the captain walked aft to pick up the spanker sheet and stand beside the wheel.

Dunbar drew in his breath, then bellowed, 'Lee-Oh!' and, turning aft, called to Grant, 'Down helm!'

'Down helm,' came Grant's resentful response and, despite his preoccupation, Dunbar grinned inwardly; Grant's hostility could not transcend the master's proximity.

Grant spun the wheel, pushing the rudder over and turning the *Fort Mackinac* slowly into the wind. As she came round, the cook and carpenter eased the fore and headsail sheets to prevent those sails inhibiting the swing, while Crawhall, forsaking his dignity, hauled the spanker to windward, chapelling it in order to force the barque's head up into the wind.

As the windward leeches of the square sails passed through the eye of the wind, the sails shook and the whole ship felt the power of their trembling. Then the wind came ahead and all were taken flat aback, only the fore and aft headsails set on the forestays continuing to flutter in the light breeze.

The next seconds were crucial, and Dunbar's heart hammered uncomfortably within his chest. If the *Fort*

Mackinac lost the momentum of her swing, she would be taken flat aback and start to make sternway with a humiliating acceleration. The trick was to keep the vessel swinging, and at the very moment her spike bowsprit passed through the direction of the wind, when the exposed wings of the sails of the main and mizen were aback and the rest in the lee of the foremast, to haul the after-yards round, ready for the new tack. Dunbar chose his moment.

'Mains'l haul!' he roared with unnecessary volume. The men in the waist jerked into furious action, the great steel yards above his head on the mizen-mast, and further forward on the main mast, swung with surprising ease. Right forward the carpenter was assisting him by keeping the headsail sheets aback, and the jibs out on the bowsprit were exerting considerable leverage in speeding the barque's movement across the wind. This turning moment increased with every passing second. Dunbar breathed easier. In the waist the braces on the after two square-rigged masts were being frantically overhauled and quickly belayed, as were the sheets of the staysails set between the masts. Then the men ran forward to attend the fore braces, which still held their sails aback to help the accelerating swing.

Above Dunbar's head, the main and mizen-sails filled with wind.

'Leggo and haul all!' he bellowed again.

The cook let fly the fore sheet. Andrews threw the windward fore-brace off its belaying pin before stepping smartly across the deck to help the men on the lee fore-brace, while the carpenter and his men hauled the windward fore tack hard down to the cathead by taking it round the capstan. As the *Fort Mackinac* gathered way on the new tack, the men came aft again and let go the main and crossjack clew garnets and buntlines. The big courses fell with a deep rustle, to be tamed by their windward tacks and leeward sheets.

"Midships,' Dunbar called to Grant and then, 'steady . . . Steady as she goes. Keep her full and bye.'

Grant mumbled his repeat of the order.

'Speak up, man, and tell Mr Dunbar the ship's head!' Crawhall snapped in his ear and Dunbar was gratified to hear a chastened Grant tell him the barque was steering her new course, some six points off the wind blowing down the gulf.

In the waist and on the forecastle the men were fine-trimming the sails and Dunbar found Crawhall beside him again, the master having secured the spanker. The stink of Crawhall's pipe was sharp in Dunbar's nostrils.

'Ship tacked, sir,' he reported.

'Very well, Mr Dunbar. How d'you feel?'

'Bloody marvellous, sir.' The remark had escaped him before propriety regretted it. To Dunbar's surprise, Crawhall chuckled.

'Think you could do that in a blow?' he asked.

'With a bit more practice, I don't see why not, sir.'

'Nor do I. Very well, you may work the ship right up to the roads.'

'Thank you, sir,' responded an enthusiastic Dunbar, only realising after due reflection that he would be doing what was commonly called 'Paddy's watches' – going on duty and staying on duty. Thus James Dunbar, acting second mate of the four-masted barque *Fort Mackinac*, remained on deck for eleven hours, slowly working the ship towards Adelaide where at last, after three months at sea, she was taken in the charge of tugs and berthed alongside to discharge her cargo of coal.

For the next twenty-one months Dunbar remained as acting second mate of the *Fort Mackinac*. Captain Crawhall had been unable to find a suitable replacement for the dead Wilson at Adelaide and had telegraphed Bullard,

Crowe and Company to state that, if he could obtain a dispensation for Mr Dunbar from the Board of Trade representatives in Australia, he recommended retaining the young man's services in the capacity of second mate. Crawhall added the cogent rider that, as an acting officer, Mr Dunbar came cheaper than a fully certificated man. Since the owners had great faith in Crawhall, both as a judge of men and as a business manager, they endorsed the master's decision, whereupon Crawhall ferreted a little and obtained for Dunbar an oral examination. Such an examination was predicated on sea-time and experience, and Dunbar was required only to demonstrate a theoretical knowledge to the examiner. During the hour and a half interrogation he satisfactorily proved himself worthy of a dispensation, a temporary certificate that effectively converted his steam certificate to cover service as a second mate in a sailing vessel.

Dunbar was never to know that a case of whisky had eased the examiner's decision, nor did any subsequent conduct of the young officer prove that either the expense of the Scotch or the issuing of the dispensation was a mistake. And at the end of the twenty-one months, when the *Fort Mackinac* found herself in Hong Kong, Dunbar went ashore and, having by now the requisite sea-time and a fine testimonial from Crawhall, sat the full examination as a first mate in sail. Here, too, the vessel went into dry-dock for a quadrennial survey, the articles were closed and the crew, those of them that wished to, were signed on for another two years. The plenitude of Chinese and Lascar seamen in the smart steam ships that served the Crown Colony gave British seamen few opportunities for employment, and while a few remained ashore to enjoy the delights of the Orient, most returned to the *Fort Mackinac* and were back on the articles by the time the junior apprentice was sent forward to hoist the Blue Peter at the foremasthead. It was three days before Christmas, 1910.

During the intervening period the *Fort Mackinac* had tramped about the world. From Adelaide they had crossed the Spencer Gulf to Port Lincoln and loaded a full cargo of grain for Philadelphia. From Philadelphia they had loaded cased oil for Kobe, in Japan. Crawhall and his owners were shrewd: passages in ballast were rare and the *Fort Mackinac* enjoyed tolerable freight rates with cargoes of rice and jute, of sugar from the Philippines to the United States and cased oil back across the Pacific again. Thus the barque had found herself in Hong Kong and Dunbar submitted himself for examination.

They left the colony and were at sea for Christmas, arriving in San Francisco by the end of March with a cargo of sugar and copra from Manila. From San Francisco, it was rumoured, they were to sail south to load guano from desolate islands on the coast of Chile. Here the droppings of innumerable sea-birds had built up over the years to a valuable encrustation, which was removed with shovels by the barque's own crew for eventual use as fertiliser. It was a tedious, stinking task reminiscent of their labour in the 'tween deck when their ship had been knocked down in the Southern Ocean by the white squall.

But in San Francisco another of Bullard, Crowe's ships, the *Fort Ticonderoga*, had lost her master. The seductions of the shore, the women, booze and the lure of the gold fields caused the majority of the inbound ships' crews to desert. They rarely got far, exhausting their money in the first binge, to be picked up by the crimps and sold to the first loaded and outward-bound ship wanting a crew. A seaman's eagerly anticipated shore-leave rarely extended more than a day or two before he was shipped out, often in a hard-driven American 'Down Easter', with only the clothes on his back, a rampant hangover and a latent dose of venereal disease to remind him of his visit.

Disputes over the effective abduction of crews were frequent. The authorities of the port were corrupt and unhelpful. Having lost most of his crew, the master of the *Fort Ticonderoga* had gone ashore to remonstrate. His ship was loaded and ready for her homeward passage. He required a crew, but was damned if he would pay the ludicrous blood money demanded by the boarding-house crimps, who held the majority of his crew drunk or debauched in their brothels, dens and gaming houses as virtual prisoners. Captain Mitchell, the outraged master, had quickly got into a fight and had been killed in the mêlée. A doctor was found to certify that the captain had died of a heart attack, and Bullard, Crowe were so informed.

It was at this juncture that the *Fort Mackinac* arrived. Embarrassed, the port authority compelled the leading crimps to provide a crew for the *Fort Ticonderoga*, and Captain Crawhall was contacted by his owners to provide a replacement commander. It was Mr Snelling's moment; he departed the *Fort Mackinac* in a smart gig pulled by the apprentices of the *Fort Ticonderoga*. Snelling's new command was a beautiful four-masted ship, the last of her rig in Bullard, Crowe's service and due to be cut down to a barque on her arrival home, but she still carried a third mate and this officer was exchanged for Snelling, joining the *Fort Mackinac* in a very depressed condition.

Snelling's departure meant promotion for Dunbar, too. As the *Fort Mackinac*'s mate, he now greeted her new second officer. His name was David Massey, and he had been eager to return home, but the *Fort Mackinac*'s movements were less predictable than those of his former ship, for Crawhall had an eye on a grain cargo from Australia to Britain to be loaded after the harvest of the late southern summer of the following year. Learning this, poor Massey was quickly deprived of any joy in his promotion.

'I was going home to transfer into steam,' he grumbled to Dunbar as he moved into Dunbar's cabin. 'I'm due to marry too,' he added, revealing a greater, more personal misery.

'Oh, I'm sorry to hear that. But she'll wait, surely?' Dunbar asked, thinking of his own disjointed, unsatisfactory and irregular correspondence with home.

'I hope so,' Massey replied disconsolately.

'Oh well, it doesn't do to dwell on these matters . . .'

Massey sighed. 'Where the hell are we going anyway?'

'To load guano.'

'Oh, Christ, no! Please God, not a cargo of bird-shit.'

'I'm afraid so,' Dunbar said, grinning.

'There's bugger-all funny about it,' Massey said morosely and, picking up a large canvas dislodged from its hiding place by Dunbar's removal, asked, 'Did you do this?'

It was the dust-covered portrait of Alan Moorehouse. 'Yes.'

'It's Alan Moorehouse, isn't it?'

'Yes, yes it is.'

Massey snapped his fingers, his face brightening, as though with a pleasing recollection. 'Of course! How stupid of me, I'd clean forgotten he's aboard this ship.' Massey smiled at Dunbar, the grin transforming his face. 'I'd quite forgotten; the bloody transfer drove the matter clean out of my mind. We sailed together in the half-deck of the *Fort Anne*. It was his first trip.' Massey chuckled and looked down at the portrait, then up again at Dunbar. 'Well, there's one good thing about this mess, we'll both arrive home together and he can come to the wedding.'

'Massey, I'm sorry to tell you, Alan Moorehouse is dead.'

Massey looked up from the portrait in disbelief. 'But he can't be . . .'

'He is, I'm afraid.' And Dunbar told Massey of the circumstances.

162

When he was finished, Massey looked up at him. 'How come I never heard of it?' he asked miserably.

Dunbar shrugged. 'I suppose Captain Crawhall contacted his people, but . . . were you close?'

Massey nodded. 'I'm to marry his sister. It was through me that Alan was sent to sea with Bullard, Crowe.' He sighed and looked down at the portrait. 'I can see the resemblance . . .'

'You'd better have it, if you want it,' Dunbar said, indicating the canvas. 'I was wondering whether his family would like to have it, or whether I should simply pitch it over the side.'

'Oh no, don't do that. Of course I'll have it.' Massey paused, then went on, 'I'm sorry; when I mentioned the resemblance, it wasn't Alan to whom I referred, but his sister Eleanor. They were remarkably alike. I'm certain she would wish to have the painting,' he paused again, 'particularly in the circumstances.'

'Yes, of course. Well, I'll get the rest of my gear out of your way.'

'Thanks. Oh, and congratulations on your promotion. I think we're wasting our time in sail, but a leg up is always a good thing.'

For Dunbar the months of his service aboard the *Fort Mackinac* as second and then first mate were hard but rewarding work. Only on the passage south from San Francisco, bound in ballast for the Chilean archipelago and the odious business of loading guano, did he suffer emotionally. Even this, he was compelled to acknowledge, was self-indulgence, for they were coasting southeastwards, down the length of the peninsula of Lower California, upon whose inner shore lay Puerto San Martin. Such close proximity to the scene of his youthful induction into the life of the waterfront excited him. He wondered if Dolores Garcia was still alive to remember him and if she was, whether she retained any of that voluptuous beauty that had so attracted him all those years ago when he was, he had to admit, a callow and gullible youth. But the long spine of intervening mountains lay like smoke upon the eastern horizon, then vanished as Crawhall took them further out into the blue Pacific in search of stronger winds. Dunbar would never know, never see her again and gloomily he meditated on the transience of all human affairs.

The guano cargo was shipped to the States and by mid-summer they were back in San Francisco, Crawhall having secured a lucrative freight of general cargo for the port, which was still recovering from the ravages of the earthquake of 1909. The passage from the east coast of the United States to the west coast was by way of Cape Horn, a passage made in mid-winter, but they had doubled the promontory without mishap and anchored safely in San Francisco Bay. Here they were greeted by the usual crimps' boats, from which their boarding-house runners offered the blandishments of the shore. By the next morning the *Fort Mackinac* had lost half her crew, despite the best efforts of Crawhall and his young officers.

Unlike the master of the *Fort Ticonderoga*, Captain Crawhall's reaction was less emotional. When Dunbar reported the depletion of the ship's company, Crawhall shrugged. 'The longshoremen will soon have us discharged, Mr Dunbar. They desire the geegaws of the east in the stores of Frisco and want their whores able to parade in the latest New York modes, so let's bide our time. Don't say a word to anyone, but you and I will take a stroll ashore tomorrow evening, just after sunset.'

The following evening Dunbar joined Crawhall and Massey in the saloon for dinner. The *Fort Mackinac* lay alongside, a privileged position for a lime-juice ship, but her cargo was, as Crawhall had predicted, eagerly sought by the consignees, who regarded its value and the urgency of its discharge somewhat in the manner of an earlier generation of Londoners eager for the season's first cargo of tea. The chief concern of the recipients of the furniture, fashions and haberdashery that were withdrawn by the caseload from the barque's holds was that their competitors would get their orders delivered, and thus show the newest merchandise, first.

'The market-place,' Crawhall sagely observed, 'is always the most likely place to get your throat cut.'

That evening Crawhall was in unusually good mood. He made fairly free with a bottle of brandy, which he produced 'in honour of the encouraging freight rates' he had obtained for this particular cargo. With an inward smile, Dunbar shrewdly and accurately concluded that Crawhall had enriched not only Bullard, Crowe by his transactions.

'Now, gentlemen,' Crawhall said after dismissing the steward and corking the brandy bottle, 'we have work to do. Mr Massey, I hope we have a brace or two of apprentices on board?'

'We had, sir, at least an hour ago, though I heard them discussing where they were to go this evening.'

'Thank God this lot aren't as bad a set of brass-bound buggers as some I've known. Well, cut along and see what you can muster, then bring 'em back aft in their shore-going togs.'

When Massey had gone, Crawhall lit his pipe and, having generated a substantial fog, said to Dunbar, 'I intend to sail from here with my crew, mister. Ballast is ordered for the day after tomorrow, and as soon as we can we'll haul off to the anchorage. You and I are going ashore this evening. Go and fit yourself out in a plain rig. I want the boys as decoys.'

'Decoys? What exactly are your intentions, sir?'

'The less you know, the less you are an accomplice but,' and here Crawhall removed his pipe for emphasis, 'I absolutely depend upon your loyal support. Without it, I'm sunk. You owe me that much, Mr Dunbar, don't you think?'

Dunbar looked at Crawhall and found himself infected by the master's recklessness. 'Yes, of course.'

'Good.' And as Dunbar retreated into his cabin to change, Crawhall rose and disappeared into his own accommodation. By the time Dunbar returned to the saloon, Crawhall was reseated at the saloon table with a small bundle wrapped in a soft cloth before him. He folded back the rag and exposed a revolver. 'Don't worry, Mr Dunbar, I'm not about to imperil your immortal soul.'

Crawhall broke the gun and shook the shells out of the chamber. He scooped five of them up and slipped them into his pocket. Then he carefully reinserted one and put the pistol into his pocket. At that moment Massey led three of the apprentices down the charthouse companionway.

'Well, gentlemen,' said Crawhall, swivelling to regard the youngsters. 'That all you bagged, Mr Massey? There seems to be one missing.'

'Yes, sir, Kemp got away early.'

'I hear Kemp's got a girlfriend here, is that correct?' There was hesitation among Kemp's fellows, then Crawhall prompted them. 'She's a blonde who used to be a brunette, her name's Angela, which is a travesty, but shows that the lady has a sense of irony. Well? Am I correct?'

'Yes, sir.'

'I think you'll find, Kinross,' Crawhall said to the spokesman, 'that she is quite well known. Mr Kemp will be urinating through something like a cauliflower in a fortnight's time, I shouldn't wonder. Well, well, true love never did run smooth, eh?'

'No, sir.'

'Now tonight . . .' Crawhall reached into his waistcoat pocket and withdrew a few dollars, 'you young men are going to go ashore and stand yourselves a round of drinks at my expense. I expect the best place will be the Diamond saloon. D'you know where that is, on Green Street?' The apprentices nodded. 'D'you know who runs the Diamond saloon?'

'No, sir.'

'Of course not. He keeps out of the way, but I'll guarantee he's watching you. D'you know, boys, long before any of you were a gleam in your fathers' eyes, I brought out a general cargo that included glass mirrors through which you could see, if you were the right side of them . . .'

Crawhall looked round them and Dunbar thought of the mirrored gallery in the Hotel Paradiso in Puerto San Martin where, for a small fee, you could watch the 'exhibition' in the bed below. Perhaps Crawhall had had a hand in the shipment of those mirrors, too.

'Right then. You buy a drink and when the barflies gather round, you ask to see Mr Joe, understand? Mr Joe. Insist on seeing him personally. Say you've a proposition to make to him concerning a part of the cargo of the *Fort Mackinac* lying alongside. He'll know where we are and all about us.

'Now tell him that the stuff can be got by coming alongside at ten o'clock tomorrow morning with this note.' Captain Crawhall withdrew a slip of paper from his breast pocket. 'It's a consignment of ball-gowns. The only thing is, you tell him you won't release them to anyone but himself and you want five hundred dollars for them. No more, no less. Tell him you're risking your careers by dealing with him, but if he asks, you want the money for a good time. Do this and I'll make sure ten pounds is paid to you when we pay off at a British port. Understand?'

The three apprentices nodded. 'Not a whisper to anyone about this. If word gets out you'll be in trouble with me. Now, off you go.'

As soon as the youths had gone ashore, Crawhall got to his feet. 'Mr Massey, I want you to stay aboard. Here's the key to the lazaretto. The hatch is in my cabin under the carpet. Get it opened up.'

'You're not intending to kidnap Paradise Joe, are you, sir?' asked Massey.

'Ever seen a Chinaman doing up his flies, Mr Massey?'

'Pardon?' Massey frowned.

'Ask no questions, tell no lies. Come, Mr Dunbar, we've work to do.'

Dunbar followed Crawhall up the companionway into the charthouse, where the master paused. 'Slip this up your sleeve,' he said, picking up from the settee and handing Dunbar a short length of heavy lead piping.

The Diamond saloon was a shabby establishment compared with the Hotel Paradiso, a long, rambling wooden building of two storeys, which had suffered some damage in the earthquake, but showed signs of repair and extension, even in the darkness. Inside it was crowded and lit by suspended oil lamps, which added their odour to the stronger scents of working men, tobacco, cheaply perfumed trollops and even cheaper liquor.

Crawhall elbowed his way towards the bar and, spotting the three apprentices in conversation with a man at the bar, veered aside to the opposite end. He took up station where he could keep an eye on his youngsters and ordered two whiskies from a large Negro barman.

When he had been served, Crawhall turned to Dunbar, handing him a glass tumbler, and said, 'Whatever you do, don't drink the stuff, it's probably spiked.'

Dunbar nodded, conversation in such a scrimmage

being impossible, so he looked about him, filled with a curious longing to record the scene. It was so like, and yet so different from, the Hotel Paradiso that it stirred a curious nostalgia in him. A whore sidled up to them, a cigarillo in her fingers, looking for a light.

'Wanna light me up, sailor?' she crooned and Dunbar looked down at the deep, inviting cleavage of her décolletage.

'Later, later,' snapped Crawhall, still watching the boys.

'I wasn't talking to you, fella,' she drawled. 'I was talking to sailor boy here.' She leaned against Dunbar so that he smelt her body and felt her rasp a long nail down his cheek. 'I ain't seen a sailor as cute as this for a long whiles . . .'

Crawhall nudged Dunbar none too gently in the ribs and jerked his head.

'Forgive me, ma'am,' Dunbar said ironically, patting her rump. 'I have an appointment. Perhaps tomorrow.'

'Gee, you're a limey gent . . .'

'Tomorrow.' And he followed Crawhall as the captain began once again to force his way through the rowdy press of bodies. Over the captain's shoulder, Dunbar could see the three apprentices being led off to a doorway at the far extremity of the bar. The minute they had disappeared behind it, Crawhall accelerated his progress, provoking complaints from the disrupted clientele.

'So sorry, so sorry,' he shouted, edging through until he broke out of the press. The door lay ahead of them and only the nearer barman was in the way, a small Hispanic half-breed with a sad face and lugubrious expression.

'I've an appointment with Mr Joe,' Crawhall called confidently, and a second later he had the door open and was stepping through into a dark lobby. Dunbar followed, aware that the half-breed had shrugged and turned away to serve an impatient customer. Inside a set of stairs led upwards. Quickly they ascended and Dunbar's sense of *déjà vu* increased, then they emerged onto a long landing. Voices came from the nearest of several doors.

'Ready?' whispered Crawhall and Dunbar nodded, sliding the length of lead piping down the sleeve of his jacket into his fist.

Crawhall kicked the door open and snarled, 'Hands up!'

Mr Joe, Paradise Joe as he was known, sat across the far side of a large table, upon which he had put both elegantly booted feet, and was regarding the *Fort Mackinac*'s three apprentices through a haze of cigar smoke. He was flanked by a large man with a brutalised face. Dunbar recognised the man as one of the boarding-house runners who had boarded the barque on her arrival. The only other man in the room was the barman who had taken the boys upstairs. Negotiations had clearly reached a critical point, and the sudden intrusion took them all completely by surprise. No-one moved for a moment, then Crawhall said sharply, 'Get 'em, lads!' and he drove forward, thrusting the table backwards and oversetting Paradise Joe's chair so that the crimp fell backwards with an oath and a clatter. Dunbar moved to the right as the ugly runner came round the end of the table, while the apprentices nearest the barman took the hint and fell upon the unfortunate fellow.

Dunbar confronted the runner, who now had a knife glittering in his hand. With all his might Dunbar brought the length of piping up, hoping to disarm the runner and then get in close and wind him, but the runner easily avoided the clumsy blow and Dunbar saw the knife blade thrust up to his face.

Once, long ago, he had felt the keen edge of such a weapon across his breast and bore the cicatrice to prove the fact. Now his reaction to the horror of succumbing to a second such assault was so fast that he dropped the lead pipe and brought both hands up to grab the runner's thrusting wrist. With his thumbs driving into the back of his assailant's hand, Dunbar dug his fingers into the palm holding the knife. Then he twisted with all his might, swinging upwards and outwards with all his power, roaring with the effort.

The sinewy strength he had gained aloft on the *Fort Mackinac*'s yards now came to his aid. He felt the click of breaking bones and saw the knife blade fall from the runner's grasp. Then he felt the fight go out of the man as he screamed with pain. It was all over. Already Crawhall was leaping over the table to sit on top of Paradise Joe, until an apprentice arrived to take the length of sennit that Crawhall had brought with him to tie the crimp's hands behind his back.

Dunbar bent and picked up the runner's knife and knelt on the man's chest, pricking him and commanding him to be silent. Then he looked round. The poor barman was sitting terrified, as he too was gagged and bound to a chair.

'Have we got 'em all? Right, your ugly bugger, Mr Dunbar, must be gagged and bound. Here, Kinross, there's more sennit and codline in my pockets. Take them over to the mate.'

They ripped up a curtain to fabricate gags and within a few minutes had Paradise Joe on his feet.

'Now, you two,' Crawhall said, standing over the runner and pointing the gun at him. 'Listen carefully. If you make a sound, your boss is dead. And if you come after us and try anything, he's likewise dead. I'm a very angry man and Captain Mitchell of the *Fort Ticonderoga* was a particular friend of mine. It's a small world. I know all about the activities of you bastards, so I'm going to give Mr Joe here a sea-trip for his health. Just think, if I take him off with me, you can run his show here, and no-one will ever know any better. Understand?' Crawhall paused, giving comprehension time to sink in, then he jerked the crimp to his feet and said, 'Show us the way you spirit the men out, Mr Joe.'

A week later the *Fort Mackinac* stood out through the Golden Gate with all her crew returned on board. Almost the last man ashore down the pilot ladder into the cutter, just before the pilot himself, was Paradise Joe.

Dunbar had come aft from the forecastle and climbed the poop-ladder to stand alongside Captain Crawhall as they discharged the pilot. 'How did you know it would work?' he asked, as the pilot cutter swung away from the ship and pilot and master exchanged valedictory waves.

'Greed, Mr Dunbar, works an infallible magic upon mankind. I offered Paradise Joe a case of Fifth Avenue gowns, or at least I pretended to. He's used to corrupting youth, so I thought youth might be used to corrupt him. Apprentice boys have been known to sell items of cargo before now; that the *Fort Mackinac*'s brass-bounders would do so was almost predictable, given the commercial nature of our cargo.'

'Well, it certainly worked. Every man is accounted for.'

'Including Grant,' said Crawhall ruefully. 'We could have done without him.'

Dunbar looked across at the helmsman. It was Andrews, not Grant, and Dunbar moved to peer into the steering compass, then crossed and checked the course.

'Saved you from a fate worse than death, Bill,' he said quietly.

'Perhaps,' Andrews responded, 'but sometimes a grown man likes to wallow in the shit for a while.'

Dunbar stared at Andrews; he looked terrible, his skin pale and his eyes bloodshot and dark-rimmed. A growth of stubble adorned his chin and jaw and even at a distance his breath stank of liquor. Andrews remained a complete mystery to him, even after all this time.

He went back to Crawhall. 'Well, it's my watch sir. I can take her when you're ready.'

Crawhall was lighting his pipe, sucking the match flame down on the bowl and puffing out aromatic clouds of smoke, allowing the flame to leap up before he dragged it down again. Satisfied, he shook the match and flung it over the side, then pulled the pipe from his mouth.

'You'll have your time in for your master's certificate when we get home, Mr Dunbar. Are you going to stay in sail?'

Dunbar nodded. 'For the time being, sir, if you'll have me.'

'Me? It may not be up to me. I may be in steam myself soon.'

'I don't believe you'd like it, sir.'

'What? Not like a life of idleness, with a Chinese tiger to bring me a gin-sling when I wanted one? How could a man not like it? Eh? We none of us grow younger, Mr Dunbar. Anyway,' he sighed, 'you may take the ship. Call me at the next alter-course position.'

'Aye, aye, sir.'

Crawhall stuffed the pipe back in his mouth and made to go below. Then, as though suddenly thinking of something, he swung round. 'Where did you learn to disarm a man like that, Mr Dunbar?' he asked, the pipe bobbing in his mouth.

'I'm not sure I did learn it. It just happened, sir.'

'Good job it did.'

And Crawhall went below, leaving Dunbar to pace the poop as the *Fort Mackinac* gathered way and crept out into the Pacific Ocean. He felt a sense of unease after his conversation with Crawhall; of course he wanted a career and he loved the life in a sailing ship, but it was true, time was passing, and although he must obtain the master's certificate without which all this would be wasted, the title of master mariner that went with it had in itself no intrinsic worth. The brief and bloody fracas in the Diamond saloon had reminded Dunbar of another life, not just of the debauched excesses of the waterfront, but of that other life of the shore; the life of which Julia Ravenham and Maureen Fletcher were a part, the life to which men like David Massey aspired, married and with children. He looked astern. Already the coast had lost its form. It was a plane surface, a single tone that continually faded as they drew offshore. It was possible to believe that it was an illusion.

Perhaps nothing existed at all except the ship under sail, gliding across the vast surface of the ocean.

CHAPTER NINE

Arrival Home

Having carried a cargo of coal from Norfolk, Virginia, to Honolulu in the Hawaiian Islands for the use of the United States Navy, the *Fort Mackinac* made a rare passage in ballast back to Port Lincoln to load a full cargo of grain. At the end of March 1912 she sailed from the Spencer Gulf bound towards Falmouth for orders. Although Captain Crawhall could be instructed to discharge his cargo anywhere between Brest and the Elbe, the whole ship's company was confident that they would be discharging at a British port. Liverpool was the favoured destination, though others reckoned on London or Hull. In the event it was Ipswich, and they towed round Landguard Point into the beautiful River Orwell to berth at Cliff Quay on a sunny afternoon in late June.

Boarding at the Sunk, the pilot had brought out a few newspapers and they learned of the court of enquiry sitting in judgement on the loss of the White Star liner *Titanic*. This news seemed to confirm the dangers of excessive speed and over-confidence inherent in steam ships, and of an inevitable judgement by sailing-ship men in the foolhardiness of maintaining schedules in a foggy, ice-filled North Atlantic.

'In foggy calms,' old Sails expostulated, when he heard the news, 'a sailing scheep she cannot move, ja? And so all is vell,' an opinion that found wide favour in the forecastle, where the resident wiseacres had conveniently forgotten the growlers of the Southern Ocean and the trap they set for big windjammers running their easting down at thirteen knots.

'I tell you,' Grant asserted, 'steamship officers are bloody murderous!'

Inured to hardship and with danger a constant companion, the men of the *Fort Mackinac* were unshocked by the loss of life. Even the story of the gallant band who played on while the giant liner settled in the water struck them as foolish. 'Who de fook want a band at sea?' old Sails asked, and no-one could provide him with an answer.

They were even more indifferent to the news of political wrangling in the Balkans, though mention of trouble by the pilot made Dunbar, who was standing on the poop alongside Crawhall, think of the Montenegrin restaurateurs he had once patronised with Julia and her friends. Since among the Balkan peoples only the Greeks had any sort of maritime reputation, Captain Crawhall regarded the squabbles among Serbians, Montenegrins, Bulgarians and Macedonians as a matter outside his opinion, sharing the deep-held prejudice of the time that, since such people were not of the Nordic race, they were inconsequential. Unless, of course, they claimed the benefits of British imperialism, in which case, the captain declared expansively, touched as he was by the quiet satisfaction of homecoming, matters would soon be sorted out by the appearance of a British cruiser and the landing of a naval brigade. The pilot, long accustomed to the ways of deep-water men just in from a passage of a hundred days, agreed and adjusted the course of the big barque to round the Harwich Shelf, while aloft the hands fisted the stubborn canvas into a neat harbour stow. For the crew of the *Fort Mackinac*, their horizon had been too long bounded by the straight-edged rim of the visible world for them to feel anything other than a great contempt for the apparent pettiness of landsmen who wanted too much and understood nothing.

But that great majority who live on the land equally misunderstood the squabbles in the Balkans, as Dunbar found out when he received an unexpected visit from his family. They arrived three days after the barque's arrival, on a fine, warm Sunday afternoon, driven from Clayton Dobbs to Ipswich in Colonel Scrope-Davies's car by Julia Ravenham.

Dunbar was called on deck and saw his father, shockingly bent with age, stepping down from the car and handing his mother out after him. They stared up at the ship's masts and then caught sight of their son, just as he saw Julia come round the high rear of the vehicle, her hat held on by a scarf, her waist slender as a willow stick. Somewhere along the deck a seaman whistled appreciatively.

Dunbar went down the gangway and helped his mother aboard. 'We received your note, dear. Why didn't you come home?' Anne Dunbar greeted him, her voice full of censure.

'I'm sorry, mother,' he said kissing her cheek, 'but I'm the only officer on board. The captain's gone home on leave and the second mate has gone home to get married.'

'So you *are* an officer?' She turned to her husband, who was just stepping uncertainly down on deck behind Julia. 'There, dear,' she rattled on, 'what did I tell you, James *is* an officer.'

'Father . . .' The two men shook hands.

'Julia.' Dunbar took both her hands and leaned forward to kiss her. 'How splendid to see you again. You look lovely.'

'It's been almost four years, James,' she said reproachfully.

177

'Yes. It's a long time but,' he turned to include his parents, 'I've time in for master and shall sit for it as soon as possible.' The importance of this news seemed incomprehensible to his visitors.

'You see, dear,' Anne Dunbar repeated, turning to her husband, 'I said he was an officer.' His father nodded and Dunbar realised that more than the rector's body was worn out by age. He caught his mother's eye and saw the anguish in it. He should not judge them too harshly; they had absolutely no knowledge of his way of life.

'Do come home soon, James,' his mother implored, as though sensing him weakening towards them.

'Yes. Yes, of course.' He faltered, wondering what on earth to do with the visitors when his father, looking down on the deck, asked, 'Is this wheat all over the floor?'

They had begun their discharge and it had been suspended for the weekend, but a golden dust covered every surface adjacent to the hatches. 'It's grain, Father,' Dunbar explained at this sudden interest. 'We have brought four thousand tons of it from Australia.'

'Why on earth have you done that?' His father looked up at him, his expression querulous, as though the *Fort Mackinac*'s arrival with her cargo was a product of his wayward son's insolence.

'Because it's needed in this country, Father, to feed the population.'

'It's why we have an empire, dear,' Anne Dunbar explained in a loud voice, patting her husband's hand in a patiently tender, yet patronising manner. Julia and Dunbar exchanged glances that mixed pity with exasperation and were the first intimacy between them.

'Come along,' Dunbar said, encouraged by this brief, unspoken allusion to their relationship, 'let me take you down into the saloon. I'll show you where I live.' He pointed vaguely up the foredeck. 'I started by living up there in that deckhouse, but unfortunately the second mate was washed overboard and I took his place.'

'Oh, how horrible,' said Julia, 'I had no idea . . .'

'I mentioned it in a letter.'

'Yes, yes,' Mrs Dunbar said, interrupting, 'I remember. Watson, a Watson, that was it. Up here, dear?'

'Wilson, Mother. Yes, follow Julia up this ladder.' Dunbar handed Julia up and ushered his parents to follow, watching as his father made heavy weather of the ascent.

They paused at the break of the poop and Dunbar gestured forward. 'This is where the officer of the watch spends most of his on-duty time. From here he can see the length of the deck.'

The party dutifully swung round and stared up Ipswich dock. Sunshine lent the scene a little colour.

'Goodness,' Mrs Dunbar said, 'what a lot of ropes!' And, turning to her husband, she remarked a little louder for his benefit, 'What a lot of ropes, dear. I suppose James has to know the names of all of them.' She did not confirm whether or not her supposition was correct, but turned as though having paid a sufficiently dutiful attention, and Dunbar felt the awkwardness of a boy trying to infect an indifferent adult with an enthusiasm for looted bird's eggs. Explanations, it seemed, were a waste of time, so he led them through the charthouse without a word. The tiny hutch, neglected now they were in port, seemed insignificant as the place where he had passed his first real professional test. The air of slight disapproval exuded by his visitors seemed to make even a mention of the absent Captain Crawhall inappropriate. Instead, Dunbar led them down to the saloon, where his mother's interest was briefly awakened by the neatness and practical cleverness of the domestic arrangements.

'Before we have some tea, let me show you my cabin.'

It was the conclusion of the grand tour and by chance it was his father who shuffled breathlessly along the alleyway and first stuck his bowed head in through the sliding door to regard the mate's accommodation occupied by his son.

The rector peered round like some strange, inquisitive bird. 'Like a monk's cell,' he pronounced, as though deprived of discovering his son languishing upon a bed of iniquity. Then a dry, satisfied chuckle escaped him and he turned back to the saloon. 'No need to have a look,' he said discouragingly to the two women, 'it's like a monk's cell.'

'Well, well, how interesting . . . Now, you sit down and I'm sure James will find a servant to get us some tea.'

'Yes, of course,' Dunbar said, following his father back into the saloon.

'I'd like to look,' said Julia, who had remained in the background during these exchanges.

'Yes, of course. That door there. I'll just pass word for the steward.' Dunbar slipped on deck. When he returned with promises that the kettle was brewing in the galley and that tea would be along in a moment, Julia was still absent. He found her in his cabin, where she in turn had discovered his paintings, rough rectangles of hatch tarpaulin or sail canvas stacked at the foot of his bunk, encrusted with the thick impasto of his crude technique.

'I'm glad to see you still paint,' she said, pulling them out one at a time.

'Yes,' he replied diffidently. 'I take them off the stretchers for lack of space and to economise on wood. I hadn't realised there were so many.' The warm scent of her filled the little cabin and he felt the prickle of lust at her presence. 'It's been a long time . . .' he concluded lamely.

Julia remained in silent contemplation for a moment,

180

then, without taking her eyes off the paintings, she said, 'I wrote regularly.'

'How regularly?'

'Every month, to start with . . .'

'And I wrote back.'

'I have had two letters from you, James,' she confronted him, 'two letters in four years!'

He frowned. 'I wrote more – perhaps not as many as I should have – but I wrote many more than that. Besides, I don't think I received more than ten or a dozen from you in the same time.' He shook his head, 'I'm sorry, Julia, these things often go awry.'

'Well, don't we have a Royal Mail and mail steamers, or something?'

Dunbar shrugged and tried to disarm her rage with a smile. 'This is a sailing ship, Julia. We're like the wandering albatross, we could end up anywhere. There is probably a great bundle of your letters lying awaiting collection in Sydney, or Hong Kong, or San Francisco.'

'Can't you wake up, James? This is the twentieth century, even if you persist in remaining in the nineteenth.' Julia waved a hand at the constricting bulkheads and spoke in a low, angry voice, muting her fury only in deference to Dunbar's parents in the adjacent saloon.

'Julia, please . . .'

'Oh, damn you, James,' she hissed. 'How long are you going to be on this confounded ship?'

He shrugged again. 'Not long now. I'm due to go on leave when the captain returns. Or at least, after we've towed round into the London River, where we'll dry-dock.'

Julia bit her lip and glared at him with tear-filled eyes. Dunbar, conscious of his waiting parents but urged on by the power of Julia's feelings, impulsively slipped his arm about her waist and drew her to him.

'Julia,' he breathed, 'it is *so* good to see you again.'

181

But she went rigid in his arms and thrust him away, adjusting her hat, which had become ridiculously cockbilled in the confined space. Incredulous, he released her. She turned away and stepped out into the alleyway.

'I am glad to see you are still painting, James,' she called over her shoulder as she passed into the saloon with a frigid little smile at Mrs Dunbar. Anne Dunbar was undeceived by the silence from the cabin or by the two points of colour on Julia's cheeks, but propriety was quickly re-established, for the steward arrived with a tray of tea and the conversation became dominated by Anne Dunbar's account of the highlights of life in Clayton Dobbs in the previous forty months.

It had not been a happy encounter. Apart from briefly caressing the rump of the whore in the Diamond saloon many months earlier, the rector's evaluation of Dunbar's cabin had been painfully apt. It would have taken a saint not to have attempted to re-establish a by-no-means improper or compromising intimacy with the beautiful young woman who, almost on the last occasion he had seen her, had been naked. But Julia was no more the same creature than he was himself. As the party returned to the colonel's car, Julia had spoken briefly to him as she pulled on her gloves before climbing into the driver's seat.

'Tell me, James,' she asked with a muted but unabated fury in her voice and a stare of unveiled anger, 'are you *ever* going to make up your own mind about yourself?'

'I don't understand . . .' he had stuttered foolishly, aware that he was out of his depth, unpractised at this kind of verbal fencing.

'No,' Julia almost spat at him, 'of course you don't! How damnably foolish of me to ever think you did!' She gave a look over his shoulder at the masts and spars of the *Fort Mackinac* and hissed at him, 'You're such a confounded bloody fool.' Then she got into the car.

'Julia . . . !'

But his parents were staring at him and he was compelled to manufacture a smile, before Julia leaned out and commanded him to start the vehicle.

Dunbar went to the front of the bonnet, bent and swung the handle, venting his unhappiness on the engine, while its igniting roar echoed his own misery.

'Lovely bint that, chief,' said Grant, meeting him at the head of the gangway with a broad and insolent grin. 'Bet you can't wait to slip her a length.'

'Hold your damned tongue, Grant!' Dunbar snarled.

The *Fort Mackinac* dry-docked in the Orchard Graving Dock at Blackwall where, much to Dunbar's relief, the marine superintendent of Bullard, Crowe, a retired master named Keith, took over the vessel. Captain Crawhall left again to resume his leave, prior to rejoining when the ship completed her refit, and he had left before the *Fort Mackinac* had taken the blocks or Captain Keith had had the dockyard labourers place all the side-shores.

The master's departure delayed that of his chief mate, but the arrival of an ancient ship-keeper signalled that moment when a deep-sea windjammer surrenders herself to the shore and becomes a dishevelled drab. Almost all her people left, except the old sailmaker, who had no other home and refused to spend his time and money in the Seamen's Mission.

'I haf plenty of vork, Mister Mate,' the old man explained sadly, indicating the long rolls of canvas that had all been sent down from the lofty spars.

'Of course, Sails.'

'You come back next trip, ja?'

Dunbar nodded. 'I hope so.'

'So do I. You good officer. Make good captain one day, I t'ink.'

Dunbar blushed. 'Why thank you, Sails, it's kind of you to say so.'

The old man held up his hand and shook his head. 'No t'anks. Old Sails only speak true. You have good missee. I see her at Ipsvich. You soon be captain.'

In his voyage report, Captain Crawhall had indicated Dunbar's desire to sit for his master's certificate, along with a testimonial as to the wisdom of retaining the young officer's services. Dunbar was thus summoned to report to Bullard, Crowe and Company's offices in St Mary Axe as soon as he was released by the marine superintendent.

On arrival, an ancient clerk who bore a striking resemblance to the equally ancient ship-keeper, asked him to wait. The outer office displayed a waterline model of the handsome four-masted ship *Fort Ticonderoga* and a painting by a Chinese artist of the full-rigged ship *Fort Oswego*. The handsome clipper showed her identifying numbers in a four-flag hoist beneath her vermilion ensign and the company's house-flag at her main truck. Since the original partnership was Anglo-Canadian, the two founders had named their vessels after frontier forts and invented as their company's device a house-flag consisting of St George's cross surmounted by a scarlet maple leaf.

Dunbar was left kicking his heels for only a few moments before the young Mr Crowe, too long a Londoner to have retained any trace of his native accent, which he had barely gained before his father shipped him and his mother to the imperial capital, came in person to call Dunbar into his office.

'Mr Dunbar,' Crowe began, offering a glass of sherry, which Dunbar thought it proper to refuse, pleading the earliness of the hour, 'Captain Crawhall has expressed most strongly the desirability of retaining your services. I have heard the sad circumstances of your promotion, but,' Crowe shrugged, betraying the high pads with which he had his black frock-coat fitted, 'one man's meat is, alas, another's poison.'

Dunbar, awkward in his shore clothes, coughed a discreet agreement. The owner, a painfully thin, small man of middle years, with a head that seemed too over-stuffed with brains for so insignificant a body, smiled unpersuasively. He looked to Dunbar singularly unlike the strapping colonials he had met in his voyaging, and bent over his paper-strewn desk with an attentiveness that emphasised the claustrophobic nature engendered in men who live and work in offices. Dunbar won-dered whether Mr Crowe had any appreciation of the reality of the distances between the ports marked on the global wall-map mounted behind him. There were neither models nor pictures of ships in Mr Crowe's office. Instead the gloomy portraits of Messrs Bullard and Crowe senior, those rugged founders who had selected the names of frontier forts for their investments, glared sternly out of their gilt frames.

'There is an examination for master next week, if you feel fitted to submit yourself, at Dock Street,' Crowe was saying. 'I would be happy to instruct staff to process your application if you wish. What do you think?'

Crowe was unexpectedly obliging and Dunbar sensed an ulterior motive. 'That is most kind of you, Mr Crowe. I confess the matter of sitting immediately is a sur-prise, but yes, thank you, I shall take advantage of the examination.'

'Excellent. Now there is another matter.'

'I thought there might be.'

Crowe gave him a thin smile. 'The matter of Moorehouse. I understand you were close to him when he died.' Dunbar nodded. 'His family are investors in the company,' Crowe went on rapidly. 'The young gentleman was only to serve a few voyages, to knock the corners off him, as his father said. The Board is conscious that, in the circumstances, some explanation of the young man's death would ease the grief of the parents. We should therefore be obliged if you would travel down to Haverfordwest on our behalf. We shall, of course, pay all reasonable expenses.'

'May I ask, Mr Crowe, why Mr David Massey did not explain the circumstances? I should have thought as prospective son-in-law . . .'

'Mr Massey was not on board at the time, Mr Dunbar. It was thought the matter more appropriately done by yourself. After all, Mr Massey has gone home to marry. It was scarcely appropriate.'

It was clear that the good opinion of Bullard, Crowe and Company rested heavily upon Dunbar carrying out this unpleasant duty. Perhaps there was some latent threat to the Moorehouse investment, a supposition that seemed to be confirmed by a final remark of Mr Crowe's that times were difficult for the owners of sailing vessels. In fact, Crowe's allusion was as much an expression of the uncertainty of continuing employment. But either way, contemplation of the duty caused the spectre of guilt to rise again in Dunbar, even after all this time. The spectral visitation shook him; this was a fateful consequence of those few moments of concern for the mortally injured boy. Dunbar felt he must oblige Mr Crowe in expiation of what had followed, to prise out of his soul the liability that Grant had planted there.

'Of course, Mr Crowe. It's the least I can do.'

'Splendid! And then you *must* have a spell of leave.' Crowe's concern was specious. 'Please leave the address of your lodgings with the chief clerk. We shall submit your papers for the examination today.'

'And I am to return to the *Fort Mackinac* as mate?'

'I'm afraid it is perhaps peremptory to consider a command—'

'No, no, Mr Crowe, I did not mean that,' Dunbar interrupted hurriedly. 'I should just like to know, that's all.'

'Very well. I see no problem with that, Mr Dunbar.'

Dunbar shook the parchment-dry hand and left. In the outer office he explained to the ancient clerk that he had yet to find lodgings, and left his certificate of competency and discharge papers for the application for examination to be made.

'It is not necessary. If you call back on Friday, Mr Dunbar, I shall confirm matters. Oh, Mr Dunbar, before you go, I have some mail for you.' He handed over a bundle of letters tied up with document tape. 'We are not used to such a volume of correspondence,' the chief clerk remarked with a thin smile that seemed endemic in this place, suggesting that the matter was entirely Dunbar's fault. 'There is a considerable surcharge for forwarding mail. Please tell your correspondents that they should affix a sufficiency of postage stamps. The company is not to be put to the expense and cannot be held liable—'

'Thank you,' Dunbar said cutting this lecture short. He recognised Julia's writing on the uppermost superscription.

Unwilling to read the mass of letters until he had achieved a degree of privacy, Dunbar drifted west and found a small hotel in Victoria, where he took a room for a week. Once admitted to his room, he carefully arranged the letters in chronological order and began to read them.

The experience was even less pleasant than the visit at Ipswich. He had left Julia to join the *Fort Mackinac*, aware that their friendship had miscarried, disappointed in the lack of enthusiasm of Conrad Strachan and disjointed by their separate, disparate expectations from it. For his part, Dunbar had quietly disappeared, almost embarrassed by the intensity of Julia's advocacy of a talent that he did not feel he had, not to mention the oddly unsatisfactory physicality of their occupancy of the Pimlico rooms, and the surrender of modesty explicit in Julia's voluntary modelling.

He had, of course, utterly failed to understand anything about Julia. He had not begun to consider, let alone grasp, the complexities of her personality, her motives or her objectives. Apart from an initial, callow, yet arrogant assumption of her faith in him, he had no real understanding of her. His own regard for his skill as a painter and draughtsman was lop-sided. The burden of his upbringing, his inhibition, the lonely self-sufficiency of his profession – even the breadth of his experience of events in the Hotel Paradiso, about which he could not talk and which formed a secret inner and hermetic part of himself – all combined to make of him an introvert. Nor had he understood anything about high art. All he knew was that images moved him emotionally with a prompting urgency to commit them to paper, and if he understood anything about this, he equated it with the compulsion that drove some men to gamble, some to drink and others to visit brothels.

But Julia's letters compelled him to reconsider himself and he emerged with her perspective of him as a brutish, insensitive ingrate. It was true that he had earned this disapprobation largely by default. For not having received and therefore not having responded to her letters, he was falsely accused, except that some of the mud stuck on the prickly hackles of his conscience.

After his departure Julia had written a summation of Strachan's reaction. She had reiterated the warm optimism that she felt should have been drawn by way of conclusion from their encounter. Strachan, she suggested, might even have been tinged with jealousy, just as any old lion might view a challenge to his mastership of the pride. This encouragement, it has to be said, went with an understated but unveiled love for Dunbar. It was not for a proud and independent young woman like Julia Ravenham to confess to girlishly frivolous preoccupations with him. Nevertheless she spoke of 'warm affection' and the prospect of a 'great happiness' attending 'a partnership in which art and friendship would build indissoluble bonds between kindred spirits'. Such fulsomeness was, Dunbar thought, under the circumstances of his curmudgeonly self-absorption, more than generous, but he was unable to imagine the true state of Julia's affections in the sad, sweet sorrow after his departure. She too had her regrets. The passion of her nature vied with the strong streak of independence that life had grafted on her, and while the former caused her to pose naked before a man whose talent she much admired, the latter could not permit her to throw herself utterly at him. Unbeknown to Dunbar, it was this reserve that ensured her standing among her almost exclusively male circle. Julia, from a good enough family to avoid opprobrious comments, was known to Dacre, Retyn and the rest as a good sort, a sport. Dacre had been known to refer to her as Elizabeth the Second, for she had 'the heart of a man' and in the bohemian circles in which they all moved, and in which subjects such as women's suffrage and sexual freedom were frequently discussed, deference to Julia's intellect and person as a free-being was quite compatible. It relinquished none of their masculinity, for she was an equal in the sense that she came after them and was perceived, as it were, as they would perceive a junior partner.

For Julia, the final surrender did not await the right person – that last redundant and unhelpful remnant of chivalry. She had no theoretical allegiance to monogamy; rather, she felt her favours best bestowed on a select band of men, not as a courtesan, but as one who dispenses friendship's greatest and most intimate gift. And although she had yet to select any among her friends to found this fortunate circle, it was James Dunbar who had awakened a potent sexual reaction in her, a reaction that frightened her and, in the contrary nature of human response, prevented her from enjoying it.

She had had every intention of seducing him when he joined her in London, but in the event he had failed to meet her mind. In the manner in which a lover may be discouraged by some unexpected deficiency in the beloved, Julia had, despite her nudity, recoiled from total commitment. Had Dunbar been less diffident, had he had the courage to employ the techniques taught him by Dolores Garcia, he might have overcome all Julia's inhibitions, but neither Señora Garcia nor any of the events in the Hotel Paradiso had taught him the subtleties of *social* foreplay. Thus, when he had assayed an advance in the mate's cabin of the *Fort Mackinac*, he had received the full brunt of Julia's displeasure. Time and distance had not made her heart fonder, but had shrivelled it. And now the contents of the bundle of letters lay between them as surely as a brick wall.

At first Julia had regretted the failure of the intended consummation. Her letters had sought to right the affair, an easy matter without Dunbar actually present, for the absent, recipient lover could be imagined as being in any state of mind, engineered to suit the writer. But his lack of response was seen as wilful, and those few letters that did arrive from him were full of mundane and trivial inconsequences, for Dunbar had no gift for literal expression and wrote with a stilted formality of the ship and its progress, not even mentioning his continued activity as a painter, save for a single reference to painting Crawhall's portrait.

There was, of course, the occasional, unfortunate and curious reference to a rival. The phrase 'please remember me to Maureen Fletcher' struck Julia with a pain of which the lovely Maureen's eponymous ancestors would have

190

been proud. To Julia Ravenham, Dunbar's clumsiness became indifference. This in turn faded into abandonment as the intervals between his letters grew even longer. Her own correspondence became accusatory and poor Dunbar became not simply her lost lover, but her whipping boy for other frustrations. Fortunately, unlike the old, the young have other preoccupations which supervene and mollify hatreds. Julia's venom ran out of steam. Her own energy was diverted to other things; frustrations were converted into opportunities. In partnership with Icarus Dacre, she opened a gallery and removed herself to Hampstead, where Dacre's dead parents had left him a property along with the remains of their fortune. While Dacre lived in the family house overlooking the west Heath, Julia occupied a small apartment over the gallery in the High Street.

Oddly, it was commerce that revived Julia's correspondence with Dunbar, although the revival was short-lived, for she had received no reply. The gallery, which had opened to provide exhibitions of *avant-garde* work, was running into financial trouble. Julia, to whom Dacre had surrendered most of the executive power, had decided that she must attract buyers by occasionally exhibiting more traditional work. To this end she was able to persuade Ernst Ketlar to change his style, a change that brought the German artist almost overnight success with a lucrative crop of sales and a subsequent exhibition in Berlin. Münck too enjoyed a modest prosperity, though not to the extent of his fellow-countryman, for his work was sensitive and subtle, where Ketlar's was not. Having failed to sell anything at all, a disappointed Retyn took increasingly to drink and opium, plaguing his former friends with loud and dissolute scenes.

Julia also resolved to act as an agent, and to bring together potential customers wanting their family's portraits painted with those capable of satisfying this vanity. While Münck proved tractable, it was James Dunbar's skills that Julia most wanted, so she had written her last letter to Dunbar outlining the proposition, and urging him in conciliatory tones to visit her in Hampstead on his return.

Why she had mentioned none of this on her recent visit to Ipswich, when presumably she had been out of London and staying at Claydon Hall, he had no idea. Had he known more of women he might have guessed, but that knowledge was denied him. Instead he felt a deep obligation to re-establish the friendship that Julia had once hinted lay predestined between them, and the unsatisfactory nature of their last encounter moved him to resolve to visit the gallery without delay. In fact, he suddenly thought, the matter had better be concluded before he turned his thoughts to sitting for his examination.

Now he regretted settling on Victoria for his lodgings; it was not far from Pimlico, but a damnable distance from Hampstead.

PART THREE

Coasting

London, Suffolk and at Sea, 1912–14

CHAPTER TEN

The Ambush

The gallery had two brilliant canvases on display. They showed no discernible form to Dunbar's eye as he approached, but the rich colours of red and blue held a certain suggestion which, when he saw the titles, seemed oddly appropriate. They were called 'Macaw I' and 'Macaw II'. In the bottom left-hand corner was a black squiggle which he deciphered as *Retyn '12*.

He went in. It was immediately clear that Retyn's two paintings, foundlings of Julia's charity, concealed a dearth of material in the gallery, for the walls were bare and no-one occupied the neat table that stood with its accompanying chair at the rear of the room. For a moment Dunbar too stood with the same uncertain abandonment as the furniture, then Julia appeared from the rooms above, alerted by the jingle of the door-bell. As she recognised him, she stiffened, a tall, elegant figure in a dark blue dress whose pale features were crowned by the mass of her luxuriant red-gold hair.

Dunbar broke the silence. 'All your letters were at the ship-owner's offices. I've read them all. Julia, I'm most dreadfully sorry.'

She seemed to deflate, to lose her self-possession and that aloof remoteness which he realised now he had seen as an intimidating barrier, compounded as it was of her femaleness, her beauty, her social difference and her intellect.

'Julia, I was a fool.'

'You shouldn't reproach yourself,' she said as the distance between them diminished.

He shook his head. 'I feel quite inadequate to this moment,' he confessed.

She laughed, smiling up at him as they each slid their arms about the other. 'You are; you don't understand women.'

'Women always say that to establish their inscrutability and their superiority to men.'

'If you were in love with me, you might be more intuitive.'

'In love?' He thought of his unhappy obsession with Conchita. 'As far as I have ever understood it,' he said, with a hint of embitterment, 'love is an altered state of consciousness which is almost entirely self-centred and seeks to consume the object of its passion.'

'You would say that,' she said, looking away. 'Perhaps that's true for men.'

'Well, it seems to me that you see my misunderstanding as such only because in reality there is no common ground between men and women, with the exception of a kind of elevated and expedient perception that we cosily call *being in love*. The obsession with one person cannot possibly prove durable.'

'So,' she said with a rueful smile, 'you are not in love with me?'

'I didn't say that.'

'Then you are . . .'

'I am in an altered state of consciousness, utterly beside myself with a desire for you, yes.'

'But it will not prove durable?' She drew back, still holding him, but looking directly into his eyes.

Dunbar shrugged. 'I cannot say. Can you?'

'I don't know, it is not me who is making this declaration.' He bent to kiss her. 'Am I to be set aside for Maureen?'

'Julia!'

'Well?'

'Julia, for God's sake, I know nothing about the girl.'

But Julia had withdrawn from him and he felt a sudden desolation, a foreboding. The figure of Maureen Fletcher interposed between them, or so it seemed to Dunbar, until Julia repudiated him utterly.

'It doesn't matter, James. I'm sorry, but,' she paused and sighed, 'I'm engaged to Icarus.'

On the train rocketing westwards ten days later, he realised that he should have left her at that point, cut and run, walked out, turned his back, shipped out, gone.

Instead he had remonstrated; asked why, in God's name, she had done such a thing.

'Why not?' she had snapped back. 'I have known Icarus a long time, know him better than I know you. We enjoy each other's company. He is wealthy.'

'How very practical,' he had said, masking his hurt with a half-sneer. 'But why marry?'

She had snorted a brief, contemptuous laugh. 'Because I will be taken more seriously in business, even if married to poor Icarus, than ever I will be as *Miss* Julia Ravenham. Apart from that not inconsiderable advantage, I have no other way of supporting myself.'

'What about Clayton Hall and the estate?'

'Uncle will live for ten or a dozen years more and, even when he is no longer with us, do you really see me as mistress of Clayton Hall?'

'But . . .'

'You have been away in your ship for four years, James. So much has changed.'

'Oh, Julia.'

'Let us not be angry with each other. Perhaps this is the best way. Perhaps life with Icarus will prove durable despite your pessimism.' She had smiled at him, though her eyes were full of tears.

'If it is not love,' he had smiled sadly back at her, 'it may well prove as durable as any millstone.'

'James! Is that really you?' Their intimacy had been ruptured by Dacre's arrival. Immediately, upon Dacre's insistence, they then withdrew to a restaurant for a celebratory dinner. Conversation was awkward until Dacre had enquired after James's painting.

'He still does it,' Julia had said, 'and is still very good.'

'Better, I hope.'

'But,' Julia had asked with sudden alarm, 'where is all your work at the moment?'

'Still on the ship,' Dunbar had replied, 'in dry-dock at Blackwall.'

'That's no good! Let us at least store them here,' offered Dacre.

'No,' Julia had put in, brightening with a sudden brittle, but inspired enthusiasm, 'let us exhibit them! Tell Icarus what you have done.'

Dunbar had shrugged. 'Oh, the usual portraits of my shipmates . . .'

'Including one of the captain of his ship,' Julia had explained. 'Oh, James, don't be so bloody self-deprecating.'

Dunbar had shifted awkwardly in his seat. 'I have only the drawings for that. Captain Crawhall bought the finished picture from me.'

'But you could do another.'

'I suppose so.'

'There's plenty of room at my house,' Dacre had

said helpfully, adding, 'D'you have any pictures of the ship itself?'

'*Her*self, Icarus. The *Fort Mackinac*, despite its name, is female.'

'Damn it's – *her* – gender. D'you have any portraits of the ship?'

Dunbar had shaken his head. 'No, not really. I've done a lot of drawings of activity about the decks, but one never properly sees one's own ship except when she's alongside or at anchor, and then she's a passive thing.'

'But you've seen other ships at sea. Surely you could produce one painting of your own ship?' Dacre had been leaning forward persuasively and he had looked at Julia.

'What is all this about?'

'To be truthful, James, we could do with a figurative exhibition. Eric Retyn's abstractions, wonderful though they are, do not sell. I think Icarus wants a picture of your barque, or whatever it is, as a central feature of an exhibition that tells people about your life at sea.'

'Absolutely!' Dacre had confirmed, placing his hand over Julia's in a possessive, confirmatory gesture. 'Isn't she wonderful?' he had asked rhetorically, lifting Julia's hand to his lips so that the candlelight caught the diamond ring about her finger.

'Oh, by the way,' Dunbar had said hurriedly, raising his glass, 'I understand congratulations are in order.'

He had drowned the memory of that evening in his hasty and unconfident preparations for the examination at the Board of Trade offices in Dock Street. The instant he had completed his orals he had checked out of his hotel and taken the train from Paddington. Now he had perforce to thrust from his mind his abysmal showing at the oral test with which he had concluded the full examination. His stupidity in forgetting what lights and daymarks were shown by a trawler fast by its nets to a rock had resulted in him failing, a circumstance that he would have to rectify in one month's time, if Bullard, Crowe and Company did not demand his services before then.

He informed their ancient clerk that messages might be left care of Mr Dacre in Hampstead, but that he was proceeding west, to carry out Mr Crowe's mission. During the journey he drowned all his manifold disappointments in considering that part of his life that offered him some possibility of progress and alighted upon the proposition of Dacre's. Dunbar had done nothing to rescue his work from his cabin, but had thought of executing a second portrait of Crawhall. He recollected that the captain had chosen a less satisfactory composition from the alternatives Dunbar had offered him than the artist himself would have liked.

'I could use the best,' he muttered to himself, his imagination taking refuge in the concept. The ship, however, was more difficult. He would need a large canvas, but he could see the impact that such an exhibition might have if . . .

But no, this was pure speculative folly. How could he breeze ashore and think he could take the world by storm? He was, in so far as the sophisticated and critical artistic world was concerned, a gauche sailorman. They would tear him to pieces!

Yet there had been mute appeal in Julia's eyes. How much did the success of the gallery mean to her? He need hardly ask the question. What did he care about the world of art critics and aesthetes? He could at least escape their scorn and derision by shipping out. Besides, he would probably be away at sea by the time Dacre and Julia got the thing off the ground, and in any case he had first to paint two pictures.

*　　*　　*

Dunbar sent word from Haverfordwest to the Moorehouse family home, which lay off the road to Fishguard, near the village of Wolf's Castle. He received a reply that he would be welcome to call the following morning and was ensconced in the bar of his hotel, somewhat disconsolate at the prospect of a lonely evening with an even less pleasant forenoon to follow, when he received a visitor.

David Massey breezed into the place asking for him by name. 'James, how good of you,' he began, clearly a far happier man than on their first acquaintance.

They ordered drinks and exchanged general pleasantries, then Dunbar asked, 'Now that you're married, where have you settled? Down here, I presume?'

Massey nodded. 'Yes, there's a dower house on the estate. It's ideal for Eleanor,' he pulled a face, 'while I'm at sea.'

'Will you swallow the anchor? I imagine with your connections you might be able to.'

Massey shook his head in denial at the seaman's phrase for giving up the sea. He lowered his glass. 'No, Alan was the youngest of three, so there are two other brothers to run the farms, though one is in the army. I'm from landed stock myself, but I've no interest in farming. I suppose I sort of ran away to sea – not literally, of course, I was sent to the *Conway*, but it was rebellion of a kind.'

'But you don't truly like it at sea, do you?'

'No, not in sail. The predictability of a steam ship would suit me. The minute I've my master's ticket I'm applying to Cunard.'

'Well, good luck to you. I've just made a glorious mess of my orals . . .'

The conversation drifted off into the esoteric concerns of aspiring officers of the mercantile marine. When it was time to go, Massey rose and said, 'James, I'm sorry I didn't know you were coming, you would have been welcome at the dower house. I understand you're meeting the old man and the family tomorrow. I'll come down for you in the car. Check out and come and stay with us for a day or two after you've, well, you know, seen the old man.'

'What's he like?'

'Oh, a thoroughly decent fellow, but he has taken the loss of the baby of the family very badly, though he's been better since the wedding.'

'What about your mother-in-law?'

Massey sighed. 'Well, of course, it's been worse for her. She really did dote on the boy. Frankly, I think that's why he was so wayward, and his father sent him to sea to knock some sense into him. You can imagine . . .'

'She's blaming him and he's blaming himself?'

'Absolutely. Anyway, I'll pick you up about nine-thirty.'

The house lay in a coombe not far from the sea, a flat-roofed building built a century earlier. Massey had taken Dunbar into the morning room and introduced him to his new family. Alongside Mr and Mrs Moorehouse stood a man of about thirty, clearly the elder son, who was introduced as Thomas. Next to her mother sat a strikingly handsome, dark young woman, Eleanor Massey. It was clear that Dunbar's visit had reopened old wounds, for Mrs Moorehouse wept quietly, while her husband's fleshy face trembled with emotion.

'Please sit down, Mr Dunbar,' said Thomas Moorehouse. 'I think, under the circumstances, we should all have a glass of sherry. David, would you?'

'Of course.'

Dunbar accepted the glass of *fino* and, after a moment, said, 'I'm truly sorry to call on you like this. I was asked by Mr Crowe to come and explain the circumstances of your son's death.'

'Yes,' said Mr Moorehouse, 'we asked to hear the particulars from someone who was aboard his ship. You were aboard the ship at the time, were you not?'

'Yes, sir, I was. More to the point, I am uniquely qualified to tell you exactly what happened, for I witnessed the whole sad business.' Dunbar focused his attention upon Mrs Moorehouse. 'Perhaps I can offer you some comfort, ma'am, in that the whole thing was over in an instant. You see, we were in the Southern Ocean and . . .'

Diffidently he explained the broad circumstances of Alan Moorehouse's death and, when he was finished, Thomas asked, 'And was there nothing that could be done?'

'Nothing, I'm afraid.'

'But you did try something, you did try and do something?' Eleanor asked.

Dunbar nodded. 'Yes, I left what I was doing and went to him. He was already dead.'

'How did you know he was dead?' Thomas asked sharply.

'It was obvious. I have seen death before, Mr Moorehouse. Your brother was quite dead. There was no doubt about it.'

'Wait a minute,' Massey put in, 'you say you left what you were doing?'

'Yes.'

'If I understand you correctly, James, you were alone at the wheel.'

Such was the emotive atmosphere in the sunlit morning room that Dunbar hung his head. 'Yes, I was.'

'Then you, I mean . . .'

'I'm sorry, I don't understand,' broke in Thomas Moorehouse, 'does this have a bearing on Alan's death?'

'No, no,' Massey said, 'you see . . .'

'Let *me* explain, David,' Dunbar said with a sigh that was clearly affecting, for Mrs Moorehouse was in floods of tears and Eleanor had her arm about her. Dunbar felt trapped; in his desire to do the decent thing he was aware that he was walking into an ambush, but was quite incapable of avoiding the absolute truth. 'The ship was difficult to steer under the conditions. The mate had been helping me and, because of the weather, had run forward to help the master. He hadn't abandoned me exactly, but he had left me alone for a few minutes. It was his intention to send someone aft to take his place, and he sent Alan. As I've said, Alan did not make it. Things were very bad, you see.' He paused, then added, 'but I made them very much worse. You see, we were running with the wind astern . . .'

'The *Fort Mackinac*'s very difficult to handle in those circumstances,' Massey put in didactically.

'I had let her yaw slightly off course,' Dunbar went on, ignoring the well-meant interruption, 'just as Alan stretched out to get a line to lash the pair of us to the helm, and he lost his footing at the same moment.'

There was a moment of terrible silence, then Thomas Moorehouse said, 'So, you contributed to his death.'

Dunbar nodded. 'In a sense, yes,' he whispered.

'That's ridiculous,' put in Massey. 'Thomas, you have no idea what it's like to try and steer a big, griping barque like that. James wasn't to blame, for God's sake!'

'What did you do next?' Eleanor's cool voice sought the middle ground between the accusations of her brother and the excuses of her husband. She could quite see how the thing was a mishap, even if the conduct of the miserable young man before them had contributed to it. It was what he had done afterwards that would denote his character, and against which she could measure her forgiveness, or hone her enmity.

Dunbar looked up. The face of Mrs Moorehouse was

204

shocked; her husband was horrified; Thomas Moorehouse bore the heartless expression he might bear as he condemned a fox to be torn to pieces by his hounds. Of the close family, only his sister remained undecided. He sighed.

'I let go of the wheel and went to your son. As I have already said, the cargo had shifted when the squall hit us. That was bad enough, but when I left the helm, the ship broached and came round beam-on to the wind. The cargo shifted further and the ship heeled over further. She nearly capsized. I don't know how she didn't. It was my fault.'

'Because you went to Alan's help,' Massey added.

'And Alan needed help because you had caused him to lose his footing,' countered Thomas.

'No, I didn't do that!' Dunbar replied, standing up. 'The invariable rule is one hand for the ship and one for yourself. But to say that Alan contributed to his own fall is as stupid as saying he committed suicide. Conditions were atrocious. I could hardly stand up at the wheel, let alone steer. The ship was over at a steep angle, due to the first shift of cargo, and gave another leeward lurch as I brought her back on course. The seas running up under our stern were as high as this house. I was not supposed to look round . . .'

'What the devil d'you mean you're not supposed to look round?' Thomas scoffed.

'It's true, Tom,' Massey confirmed. 'Those seas are so huge that they can unnerve a man if he turns round and sees what's looming up behind him. Lots of sailing-ship masters pass a standing order that the helmsmen are forbidden to look round. It's quite clear that Alan's loss of footing was pure misadventure. Don't forget, Alan's wasn't the only life lost that day. My own transfer and promotion were basically consequent upon the loss of the *Fort Mackinac*'s second mate, Chris Wilson.'

'How did he die?' asked Mrs Moorehouse.

'Nobody quite knows, ma'am,' Dunbar replied, 'though it was thought he was washed over the side at some point.'

'No-one knows . . . how terrible.'

'It must have been awful,' said Eleanor Massey.

'It was. The fact that Alan fell right at my feet enables me to tell you exactly what occurred. In fact, Alan was acting in a thoroughly responsible manner by trying to reach the lashing that might have secured both of us.'

'Well, I don't know,' Thomas said doubtfully.

'Tom, you really have no idea . . .' said Massey.

'You've seen St Bride's Bay,' broke in his wife, 'with a westerly gale lashing the rocks at Skokholm and Skomer, Tom. Surely you can imagine what it must have been like. Remember when the *Star of Galway* drove ashore on Old Castle Head,' Eleanor went on, reminding her brother of a shipwreck they had witnessed some seven years earlier. 'You said then you could hardly conceive of the power of the sea, breaking up an iron ship like that.'

Thomas Moorehouse grunted and then Mr Moorehouse, who had remained silent throughout the proceedings, coughed. 'Well, young man,' he said to Dunbar, 'it seems to me you have been unusually brave by telling us all this. I attach no blame to you. Perhaps if you had not been left alone, Alan would not have been sent to the wheel and perhaps you would not now have to confess these sorry events. At least we know Alan's death was manly. Thank you for coming down here. Now, David, let us have another glass of sherry.'

'What did you think of my brother, Mr Dunbar?' Eleanor cut in quickly.

'I liked him. He was a fine young man. I understand it was not his intention, or yours, that he would stay at

206

sea, but he was a credit to you all and had the makings
of a fine seaman.'

'He wrote to me once,' Eleanor said, 'to say that he
liked the life, but could not decide whether to stay, or
whether to jump ship and raise sheep in Australia.'

'He would not have been the first brass-bounder to
do that!' Massey confirmed as he refilled their glasses.

'That, my dear,' added Mr Moorehouse, turning to his
wife, 'would have broken your heart just as certainly
as this.'

'Oh, don't say that . . .'

'Mr Dunbar, wasn't it you who painted Alan's portrait.'

'Of course it was,' Massey said, 'I told you last
night . . .' His wife gave him a sharp glare, but her
remark had done its work.

'What's that? Was it you, Mr Dunbar, who painted
Alan's portrait?'

'Yes, ma'am, it was.'

'Oh my,' her hand went to her breast, 'what a strange,
small world this is, to be sure.'

The gallery was crowded when Dunbar arrived. In his
innocence he knew nothing of the network of contacts,
of the lists of former and potential patrons and critics
that between them Julia and Icarus Dacre had acquired.
A disquieting sensation filled him as he pushed through
the throng that chattered animatedly before his pictures.
Julia's staff of a jobbing carpenter and Eric Retyn, when
sober, had restretched and framed them and they hung
now in imposing array. After the visit to Pembrokeshire,
the reawakened misery of his involvement in the death
of Alan Moorehouse and Christopher Wilson had robbed
him of any sense of triumph. Rather, this brash display of
images generated by his life aboard the *Fort Mackinac*

seemed to embody a wilful, insensitive contempt. Their impact, seen now for the first time as an *oeuvre*, came to him as a reproachful shock. He was conscious of suffering a second ambush, this time constructed entirely of his own pride.

Between the heads of the crowd, Dunbar caught glimpses of Captain Crawhall, pipe aggressively clamped between his yellow teeth and hard, purplish mouth. The old master was haloed with a black sou'wester, with a heavy breaking sea rearing up astern of his hurrying ship. The painting was barely dry. Then there was Bill Andrews, his good looks featuring several times – in oilskins, at ease reading in the forecastle and, in a small neat oil, climbing into the weather rigging as the *Fort Mackinac* dipped her lee rail and a green-white avalanche of water poured into the waist. Even Grant – insolent, unhappy and fractious Grant – stared with an Odyssean glare at an imaginary horizon somewhere behind the head of the observer. Dunbar could hear his voice, heartlessly linking Dunbar with death. The memory and the almost spectral impact of Grant as a *bête noire* made him shudder involuntarily.

Dunbar forced himself to look away. Between the oil portraits, Julia had hung the drawings. He had forgotten how many of them there were: men chipping, men painting, men sewing sails and splicing wire, men aloft taming a flogging top-gallant or hauling on a brace; the steward going aft from the galley up to his waist in a green sea with the officers' soup tureen held aloft; Crawhall and Snelling shooting the sun at apparent noon; the figure of the carpenter outlined against the sky as he shifted the headsail sheets, while the barque threw her head up into a head sea as they tacked; and the same man striking with his maul the pin that let the starboard anchor go. On an elegant easel at an angle to the gallery, Dunbar's large portrait of the

Fort Mackinac herself was roped off, for it too was still wet.

The whole impression, with its attendant crowd, was overwhelming. Dunbar was aware as he shouldered his way forward that he had no idea where he was going. He hesitated, out of his depth. What, he wondered, did all these people think of his pictures? He suddenly overheard a conversation between two overdressed, middle-aged women whose headgear seemed to contain several slaughtered birds of paradise; they were discussing a mutual acquaintance. Dunbar turned away, only to hear a further couple, an elderly man with a much younger woman whose back was to Dunbar, but whose cream dress revealed her slender figure and a narrow waist, saying '. . . of course, the appeal of such work is terribly limited.'

Dunbar suddenly wanted to retreat, to gain the street outside. This had all happened so quickly. He had returned unhappily from west Wales and, in response to an invitation made on the eve of his departure, had returned to lodge with Dacre. In the house overlooking Hampstead Heath, in an opportunist whirlwind, Icarus had persuaded him to recover his canvases and drawings from the *Fort Mackinac* and leave them with him. Distracted by both his reception by the Moorehouse family and the compulsion of revising for retaking his oral examination, Dunbar had surrendered his work and left London to visit Clayton Dobbs. The week in Suffolk only increased his depression. The rectory was suffering from neglect and grew as shabby as his parents, who were deprived now of even the occasional support of Jenny Broom. Less and less able to cope, they were nevertheless touchy about their independence and almost resentful at his concern. He had felt more a stranger than ever, concluding gloomily that his father was on the verge of mental decline and that his own presence seemed to irritate the old man beyond endurance. Julia's telegram that he should return to London came as a welcome relief.

Now, standing foolishly amid a press of people whom he did not know, but who were commenting freely upon or utterly ignoring his exposed work, he wished he was back at sea.

At this moment of lonely indecision, Dacre saw him and, with a loud, 'Ahhh, the conquering hero . . .' approached Dunbar, arms outstretched in a flamboyant and conspicuous greeting. The gallery grew suddenly quiet and Dunbar's heart sank.

'My Lord, ladies and gentlemen, may I present the artist, James Dunbar.'

Dunbar flushed at the liberty Dacre took, as a ripple of polite, restrained applause filled the room. He nodded and muttered his thanks.

'Say a few words, James,' Dacre murmured into his ear.

Dunbar glanced around; people were looking at him expectantly and he felt intimidated, avoiding the curious stares laid upon him. His eyes suddenly fell on the sardonic Grant, gazing above their heads from the far wall.

'Come on, man,' Dacre hissed as Julia arrived alongside the two men.

'I, er, I must thank you all for showing an interest in my work.' Dunbar faltered, coughed, cleared his throat and remembered his manners. 'I should also like to thank the proprietors of the gallery, Julia Ravenham and Icarus Dacre, for the opportunity to exhibit these paintings and drawings. They were all done during the last four years, which I spent aboard the four-masted barque *Fort Mackinac*. I hope you like at least some of them.' He could think of nothing to add, except to repeat the words, 'Thank you.'

The applause was more enthusiastic, people were smiling at him and he found a glass shoved into his hand, took a deep swig of the Burgundy, smiled back and nodded.

'Well done.' Julia, coolly professional, slipped a hand under his elbow, 'Come and meet a few people.'

Now, instead of forcing his way through the press, Dunbar found that people drew aside, smiling with murmured compliments. He heard 'well done', 'congratulations' and 'a *tour de force*'.

'Lord Fowey, may I present James Dunbar; James, Lord Fowey.'

'How d'ye do, Dunbar . . .' Fowey was in his late thirties, a man of medium height and compactly powerful build, with dark hair that was already greying. His weathered complexion was set off by a short, clipped beard.

'My lord,' Dunbar shook the offered hand.

'I'm a sailor myself, Dunbar, and I must say that these are particularly fine studies, particularly fine. It's time someone showed what it's like bringing the bacon home, don't ye think so, m'dear?' Fowey's head jerked forward and Dunbar caught the faint pungency of toilet water. The woman next to him turned round. She was much taller than her husband, wearing a long grey dress and tip-tilted turbaned hat with a flaring aigrette. But Dunbar was transfixed by her face, for it was extraordinarily striking. Lady Fowey's complexion was pale, her features almost fleshless, so closely was the fine skin drawn over the skull. Most prominent was the huge aquiline nose, which dominated her appearance. Her deep-set eyes were so dark that they seemed as black as her hair which, where it showed beneath her head-dress, swept from her exposed brow like a wave to curve behind her head, where it was gathered and pinned by a silver stiletto. This fantastic head was held in a regal, rather than a haughty manner by a long neck, which rose from an emerald green silk cravat.

'My wife, Dunbar . . .'

Dunbar took her hand and managed a meek half-bow over it. 'A pleasure, Lady Fowey.'

'I was saying that the paintings are very fine, m'dear,' Lord Fowey repeated.

'They are splendid, Mr Dunbar,' said her ladyship, smiling, 'truly splendid,' and Dunbar felt himself bewitched by the curve of the carmine lips. 'I was particularly struck by this one,' Lady Fowey pointed at Andrews. 'Who is he?'

'Andrews, your ladyship, William Andrews, an ableseaman, but an odd case,' he broke off, but Lady Fowey turned back to him.

'Odd? How so?' Lady Fowey looked at Dunbar attentively.

'He was – untypical, an enigma. I have no idea why he was at sea, but it did not seem to me that he was from the normal background from which the majority of seamen come.'

'Which is?'

'Oh, wide enough, but from seafaring families generally – rough men mostly, and by that I do not speak ill of them. Most were kindly enough, but alongside them Andrews stuck out. He said little enough; I have no idea what part of the country he called home, or, for that matter, where he is now, who or what his family was. In the manner of these men, he paid off and will turn up again when he's run out of money and a ship wants a crew.'

'How strange,' Lady Fowey murmured, turning again to look at the portrait and an idea occurred to Dunbar.

'You don't think you recognise him, do you?' he asked.

'Do you know,' she turned back to him with her strangely striking face, illuminated by her smile, 'I rather thought I might, though I cannot for the life of me . . . Johnnie!'

Her husband turned from his conversation with Julia. 'Eh, what's that, m'dear?'

'Does that fellow over there,' Lady Fowey indicated Andrews's portrait, 'remind you of anybody?'

Lord Fowey frowned and regarded the picture for a moment or two before vehemently shaking his head. 'No, not at all.' He turned to Dunbar, 'Never forget a face, Dunbar – once seen, never forgotten. You must be mistaken, m'dear, unless of course he's someone I don't know.'

The possibility had not escaped Dunbar as he listened to this exchange, but then there was somebody else to meet, a familiar, elderly man who was bending solicitously over Lady Fowey's hand. 'Lady Fowey, how delightful to see you. I gather you are enthusiastic about the young lion here.'

'I am indeed. You may well have to look to your laurels if Mr Dunbar gives up the sea and offers his services as a portraitist.'

'I shall take heed of your warning, Lady Fowey, though I am sure Dunbar is happier at sea than he would be ashore.'

Seymour Conrad Strachan smiled thinly at Dunbar, who submerged his surprise under a courtly 'Good evening, sir.'

'Now, James, we were not so formal at our last encounter. You have come of age, since then. These are very fine, very fine. In the event, Julia was right,' Strachan made a deferential bow towards Julia, who smiled graciously. 'I saw some earlier work of James's,' Strachan explained to the Foweys.

'And misjudged the artist?' Lady Fowey asked with a slightly sardonic expression, one black eyebrow arching dramatically.

'No, not exactly. I sought to discourage him, because only by placing the obstacle of discouragement before him would I enable him to prove his mettle. As you see,' Strachan gestured around them, 'there was method in my madness.'

'You talk a lot of rum nonsense, Strachan,' Lord Fowey put in. 'I dare say in your business every competing talent's a threat, eh? Well, looking about, I'd say you'd got your work cut out to keep up, eh?' Lord Fowey grinned at Dunbar.

Dunbar could hardly bear the expression on Strachan's face. The artist went very pale and stared at Fowey with eyes that glittered with affront. 'As your lordship pleases,' he said in a low voice and withdrew with a curt bow to Lady Fowey.

'That was unforgivable, Johnnie,' her ladyship reproached her husband.

'Oh, don't fuss, m'dear, he shouldn't be so damned touchy. He'd be able to take a knock if he'd been at sea, wouldn't he, Dunbar?'

'I dare say, my lord.'

'There you are then.' Fowey took a gold watch from his pocket.

'It has been a pleasure to meet you, Mr Dunbar,' her ladyship said as Fowey grunted agreement.

'Thank you so much for coming,' Julia smiled and Dunbar felt her ushering arm under his elbow again as the couple left.

'How much more of this do I have to do, Julia?' Dunbar asked.

'Another hour.'

'Another hour!'

'Yes. For me, for friendship's sake, for your own sake. You're selling, James. I didn't expect to sell a single one of these portraits – people usually only commission the things. Perhaps it was the loss of the *Titanic*. Who knows how people's whims are generated? But these are selling and you must capitalise upon it.'

Dunbar was touted from group to group, Julia introducing him to each with a tireless courtesy. Among those he met was the elderly gentleman he had seen talking earlier to the slim-waisted woman. He had bought the portrait of Crawhall, 'Because', he said, 'it epitomises the spirit of this nation, Mr Dunbar, and in particular, it kills the lie that trade follows the flag. The flag has gone wherever trade went first, and don't let them pretend otherwise. That fellow,' the elderly gentleman pointed at Crawhall's stern image, 'affirms it.'

'Who is he?' Dunbar whisperingly asked Julia as she moved him on.

'Frederic Maddox is a self-made man, a grocer I believe. He owns numerous shops and a retailing empire. He's also a notable yachtsman, hence his sentimental attachment to the sea.'

There were several more such encounters, then the crowd thinned, the occasion became less formal. Dunbar found himself alone, Julia being occupied in saying goodbye to a trio who, without buying, had been suggesting that Dunbar should take up portraiture as a living. He avoided their fulsome enthusiasm, retrospectively embarrassed for Strachan. He looked round, eager to make amends and apologise for Lord Fowey's rudeness, but the painter had gone. The slender woman in cream to whom Maddox the grocer had been talking was standing alone before the large, wet oil of the *Fort Mackinac*.

For no accountable reason, other than an acknowledged curiosity as to why so material a thing as a four-masted barque should interest a woman by herself, or perhaps because of a lingering sadness at the most vividly remembered events aboard her, Dunbar felt compelled to speak to her.

He crossed the emptying gallery to stand beside her

and, without looking at her, said, 'I'm afraid it's not very good. It was done here, for the exhibition, in a hell of a hurry.'

'I know,' she said, and Dunbar looked up into the dark eyes of Maureen Fletcher.

CHAPTER ELEVEN

The Attaché Case

The success of Dunbar's exhibition stunned him. There was no doubt that much of this success was directly attributable to Julia, whose nurturing of her protégé's talent was coolly, even ruthlessly commercial. Indeed, she seemed to Dunbar during the few heady days succeeding the exhibition's opening to revel in it, as some perverse weapon with which to berate him for his foolishness and insensitivity. Clearly she thrived on her relationship with Dácre, who kept largely in the background and gave her the freedom that Dunbar knew he could never have given her. Dunbar quickly doubted whether either of them had really considered that anything more significant than a brief, frustrated, but lustful passion had ever existed between them.

To Dunbar, Julia was efficiently friendly, as befitted two people who had known each other for a long time and between whom now lay a bond of financial success. If he had been in a mood for regret, he might have thought himself courteously thrown over for Dacre, but the truth was that the reappearance of Maureen had quickly distracted Dunbar from any lingering regrets over Julia. The four of them, Julia and Dacre, Maureen and himself, had had dinner at a Hampstead restaurant after the gallery had closed for the night and he had been captivated all over again by the dark young woman's outstanding beauty. Only once during the conversation had the old relationship with Julia intruded when, during a moment when both Dacre and Maureen had left the table, Dunbar had asked Julia about Strachan.

'I suppose,' he had said, 'you are not dependent upon poor Strachan any more.'

'No,' Julia had replied, shaking her head, 'though you've no need to pity him.'

'I did think the Foweys handled him rather roughly.'

Julia laughed. 'I think Lady Fowey wanted him to paint her, but Conrad has grown greedy and asked too much, I believe. I don't think Fowey's got a lot more than his naval pay to live on . . .'

'Oh, I see.'

'What's the matter, James? I can see there's something on your mind. Is it to do with me and Strachan?'

He looked at her, astonished. 'How the devil did you know?'

She sighed. 'I don't know; I sensed your antipathy towards our relationship all those years ago, when you first came to London and I stupidly took you to see him. Like most men, you don't like the idea of women enjoying the same kind of easy freedoms that you take for granted.'

Dunbar avoided this generality. The subject was, he knew, often being debated among Julia's circle. Theoretically he had no objection. Emotionally, though, he clearly found his objection unavoidable. Instead he said, 'I didn't like the idea of you posing for Strachan . . . I thought you were modelling for him, just as you had for me.' He coloured, feeling embarrassed.

Julia smiled contemptuously. 'You're embarrassed! My God, James, you are a terrible hypocrite!'

'No, I'm not. I'm embarrassed because of the change between us . . .'

'And that change occurred, or at least started, with your stupid suspicions about Strachan and me?' Julia looked astonished. 'Well, I did model for him, though not as you imagined.'

'I'm sorry, I don't understand,' he frowned.

Julia shook her head. 'Oh, James, what fools we make of ourselves when we should least like to. Of course I modelled, but not in the way I posed for you. That,' she said with emphasis, 'that was scandalous. Enjoyable even,' she admitted, leaning across the table. 'I did it for you. What I did for old Conrad was innocent in the extreme. When he received a commission, and I think he was painting the Countess of Linlithgow at the time, it was my job to help with the clothes.'

'I still don't understand.'

'The countess and her ilk don't want to sit all day having their ball-gowns, or their ermines, painted. Cheap little country girls like me can do that. Not only was I fully dressed, you stupid man, I was positively overdressed!'

'I'll be damned!'

'Would it have made a difference if you had known? Would I have seemed less of a trollop than you thought me?'

'I didn't think of you as a trollop,' Dunbar protested, but he got no further. The brief interlude of intimacy was over, for Dacre, having visited another table to which several patrons of the gallery had withdrawn, rejoined them.

'They asked us to join them,' Dacre said confidentially as he sat down, 'but I explained, James, that you were leaving in the morning and we had some business matters to conclude.'

'I see. And is that a hint, Icarus?'

'Not at all, but I supposed you wished for some privacy after your evening of triumph.'

'That was thoughtful of you.'

'What he means, James,' Maureen said quietly, reseating herself, 'is that he does not want you talking about art. Only Icky knows about art?'

'Maureen, how can you?' Dacre protested insincerely.

'Maureen is right, Icarus. You are dreadfully pretentious about aesthetics. Anyway,' Julia said briskly, nodding at the neighbouring table, 'they failed to buy anything, so there is no need for us all to mortify ourselves.'

Preoccupation with the oral examination for master prevented Dunbar from revelling in his brief fame. To his surprise and no little regret for the extra hours of anxious revision, he passed in twenty minutes, appearing before the same examiner who had thrown him out for his failure on his first attempt. As Dunbar rose to go, Captain Piggott, a short, rotund man, whose black frock-coat failed to give him stature and seemed, if anything, rather too long, held out his hand. 'Well, young man, good fortune. It will have done you no harm to stumble here. Now you are a master mariner, your mistakes may have greater consequences, so always think before you act.'

The remark was well meant, but the effect was to recall the death of Moorehouse and the jeers of Grant, so that Dunbar's professional triumph was also robbed of its climacteric. Nevertheless, he dutifully reported his success to Bullard, Crowe's ancient clerk and was told that the *Fort Mackinac* had been delayed in dock and that he might take a few more days leave.

'She will be making a passage in ballast, Mr Dunbar, to Newcastle, then loading coal for San Francisco.'

He left St Mary Axe with a sense of *déjà vu* and, leaving Dacre's address, went west towards Pimlico where Maureen Fletcher still occupied the same rooms.

She was not in when he called and he retreated to

a public house to kill an hour impatiently. He was in a ferment now; the passing of his examination had freed him from worry, and news of his now imminent departure compelled him to seek out Maureen. He had thought, during the evening they had spent together, that she was not indifferent to him, and while he nurtured no silly romantic hopes, her image, which had drifted in and out of his consciousness for many months, had been a pale tribute to the reality of her. For where Julia, for all her flaming head of hair, possessed a cool and elegant beauty, Maureen's was a darker, more touching and haunting loveliness which, to Dunbar's eye, was utterly compelling. He doubted, had Maureen posed for him as Julia had, whether he could have painted a single brushstroke. And where Julia's character was independent, there was something appealingly dependent, even poignantly vulnerable, about Maureen. Even on his brief acquaintance with her, this quality exerted a powerful attraction upon him.

She had withal something of the beauty of the whore Conchita allied to the sensuous grandeur of Dolores Garcia. Such a combination was, for James Dunbar, irresistible.

When he returned to her rooms she answered the door. To his delight she smiled at the sight of him.

'I hope you don't mind, I . . .' he hesitated, stumbling foolishly.

'No. It's good to see you. Come in.' A quick look of irritation crossed her face, producing a small pucker on her brow, gone as soon as summoned. It did not escape him, however.

'Look,' he said, stopping on the threshold, 'if this is inconvenient . . .'

'Inconvenient?' she asked quickly.

'I thought you looked cross with me.'

She smiled, and Dunbar was bewitched by the languorous

curve of her mouth. 'I am cross, but not with you. Ernst is due . . .'

'Ernst Ketlar?'

'Yes.'

'Oh.' He paused again, but she plucked at his sleeve with a curiously plaintive gesture and he admitted impetuously, 'I wanted to see you again.'

Maureen nodded, as though the remark was familiar. 'Yes,' she said resignedly and Dunbar was uncertain whether she meant, as she seemed to, that she was used to being pursued. 'Please, come in.' She led the way into the living room. Little had changed; it remained untidy and the curtain concealing the drawers of paints was half-drawn. A canvas leaned against the wall, just as it had done all that time ago. 'I will make some tea. Please sit down. I'm sorry about the mess.' Dunbar made a deprecating gesture. 'I can see you don't like it,' Maureen remarked, sweeping out into the kitchen.

Dunbar sat down and Maureen reappeared. 'Ernst wants to paint me again. D'you remember his ridiculous idea of painting the ultimate female nude?' She chuckled, a low, engagingly amused sound. 'He's no nearer accomplishing his ambition. Have you been to Clayton Dobbs recently?'

The change of subject surprised him. 'D'you know it?'

'I visited there once. It was quite a long time ago.'

'Where did you stay?'

'At the Hall,' she said, matter-of-factly.

'Ah. You've known Julia a long time then?'

'Yes, quite a long time. She joined me here when she came to town. I used to live in Suffolk.'

'I see.' He gestured up at the watercolour odalisque. 'Does Ernst still paint you like that?'

Maureen laughed again. 'No. He hasn't painted me like that for a long time. All Ernst wants these days is to paint me in the nude.' She rose. 'The kettle . . .'

222

'D'you sleep with him?' he asked, as though her retreat to the kitchen presaged some final, irrevocable disappearance that drew the impertinent question from him in defiance of good manners. But it seemed not to faze her. She paused, one hand on the kitchen door-jamb, and swung round towards him, her large dark eyes regarding him sadly. 'I suppose that is what you have come for,' she said.

He shot to his feet, confused, protesting his stupidity, stumblingly apologetic, like the adolescent boy who had stood staring at the naked Jenny Broom while she, lonely and hopeful, had stared back. But Maureen smiled again and told him to sit down, then she disappeared into the kitchen, leaving Dunbar feeling ridiculous. The woman tied him in knots!

She emerged with a tea-tray and had begun to pour when the sound of a key turning in the door-lock announced Ketlar, circumstantially revealing the relationship between Maureen and the German artist.

'My dear James! What a very great pleasure!' Ketlar's greeting was effusively sincere. 'I hear you are enjoying a great vogue at the moment, my congratulations. Rollo is also pleased, but Eric,' Ketlar tut-tutted, 'I should keep out of Eric's way. He is not the man he was and, in his present state of mind, can be,' Ketlar paused, 'unpleasant. Most unfortunate, of course, but in the circumstances understandable. Eric is ahead of his time. We will all admire him when he is dead, like Vincent Van Gogh. Ach, tea,' he bent over Maureen and kissed her soft, dark hair.

'You are very pleased with yourself,' Maureen said to Ketlar, handing a cup of tea to Dunbar. '*He* was the jealous one the other day,' Maureen revealed, laying emphasis upon the personal pronoun. 'He would not come to your exhibition.'

'But now I *have* seen it,' Ketlar broke in, waving a

223

dismissive hand at Maureen. 'It is excellent. You are not a Fauve, nor an *avant-garde* Cubist, but the work is good. I shall beg a drawing of you when it is over; as a memento.'

'Why don't you buy one? You can afford it,' Maureen said as she kneeled beside the tea-tray on the low, occasional table. Ketlar's look of annoyance at this remark struck Dunbar for its expression of extreme irritation, quite at variance with the apparent accord between them.

'Ach, Maureen, an artist does not buy the work of another artist, does he, James?' The repartee did not seem to justify the undeniable venom in Ketlar's quick glance.

'If you would truly like one of my drawings,' Dunbar said placatingly, eager to maintain the atmosphere of good-natured levity, 'I shall be happy to exchange it for a drawing of Maureen. I understand you are about to do another painting of her.'

Ketlar spluttered into his tea and looked at his model and mistress. 'Him too?' Dunbar saw Maureen's eyes lower and he looked at Ketlar. The German was now staring at him. 'So you also are in love with Maureen?' Ketlar asked. 'I suppose it is to be expected.' The hawk-featured German shrugged and raised his tea-cup again. 'She is beautiful. It is the fate of a beautiful woman to be loved by many men.' Ketlar returned his cup to its saucer. 'But you are wrong, James. I am not going to paint Maureen. Not at once anyway.'

Maureen looked up at Ketlar. 'I thought you said . . .'

'I,' Ketlar cut in, looking pleased with himself, 'I have secured a very good commission. I am to paint Lady Fowey.' He smiled and turned to Dunbar, 'You will not know Lady Fowey . . .'

'On the contrary, James does know Lady Fowey, don't you, James? You were much taken with her, from what I saw.'

Dunbar grinned shamefacedly, but Ketlar was unde-terred. 'So, you fall in love with many women at the same time, James, eh?' He turned to Maureen. 'He is as fickle as the rest of us, my dear. You should not trust him.'

The edge of venom had crept back into Ketlar's tone and Dunbar, sensing again Maureen's vulnerability, sought to divert what he considered an unpleasant revelation of Ketlar's character. 'Lady Fowey,' he said distractingly, 'is a striking woman, wouldn't you say? Anyway, the fact that that is how she appeared to me does not quite make a libertine of me.'

Ketlar gave a hard chuckle. 'I should hope not indeed. She is, in any case, married, not only to a lord, but to a captain in His Britannic Majesty's Royal Navy. One supposes,' Ketlar added with malicious irony, 'that there are easier men in London to cuckold than Captain Lord Fowey.'

'I was not intending to cuckold anyone,' Dunbar said with a forced laugh that he was far from feeling. Beside him Maureen had fallen silent, into a mood of almost palpable withdrawal.

'Well, that is good news!' Ketlar said briskly, rising to his feet. 'I, I must confess, am tempted, but I must behave myself. Maureen my dear, I am invited to dine with the Foweys this evening, for the purpose of discussing the sittings. Make sure you two behave yourselves with equal propriety.' Ketlar clicked his heels, smiled and added, 'Do not waste a good model, James. She likes you. Paint her, but do not sleep with her. Goodnight.'

For a long time after Ketlar's departure they remained silent, then Dunbar reached his hand out and the move-ment caused Maureen to look up from the floor. Dunbar saw tears in her eyes. 'I am sorry to have been the cause of unhappiness between you,' he said.

'You?' she looked up, smiling through her tears. 'You are not the cause. It is Ernst; I do not know . . .'

'You are obviously fond of him,' Dunbar said, half-consoling, half-fishing.

'Fond? What is fond? You came here tonight because you thought I was someone. Whether or not I am the person you supposed does not matter, but it was what you think I am that keeps you here. It was the same for me. Ernst was my first,' she sighed, 'for someone like me it was foolish. With someone like him, it can only have one outcome. Do you understand?'

'No, my dear,' he said, shaking his head and taking her hand, 'I don't. At least I don't think I do. What is it about him, apart from his nationality? His cruelty? He is cruel, isn't he? I sensed it in him; I could see something of it tonight.'

Maureen nodded. 'He can be. But it is what he is . . .'

'And what is he?' Dunbar thought of those men who enjoyed maltreating women for their own lascivious pleasure.

'He is not only an artist, he is of good family, a very good family.' She spoke in a low voice and, reaching under the settee upon which Ketlar had lately sat, drew out a small leather attaché case, which bore a monogram: *E.V.C.v-K.* 'Ernst Victor Christian von Ketlar,' she said, tracing the gold tooled letters before shoving the leather case out of sight. 'He will marry a German of equal birth. I am just an amusement to him. A trollop!' Maureen uttered the last word with a sudden fury.

'Give him up, Maureen,' Dunbar said quietly.

She shook her head. 'It is not easy for me. I have little income and he pays well.'

'As his whore or as his model?' Dunbar regretted the question as soon as it was uttered. This young woman affected him oddly. In her presence he was unable to keep a rein on his tongue. How different it was with Julia, when sometimes he could scarcely think what to say, so overcome with diffidence did he feel. 'I'm sorry. I am saying all the wrong things.'

'No. It does not matter. I say them to myself. It makes little difference for you to know. Besides, I am a whore, at least to Ernst.'

'And to others?'

'I have slept with Rollo Münck,' she smiled, a private, inward smile.

'And he is not like Ernst?'

'How do you know.'

'Your tone of voice and your smile tell me so.'

She gave him an odd look and said, her eyes narrowing, 'Ernst would be furious if he knew.'

'Why? He seemed remarkably relaxed to me, even if he did tell me not to sleep with you.'

'Because Rollo is a Jew!' she said. 'Did you not know?'

'Well, yes, I knew he was a Jew, but I got the impression that Ernst would not be entirely surprised if I defied him and slept with you tonight. Indeed, I almost think he expects me to, despite what he said.'

'But you aren't a Jew.'

'Well, that's true, even if it doesn't make sense . . .'

Maureen gave a bitter laugh. 'Count von Ketlar,' she said sardonically, 'would not wish to share his mistress with a Jew.'

'Count von Ketlar, well, well . . . So, *Graf* von Ketlar is a fastidious anti-Semite, is he?'

'Aren't you?'

'An anti-Semite? No, why should I be? Besides, Rollo Münck struck me as being a very kindly man. It does not surprise me that you found him attractive, nor that, in the circumstances in which you live, you loved him.'

'He is kind and he was lonely.' She fell silent and then threw up her head. 'Ernst Ketlar is not a kind man at all, but . . .'

227

'But you love him?'

She looked at Dunbar and shrugged. 'I was infatuated. I do not know why. I have no reason beyond saying he made me feel,' she broke off and searched his face, judging whether or not he could be trusted. It was her weakness to trust men at face value. 'But that is not a thing a man can understand. Now, I do not know.'

Dunbar felt a great tenderness for the young woman curled up at his feet whose hand he held like a trusted friend. Perhaps a man could understand a little. The news that she had slept with Ketlar and Münck came as no surprise. He had thought Julia similarly promiscuous; Maureen was less a mistress of her own destiny than Julia. And what business was it of his, anyway? If he loved her now, her past was irrelevant. Besides, he had not cared how many men Dolores Garcia had slept with. His contrary attitude towards Julia, his prejudice against her enjoying the same freedom, was a paradox. Did he think the less of Maureen for this condescension?

'Maureen,' he began, but she shook her head and pulled her hand away.

'Get out, James,' she said vehemently, sensing her attraction for him. 'Get out while you can!'

'I can't do that . . .'

'I shan't let you sleep with me, even,' she added desperately, 'even if you offer to pay me.'

'Then you aren't a whore and I shall never do that!'

But she wasn't listening. 'They say the sins of the fathers are visited on their children,' she murmured, half to herself.

'What on earth d'you mean by that nonsense?' Old visions of hell and his father's parochial prophecies of doom came to Dunbar. 'Whose sins are you being visited with, and what form does this visitation take?'

'It doesn't matter . . .'

'Come, Maureen,' he remonstrated gently, 'you have fallen for a German aristocrat and taken pity on a lonely man who was, quite incidentally and quite irrelevantly, Jewish. Neither of these is, I think, the visitation of a paternal sin.'

'But you must believe these things. Your father is a parish priest.'

Dunbar laughed. 'How on earth do you know that?'

Maureen seemed momentarily flustered and replied, 'Oh, something Julia said.'

'Well, I don't believe it at all. God alone knows why our heads are filled up with this stuff. It may be true that we inherit disabilities or disease, just as we inherit blue eyes or blond hair, but what has happened to make you unhappy is the unkindness and inhumanity of Ernst. Even the fact that Ernst is a count is, I suspect, quite irrelevant. He might have been a sailor or a miner,' Dunbar laughed. 'I have seen men of those classes ill-treating women.'

'I forgot, you are a sailor yourself and have travelled a lot.'

'I have seen a great deal of salt-water,' he admitted, which made her smile and put her hand up to his face.

'You are a kind man too.'

He placed his own hand over hers. 'I feel I have known you a long time, Maureen.'

She smiled. 'I would like you to stay here tonight. Not,' she added hurriedly, 'to sleep with me. Not yet . . . But I spend so much time alone, now that Julia has moved, and I do not want Ernst to come back late and . . .' She broke off.

'Of course. I have slept on this settee before.'

He woke crick-necked in the dawn, a mood of pure, unalloyed joy seeping through him. He felt strangely elated. An expectation of sensual pleasure was enshrined in happy anticipation, yet he was conscious of not taking advantage of Maureen, of being first a friend when it was a friend she most needed. Perhaps that is what Rollo Münck had been to her; perhaps that is what he still was. He dismissed Münck; he should treat Maureen on the profits from his exhibition. It would do no harm, and it need not look like some cynical investment in future carnality.

He lay there in modest self-congratulation, taking a warm, personal comfort in the security that acquisition of his master mariner's certificate had given him. But then, as quickly as the thought occurred to him, another utterly sinister and desolating consideration roared into his consciousness: his imminent departure!

How was it that he had not thought of it before? Had he been so besotted with Maureen that he had cast it from his mind? And when he left, would Ketlar continue to play upon Maureen's emotions and do God knew what with her, as he pursued his ridiculous dream of painting the ultimate female nude?

Distracted, Dunbar's thoughts raced in circles. Ketlar and Lady Fowey, that strikingly elegant yet almost grotesque figure. By God, perhaps she would provide the catalyst! Perhaps, in a malign conspiracy of aristocratic symbiosis, she might provide Ketlar with the catalyst to achieve his ambition! Was that why he had been so cock-certain last night? Perhaps! And here Dunbar's fantasy ran wilder; perhaps Ketlar had dissuaded Lady Fowey from having himself, James Dunbar – the admired portrait painter so lately arrived upon the London scene – from executing her likeness!

He sat up and shook his head. He was being stupid. This was a waking nightmare induced by infatuation and foolishness. He lay back again. Notwithstanding the assertion of sanity, he wondered what progress Ketlar had

CHAPTER TWELVE

The Admiral

ng, unnerving doubt seized Dunbar. He felt sud-
endangered, uncertain of this woman who sank
to kneel beside him. Alarmed, he watched her as,
sigh, her bottom lip caught between her teeth, she
d for the obscene drawings.

s heightened state, it was with a palpable flooding
f that Dunbar realised – the evidence far more
nt than any virtuous denial – that Maureen had
erred to the annotated drawings of British naval
So unnecessary was Dunbar's anxiety, for her
is full of the profoundest regret for his discovery of
meful secret, that its remission brought on a wave
most irresistible lust. Handling Ketlar's drawings,
n unconsciously touched him.

absorbed, she was momentarily oblivious of the
Dunbar was overcome with the scent and the
of her so close. The appealing dishevelment of
r, the shortness of her breath and the silk of her
ess swollen with her body were too much for him.
a strong compulsion to push her gently on her
d part her thighs. She looked up and immediately
ashamed and confused. Urgent though the desire
did not want her to think he was moved by the
that had stirred Ketlar. But Maureen had her own

made upon his fantastical project. Then he remembered the attaché case and, rolling half off the settee, dragged it out from underneath. It was locked.

Dunbar sighed. It served him right. He was being as arrogant as Ketlar with his crazy notions. Why did a rich German count need to be in London painting, if not to indulge himself? And how did rich, dissolute young men indulge themselves, but by fornication? How fortunate some people were! To be able to do simply what they liked, when they liked.

As for art, it was a sham. If he had considered it at all, Dunbar had thought of it as some tributary to the great river of history. But it was dependent upon patronage or the whim of the self-indulgent. It made no material contribution to the advancement of mankind. Yet surely there was something else? Surely real art had no truck with such dependency? Was not this what poor Retyn was trying to say, except that he said it in such a jarring, unlovely, contemptuous way? 'Macaw I' and 'Macaw II' seemed to ask, 'Who's a pretty boy then?' in tones as self-indulgent as Ketlar's foolish pursuit of his own conception of the sublime!

So, what of his own work? Was it honest? A pure expression of a pure emotion? Was that why Mr Maddox, the self-made man, admired it? Dunbar was too naturally honest a being to debate long about his own moral rectitude. He was too English, too easily embarrassed by unseemly realities. His thoughts sprang eagerly back to Ketlar and the locked attaché case. Even a man of integrity, however, may weaken over small matters of curiosity, particularly where a rival in love and art is concerned.

Dunbar freed his legs from the blanket and went into the kitchen, returning with a short-bladed fruit knife. With a twist of his strong wrist, he had the brass hasps open in a jiffy. With a beating heart, for he could not escape the sensation of excitement, he lifted the lid of Ketlar's hide attaché case.

Inside, the case was stuffed with drawings. All of them, as far as Dunbar could see as he riffled quickly through them, were of Maureen and most of a touchingly pornographic nature. Dunbar understood something of the abuse to which Ketlar had subjected her: it was startlingly obvious. Clearly Maureen's love, if love it was, had betrayed her. What Ketlar had put her through was not sadistic, merely profoundly humiliating, but it contained the power to shock. There was a superfluity of it, oddly degrading to one as lovely as Maureen, yet it degraded her only insofar as she had acquiesced. Looking through the drawings, Dunbar felt himself touched by this sullying, for there was no compulsion for him to review the work. Ketlar was degraded absolutely.

Here was the nobility revealed as utterly ignoble, corrupted by the power that it exerted over its victim. If this was Ketlar on his quest, if this was the end of that art first spawned by Botticelli, Titian and the rest, then poor Retyn's daubs were infinitely preferable; they were colour, optimism, energy, life . . .

Ketlar would claim there was nothing to be ashamed of, that regeneration was the very core of life, familiar to all humankind, dwelt upon in the secret recesses of every man. Ketlar would claim that this work of his swept away hypocrisy and all the canting misery of repression and religion. He, Graf von Ketlar, was, for God's sake, only being supremely, even courageously honest!

And perhaps, faced with his father's unconvincing certainties, Dunbar might once have applauded this as being liberating and modern. Might have; until, that is, he had held the dying Conchita in his arms and, only last night, seen the misery in Maureen's face.

Did she know what was in the case? Had she drawn his

attention to it in order that he would c
its contents for himself? And if so, v

To tell him what she truly was, wh
tion, had exposed her to, or to dare hi
her, to persist in his desire for her, afte
extremes she had been put? As these
Dunbar, a dark and shamefully con
made him lift sheet after sheet, as if
ultimate clue to Ketlar's ultimate mas

Then, at the bottom of the attaché ca
the loose lining. There was no atten
properly; perhaps that would be done b
final departure, when the collection of c
would either have been burned or rende
great work, for no customs officer, not
and foreign *douanier*, would let that co
frontier!

Here, quite by mischance, Dunbar stu
von Ketlar's grail.

Not the intimate, sensitive and regene
woman, but two dozen equally intimat
drawings, revealing the sacred inner deta
their guns, a torpedo and what Dunbar kn
he had never seen one, a submarine.

'I hoped you would not find those.'

So startled that he jumped, Dunbar lo
unhappy, lustrous eyes of Maureen.

A gr
denly
slow
with
reach

In
of r
eloq
not
secr
face
her s
of a
Mau

S
cont
war
her
nigh
He
back
he v
was.
mot

preoccupations, her own motives.

She turned towards him, her lips now parted in tremulous expectation. They kissed and she relinquished the drawings, to slip her hand about Dunbar's neck as he pressed gently upon her shoulders and she lay back, her expression one of uncertainty, her body all soft acquiescence.

He lay upon her until his shrivelling retraction released them and he swam into his own individual consciousness, rolling onto his back with a long sigh.

He felt shame now, unalloyed by any triumph; had they both been moved by the utter shamelessness of Ketlar's disturbing drawings? Were they both the humiliated victims of pornography's corrosion? Then thoughts of a more personally undermining nature flooded through him again. Why had he felt it so easy to ravish Maureen, when he found Julia surrounded by an impenetrable barrier? Had there not been moments of equal propinquity with her, when their own sensuality had been awakened by the power of an image? Was this emotional communication the sole purpose of art, and were Ketlar's drawings therefore art? If so, in doing them, had Ketlar actually reached his desired climacteric?

Dunbar was snatched from this thought by the sad consideration that Julia, for all the raffish worldliness of her behaviour, was not known to him as an easy lay. The woman breathing beside him was, by her own admission, at least the mistress of two other men. Was he, James Dunbar, only able to find fulfilment with women of this quality, women who were said to be fallen, the degraded harlots of his father's biblical condemnations?

He slowly raised himself up on one elbow and looked at Maureen. She felt his gaze upon her, opened her eyes and, without moving her head, looked at him. 'I'm so sorry.'

'Why?' he asked, astonished at her apology to him.

'Because it should have been different with you . . . Those pictures . . .'

'Did you mean me to see them?'

She shook her head. 'I did not know they were in that case.'

He was about to ask her if she knew what else was in the attaché case, then postponed his patriotic duty. 'Why should it be different with me?' he asked, tracing a finger down her cheek.

'How many women have you slept with?'

'Only one,' he said truthfully.

'What was she like?'

'Dark, like you, and older, but beautiful nonetheless.'

Maureen smiled. 'You seemed experienced . . .'

'And you?'

'What about Julia?' Maureen asked, avoiding or ignoring the question.

Dunbar shrugged. 'We were once close, but that was more an obstacle between us than an intimacy.'

'She will not be happy with Dacre.'

'Perhaps not; but I do not think Julia has the capacity for happiness in that sense. A kind of contentment, yes, but not happiness.'

'I wonder if any of us has the capacity for happiness. It usually seems just beyond our reach . . .'

'Or we realise we should have enjoyed it last week, or last year.'

'Will this be one of those moments? Or will you despise me as a whore?'

He looked at her, holding her gaze. 'Maureen, I could never despise you, even if you were the greatest trollop in history. Your beauty has too profound an effect upon me. Perhaps if you were to lose your loveliness I might find it difficult, but then I suspect I should feel pity.' Dunbar paused and pulled a self-deprecating face. 'These things have almost nothing to do with you, the person you are. It is all in my head.' He smiled. 'I think it is you who should despise me.'

'Dear James . . .' She pulled his head down and kissed him. For a lascivious moment he abandoned himself to the pleasure and then gently detached himself.

'You know I have to go back to sea.' She nodded mutely. 'It is not for me to expect you to answer this, but will you see Rollo or Ernst again? I mean to sleep with?'

She turned away and Dunbar's heart sank. He had no right to expect her to repudiate her lovers, particularly if she was economically dependent upon one or both of them.

'I was a little in love with Rollo,' she whispered, 'but he took me only as a consolation. He loves someone in Germany; she did not want him to come to London and he was unhappy. They are reconciled now. He is to go home by Christmas, though he says he will bring her to live in England.'

'And Ernst . . . ?'

He thought she shuddered; then she turned back and looked up at him with a frown. 'I hate him,' she said, her voice cracking with vehemence and ending on a choking sob. 'But I cannot tell him to go . . . Don't ask me why . . .'

'Is it money?' he asked tenderly. 'If so I can help you.' He stilled her protest. 'No, I should not regard myself as purchasing you. I should merely help you, as you might help me if I were in trouble.'

Maureen shook her head, smiling and crying at the same time. 'How do you know I would help you?' she asked.

'Because I judge you to be a kind person,' he said simply. 'Anyway, I would do anything to prevent you having to debase yourself and submit to any more of

Ketlar's beastliness.'

'Poor James. You do not understand. I was not *compelled* to pose like this.' She reached out and picked up the top few sheets of Ketlar's drawings.

Dunbar was horrified. A slow queasiness rose like bile in his throat. 'But you said you wished—'

'I said I wished you had not seen them. They are an unpleasant part of me, a part I am not proud of, but a part Ernst found. I cannot tell you how, but he did. Why did you love your older mistress? Was it just because she seduced you, or did she show you something about yourself which came like . . .' Maureen fought to express herself, then suddenly got to her knees and, kneeling beside him, exposed herself, 'like the shock of this?'

She smiled triumphantly, drew her knees together and bent over his white face, the loose braids of her hair falling about his face.

'I knew you would despise me, James.' She stilled his protest. 'You see, pleasure, the irresistible and most ultimate pleasure of one person, can rarely be shared except with someone of similar inclinations. You and Julia have a barrier between you because you do not understand this; you would never be content in bed with Julia. Perhaps, as you said, you have enjoyed your happiness with your older lover. I do not think any of us can expect more than one chance in life, do you?'

Dunbar remained silent. He was choking on disappointment and disillusion; felt the knife turn in the wound that Maureen, unwittingly, had made.

She shook her head. 'I am a whore, James. It is no good you thinking otherwise. I shall always think of you as a kind and sympathetic man, but . . . Oh, my dear, I am so sorry.'

He lay silent for a long while, then rose to his feet and, bending over her, picked up a complex drawing of a torpedo, showing the gyro-control mechanism.

'Do you know anything about this?' he asked, holding it in her face. 'Do you know what it is?'

Maureen shook her head. 'Some sort of a machine?'

'Where does Ketlar live?'

'He has rooms in the West End.'

'And how often does he sleep here?'

'Never.'

'But you said . . .'

'He comes here to paint and draw me. I am his model.' She was colouring with anger at his line of questioning. Rejection added an unpleasant edge to his voice and Maureen was confronted not with the amiable, overgrown boy-sailor, but with a man who knew the strength of his own resolution.

Dunbar lowered his face. 'Then when,' he asked with unconsciously pointed menace, 'when exactly do you fuck?'

'What has that . . . ?'

He grabbed her hair and held her head. 'Tell me!'

'James, you're hurting me.' He was torn with self-contempt and yet the potency of her vulnerability and the righteousness of his interrogation caused him to give her head a vicious little tug. 'Tell me!' he reiterated and then, with a low moan, let her go.

'In the afternoons,' she confessed, looking at him with a shocked curiosity. 'Ernst would never stay the night.'

'Yet he leaves paints, canvases, a portfolio of drawings, an attaché case . . .'

'I don't understand.' She was frowning and weeping.

'Your sacred lover,' Dunbar said, holding up the fruits of Ketlar's espionage for Maureen to see, 'the man who releases you from yourself and brings you to the boil so that you would eat shit for pleasure, is a spy!'

There was a moment's silence, then he turned away to the bathroom, eager to wash himself and rid himself of her. At the door he paused and looked back. She

239

was kneeling among the drawings, her soft red lips parted in incomprehension, the tears streaming down her cheeks.

Still her beauty stung him like a blade. 'You should douche,' he called out cruelly. 'I should hate that we should have a child between us.'

Dunbar waited impatiently for Lady Fowey to receive him. He thought, as he approached the great house off Belgrave Square, that she might already be sitting for Ketlar, but apart from the soft comings and goings of servants, the house seemed devoid of visitors. He had asked for Lord Fowey, but the footman had informed him that his lordship was not at home. However, if the matter was important and he left his name, her ladyship might receive him. He had been asked to wait.

It was twenty long minutes before Lady Fowey entered the drawing room, twenty minutes during which Dunbar relived the events of the early morning, burning with a shame that he buried under an equally burning zeal to expose Ketlar for at least a part of his infamy.

'Good morning, Mr Dunbar. I understand you wish to see my husband. I must confess I am disappointed.' She smiled and he felt touched by the compelling style of the woman, odd though her features were. 'I had thought it might be me you wished to see.'

'I would not be so impertinent, Lady Fowey.'

'Oh,' she pulled a wry face, 'I should not think it impertinent. You are after all an artist of distinction.'

'Your ladyship is too kind. I am afraid I do not think of myself as an artist, though artists are, I confess, apt to be impertinent. I understand Ernst Ketlar is to execute a portrait of you.'

'What an awful expression that is,' Lady Fowey laughed. 'I suppose you know him. He is very talented and very fashionable.' She smiled. 'And his work is very different from yours.'

Dunbar thought of the drawings of Maureen. 'Very different.'

'But you have not come to discuss art, I gather. My husband is at the Admiralty. He was gazetted a rear-admiral only this morning and is due to take command of a cruiser squadron very shortly,' she explained. 'Perhaps,' she added with a tantalising laugh, laying droll emphasis on the verb, 'he might like you to *execute* his portrait in his new epaulettes, or whatever it is rear-admirals add to their wardrobe.'

'I am sure Lord Fowey would not choose me to record his success . . .'

'You'd be wrong, Mr Dunbar. He liked your work. Called it,' she frowned as though finding it difficult to recall her husband's phrase, '"damnably unlubberly work" which, being a sailor yourself, if a mercantile one, you will understand as something of a compliment.'

Dunbar could not resist smiling. Lady Fowey's charm was potent. Her fascination illuminated her strange features and her guileful manner, even while she set him in his place as a mere mercantile sailor, gave the impression of enjoying his full attention. After the unpleasantness with Maureen and a brief conversation with Julia, who had given him Lord Fowey's address, he felt himself relax in the company of this utterly enrapturing woman.

'Anyway,' her ladyship said, as though sensing her uninvited guest's relaxation, 'my husband will be back for lunch.' She looked at her watch. 'He should not be long; he is a stickler for punctuality, claiming it to be the courtesy of a captain. I suppose we shall have to consider that a prerequisite for admirals now, shall we not?'

And Dunbar felt himself admitted into the intimacies of Lady Fowey's marriage, basking in her condescension, all the while knowing that she was playing him, just as he had seen Skipper Hopton play fish, or old Sails a shark.

'Are you to sit soon for Graf von Ketlar, Lady Fowey?' he asked, as if politely interested.

'Next week. He was here for dinner last night. A charming man; something of an enigma. He is not quite incognito, but I suppose an artist eschews rank. There was that little Frenchman who was a count, wasn't there . . . ?'

Dunbar, who had never heard of Comte Henri de Toulouse-Lautrec, kept his mouth firmly shut.

'And might one know what, if you have not come to offer to paint my husband, it is that you wish to see him about?'

'I, er, hope you will not think me rude, Lady Fowey, if I ask you not to press me upon the matter. I am sure that your husband will explain, but it would be truly impertinent if I were to speak of the matter to you first.'

'I hope,' Lady Fowey said sharply, 'you have not come to ask for money?'

'Good heavens, no, ma'am,' Dunbar said, horrified.

'That's a relief then. Ah, I think I hear Johnnie now. Yes, here he is.' Rear-Admiral Lord Fowey, his brick-red sailor's face at odds with the monochrome of his morning dress, kissed his wife's cheek and turned to Dunbar.

'You recall Mr Dunbar, Johnnie, whose paintings you much admired.'

'Ah yes! Yes, of course. Dunbar, how are you?' The admiral seemed displeased to see him.

'Very well, sir, and my congratulations on your promotion.'

'Yes, yes, thank you.' Lord Fowey was testy. 'Bit quick off the mark, aren't you?'

'I'm sorry, my lord . . . ?'

'It's all right, Johnnie. Mr Dunbar hasn't come to ask

you whether you want your picture executed. I'm not sure what he wants, except that it's for your ears only. I'll leave you two to your tittle-tattle.'

'I hope,' said Lord Fowey crossing the drawing room to a table with a decanter and glasses upon a silver tray, 'you *haven't* come to tittle-tattle.' He helped himself to a glass of whisky.

'Believe me, my lord, I should not bother you unless it was a matter of importance. I am only profoundly grateful that our fortuitous meeting last evening enables me to bring this matter to the notice of someone of influence.'

'For God's sake cut the cackle, Dunbar, and come to the point.'

'Lord Fowey, please take a look at these and tell me if you think anything improper in them.' Dunbar drew the drawings in a roll from his breast-pocket and handed them to Fowey. Fowey put his glass down and cast his eyes over Ketlar's studies.

'How did you get these?' he asked sharply, fixing Dunbar with a penetrating glare.

'I was with a girl, Lord Fowey, a friend who models . . .'

'Dunbar, I don't give thruppence for the quality of girls you spend your evenings with. Where did you get these, man?'

'From an attaché case in the girl's rooms. The case belonged to another friend of hers, her true lover in fact. He did them—'

'Then what the devil is this girl's name?' Fowey interrupted.

'It doesn't matter . . .'

'The devil it doesn't! Look here . . .'

'She knew nothing about them. I broke into the case. I was,' Dunbar hesitated, then said, 'impertinent.' Then he shook his head. 'No, sir, actually I was jealous. I broke into the attaché case out of jealousy and anger.

The important thing is I know who did those drawings and to whom the case belongs.'

'Well?'

'Graf von Ketlar. I understand he had dinner with you last night. He seemed very pleased to have received your wife's commission.'

Rear-Admiral Lord Fowey's brick-red countenance took on a sickly look. 'Good God!'

There was a long silence, then Fowey said, 'Forgive me, Dunbar, I was most uncivil to you. A drink?'

Fowey laid the drawings down alongside his half-empty whisky and played the attentive host. 'What are you on board your barque, the *Fort* . . .'

'*Fort Mackinac*, my lord. I'm the chief mate.'

'She's one of Bullard, Crowe's, isn't she?' Fowey asked as he handed Dunbar the glass. 'You're not in the Reserve?'

'No, I'm not.'

'But you're a master mariner.'

Dunbar nodded. 'A rather new one, I'm afraid.'

'I'm a rather new rear-admiral,' Fowey said, picking up the drawings again, 'and rather a lucky one, I think. I'm damned glad you brought these to me. What d'you know about von Ketlar?'

'Nothing,' replied Dunbar, the whisky on his empty stomach making him feel expansive. 'I didn't know he was a count until last night. That's about all I know, oh, apart from his desire to paint the ultimate female nude.'

'Good God! What the devil does that mean?'

'I've no idea.' Dunbar frowned. 'Oh, and he did once admit to me, quite in passing, that he was a yachtsman.'

'A yachtsman,' Fowey rubbed his bearded chin and Dunbar smelt the scent of toilet water and heard a faint creaking, as of stays. 'Interesting,' Fowey ruminated. 'You've known him for some time?'

'I met him in London some years ago.'

'When precisely?'

'About the year eight, I think. Yes, yes, it was, I had just passed for second mate.'

'So he's been here at least four years?'

'At least.'

'But he kept his nobility a secret, at least from you and your circle?'

'It would seem so. His mistress knew of it, but I don't know how recently she found out. I suspect she had known for some time.'

'An opportunist fortune-hunter, I dare say.'

Dunbar shook his head. 'I don't think she is under any illusions about Ketlar, though she had no idea what those drawings show.'

Fowey grunted, tugging his beard reflectively. 'You know, of course,' he said after a few moments, 'that we are having a problem with the Germans?'

'To be honest, Lord Fowey, I don't have much of an interest in politics. I'm away at sea most of the time; it seems the world gets on with its affairs whether or not I read the newspapers.'

'Well, you should. The Kaiser thinks he's a naval man and his naval chief, von Tirpitz, has played on the Kaiser's vanity to increase the size of the German navy. You may consider sharing a mistress with a German officer preferable to the closer acquaintance with the Boche that you might yet have as chief mate of your barque.'

Dunbar frowned. 'You mean war?'

Fowey shrugged. 'I was lately naval attaché to the Ottoman Sublime Porte; the Germans are much embroiled with Turkey and in the Balkans. Their policy could best be described as bent upon provocation.' Fowey paused and looked again at the drawings. 'Anyway, thank God you had your jealous fit and broke this bounder's attaché case open. D'you know what these drawings show?'

'Well, only generally. A submarine, some gunnery

details and some sort of submersible weapon. I suppose a torpedo.'

'A pretty advanced Armstrong modification of White-head's original Fiume machine, but that need not bother us now. The point is, I don't suppose this is all he's been up to. This is just the tip of a very sinister iceberg.'

'I understand Lady Fowey is sitting for him next week.'

'Yes,' ruminated the admiral. 'I am just wondering whether you should replace these, to allay his fears for a few days.'

'That might be difficult.'

'Oh, why?'

'Indirectly, my assault on Ernst's case caused a row between the girl and myself.'

'Ah,' smiled the admiral. '*Persona non grata*, are we?'

'Sadly, yes.'

'And when are you rejoining your ship?'

'Any day now.'

'Then I can't ask you to paint my portrait?'

Dunbar shook his head. 'I'm sorry, Lord Fowey. I'd be delighted, but, well you know how it is . . .'

'Absolutely: duty calls. Well, thank you, Dunbar.' Fowey held out his hand. 'I'm damned grateful to you. I shall let what you've done be known where it matters. If you decide to join the Naval Reserve, do let me know.' He held out his hand.

It was only afterwards, when he bent his steps towards Hampstead, that Dunbar thought that his lordship could have extended his gratitude to a bite of lunch.

CHAPTER THIRTEEN

The Apostate

Word was waiting for him at Dacre's that he should rejoin the *Fort Mackinac* at the end of the week. Initially Dunbar was equivocal about the order and briefly contemplated leaving the ship, but then he recalled her, conjuring her into his mind's eye under a press of sail and thinking of Crawhall and Bill Andrews, and of the camaraderie and opportunity that went with her. Subject to that contrary emotional tug by which every seafarer is seduced, he forsook the crazy notion. Hampstead galleries and the blandishments of the arty set were ephemeral pleasures. He did not belong among them and, even if he felt some desire to linger with Julia and Icarus, he knew he derived his inspiration from his experiences at sea. In reality, he had little of substance to bind him to the shore.

Dunbar had dismissed the affair of von Ketlar from his mind; Rear-Admiral Lord Fowey would deal with it. He himself was beset by more personally touching and shameful considerations. The rupture with Julia had been superficially patched over by the success of the exhibition, but there were no mitigating consolations for the break with Maureen. He felt ashamed of his conduct towards her: he had been unkind, cruel even, and yet he had not meant to be. He felt passionately towards her, dangerously so, he thought, as he found himself travelling to Pimlico with abject apologies forming themselves in his mind.

As if in response to his high expectation, she was not in. He retired miserably to the public house in which he had killed time on his last visit, but even an hour's delay did nothing to alter Maureen's obvious absence.

'She's gone away,' a neighbour finally informed him, as he dithered on the landing.

'When will she be back?' he asked.

'Are you one of her gentlemen friends?'

'Yes.'

'She didn't say. I think she went home.'

'Home?'

'Yes, home.'

'Where's that?' But the question elicited only a dismissive shrug.

Dunbar stepped out into the street. She had said she came from Suffolk, like himself, and thoughts of Suffolk pricked his conscience further. Before he sailed he ought to visit his parents again, to make his peace with them. Maureen had left his life as quietly as she had entered it.

Liverpool Street Station was crowded with travellers burdened with luggage as they swarmed around the waiting boat-train. Thoughts of continental travel reminded Dunbar of Lord Fowey's warnings of war. Surely there was no question of war; what would be the point? The German navy was no match for Great Britain's fleet of dreadnoughts and super-dreadnoughts, her cruiser squadrons and flotillas of destroyers. Dunbar dismissed the admiral's fears. Was it not in Lord Fowey's professional interests to war-monger? His destiny as a naval officer lay in the possibilities open to him in a war, particularly if it was true that he had little more than his pay to live on, though the house in Belgravia seemed evidence to the contrary. Perhaps, Dunbar thought parenthetically, the property was Lady Fowey's. It further occurred to Dunbar that Fowey and his like must spend a considerable portion of their waking day just dreaming of war. Seeing the happy crowd of travellers entraining for Harwich, it seemed inconceivable that the civilised world would embark on a European war. There had not been a real war in Europe since Napoleon, and that was history!

'Maureen!'

Dunbar forgot Lord Fowey; his thoughts switched to Suffolk and Maureen's journey 'home'. Surely the woman he had briefly caught sight of was Maureen in her cream dress! He began to thrust eagerly through the crowd, but already he had lost sight of her. Looking up at the indicator board, he located the Ipswich train and, finding the platform, walked the length of the carriages. He would travel home with her! It was a God-given opportunity to apologise and convince her of his love for her!

She was nowhere to be seen, though an elderly woman in a cream dress peered back at him through a third-class window and a slightly younger lady stepped out of a first-class compartment and waved to a departing friend. He had been misled by his own wishful thinking. Despondently Dunbar climbed aboard the train himself.

He had to change at Ipswich for Woodbridge and the Lowestoft line. Crossing the bridge, a figure with whom he was familiar waddled ahead of him. He accelerated and caught her up.

'Jenny! How nice to see you!'

Jenny Broom looked round, her face a picture of sudden anxiety, as though Dunbar had caught her acting improperly, then she recognised him and relaxed.

'Oh, Master James, what a surprise!'

'Are you all right, Jenny?'

'Oh, yes, yes, of course I am.' She took his arm and Dunbar felt the same compulsion that he had felt under

Julia's guidance as she had steered him through the crowd at the gallery.

'What's the matter?' he asked.

'We'll miss the connecting train,' Jenny said practically, bustling him along. In the event they had plenty of time and sat for fifteen minutes, waiting for the guard's piercing whistle to set the branch-line train in motion. By then Jenny had become her old self. She sat back, smiling at him, waving her handkerchief across her broad, freckled and pleasant face. 'I get so flustered these days,' she admitted confidentially. 'You'll be going to see the rector,' she remarked.

'Yes. Is there something . . . ?'

'You don't know?'

'Know what?' A sudden irrational apprehension seized Dunbar.

'Oh, my dear. He's very ill; very ill. He isn't expected—' She broke off, the unspoken word lingering between them.

'I had no idea,' Dunbar said, gazing out of the window as he caught sight of the silver ribbon of the River Deben between the trees.

Clayton Dobbs basked under the summer heat. Like the Deben, the estuary of the Clay shimmered in the distance and overhead the leaves of the old chestnuts rustled in the gentle sea breeze. Dunbar was met by his younger brother Michael.

'Michael, this is a surprise!'

'You are just too late.'

'I knew nothing about Father. I met Jenny Broom on the train. Why didn't you let me know? You must have known I was in the country.'

'I sent word to your ship's owners. It was the only address Mother had.'

'Oh, Lord . . .' Guilt overwhelmed Dunbar. He thought of the ancient clerk at Bullard, Crowe and Company and that worthy's complaints about forwarding mail. Clearly he did not consider it a duty incumbent upon the owner's chief clerk; nor of any other clerk for that matter. No, that was unjust; Dunbar had himself made little attempt to keep in touch with his parents, beyond his dutiful visits. 'I was only down here a week or so ago.'

'The last phase,' Michael said, running his hand through his long, blond hair, 'was mercifully quick.'

'What happened?'

'A stroke, followed by a second, fatal one.'

'And Mother?'

'She'll feel the worst of it in a week or two. At the moment she's coping very well. Come in, anyway. David's inside; the funeral's the day after tomorrow. Mother will have to move out.'

'I see.' Dunbar paused. 'Look, Mike, I'm due to sail. I can stay for the funeral, but winding up Father's affairs . . .'

'We'll attend to that,' Michael said shortly. 'We didn't expect you to be here at all.'

Dunbar looked at his reproachful younger brother and let the matter pass. The twins had always been closer to his parents than he was himself, adding to that sense of alienation he had always felt as his due portion of familial guilt. He turned away and led Michael into the house.

He embraced his mother in silence. She clung to him for a long, surprising moment, then drew back with a sniff and looked up at him. She was hollow-eyed, determined, full of courage.

'I am so glad you came back. I thought after you left the other day that we should not see you for a long while.'

Dunbar smiled. 'Well, Mama, you should have known better. The bad penny always turns up.'

'I'm glad he saw you on your ship. He was very proud that you had become an officer.'

His father had seemed so incapable of showing any interest in his first-born's career on that Sunday afternoon in Ipswich that Dunbar doubted the truth of his mother's remark. But he nodded and said, 'I'm glad of that, Mama.'

'I've got a little cottage, thanks to Colonel Scrope-Davies, the white one at the end of Spur Lane,' she said with a brittle eagerness. 'It will be sad to leave here, though,' she added, looking lovingly round the big old kitchen. 'You all grew up here. I remember you cutting your knee . . .'

The funeral took place on a beautiful summer's day and it seemed the entire parish was in attendance. Michael's twin brother, the Reverend David Dunbar, took the service. As he stood by the grave beside his mother, James Dunbar felt an extraordinary and unexpected sensation. So far had he drifted from a close relationship with his father that he felt unable to mourn the passing of the rector, experiencing nothing but a deep sadness on behalf of his ageing mother. Yet he had expected grief in some tremulous form to manifest itself as he stood amid the members of his family and, with his father's parishioners, gathered to pay their last respects to the man who, whatever his faults, had presided over their own rites of passage and who now passed from them amid his own obsequies.

Dunbar had no belief in the soul as a unique gift, vented to Heaven at the moment of death, and wondered if his father had, at the end. The shrivelled man who had boarded the *Fort Mackinac* only a few weeks earlier had somehow failed to convey any generosity of spirit towards his returned son. Moreover, his wife's desperate confirmation that James had at least attained the status of an officer seemed merely to confirm the rector's retreat into a miserliness of spirit, emphasised by the only intelligible comment his father had made upon that dismal occasion. That his son seemed to have become a kind of monk appeared to gratify the old man. It was scarcely the welcome afforded the prodigal, Dunbar thought ruefully.

David completed the committal and Michael took Anne Dunbar's arm and led her from the graveside. Dunbar stood back, allowing others to come up and perform their last act of respect.

As he finally threw soil onto the coffin and turned away, he felt a great burden lifted from him. The weight of his father's faith, the inhibiting mass of tortuous, uncertain theological supposition seemed already etched upon the worthy brows of his two brothers. It occurred to Dunbar that the childhood attraction of the sea had been, to his unformed intellect, the only refuge for an apostate who had been conceived and born in the rectory and made to submit to the lugubrious rites of the Church of England. Whether or not the elder Dunbar's soul rose to heaven, the spirits of his son soared blasphemously upwards.

'I say, James . . .'

Dunbar turned. Colonel Scrope-Davies was behind him, walking with difficulty and leaning upon a stick.

'May I help you, Colonel?'

'That's good of you. Confounded legs . . .'

'You're coming back to the rectory?'

'Of course, my boy, of course.' The old man puffed alongside Dunbar, leaning on his arm as they traversed the graveyard. 'Not long before its my turn.'

Dunbar thought of Julia. 'You'll go on for years, Colonel.'

'Not sure I want to. Sorry Julia didn't come down from town. I telegraphed her.'

'Yes. Never mind . . .' Dunbar thought of explaining

that it was probably his own presence that prevented her.

'She's getting married. Fellow named Dacre. Did you know?'

'Yes. I've met him.'

'What d'you think of him? Arty type, I'm told.'

'Well, yes, that would be one way of describing him. You could say he was cultured and kind, fairly wealthy I believe, with a fine house overlooking Hampstead Heath. I suppose Julia will make it work.'

'What the devil does that mean?'

'That she's an ambitious woman and that Dacre has the means and outlook by which she will be fulfilled.'

'Fulfilled? I know she's behind women's suffrage and all that damned nonsense. What the devil women want the vote for, I don't know,' Scrope-Davies said as they passed from the churchyard into the overgrown rectory garden, following the procession of parishioners. The two men, the one leaning upon the arm of the other, took a few steps in silence and then Scrope-Davies said, 'You never got on too well with your father, did you, James?'

'No. No, I suppose I didn't. There was something about me that he didn't approve of. I suppose I failed him in some way.'

'We all expect a great deal from our first-born son.'

Dunbar thought of the colonel's long-dead heir. 'Yes, I'm sorry. I'm not complaining.'

'Never thought you were. Always thought your father was too hard on you.' The colonel shook his arm and stopped. 'You and Hugh would have been friends.'

Dunbar looked down at the old man. He could think of nothing to say except, 'Yes.'

'You know Hugh had a child, a love-child?'

'No!' Dunbar was shocked. 'I had no idea.'

'Your father helped get the child adopted. He was very

254

discreet, very helpful. It brought us close. He was a good man, James. I'd like you to know that.'

Dunbar nodded. 'Yes, of course.' He felt swamped with guilt. It was as if his father's ghost had chastised him for his lack of charity; as if his unbidden sense of liberation was a temptation of the devil; as if this other old man, in revealing the existence of an adopted heir to the Scrope-Davies estate, sought to assert the obligation of filial obedience that lingered after death.

They were alone in the garden now, though Dunbar could see a press of people inside the rectory.

'The living lies in my gift,' Scrope-Davies went on, looking up at the rectory and resuming his interrupted progress towards the front door. 'D'you think I should keep it in your family?'

'I think, Colonel,' Dunbar said with an ironic twist to his mouth, 'that I am the last person you should consult on an ecclesiastical matter. Perhaps David might have a view . . .'

'Well, it was David I was considering,' the colonel said as they entered the porch and the loud babble of chatter met them. 'It would be a pity for your family to leave this place, just as it would be a damned pity if mine had to abandon the Hall. My God, what do people find to talk about so inappropriately on these occasions.'

Dunbar endured the following hour making small talk, acknowledging the compliments paid to his father and listening to the small anecdotes of the rector's life. Towards the end, he was approached by the colonel.

'Damn silly thing to do, James, but I took it into my head to walk down. Don't know whether I can make it back unaided. D'you think you could oblige?'

'Of course. Happy to.'

'It's such a damned lovely day.' The colonel excused his foolhardy conduct as the two men walked slowly up the tree-lined drive, punctuating their progress with short

255

halts and brief asides. 'I couldn't resist the temptation. At my age one begins to think every action is the last one you're going to be able to make. I also thought it would put me into the right frame of mind for your father's funeral. But I'm not sure anything puts you into the right frame of mind for a funeral.'

'No.'

'I love this place. Family been here for generations. Imagine all the tradition, all the *life*! Very remarkable. Don't suppose you feel the same, eh?'

'No. But I think many people in the village do. My father did. For myself, well, I've rather cut myself off by going to sea, I suppose.'

'You'll lose your roots. Your family's had the living for over two hundred years.'

'Yes. But my family's traditional occupation wasn't mine.'

'Unbeliever, are you?'

'Yes, I think so.'

'Your father wouldn't have tolerated an apostate.'

'I don't think he did.'

'That was the problem between you, eh?'

'Yes, I think so. I don't recall it being a conscious act, as he would have imagined it. I simply grew up thinking like that.'

'Perhaps you had too much of it,' remarked the colonel with a short laugh that turned into a cough and brought them to a wheezing standstill. 'Boys will be boys and fathers should remember their own youth.'

'I think he did sometimes,' replied Dunbar. 'That's why he didn't really care for me. I say, are you all right?'

Scrope-Davies nodded. 'Fit as a fiddle really. Yes. I gave Hugh hell when he told me what he'd done, but I'd had a narrow squeak or two in my own time. Wild oats will out.'

'Yes.' Dunbar thought of Conchita, Dolores and Maureen

256

as they moved off again in silence for a while. And he thought of his father; it was an incongruity.

'World's changing,' Scrope-Davies said, waving his walking stick in an encompassing arc. 'Women's suffrage is the least of it. I'd not be surprised if we didn't have a war soon, perish the thought.'

'Amen to that, though you're in good company. It seems to be a growing preoccupation among the better informed.'

'We were damned close over that business at Agadir, though why the Admiralty had to get up a head of steam over one confounded Boche gunboat anchored off Morocco, I'm damned if I know. Threat to Gibraltar, or some such nonsense. I suppose you know nothing much about it?'

'Not really; not until it had all blown over.'

'It took some time to do that,' Scrope-Davies said, shaking his head. 'If it ever really did. I think further trouble with Germany is very likely. The Kaiser's a jealous little man and the more he's bound to us by ties of blood and interest, the more he's likely to resent running at the wheel of our chariot. Same sort of thing as boys being boys. Too much power in the little blighter's hands.' The colonel paused, then added, 'I recall some words of Tom Paine's that my old brigadier used to quote to subalterns: "men who look upon themselves as born to reign, and others to obey, soon grow insolent."'

Dunbar suppressed a smile. Scrope-Davies was leaning surprisingly and dangerously to the left; he would be advocating women's suffrage next! But women's suffrage was very far from the colonel's mind.

'This war in the Balkans is a bad thing, you know. This isn't the age of Byron, with romantic tribesmen running around with antique *miquelets*. This is the age of the Nordenfelt, the Mitrailleuse and the Vickers machine-guns. And we're so damnably tied up in a web of alliances that if the Balkan fly tugs at one end of the European web, God knows what the consequences will be at the other.'

'You think it that serious?'

Scrope-Davies stopped and faced Dunbar. 'I do, James, I do. We took a damned drubbing in South Africa. If we hadn't had the imperial troops to help us, we'd be taking our hats off to Mr Kruger. We're an old power, James, a tired old power, which has grown fat and inert like our late, lamented King. Many of our best young men caught it in South Africa. A war in Europe won't be like the defence of Duffer's Drift; it will be Oudenarde, Malplaquet, Austerlitz, Borodino and Waterloo all over again. We couldn't stand that, not with all the old certainties under attack. I've no objection to women like Julia having a vote, but not all women are like Julia, any more than all men are like me . . . and you, of course.'

They had emerged from the end of the drive, the chestnuts had fallen back behind them and they had begun to cross the low, formal garden about which the gravel drive swept. Before them stood the façade of Clayton Hall, just as it had that evening when Dunbar had walked Julia home, though today the old brick was warm in the sunshine and the neat white rectangles of the windows bore no lights, only the reflections of the clouds and blue sky.

Dunbar bit his tongue. No socialist, he was yet sympathetic to the aspirations of ordinary people. He wondered if Scrope-Davies knew of the poverty that clung to the flanks of the shipping world in which he had an interest – or was poverty something he had left behind in India? Or was he thinking only of his lost heir?

They crossed the gravel in silence, their feet scrunching in companionable step. At the door Scrope-Davies asked, 'So, do I gather you're going back to your ship tomorrow?'

'Yes.'

'I'd ask you in for a drink . . .' There was reluctance in the colonel's voice. He looked tired.

'It's kind of you, Colonel, but I have a few matters to conclude with my brothers.'

'Well, it's good of you to see an old bugger home.'

'It's a pleasure.'

'I feel I can talk to you, my boy. I suppose it's because you've knocked about a bit. Not spent your life tupping the gels round the parish pump, eh?'

Dunbar grinned. 'No.'

'Come and see me when you get home.'

'Yes, of course.' Dunbar watched the old man approach the door and saw it open as if by magic. The pale features of Clyde, the butler, peered from the gloom of the house. Scrope-Davies turned.

'I nearly forgot,' he said. 'David shall have the living, if he wants it. You'd better tell him when you get back to the rectory.'

'Oh. Yes, very well. Thank you.'

Later that evening, as the sun drew westwards, Dunbar wandered through the old house. He felt no resentment at David inheriting the living, but wondered vaguely if Michael minded. He had been more disturbed by Scrope-Davies's worrying references to a war with Germany; they were fearfully congruent with those of Lord Fowey. But he was a young man, and the shadow of war soon receded. He was more intrigued by the colonel's reference to Hugh's bastard and to his father's involvement in dealing with the embarrassment. Now he knew the root of Julia's assumption that she would not inherit Clayton Hall and the estate: the colonel must be considering legitimising his lost heir. Curiosity made him regret not pressing the colonel on the matter: who and where was this lost heir, whose emergence would, Dunbar realised with a sudden wry mischievousness, prevent Icarus Dacre presiding over the acres of the Clayton estate?

Dunbar reached the attic. The door protested with a dry creak, opening on a shaft of sunlight alive with dust motes. Here he had seen the naked Jenny Broom and here he had shown Julia his first paintings. How distant those two events now seemed, and yet time had almost blurred them, giving them a specious inter-relationship.

He sat upon Jenny's old bed, which creaked with even more ferocity than the door. Above him the boards lining the roof timbers had cracked the old paper and the floor-boards showed the undulations of wear, proud where the steel nail-heads protected the grain. How many maids, eking out a life of servitude on the ministers of Christ's church, had buried their private dreams up here, he wondered? He thought of the colonel's incongruous quotation from Tom Paine's *Common Sense*.

He rose and, stooping, went to the small quartered window. Its panes were dusty and cobwebbed, its casement too rotten to open. The trees on the skyline beyond the rear garden were purple against the flaming scarlet of the setting sun. Below him the house had sunk into silence, though he had left David, Michael and his mother talking quietly in the kitchen.

He would have to go down and tell them he was leaving for London in the morning. Tomorrow he would rejoin the *Fort Mackinac* and suddenly the seduction of the open sea, of being under sail in the keen, cold wind, overwhelmed him.

Most of the old hands were back. Bill Andrews appeared in the saloon when the crew were signed on, looking like a man who had so reduced himself by excess that he offered the ship no advantage by his employment.

Afterwards Dunbar expressed his concern to Crawhall and the shipping master. Captain Crawhall shook his head.

'Andrews has signed on with me without fail for the last eight years. He always looks like that. God knows what he gets up to, though a fool could guess, but a week at sea will sort him out.'

'Yes, but it must take its toll on his constitution,' Dunbar persisted.

'There used to be an old bosun in the Blackwallers,' the shipping master broke in to remark as he gathered up his papers, 'name of Wade, I think, who must have been over seventy, though he was active as a cat aloft. They used to ask him his age when he signed on and he used to say, "Oh, put it down as before, fifty-three, sir!". "But you don't look fifty-three," they'd say, to which the old buzzard'd reply, "Of course I don't! But I'll look it when I've worked the women and whisky out of my system!" And d'you known, Captain, old Wade was right.'

Crawhall chuckled and poured the shipping master a peg of whisky in response to the heavy hint and to mark the conclusion of their business. 'One for you, Mr Dunbar?'

'No, thank you, sir.'

'You won't celebrate not having Grant back?'

'I think it's better if I don't smell of whisky, just at the moment.'

'As you please.'

'If you'll excuse me . . .'

'Of course, Mr Dunbar.'

'Fine young man you've got there, Captain Crawhall,' the shipping master remarked when Dunbar had gone.

'Indeed he is, Cap'n Whall. I confess to a great liking for him. He's a bright fellow and thoroughly dedicated. Treats his work with a religious fervour.' Crawhall nodded to give emphasis to this assertion as though the slug of whisky had unlocked it from his perception.

'I guess it's because he comes from a Church background.'

'He doesn't seem to have anything of the religious fanatic about him. I've seen a few of them, and they invariably come to a bad end.'

'No, he's no God-bothering Bible-puncher. Quite the reverse in fact, but there's a hidden side to Mr Jimmie Dunbar. He's a bit of an artist. Did a portrait of me last voyage. Not bad at all.'

Whall smiled to himself. He was used to the personal vanity of shipmasters. 'Thanks, Cap'n,' he said as Crawhall topped up his glass again. 'Who was the Grant you referred to?'

'Oh, a bad-hat of an AB who gave young Dunbar a hard time when he moved aft from the fo'c'sle.'

'Something you did yourself, if I remember correctly,' put in Whall, as Crawhall filled his pipe.

'That's true,' said Crawhall, tamping his tobacco into his pipe-bowl. 'And Dunbar went into the fo'c'sle from the half-deck.'

'Why on earth did he do that? Fail his ticket?'

'No, did his time in steam.'

'Well, that's bucking the system; it's usually t'other way round.'

Crawhall laughed as his match flared and he sucked it down onto the pipe. 'Yes, but our Jimmie's a romantic.'

'I should have thought a sailing vessel the last bloody place for a romantic.'

And Crawhall nodded his agreement from behind a dense and fragrant cloud of smoke.

It proved a tough voyage, unexceptional in its way, but hard and demanding with strong winds in both temperate zones, a relatively fast passage through the horse latitudes and a roaring beat round the Horn. The *Fort Mackinac*, laden with coal, was driven by Crawhall from latitude fifty south in the Atlantic to fifty south in the Pacific in nine days. At San Francisco, where there was no trouble with crimps, she loaded 2,000 tons of bagged wheat and barley, along with two thousand tons of canned Alaskan salmon and Californian fruit.

The homeward voyage was no better and ended worse. Bound for Liverpool, the big four-masted barque was due to embark her pilot off Point Lynas after 115 days. Backing the main yards in order to heave-to for the cutter, and having sent aloft a hoist of flags to request the Lloyd's signal station to summon a tug to meet them at the Bar, the crew were soon aloft shortening down as a gale swept up from the south-west. The pilot failed to board and Crawhall abandoned him, squaring the yards and running off to the north, hoping to seek shelter under the lee of the Isle of Man.

In the event, the following afternoon found them off St Bee's Head. In a desperate bid to save the ship from driving ashore on the banks of the Solway Firth, Crawhall brought the barque into the wind, let go his starboard anchor and veered all its one hundred and twenty fathoms of stud-link cable.

'Anchor and hope, Mr Dunbar, anchor and hope,' he called to his mate as Dunbar came aft to report the anchor having been brought up.

'Aye, sir. I shall hope most fervently!' Dunbar replied, shouting above the shriek of the wind.

There followed an anxious twenty-four hours during which, at three in the morning when the gale reached its height, the *Fort Mackinac* began to drag her anchor towards the Workington Bank. Dunbar ordered the port anchor let go and informed Crawhall.

'I remember,' Crawhall shouted into Dunbar's ear, giving vent to his anxiety as the two men stood at the top of the poop-ladder and watched the seas roaring down out of the night and breaking all about them, 'the *Hougoumont* drove ashore here about ten years ago.'

Ducking into the chart-room, Dunbar emerged with the news that the glass had begun to rise.

'I think we can soon expect a shift in the wind, sir,' he yelled.

'If it comes, we shall need all hands, in case we have to unscramble those anchors!'

An hour after daylight the wind chopped round to the north-west, driving the cloud and rain to leeward while the sun broke out over the Kirkudbright shore and dappled the land with delightful patches of green. But their troubles were far from over. The shift of wind, though blowing them off the Workington shoal, which, now being to windward, afforded them considerable protection, nevertheless caused them to have a turn in their two anchor cables, a snarl not easily remedied until the gale abated, and one made increasingly complex by the six-hourly changes in the tide as the wind fell right away.

When the gale finally abated, the tug *Cruiser* arrived from Liverpool. Crawhall ordered Dunbar to slip their port anchor and a length of cable to a dahn buoy. Having then weighed the starboard bower, they proceeded under tow south to Liverpool. Later, Dunbar caught a train north and, hiring a small tug from Maryport, recovered their missing anchor. After an absence of a week, he returned it to the *Fort Mackinac* in Birkenhead and thereby earned a further commendation from Captain Crawhall.

By the time the *Fort Mackinac* next sailed in ballast for Australia, the long foretold war in the Balkans had broken out and been terminated by a treaty, only to break out again with even greater ferocity. But it was considered, in Crawhall's phrase, 'a brush-fire', which would burn only those close to it. Such was the weight of a shipmaster's opinion, such the hermetic world in which they lived, and such were their desires and self-delusions that these events were easily forgotten.

The unremitting demands of standing watch-and-watch, of coping with the pressing needs of the daily round of fighting a big sailing vessel across the vast, grey, uninhabited spaces of the world reduced in their perception the squabbles of Turks and Macedonian Greeks, of Bulgars, Russians, Serbians and Montenegrins.

Dunbar himself had long ago forgotten to associate the Balkan brush-fire with the restaurant that he, Julia and the others had occasionally visited. Moreover, while he still wrote to Julia, his letters were usually responses to her own business-like epistles, chief among which was the one announcing that Mr Maddox had shown his interest in buying a collection of 'Dunbars'.

He did his best to satisfy this lust, sending home from Liverpool, or Glasgow, a packing case of paintings and drawings, but, for Dunbar at least, these had lost something. His technique had become more refined, but it had lost its spontaneity and with it something of the fire of its creation. Maddox seemed unaware of this, though Julia mentioned, in an aside intended to wound yet oddly encouraging to Dunbar, that the magnate seemed more interested in 'the raw political aspect' of Dunbar's work than in the purity of its artistic merit. Only Dunbar's quick drawings retained that seductive energy, that sureness of touch and quality of instantaneous capture that no camera could ever achieve.

Dunbar was not an artist who could work without a model, or at least a very recent and haunting impression of an action or activity. On several private occasions he tried to recapture the face and figure of Maureen, just as he had once done with Mrs Coxford, but the enchantment that distance and time lent his mind's eye eluded the cunning of his hand, and all he succeeded in accomplishing were some grotesques. It was as if some malignantly fateful power was depriving him of his skill, perverting his powers of recall where Maureen was concerned.

For the most part, however, drawing and painting were the only manifestation of Dunbar's private persona, and while the former might be executed at any time, the latter tended to occupy those periods of partial respite in the trades, or the enforced idleness experienced from time to time while at anchor awaiting cargo. It seemed that his occasional despatching of a packing case to Hampstead was the mature consequence of his brief encounters with Julia and her circle. If so, he supposed it was enough; an ocean gypsy had no right to expect more, and he had nothing to live on beyond his pay and the little extra that the sale of his pictures made. As time passed he forgot. It was the lot of every seafarer, just as it was in turn his own lot to be forgotten.

Occasionally memory would stir, stimulated by something read, said or seen. On a bleak morning in the southern autumn, for instance, with the *Fort Mackinac* running under top-gallants between Staten Island and the Falklands, under a lowering, leaden overcast and over a heaving grey sea, they came upon a squadron of British cruisers. A pallid yellow streak in the east told where the sun shone beyond the thick pall of overcast and the dense cloud of boiler smoke smeared across this in heavy streaks. They were four elderly ships, rigid in their station, with the familiar white ensigns of the British navy flying from their masts. The second from the van bore the flag of a rear-admiral and Dunbar, studying the warships through the long glass, thought of Lord Fowey, the scent of *eau de toilette* and the creaking of stays.

So far distant from Britain, yet extending the protection of her flag to merchant ships like the *Fort Mackinac*, enabling them in turn to pursue their lawful occasions, were these ships in fact the cruiser squadron commanded by his lordship? And if they were, had Lord Fowey expelled or arrested Ernst, Graf von Ketlar? If so, who, if anyone, had painted the portrait of Thelma, Lady Fowey?

'And how in hell's name,' Dunbar muttered to himself as he shut the long glass with a snap after the flagship had answered the respectful dip of the barque's red ensign, 'did I know the lady's name was Thelma?'

Such questions could never be answered and merely contributed to the uncurious nature of seamen. They made themselves perfect masters of their ships and all the complex skills necessary to command them, but they were dismissive of outside events, relegating the squabbles of tribesmen to 'brush-fire' conflicts, and paying a perfunctory respect to the appearance of men-of-war by the dipping of their own ensign.

Thus detached, Dunbar coasted through two years of ocean wandering, preparing himself for command. He was sanguine that, with Crawhall's promised recommendation, he might inherit the master's berth in the *Fort Mackinac* when Crawhall himself retired, which the old man promised would not now be long.

'One more trip, Mr Dunbar,' Crawhall said as they ran up-Channel on a fine spring morning in April 1914, 'and then I shall swallow the anchor.'

PART FOUR

Unpaid Excursion

The South Atlantic Ocean,
London and Suffolk, 1914–15

PART FOUR

CHAPTER FOURTEEN

The Attack

The four-masted barque *Fort Mackinac* was approaching Cape Horn, reaching to the south-south-west, reeling off the knots and heading for the Strait of Le Maire.

'How many, Wells?' Dunbar asked the apprentice of the watch, as the young man entered the chart-room from the taffrail where he had read the patent log.

'Fifty-eight for the watch, sir,' Wells replied with a gleam of appreciation in his eye, 'nearly twelve knots.'

Dunbar heaved himself out of the lad's way, allowing him to write the details of the distance-run on the log slate. Dunbar pulled on his cap and stepped out into the windswept afternoon.

'Good sleep, Jim?'

Dunbar nodded. 'Not bad, and I feel like death now,' he grinned back at the second mate whom he had come up to relieve. Mr Nicholls was a studious young officer who had recently qualified. But he had served his time with Bullard, Crowe and Company, had an uncle and an older brother at sea in sailing vessels, both of whom had served in the *Forts* at one time or another, and had had the experience of a dismasting in the *Fort Oswego* on his first voyage to sea. Despite his almost beardless good looks, Mr Nicholls was already an experienced and reliable officer.

'Afternoon, sir.' Bill Andrews went aft to relieve the man at the wheel and gave Dunbar a smile. Andrews had made his customary recovery from his two-month debauch and looked fit and lean again. Dunbar still wondered how the man did it, and how he had apparently succumbed to neither the clap nor the pox.

'Wind's dropping,' Nicholls said.

'You could have fooled me,' Dunbar replied, staring to windward.

'It's been dropping all watch. We reset the t'gallants at two bells.'

Recalling through a fog of fatigue the gale that had been blowing as he had relinquished the deck to Nicholls at noon, Dunbar grumpily agreed and looked aloft. 'I didn't hear a thing.'

'You'll be giving her the royals before the second dog,' Nicholls said, smiling.

'Why don't you bugger off and write your damned book.' Dunbar grinned encouragingly, 'though why we need another bloody seamanship primer, I'm damned if I know.'

'We need a fresh approach to technical subjects,' Nicholls began, 'to avoid excluding new knowledge from old crafts. This is a scientific age and if we ignore the fact, seamanship will not benefit from the acquisition of revision and reassessment.'

'God save us . . .'

'Come on, Jim, you know what I mean.'

'You won't need any seamanship in a steam-kettle. I hear they're fitting them with brakes now.'

It was an old argument between them, and they parted with those amiable insults that mark the banter of men who know and like each other. A few minutes later the *Fort Mackinac* flew unfalteringly onwards with a different group of men in control of her.

The little ritual of handing over the watch included

272

passing over the course and the oncoming officer checking this personally. Dunbar did not linger beside the steering compass, for Grant was the helmsman, and Grant had become a strangely embittered man since he had last sailed with Dunbar, given to frequent asides of an insubordinate nature, which Dunbar tried to ignore.

Later, however, Grant was relieved by Andrews and Dunbar wandered aft to stare routinely in the compass bowl: the card's point of *SSW* swung gently about the lubber's line indicating the *Fort Mackinac*'s heading. Shutting his eyes, Dunbar stretched, trying to slough off the woolly-headedness induced by his all too short, post-prandial nap.

'You look dreadful, Mr Dunbar,' remarked Andrews with a wide grin.

'Don't be insubordinate,' replied Dunbar, smiling back. 'You're getting as bad as Grant. I shan't be able to overlook your provocative cheek as well as his.'

'He's a pain in the arse,' said Andrews succinctly.

'I had a notion he'd changed, and not for the better.'

'Oh, that's true. He's infinitely worse; he used to be curmudgeonly, but now he complains all the time. He's become a real moaner. I asked him why, if he felt so badly about coming to sea, he bothered. D'you know what he said to me?'

'No.'

'It was a rhetorical question, sir.'

'It was a rhetorical answer, Andrews.'

'"I go to sea," he said,' said Andrews, laughing and shifting the wheel a spoke or two, '"because I'm the best seaman there is and one day you're going to need me!" Can you imagine it? What a damned odd thing to say! I'm persuaded he actually believes it!'

'Well, it's extraordinary that he should turn up again like this,' said Dunbar, looking round the horizon.

Andrews's face grew grave. 'To be serious, I think

it's bad ju-ju, Jim, what with the news we got the other day,' he said with quiet informality, relying upon their old familiarity.

'For heaven's sake, Bill; you'll be calling him the Flying Dutchman next.'

But if Andrews replied, Dunbar did not hear him, for something astern of them had caught his eye, something that might be fatefully connected not with Grant's lugubrious attitude, but with the news to which Bill Andrews had referred. Dunbar strode quickly forward and, reaching into the charthouse, picked up the long glass. Crouching down he levelled the telescope against the taffrail and brought into focus the tiny irregularity that broke the symmetry of the horizon. The smudge of black smoke rose from two distinct sources, two funnels, just forward of which rose the unmistakable silhouette of a warship's forebridge. Even as he watched, the twin funnels foreshortened, then disappeared behind the mast and bridge.

'She's seen us,' he muttered, 'just as we've seen her.' Dunbar stood up, shutting the glass with a snap. His heart thumped in his breast and he wondered if he would prove a coward. Six days earlier they had exchanged signals with a Clan Liner homeward bound from Calcutta. The *Clan Ranald* had altered course out of her way to close on the sailing ship and initially Nicholls, who was officer of the watch, had thought she had passengers on board. It was quite common for former sailing ship masters to amuse their passengers by showing them a relic of a former age and, by association, claim some kudos from the spectacle. But the *Clan Ranald*'s master was possessed of no such conceit; he bore down upon them with the message flying from his signal halliards in the gaudy international code of flag signals: *The British Empire is at war with Germany*.

They had seen nothing but a single steamer bound

for the River Plate in the succeeding days, but there was no doubt that the ship astern of them was not merely a man-of-war, but was showing an interest in the lone barque. Pleased though Dunbar, Nicholls and Wells might be with the *Fort Mackinac*'s twelve knots, it was not enough. Dunbar looked about him. The pale disc of the sun gleamed for a moment behind the cloud-bank as it westered. The overcast would bring darkness early and twilight would be short. The strange ship was probably a British cruiser, but she might not be; she might be something infinitely more deadly.

Dunbar went quickly forward, dived into the charthouse and skidded below to let Crawhall know.

Darkness closed about them with predictable suddenness. Before it did so they had confirmed that the ship astern was indeed a warship and was heading towards them. Its nationality, however, remained a mystery.

Crawhall puffed on his pipe in furious deliberation as, after he had studied the stranger and night had eclipsed his view, he stood on the windward quarter, talking to Dunbar whose watch it was again, but who had not left the deck in the intervening second dog-watch.

'I don't like it, Mr Dunbar, damned if I do. That fellow isn't using his full speed.'

'That could mean he's a British cruiser, steaming at an economical rate,' Dunbar said, joining Crawhall in altering the gender of the pursuer as they changed their reference from the passively female ship to the active male who commanded her.

'True, but he could be playing cat and mouse with us. I've a feeling in my water. We're easier game at first light with all day to sink us.' Crawhall pulled the pipe from his mouth, ever a sign that he had finished chattering and was about to utter either an order or a profundity. 'Anyway, we'll square away in ten minutes. Pity this bloody wind's dropping, but perhaps, if we shift to the eastward, he'll overrun us in the night.'

It was the best they could do.

Dunbar was called again at four o'clock in the morning. As he rolled out of his bunk and his feet hit the cold deck, his eyes fell on the canvas bag he had prepared before turning in. The sight filled his weary mind with apprehension as full memory came flooding back. Sleep had killed all thoughts and fears of the warship astern of them. Now the bag brought them back with a rush.

It contained a few necessaries – some sea-boot stockings, a jersey, a bottle of water, a flask of whisky, lucifer matches and his best, shore-going leather gloves. He had also included a notebook and pencil. Now he dressed with unusual care, pulling on his serge trousers over his pyjamas and tugging two sweaters on over a flannel shirt. Finally he put on his pea-jacket and cap, hung the field glasses that had once belonged to Hugh Scrope-Davies about his neck and went on deck. Climbing up into the charthouse, he heard eight bells ring, marking the change of watch. He was a few minutes later than was customary.

'Morning.' Nicholls's greeting was terse.

'Morning. See anything?' Dunbar asked, peering around, his eyes still unadjusted to the inky blackness of the night.

'Not a bloody thing.'

'Well, that's something I suppose.' Dunbar sniffed the air. The wind had fallen very light, no more than a faint breeze, still steady, but scarcely powerful enough to drive the barque forward at more than a few knots. 'He might outrun us, I suppose,' he remarked hopefully.

But Nicholls had been on watch for four hours, his mind had been nervously active throughout the bleakest

276

and loneliest period of the night, and he had turned over every sequence of events that an overwrought imagination could conjure up.

'Naval officers are not stupid; at least not all of them are. They can tell the wind is light and that we won't be racing about the ocean until it freshens. If they overrun us and can't see us at daylight, all they have to do is turn round and . . .'

'Yes, yes, all right. No sign of any fog. That would help.'

'As you say, there's no sign of it, so forget it.'

'You think . . . ?'

'Yes. Of course I do. The only hope is that the bloody thing is British, and to be honest, I don't think we've much chance of that.'

Dunbar sighed. 'No, to be frank, neither do I. In fact I've packed a ditty bag with a few essentials. I suggest you do the same.'

'Yes, I'd thought of that. Should we tell the men?'

'Yes. It would be best, I think,' Dunbar said. 'Better than taking to the boats with bugger-all.'

'Well, the course is still south-east, at least until daylight. The Old Man didn't turn in until after midnight. He left word to give him a shake at the first sign of twilight.'

'Fine. Try and get some sleep.'

As was his invariable practice after taking over the watch, Dunbar went aft to check the course. Once again Grant was at the wheel. The able-seaman sniffed as Dunbar peered into the compass.

'Don't make that disgusting noise in my ear, Grant.'

'Can't help it. Got a cold.' Grant sniffed again, a long, deliberate, insolent snort. 'Got to keep both hands on the wheel, to steer her properly, *Mister* Dunbar, see. If you let go of the wheel, the fucking ship might broach, *Mister* Dunbar, and *you* know what happens when the ship broaches, *Mister* Dunbar, don't you, eh?'

'Shut it, Grant.'

'Shut it. Aye, aye, *sir*.' Grant sniffed again and Dunbar turned forward, leaving the able-seaman chuckling behind him.

He walked forward and called to the watch, who were hunkered down at the break of the poop under the after-boat skids beneath him. 'I'm sending each man back into the fo'c'sle one at a time to pack a bag in case we have to take to the boats. Small bag each, warm clothes. You go first, Andrews. Two of you to relieve the wheel and lookout when you've finished. Last man to let me know you're all done. Get on with it.'

The dark shapes below stirred like disturbed animals. With a brief muttering, one of them broke away and Dunbar caught a glimpse of a pale face, lit by a flaring of phosphorescence in the sea alongside the ship as he went forward.

Dunbar began to pace the poop. Forward eight steps, balance, turn, aft eight steps. The activity calmed him. He felt better able to think. They were quite defenceless of course, passive hostages to fortune, victims of the caprice of fate, or of the malice of the commander of that putative German cruiser. What a situation to find themselves in! He raged briefly and ineffectually at the stupidity of what he knew would happen. Here they were, performing a useful task hauling the world's goods about the ocean – even if this was only a trip in ballast, the purpose was to return to Europe with a hold full of grain. And at the behest of some high-born arsehole on the other side of the world, who robbed what he was pleased to regard as his subjects of the fruits of their work to build an expensive ship armed with the latest form of weaponry, they, the crew of the *Fort Mackinac*, who owed this crowned bastard nothing, could – no, *would* – find themselves cast adrift at the mercy of the sea and the wind . . .

The insolence of it! Dunbar flared into sudden incoherent anger, recalling Colonel Scrope-Davies quoting Tom Paine. He swore a string of filth and stopped, finding himself staring astern into the impenetrable darkness, lit only by the occasional heave of the wake under the *Fort Mackinac*'s counter and an upwelling of fitful bio-luminescence.

Beside him Grant gave another low chuckle, followed by a loud snort. In an instant Dunbar was beside him, furious that this idiot could pursue his stupid, irrational vendetta at a time like this. As he confronted Grant, the seaman lowered his eyes to the compass.

'Course south-east, Mr Dunbar,' he intoned.

Dunbar swung away, mastering his temper. Then an idea struck him; he walked into the charthouse and closed the door. Behind him Grant muttered about bad luck and the smell of death.

Dawn came at last. After what seemed like an interminable wait, it grew swiftly lighter. As soon as he could make out the lines of caulking in the deck, Dunbar dropped to the maindeck. The men sheltering, half-dopey in the lee of the half-deck and each clutching his ditty bag, moved in nervous anticipation as he approached. He sensed that his footfalls on the deck woke them from their somnolent state to remind them of the danger they were trying to forget.

'Wells?'

'Sir?' The apprentice broke away from the huddle of men. He was nursing a mug of tea, his tousled hair no longer grey, but light brown, his face a pale but recognisably pink shape. 'Give the captain my compliments and tell him daylight's breaking. I'm going aloft.'

'Aye, aye, sir.'

The news caused them all to stir. As Wells put down

his mug of tea for safe-keeping, men rose and stretched themselves to wakefulness. One or two went to the rail as if expecting to see the enemy close by. Dunbar walked forward and hoisted himself up into the main rigging.

He had less cause than formerly to go aloft these days beyond the course yards, where the mate of the watch usually stationed himself when shortening sail, and found that he had to concentrate upon the climb. With the ship scarcely heeling, the clamber out over the lower futtock shrouds found him hanging back downwards like a sloth. Then he was up the topmast shrouds to the crossing. The barque had her top-gallants set and he pressed resolutely higher, not only to gain an unrestricted view, but to increase the distance of the sea-horizon, which was a function of elevation. Finally, he threw a leg over the main royal yard, braced himself and stared around. For a moment they seemed to be quite alone upon that broad, heaving, grey expanse of the South Atlantic; then he saw her, a jagged shape against the still slightly indistinct edge of the horizon to the south-south-west, betrayed by the smudge of black smoke that rose from her funnels, more prominently now that the wind had dropped.

Levelling the field-glasses he stared hard at the warship, bringing the sinister image into focus. The cruiser swung obligingly, turning into full side elevation as Dunbar watched, presenting her broadside so that although still hull-down, he recognised without a doubt and with the instinct that seamen develop that this was no British man-of-war, but an enemy commerce raider. Moreover, her identifying manoeuvre was but part of a turn of some 120 degrees which, when her commander or officer of the watch had completed it, left his ship heading almost directly towards the barque, on a course that would intercept them a few miles ahead. Their gunnery sights, Dunbar knew as his heart hammered painfully in his breast, would give them the precise offset to steer in the same way that it would direct the elevation and angle of their guns. With an effort, he stilled his shaking hands. He could see the white of her bow wave now, a great bone in her teeth as she increased speed and her long, grey hull rose over the edge of the world.

He felt an odd sensation of almost telegraphic communication with the distant intelligence that was directing the cruiser's actions. There was a fateful link between the hunter and the hunted, as though the unknown being initiating the kill was first trying to stun its victim, seeking to paralyse it with the fear that would render it supine at the moment of attack.

Why? Could it possibly be because, even when all the might was overwhelmingly on one side, there was a natural revulsion to the actual act of murder? Did the victim have, in some strange way, to acquiesce? To condescend to be killed? To submit to the logic of 'might is right'?

And did they not learn this acquiescence, if such it was, in the respect they paid to their crowned arseholes, along with the taxes they gave up to build these engines of death?

'Masthead! Can ye see anything, Mister?'

Crawhall's voice summoned Dunbar back to reality and he looked down at the narrow strip of deck far below. Crawhall, pipe already alight, stood at the starboard poop-ladder and stared upwards.

'Aye, sir! Four points on the starboard bow! He's seen us and is running in towards us!'

'How far distant?'

Dunbar estimated. He was some 150 feet above the sea, with the horizon fourteen miles away. The cruiser, which he had first seen hull-down, was now hull-up, closing the distance between them at a speed, he guessed, in excess of twenty-five knots: one mile in less than three minutes.

'Ten miles, sir!' he roared and began to clamber down,

aware that he was shaking with nervous reaction. He began to swear, a low, sustaining mutter of obscene imprecation against fate, against the God he had rejected, against every projection, ratline, shackle pin and seizing that he fouled in his hurried descent.

'Fuck the Kaiser! Fuck all kings!' he railed venomously until he heard, surprisingly loud, a voice call out, 'I can see her, sir!' and found himself level with young Wells, who had come halfway up the main lower shrouds in some demonstration of solidarity among the officers who should, he thought, as befitted their privileged rank, first set eyes upon the nemesis approaching them.

'Don't get too excited, Wells,' he snarled quite unnecessarily through clenched teeth. 'She'll be here in no time at all.'

Breathing heavily, Dunbar joined Crawhall on the poop. The master had the long glass levelled off on the starboard bow. 'I see the bastard,' Crawhall said through teeth that gripped his pipe-stem and emitted puffs of blue smoke.

'German cruiser, I think,' Dunbar said.

'Reckon you're right.' Crawhall paused, then went on, 'Dig out that Yankee courtesy ensign and hoist it up to the peak. It won't fool him for long, but it's worth a try.'

'Aye, aye, sir.'

'Don't give up till you're dead, Mr Dunbar,' Crawhall said quietly, lowering the glass for a moment and catching his young mate's eye. 'Death'll come quite naturally and you needn't worry about it at all.'

Dunbar felt the older man's influence steady him. He was still shaking a little from the exertion of his muscles and the task given him enabled him to concentrate on something specific, to quieten his crazy heart and master his anxiety.

As he bent the Stars and Stripes onto the peak halliards, he heard the noise of the shell and looked up, just in time to see the tall column of water rise ahead and slightly to windward of them. He was hurriedly hauling the brilliant bunting aloft as the rumble of the concussion rolled over the sea towards them.

'Damn the bastards!' Crawhall shut the long glass with a percussive snap. 'Main braces there! Heave her to! Watch to the main braces and call all hands!'

It was a relief to do something, even if that something was to accede to the enemy's demands and, as Dunbar had foreseen in that clairvoyant moment of understanding at the masthead, contribute to their own undoing.

With her mainyards flat aback, the *Fort Mackinac* rapidly slowed to a standstill and waited for the massive, ugly casemated steel shape of the German cruiser to come up with her.

This she did with speed and *élan*. They watched fascinated as the grey shape once again underwent its transformation and turned, to range up to windward of them some three-quarters of a mile away. Her screws boiled the water white under her ugly stern as her commander threw her engines into reverse and stopped her parallel to her prey, exposing her full primary and secondary armaments, the first in its turrets, foreshortened as the great gun barrels intimidated them; the latter, lighter but deadly for so vulnerable a target, levelled upon them from their armoured casemates. At her peak flew the black cross with its single dark quartering which, at a distance, might be mistaken for a friendly white ensign but was clearly that of the Kaiser's navy.

Dunbar could see the figures of men running about the deck, glimpsed the line of white-clad sailors walk away with the boat falls and watched as the result of their labour rose from her chocks amidships and was swung over the side. The brass funnel of the picket boat gleamed sullenly in the dull daylight, then it was bobbing alongside and men were swarming down into her.

'Boarding party,' Crawhall said shortly. 'Put the pilot ladder over. Let's not make it difficult.'

'Are you going to leave the ensign up, sir?'

'Yes. Why not? We don't want it to be *that* easy.' Crawhall's face broke into a grim smile. He shouted, 'Let 'em aboard, men, but don't talk to 'em. I'll pretend we're a Yankee for as long as possible. You all hold your tongues.' When he had finished, Dunbar ordered the watch to throw the pilot ladder over the side to maintain the pretence of being a co-operative neutral. As he turned back he noticed that Crawhall had disappeared. Dunbar assumed the master had slipped into the charthouse, but when he looked again, Crawhall was not to be seen.

A moment of pure panic seized Dunbar, and then Crawhall was in the charthouse, having clearly run down to his cabin for something. Dunbar's anxiety was evident in his face, for Crawhall muttered, 'Brace yourself, James, I'm damned if I'm going to be taken without spitting in the Kaiser's eye!'

Dunbar had no idea what this defiance portended, but he swallowed and nodded, reassured. He thought of the bag prepared in his cabin, looked over the sea at the approaching picket boat, and asked, 'Mind if I nip down to my cabin, sir?'

Crawhall shook his head. 'No, go ahead. And tell the steward to get some dried fruit and extra water to go into the boats. We may not get much time.'

Dunbar disappeared, tumbled down the companionway and bumped into Nicholls and the steward in the saloon. He passed on the master's instructions adding, 'get a move on. The bloody Germans are about to board.' He ran to his cabin, the monkish cell at which his father had scoffed, picked up the ditty bag and returned to the charthouse. Dropping the bag on the settee, he went out onto the poop.

The picket boat was almost alongside, riding up, then

sinking on the lazy swells. Dunbar could smell the distinctive odour of a steam boiler blowing downwind ahead of her, and watched the armed party of seamen clustered about the low superstructure of the boat. They all bore Mausers with fixed bayonets and were stationed behind a gun mounted on the boat's foredeck, which constantly raked the barque. He caught sight of the flash of gold on an officer's cuff lace, then turned back into the charthouse and picked up the scrap of paper he had prepared earlier, shoving it into his pocket.

When he emerged again, the picket boat was out of sight alongside. In the waist the crew were leaning over like so many sightseers. They did nothing to assist the German officer and his party of a dozen armed sailors over the rail.

'Come up here, Lootenant,' Crawhall drawled.

The German officer motioned a pair of bearded seamen to precede him and the booted and gaitered men thundered up the poop-ladder and confronted Crawhall with the naked steel of their bayonets.

'I have a deep prejudice to coercion, Lootenant. Tell these bastards to lower their God-damned rifles.'

'Stop being a fool, Captain,' the German officer said in impeccable English, appearing at the top of the ladder. He was bearded, like his ratings, and had the swarthy looks and hooked nose of an Arab. 'This vessel is the *Fort Mackinac*, she is registered in London and owned by Bullard, Crowe and Company of St Mary Axe.'

'Why you impudent damned . . .'

But Crawhall got no further. As he pulled out the revolver with which he had kidnapped Paradise Joe, he was shot through the heart by Korvetten-Kapitän Graf von Ketlar.

CHAPTER FIFTEEN

SMS Augsburg

As Crawhall's lifeless body slumped to the deck, a wild-eyed Ketlar rounded upon the others on the poop, his pistol raking them all. He was flanked by his two sailors, who presented their bayonets with an air of nervous expectancy. In the waist below, the noise of the shot had transformed the attitudes of the casually boarding German seamen and the indifferently observing British; both parties were suddenly, suspiciously hostile. Whereas the largely tolerant and detached crew of a merchant ship might have been expected to have little interest in the fate of their owner's property, the shooting of their commander was an insupportable outrage.

The production of Crawhall's own revolver was not seen as reason enough for the cold-blooded murder that they considered they had just witnessed. Crawhall's vulnerability was a measure of their own collective weakness.

For their part, Ketlar and his sailors, armed as they were, had expected no resistance: merchant seamen were practical men. The sudden appearance of Crawhall's pistol had provoked Ketlar's reaction. The orders of his own commander, Kapitän-zur-See Helmut Kranke, had been unequivocal: Ketlar was to stand no nonsense. This only compounded his nervous satisfaction at knowing, by her name, that their prize was no American, but the barque once sailed in by an English acquaintance of his own, during what Kranke slyly referred to as Ketlar's 'London period'.

As Ketlar fired the fatal shot, Dunbar moved forward to Crawhall's assistance, attracting the German officer's attention. Recognition flared in Ketlar's eyes and was as quickly suppressed.

'Ach, you are the chief mate?' The question was accompanied by a thrusting forward of his revolver as Ketlar stepped over Crawhall's body and confronted Dunbar. There was in this advance the unspoken command of compliance and, beyond an acknowledgement that Dunbar was the *Fort Mackinac*'s mate, of silence.

Oddly, Dunbar felt no coercion in this tacit command. He would himself have willed silence upon Ketlar at that moment and, since he did not hold the advantage, derived some small satisfaction from what he sensed was Ketlar's discomfiture. As Ketlar turned to bark an order at his two sailors, an order that was in turn bellowed down to the Germans in the waist and which dispossessed the legitimate crew of the *Fort Mackinac* of their ship, Dunbar stepped backwards, retreating towards the charthouse.

As soon as he had passed his instructions, Ketlar waved his pistol barrel at Dunbar. 'Inside!' he snapped. Seeing the companionway leading below, he asked, 'Is there anyone below?'

'Would you trust my answer?' Dunbar replied. Although the presence of Ketlar seemed less of a terror than that of some unknown predator, the circumstances that bound their fates gave to this strange meeting a sinister air, aided by the callous shooting of Captain Crawhall. The seizure of the barque might almost be a row between acquaintances, rather than a dispassionate dispossession between men who had nothing between them but the hostility inculcated by a state of war. But it also had all the incipient horror which so close a relationship brought in its train.

'If you lied, I would shoot you.'

Dunbar wondered what action Lord Fowey had taken against Ketlar and whether Ketlar knew the part that Dunbar himself had played in the revelation that the German officer was a spy.

'In the line of duty, I suppose,' Dunbar replied, suddenly feeling reckless and angry, referring to the summary execution that Ketlar had meted out.

'Your captain's death troubles you?'

'A lot of things trouble me, Ernst . . .'

'You will not call me that! Not now!' Ketlar retorted. 'I want your ship's papers.'

'They are in the master's cabin.'

'Then lead the way.' Dunbar descended into the deserted saloon and turned aft as Ketlar's boots clattered down after him. Inside the cabin, across the bulkhead dividing the master's quarters from the saloon, to one side of the entrance door, stood Crawhall's desk. The rolltop was open and it took only a moment to pull out the articles, manifest and outward clearance forms.

'We are in ballast,' Dunbar said sardonically, handing the documents to Ketlar. 'Not much of a prize.'

'We are not taking prizes,' Ketlar snapped. Pointing his revolver towards Dunbar, the German officer backed off a yard and cast a quick eye over the papers. Then he swiftly folded them, thrust them into the breast of his tunic and menaced Dunbar with the gun.

'I hardly dared hope we might meet.'

'How very kind of you, Ernst—'

'I have told you. Do not use that name.' Ketlar jerked his head. 'Get back into the charthouse.'

As he left the cabin, Dunbar cast a look back into the stateroom. 'The captain was a good man,' he said almost conversationally as he passed Ketlar.

'He was a fool. He paid for his folly,' Ketlar replied, following Dunbar to the foot of the ladder.

'Of course, you would know,' Dunbar said with ironic emphasis as he ran up the ladder with Ketlar close behind. 'You have great experience of making fools of people.'

'So it *was* you,' Ketlar breathed with a sense of satisfaction as both men stood in the charthouse again. 'I thought it must be.' He smiled. Outside the German seamen could be seen running aft and then forward. They were pushing the helmsman before them. Ketlar said, 'So it *is* fate that we are here, eh? She would never admit it was you, though I guessed. The balance of probabilities, you know . . .' He smiled again. 'This is more satisfactory. Between us, I mean.'

Dunbar thought of Maureen being interrogated by her brutal lover. 'What did you do to her?'

'What did *you* do to her?' Ketlar answered back. 'And why don't you ask what happened to me, eh?' Ketlar shed his smile and his eyes became cold. 'How very fitting that we should meet like this, James. How very fitting.'

Dunbar felt touched by a sudden menace; he lost the faint comfort of knowing Ketlar. Now it was quite the opposite. He attempted to claw back some initiative. 'Why did you shoot that old man?'

'He threatened me with a gun.'

'He frightened you with a gun,' Dunbar retorted quickly. 'It was a despicable act to murder in cold . . .'

Ketlar shoved his face into Dunbar's, so closely that Dunbar smelt his breath. 'Do not judge me, *Gott* dammit!'

Sweat broke out all over Dunbar's body, but he persisted in his defiance. 'I can hardly believe you ever had the sensitivity to paint!' he breathed. Ketlar's revolver muzzle punched its way painfully into the flesh under Dunbar's jaw, forcing his head back.

'I will blow your fucking head off!'

Dunbar was pushed beyond extremity. He suddenly did not give a damn whether Ketlar shot him at that moment;

he was flooded with a furious defiance that owed its existence to the affront this man had caused Maureen, to the death of Crawhall, the seizure of the *Fort Mackinac* and the adrenalin flooding his system. Through clenched teeth he sneered, 'You were going to paint the ultimate female—'

Dunbar did not finish. The cold muzzle forced his head further back so that he was able to expel only one contemptuous word: 'Pirate!'

Provoked, Ketlar swept a gaitered leg upwards, driving his knee into Dunbar's groin. With a gasp, Dunbar collapsed forward and Ketlar stepped back, bringing the butt of his revolver crashing down on the back of his skull. Dunbar sprawled on the scrubbed deck of the charthouse. Retching and gasping for breath, he received the additional kicks without protest. Only deep-rooted reflexes enabled his failing body to cling to life as his conscious self abandoned sensibility, enveloped by an overwhelming blackness.

With a kind of hopeless satisfaction, Ketlar wiped his mouth, staring down at his victim. For a moment he was pallid with indecision, then he stepped out on deck and closed the charthouse door.

Dunbar emerged into a roaring agony, rising, like a drowning man, towards a dimly perceived light far above him. He knew not whether he wished to fight his way towards it, knowing the pain that awaited him there, or submit and sink into the comfort of eternal darkness. Quite powerless, he hovered thus for some time, unable to affect matters, indifferent, a small fragment of distress, bereft of hope or motivation, clinging to life only through reflexive habit.

Afterwards, he remembered only that his existence hung suspended, meaningless, irrelevant. Had nothing else happened, he was convinced that he would have surrendered to the darkness: it offered him endless comfort.

But at that moment of suspension, SMS *Augsburg* opened fire upon the *Fort Mackinac* with her secondary armament. The shells, fired on a flat trajectory at point-blank range, thumped into the hull. The deck beneath Dunbar's body shook with the impact and bucked with the instantaneous explosion. The shock stimulated him. With a growing consciousness came natural curiosity, asserting itself at first in a detached way. But this almost abstract curiosity suddenly received the revivifying shock of fear. He might die comfortably through inertia, but his spirit revolted at being killed outright. He raised his head and though it reeled and he felt a wave of sickness overwhelm him, he found this eased if he drew his legs up beneath him and propped himself up on his arms. It was at this point that he became aware that Ketlar had gone. He was quite alone.

Kapitän-sur-Zee Kranke had awaited the return of his boarding party and the abandonment of the *Fort Mackinac* by her crew. Then, after he heard Ketlar's report, he had ordered a single gun to open fire. The four-masted barque was the seventh British ship that the *Augsburg* had sunk since she had sailed from Buenos Aires at the commencement of her cruise five weeks earlier. Kranke watched with satisfaction as the second shell exploded. The intelligence that the barque bore no radio was a relief. He disliked the necessity of putting as much distance as possible between himself and his victim, of running away before an alerted British cruiser came over the horizon and caught him; it smacked of cowardice, for all the arguments in favour of prudent conservation of a valuable commerce raider. True, it was not his business to engage enemy men-of-war: the sinking of merchant ships was his stock in trade, but the matter irked him, nonetheless. Kranke raised his glasses. The *Fort Mackinac* was already settling in the water as the sea rushed into her breached holds. Her two boats were both off the after-skids, where the davits were now swung outboard and the falls trailed untidily in the water as the ship sank. It was a pity to see any ship sink; it was a particular pity to see a noble sailing vessel founder under fire like this.

Kranke sighed; he considered himself a romantic, having been in sail himself, and the four-masted barque was going down defiantly with all her sails set. War, he mused, created sad imperatives, but, and here Kranke drew himself up to his full height of two metres, duty was duty and had to be done. He was sorry about the barque's master and her first mate, but Ketlar had behaved correctly in reacting to resistance. A merchant ship's crew were non-combatants; a lack of resistance was part of the covenant that bought them the time to abandon their ship. He would brook no interference to the expeditious despatch of even a beautiful sailing ship.

Kranke was a civilised man; war was a sorry business. He spared one final glance at the two boats, which were now crammed with men and had pulled away from the ship. On the farther side of the wreck, the crew of the barque were now resting upon their oars, watching her sink. Below him, from the port casemate, the single gun barked again and the hot gases swept over the bridge in a pungent wave. For an instant Kranke clearly saw the shell as it spun away from him. Then, just after the third explosion and the eruption of water and ballast amidships, a collective sigh swept the German cruiser as the *Fort Mackinac* broke in two.

As she did so, her mainmast fell, bringing with it all its great yards and the canvas, chain, wire and rope that made the structure work. Then both ends of the hull, the forecastle and poop, more buoyant than the ballasted and perforated hold, slowly assumed the vertical, tipping their still erect masts inwards, like the arc of swords over a bridal pair. As the stays drew taught and stresses rose within the complex web of the great ship's rigging, the whole lot fell, tugging and bowing, stretching, snapping and finally collapsing in a welter of white water, echoed by the sub-marine shimmering of the sails as they sank, weighed down by the steel yards.

The waterlogged mass of the hull now exceeded its reserves of buoyancy and air was forced out of the recesses of the ship where it still lurked. A strange roar accompanied the compression, along with some distant bangs and crashes, as doors burst under pressure and fittings broke loose and crashed through bulkheads.

'What in God's name . . . ?' Kranke's glasses were at his eyes in a flash. 'Cease fire!' he ordered. On the bridge beside the captain, Ketlar swore. A single man was hauling himself over the taffrail. He seemed to be experiencing a certain amount of difficulty.

'Do you recognise this man?' Kranke asked, handing his glasses to the young officer alongside him.

Ketlar took the proffered binoculars, re-focused them and quite clearly saw James Dunbar fall from the counter into the sea.

'No, sir,' Ketlar said. 'He must have been off watch, asleep. Our sailors did not find him.'

For a moment the two men stood in silence as the *Fort Mackinac* finally disappeared. Then there was only a disturbance on the surface of the sea, and the white shapes of the distant boats. Of the man who had slipped over the stern of the *Fort Mackinac* there was no sign.

'Poor devil,' said Kranke, holding out a gloved hand for the return of his binoculars.

Graf von Ketlar scanned the swirling sea surface one final time, then handed them back. 'The fortune of war,' he said grimly.

'Indeed, indeed,' mused Kranke in a low voice, raising the glasses himself for a last look. 'The fortune of war.' There was no sign of the survivor. He lowered the glasses. 'Now full ahead, steer due south.'

And His Imperial Majesty's cruiser *Augsburg* swung away to the southward, leaving the two boats of the *Fort Mackinac* to the further caprices of the sea.

In later life, Dunbar was unable to recollect very much of those few moments during which, in great pain, he was wakened from his stupor, to fight for his life. The shuddering of the hull as the *Augsburg*'s shells exploded forward, admitting sea-water into the ship, was the catalyst that jerked him back to a single-minded semi-consciousness and impelled him to leave the false sanctuary of the charthouse. Fortunately for him, the hinge of the charthouse door was on the forward side of the doorway and it required him only to start the door for it to fall open with a crash. But such was the ever-steepening angle of the deck, that to move aft required a great effort of will. He embarked on a kind of scrabbling crawl, grabbing first the after-corner of the charthouse then, by dint of effort, using the same corner as a step enabling him to reach upwards to the base of the steering binnacle. From here he grabbed the steering gratings and the fittings of the varnished teak cover, which housed the complex wormed shafts and yokes of the steering gear. Waves of nausea and the pain in his loins made him gasp with the effort.

But ahead of him was a far greater obstacle, that of the railings which, capped by teak, formed the taffrail round the outside of the poop. These now contained him like the bars of a cage, more securely than they had ever prevented him from falling overboard when vertical. His aching muscles cracked with the strain, for it was worse than climbing outboard, back downwards, over the futtocks on that first terrifying ascent of the masts in the River Tyne a lifetime earlier.

None of these details occurred to him then. If he recalled anything it was simply that his whole being was suffused with a single *determination* to rest his continuing existence upon this hazard of exertion. He had no strength and little rational control over what residual effort his battered frame could produce. He was shrunk to this single attempt, of clinging and clawing, mercifully unaware in any intelligent sense that he was engaged in a critical race against time and that the obtuse ship, whose fabric barred his escape, was even then descending into the abyss.

It is tempting to describe the effort called forth from him as superhuman, but it was nothing of the sort. Nevertheless, the extraordinary may be summoned from an unexceptional person, and Dunbar was far from unexceptional. In fact, it was neither superhuman nor heroic; it was merely what he was, in those extreme moments, capable of attempting.

When he had clambered painfully over the taffrail, he half-fell, half-sprawled, belly down, onto the turtle-backed counter and over its lower extremity, now a horizontal ridge.

Below him loomed the plane of the rudder, dimly perceived as he launched himself; he was aware, in that first fully apprehensive moment, that in an instant he might dash his brains out upon it. Then he fell, downwards past the rudder, so close that he bore a fleeting impression of its curved blade against the blinding whiteness of the sky, his stomach flying upwards in yet another painful eructation into the cold, black, engulfing sea.

Christ! How cold it was! And how it stung and made him gasp, forcing the salt-water into his mouth.

And now he was fully sensible, thrashing wildly for his life as only a seaman can when rudely thrust into the sea. The close and deadly embrace of the element he had spent his lifetime cheating eased the immediate pain of his wracked and torn muscles, numbed the ache in his testicles and the throbbing lump on his head where Ketlar's revolver butt had struck him. Simultaneously it conveyed a message of death more certain than the semi-conscious state in which he had found himself, in the familiar surroundings of the charthouse, for all the thump and thunder of the German shells.

Once in the water, Dunbar was granted full consciousness and surfaced just as the *Fort Mackinac*, her hull wracked in turn by the minor internal explosions of confined and venting air, slid out of sight. With one impetuous and almost joyous gasp, he realised he had survived. He gulped in air, unaware and thus uncaring of the damage to his chilled body. As this triumphant euphoria seized him, he felt the tug of the ship dragging him after it. He roared out, protesting at the injustice of it. To have come thus far and then to have the ship, his own ship, claim him as some funereal acolyte. The swirl of the sea was like a rope about his legs; he could feel the coils of it . . . No! It was a serpent, vicious and live, a malignant beast that not only took hold of his lower limbs, but had locked itself about his breast, crushing the very life from him.

He was alive now! Alive at the very moment of drowning. Fully cognisant, knowing the terror of the doomed and straining with fear, his instinct compelled him to draw air into himself, to release the constraint upon his lungs and to breathe as he had done unthinking since his birth. And yet something, some last effort of will that would kill him as soon as breathing, told him not to: in that pitiless moment intellect was pitted against instinct. His head split with the sheer struggle of these titanic forces. Panic filled him and he knew that as it grew, it would reach some boiling point beyond which he could not go and would be lost.

But panic made him fight, made him produce from the primeval being that lived in the heart of him, a few violent kicks. They were the last reflexes of the hanged man, the sublime moment for which the gawping crowd had waited, the tiny fraction of a second when the victim passed from sentient life to inert death and in which they hoped to gain a fleeting glimpse of the escaping soul. But just as the crowd was always cheated, so Dunbar broke surface, breached like a humpback whale clear of the water to his very waist, before falling back with a splash.

'There!' yelled Andrews. 'There he is! Give way, you bastards! Give way together!'

As the *Augsburg*'s engines cranked the cruiser up to full speed and she turned away, the *Fort Mackinac*'s port boat's crew plied their oars and, unobserved by the retiring Germans, pulled towards Dunbar.

Hauling the inert and exhausted mate into the boat was a desperate and tiring business, but after a short struggle James Dunbar was laid on the bottom boards of the leaky boat, awash among the water that slopped there.

'He's alive,' Andrews announced in a tone of wonder. Forward, Grant, who had taken no part in the recovery of the mate, sniffed with callous indifference.

CHAPTER SIXTEEN

Abandoned

On his recovery from the sea, Dunbar passed out again lying in the bottom of the boat. After months on the skids, the boat had been dried out and had yet to take up. Her seams leaked and the South Atlantic seeped in a steady flood into her bottom, to be pumped out at regular intervals. Dunbar finally recovered consciousness lying in the boat's bilge, cold, wet and only partially numbed to the full pain of his rough handling and his escape.

Bill Andrews had, by dint of his personality, inherited the leadership of the port boat. This had been confirmed by Mr Nicholls, who had command of the starboard boat and who set aside the claim of the inexperienced apprentice, Wells. Nicholls had given orders for the two boats to keep within sight of each other and to set the most favourable course at the best possible speed. This meant putting the boats on a reach and heading to the south-east, where they hoped they would intercept the route of the mail steamers to and from the Cape of Good Hope. The crews of the two boats therefore stepped their masts, hoisted their small lugsails and jibs and set watches of a helmsman and lookout. Meanwhile the boat leaders, Nicholls and Andrews, sorted out their resources, surging alongside one another to pass over and share those odds and ends that they discovered and which gave both boats a fairer chance of surviving, should they become separated.

Once they were under way in the light breeze they bowled cheerfully along and this raised their morale. The upsurge of spirits, gratifying though it was, put a philosophical gloss upon their predicament, which was vulnerably mercurial. The *Fort Mackinac* had been sunk in the early forenoon. Midday was warm, with a hazy sun in a clearing sky; the afternoon was delightfully sunny, so sunny that wet gear quickly dried out when hung in the wind. An issue of spoonfuls of treacle from stoneware jars thoughtfully placed in the boats reinforced the unspoken determination to survive, and every face bore an expression of fortitude.

Even Dunbar shared in this euphoria to a degree, for all the pain to which he was subject. Though chilled to the bone, the sun did warm him and his injuries subsided to a dull, throbbing ache, persuading him that no permanent harm had been done. He was divested of his wet gear by Andrews, who handled him with an almost tender solicitude. He spent that day and the following night wrapped in blankets while his clothing dried out, apart from the heavy pilot coat, and even that was only damp by the second night. He was thus quite comfortable and took a gradual interest in the boat and her equipment.

In an attempt to talk him out of the apathy with which hypothermia had touched Dunbar, Bill Andrews briefed him with what, in the hiatus allowed them by the Germans, they had stocked the boat. They were indeed fortunate. Blankets, oilskin coats, boots, water and provisions seemed to be everywhere, so that the men almost enjoyed themselves stowing items away with child-like enthusiasm, as if this were some inconsequential adventure at the end of which a hearty tea might be anticipated.

The sun was westering on the second evening when

the first misgivings arose to menace them. Predictably it came from Grant who, being on watch, was perched in the bows forward of the mast thwart as the duty lookout.

'I've just thought of something,' he announced to them all.

'Whassat?' someone asked.

'Our fucking pay stops today.'

For a moment no-one said a word and then, like a breeze through dry grass, the small oaths of comprehension ran through the unfortunate castaways.

'Christ, it's true . . .'

'That's right . . .'

'The bastards . . .'

'What? D'you mean we don't get paid because the ship's sunk?'

'That, you bright sod,' replied Grant as though pleased to confirm the fact, 'is exactly what I mean.'

'Iss right, Mr Mate?' the old sailmaker asked Dunbar, who was lolling in the stern, next to Andrews on the tiller. He frowned and then recalled the clause in the articles.

He nodded. 'Yes, Sails, I'm afraid it is.'

'For ze officers also?'

'Yes. I think perhaps the captain would be all right, but the rest of us . . .' He shrugged.

'We are in ze same boat, ja?'

It was a thin joke and Dunbar was never sure whether the sailmaker understood his own pun. In any case, no-one laughed. The others in the boat were in no mood even to recognise it as such. Beside him, Andrews swore quietly with a comprehensive eloquence.

'Christ, trust Grant to unearth that. This could be bloody dangerous, Jim,' he muttered.

'I don't see what we can do about it at the moment,' Dunbar said. 'If a lot of ships are sunk like this, they may change it, but for the time being, we're—'

'*They*,' said a seaman nearby named Kingston, 'never

300

do a fucking thing for us. *They* will be cashing in their insurance policies.'

'Let us see what happens when we get home,' Dunbar said placatingly.

'*If* we get home,' retorted Kingston.

'Of course we're going to get home,' said Dunbar resolutely. 'Now, as it's sunset, let us have a water issue and then set watches for the night. We shall need the lantern at the masthead.' He set the boat a-bustle, giving the men something to do and to think about, something more urgent than the seed of miserable injustice that Grant had planted.

He thought he had accomplished something of this as those designated as being 'off duty' attempted to hunker down in some semblance of relaxation. Then Grant raised his head and called, 'Sweet dreams, lads, this is the first day of your unpaid excursion!'

Despite himself, Dunbar thought Grant's choice of words aggravatingly apt.

The night brought an increase in wind and a dull, unfriendly overcast. The gibbous moon appeared briefly, then spent most of the night obscured, but for an occasional period when it glowed fitfully through the clouds. The chill and the dew assailed them, despite their blankets and oilskins, and their constrained situation brought on a multitude of painful cramps, of pins-and-needles, numbness and the aching agony of stirring blood where it re-entered restricted blood vessels.

Even the masthead lantern seemed to emphasise their isolation, for though it showed itself to the other boat and though they frequently glimpsed the other boat's lamp, the yellow glow seemed to throw a cocoon of obscurity about them beyond the range of its illuminance. Half-asleep, it was possible to imagine themselves cast into space, abandoned and utterly forlorn, their universe bounded by the limits of that dim glow.

'The eye of Hecate,' Andrews observed obscurely to no-one in particular. 'The goddess of the night.'

'Couldn't I just do a goddess of the night right now,' a neighbouring and unidentified voice responded.

'You've only one fuck in you,' someone else chipped in, 'and that's holding you together!'

A tiny chuckle greeted this witticism and then silence fell, a silence relative to the moan of the wind, the slosh and slap of the sea on the plank lands, the occasional hiss and muted roar as a wave broke alongside them, accompanied by the patter of spray. There was also the periodic slap of the sail as it collapsed when the boat lolled to windward, then filled again with a sharp crack as she rolled away again.

Dawn came with an increase of the wind. Dunbar woke cold and cramped in the grey twilight, confused as to whether he was supposed to be on watch. Responsibility fell upon him along with guilt that he had been asleep, but Andrews reassured him.

'You've got two hours of glorious sleep left,' he said.

Dunbar grunted and sat up. Spray hit him like spent bird-shot, making him gasp in the wind-ache that followed.

'Shit!' he swore.

'You're on the mend, Mr Dunbar,' grinned Kingston on the tiller.

'I don't bloody feel like it.'

'That bloody Boche officer duffed you up then?'

Dunbar nodded. 'Yes.'

'An' the bastard killed poor old Crawlie.'

'Yes.'

'Maybe he's better out of it.' Kingston paused, then asked, 'What are our chances, sir?'

Dunbar looked at the man. He was new to the *Fort Mackinac*'s crew, a steady, competent and experienced sailor, a pale face under his sou'wester, staring ahead and glancing down at the compass, but steering for the most part by the wind. Briefly, Dunbar stared at the image. Once his fingers would have itched for his pencil. Now duty compelled him to consider the question. Like Dunbar, it was unlikely that Kingston had ever experienced anything like this.

Dunbar blew out his cheeks. 'Realistically,' he said slowly, 'I'd say that if we are careful, if we prepare for the worst and hope for the best, I think we should make it.' Then a thought struck him. 'Somewhere,' he said plunging his hands into his jacket pocket, glad that he had taken the trouble to dress sensibly before he had come on deck the previous morning, 'I've got the ship's position . . .'

But the scrap of paper had gone. Sometime in the terror of the previous day he had lost it, flushed from his pocket by the invasive sea. He hid his disappointment. 'Anyway, as I was saying, I'm pretty confident we can pull through.'

'I hope you're right, sir.' Kingston's deference made Dunbar feel simultaneously warmed and isolated. It was a response to the order in the boat and re-established the conventions of shipboard life; it was also an indicator of the expectations that simple men had of him. He was the officer. If nothing else, they assumed that he enjoyed a superior knowledge to themselves. Knowledge might buy him a measure of scanty privilege aboard ship, but here, *in extremis*, it also placed him under an obligation to pay back the dividend required by the enjoyment of those privileges.

The thought was gloomy. Had he been fit and well, Dunbar might have embraced the responsibility with a degree of enthusiasm. Every ambitious sea-officer aspired to his first command and, on a scale of responsibility, a ship's lifeboat adrift in time of war offered him a challenge that in a former life he would have seized gladly.

But this was no adventure by Mr Ballantyne, nor by Kingston's namesake; this was the grim reality of war, of survival and of possible death. He felt ill-equipped to bear such a burden, hampered as he was by swollen testicles, a sore throat, aching ribs and a lump on his head like a small potato. In this depressed state of mind Dunbar embarked upon the third day of their abandonment.

Until darkness that evening the two boats were in sight of one another. Twice they ran alongside each other and traded cheery exchanges. Both officers, Dunbar and Nicholls, publicly agreed that their chances of running athwart the steamer routes to and from the Cape were excellent and their course the best one for such an interception.

Those most knowing or most optimistic among the boat's crews nodded their heads in agreement. Then Grant brought up the matter of their pay again. Clearly the thought had struck no-one in the second mate's boat; they were all novices at war. Thus permeated with gloom, the boats parted in poor spirits.

'Why did you have to mention that again, Grant?' Andrews asked angrily.

'Because it's true,' Grant riposted. 'This is a fucking unpaid excursion.'

'So you've told us already.'

'Well then.'

'But it doesn't help us to keep cheerful, does it?' remonstrated Andrews.

'Who the fuck wants to keep cheerful in a situation like this?' Grant asked with a convincing logic, which elicited a few grunts of agreement from the pessimists among them.

'Well, if you don't keep cheerful, you won't survive.'

'Bollocks!'

'It's true. You must think positively to sustain yourself. Think of Robinson Crusoe and Man Friday.'

'I never sailed with either of them.'

'You can scoff, you silly sod.'

'Who are you calling a sod?'

'Sit down!' Dunbar commanded. 'Andrews is right, lads.' Dunbar addressed the men generally. 'Our first priority is to look after ourselves.'

'I never said it wasn't,' put in Grant.

'Pipe down, Grant. We shall run into a steamer in a day or two, I'm sure. We're making four or five knots,' Dunbar estimated optimistically, 'that's over a hundred miles a day and the boat's taking up all the time and already making less water. If this wind holds, well, who knows? Maybe we'll be laughing aboard a Castle liner this time tomorrow!'

'May-fucking-be,' grumbled Grant.

But Grant's reminder of their forgotten status seemed to have sapped the collective morale of them all. It had the finality of financial imperative, conveying a tacit message that they were of no account. In this onset of mild hopelessness, the first serious inroads of hypothermia began to sap them of the will to live.

The last sight of the other boat, sometime before midnight, seemed to mark a turn for the worse. The superstitious would believe that the will to stay together was taken from them and that the realisation of their employer's abandonment was their martyrdom. No-one would ever know that in Nicholls's boat they had forgotten to refill the lamp's reservoir, the lamp died out and no-one could be bothered to relight it. 'We'll be in sight of each other by daylight,' Nicholls's second-in-command, the bosun, affirmed lethargically.

He should have known better: at sea such assumptions can never be made. A small divergence in course, steadily maintained during the hours of darkness, was sufficient to separate the two boats beyond their respective visible horizons. Both crews woke to an increased feeling of isolation upon the inhospitable sea.

During the next day the wind got up to a near gale and, in Dunbar's boat, the first man began to suffer severely from exposure. The drowsiness that presaged this slow form of death is, to those enduring such privation, seen by the victim as a welcome relief. The *Fort Mackinac*'s cook, John Eagleton, was ill-clad for an open boat voyage and, although he had been loaned some extra kit in the form of double blankets, he remained ill-suited to the conditions. Used to a warm galley, he was less adapted than most of the others and soon fell victim to the seductive apathy. The cold, which was not yet severe, seemed to him to be relieved by a detachment accompanied by a welcome warm feeling. This wholly false inducement was deadly; the survivor stopped shivering and his inner body temperature continued to fall. Eagleton's breathing became shallower and his heartbeat slowed.

No-one noticed the pallor on the man's face, or the uncharacteristic puffiness of his features, for they began during the hours of darkness. All their clothes had become damp and the increase in wind sped the process of evaporation, which in turn robbed all their bodies of heat. By dawn Eagleton's apathy was seen simply as prolonged drowsiness, evidence of a poor night's sleep. Others suffered to some extent, but their reflexive movements upon wakening with stiff muscles rescued them and, for a while, they staved off the onset of hypothermia.

At the change of watch Andrews, doling out the biscuit and water forming their meagre breakfast, noticed the somnolent state of Eagleton and raised a belated alarm. Dunbar reached into his coat and produced the small bottle of spirits that had mercifully remained intact and handed this forward. A slug or two was forced into Eagleton. Well meant, this specific succeeded only in enlarging the cook's capillaries, surrendering more heat to the atmosphere. It was a fatal remedy; they knew so little of the reactions of their own bodies.

Eagleton was dead by noon.

In the succeeding three days they lost four more men to the same cause. Now they were subjected to alternate sousings by spray and the excoriating of a cold wind. There seemed little they could do. Dunbar, officiating at the makeshift burials, found it hard to concentrate as they slid the bodies over the side, unweighted, to bob in their wake until out of sight, and marked only by a curious assembly of squawking gulls. It was clear they had to cover themselves, to protect their bodies from as much spray as possible, but this seemed to be extraordinarily difficult. Water got in everywhere, despite the ingenious use of their oilskins and the extra material stripped off their dead comrades. Their fingers and thumbs mutinied against the commands of their brains. So fumbled was the simple act of taking down the long-extinguished lantern and unbending it from the halliard that it took almost a quarter of an hour to carry out this simple task.

Although they did not know it, most of the boat's crew were now suffering the first stage of hypothermia. All were shivering to some extent, confusion and disorientation marking their movements which, when directed by any desire to do anything – to eat, drink, tie a knot or tuck a blanket about them, even to urinate

– were marked by a ponderous and indecisive slowness. Most fought these symptoms by excessive movement, aggravating their neighbours, so that oaths and pathetic, almost idiotic quarrels flared up and died away.

Those that had been in the watch-below when the *Augsburg* attacked and were least well clad slipped most easily into the adynamic stage of the condition, when pallor and mild amnesia affected them. Sharing the spare gear had come too late; the inner temperatures of their bodies had dropped irreversibly, fatally. They became difficult to feed, spilt their water ration in the giddily moving boat, urinated uncontrollably, slipping into torpor and rigidity with staring eyes.

It seemed at one terrible moment to the shivering Dunbar that he was surrounded by an insane crew, all of whom regarded him with a madly expectant stare. He felt that their expressions burned with accusation, imagined the turbulence of their resentful thoughts invoking hellish tortures upon himself, unknowing that such mental effort had passed far beyond them.

As the days passed, he learned too that as the eyes lost their silent accusation and the stiff muscles relaxed, these men were irredeemably lost to the world. For perhaps an hour they would lie silent, lolling in a protracted death throe that seemed like nothing else, other than a slow withdrawal from this world.

To the watching Dunbar this almost stealthy departure, devoid of the manners and customs of a noble and worthy death, seemed an affront. That his own foresight and prudence in dressing with especial care, in wearing wool and not himself drinking alcohol, had saved him could not occur to him in those long, lonely apathetic hours. If he thought logically at all, it was to wonder why, battered as he was, he had not himself succumbed. Much of the organisation of the boat he was content to leave to Andrews, who, half-aware that the duty in some way kept him active and thinking, was only too happy to carry it out.

Yet those stares affected Dunbar and fomented a deep anger, which drew its motivation from several sources. He felt increasingly a resentment and outrage at Ketlar's conduct in killing Crawhall. And it was this simmering affront that slowly became the anger that saved Dunbar. Deep anger stimulates the heart, and, just as Andrews drew his inner strength from the responsibility that Dunbar's bruised condition delegated to him, so Dunbar himself was stirred by a desire to wreak vengeance on Ketlar, if only by surviving to tell the tale.

The first manifestation of Dunbar's determination was an alteration of course. By now few in the boat were in a fit condition to argue with him as he ordered the tiller put up and the boat run off before the wind. It was clumsily done, as was everything now, but whatever rational argument was put up against the change of direction was swiftly dispelled by two things.

The first was Dunbar's argument that they had seen nothing of any confounded steamer and that their boat compass might be suffering from a greater deviation than they knew. Allied to this was the certainty that if they were to head much further south, the temperature would fall further and the weather was likely to worsen.

The second was the immediate benefit of the loss of the cross-wind. With the boat running before wind and sea, though her speed was less than it had been on a reach, the apparent wind was minimal and far less icy spray slopped aboard. It thus seemed perceptibly warmer. They were still reasonably well provisioned, though their water was giving some cause for concern, but such was the torpid state of all their minds that neither Dunbar nor Andrews could work out exactly how long this would last. They were incapable of carrying out simple arithmetical division accurately, and even when they had thought they had done so, they could never agree on a consistent figure.

Such preoccupations took a long time, and time was something they began to lose track of. As day succeeded day there was only darkness and light, and the twilit zones marked those periods when they doled out biscuit and water with painful slowness.

The progress of the boat herself was subject to similar factors. From time to time she would gybe, the loose-footed mainsail flapping across the boat and the swinging sheet occasionally flogging an unwary survivor until the boat became emptied enough for them to leave the arc of its wild swing free.

By then death had become a commonplace. Men died not of starvation or scurvy, or any of the other historic curses of seamen, though dietary deficiencies had begun their own remorseless process of attrition. It was exposure that killed them, a condition which, once it had taken hold, was almost impossible to reverse. On the fifteenth day, however, death demonstrated its own versatility.

Grant, whose steady complaining had finally subsided, greeted the dawn with low groans. Like all the other occupants of the boat, Grant was suffering from exposure, though the fittest and most active were still only partially affected. The general debility was so endemic that for a while Grant's moaning went as unremarked as Eagleton's condition had done. But after a while Dunbar became fractious. Irritated that Grant should once again dominate the boat with so depressing a noise, he bestirred himself. He stumbled forward to see what was the matter with Grant.

The able-seaman was cold to the touch, already entering the final stages of hypothermia, close to the almost total inertia of apparent death. Pallid and immobile, in a sitting position, Grant leaned against the mast. He stared unseeing at Dunbar, who recollected the unpleasantness he had suffered at the hands of this man.

'Love thine enemy . . .'

The words came into his head quite unbidden. His father's voice spoke them, echoing with that sonorous majesty which, as the rector's son, the young Dunbar had heard with a mixture of embarrassment and fear. '. . . as thyself.'

It suddenly became important to save Grant, partly because the man's perversity invited salvation, partly as the first act of defying the death sentence pronounced upon them all by the unknown captain of the German cruiser, and partly because keeping Grant alive was a snub to Graf von Ketlar.

'Damn it! I will save you, you bastard,' Dunbar muttered, 'or die in the attempt!'

He thought to stretch Grant out. With a great effort he freed a bottom board and laid it across two thwarts to form a rough, extemporised bed. Then, by dint of persuasion and manhandling, all accomplished as the boat rose and fell to the seas under-running her, he managed to get Grant horizontal on this makeshift platform. As he did so, the sodden state of the man's serge trousers became apparent, as did the stream of water that ran out of Grant's sea-boots.

The deaths had created a surplus of blankets, so Dunbar resolved to tuck Grant up. He himself was gaining strength with every minute that he worked, as the blood, surging round under the impetus of his young heart and an ancient anger, slowly warmed his own extremities.

Unable to pull Grant's boots off, Dunbar attacked them with a knife. A child knows the agony of cold feet, and it thus seemed the logical thing to try and warm Grant's wet

311

feet; in fact, Dunbar's action saved Grant's life, for the man's feet were already half-dead from immersion-foot. Removal of his heavy woollen socks exposed feet that were swollen and white, almost icy to the touch. Dunbar covered them with a spare jacket, then lit the lantern and, wrapping a blanket around its glass globe, allowed this to heat through. Then he transferred the warmed blanket to Grant's feet, repeating the process after half an hour.

'Why didn't we think of that before?' the watching Andrews asked, his voice croaking.

Dunbar shook his head and shrugged. The boat was well supplied with lamp oil. The matter was quite incomprehensible. 'I shall never take being warm for granted again,' he finally said to Andrews, looking round. 'How many men did we have when we started?'

'You made the numbers up to fifteen,' Andrews replied. Dunbar carefully counted those remaining, then, for fear of being wrong, repeated the head-count. There were only seven remaining; eight men had perished from the cold. He went round the boat, touching each man, shaking them awake if they were drowsy.

'Wake up, wake up! You're on watch, all of you, you're on watch. You're on Paddy's watches: go on and stay on! Don't sleep! From now on, there's to be no sleeping . . .' Dunbar's voice rose hoarsely until he was railing at them stupidly. But they all stirred, to swear at him.

'Come on, you two, Kingston and you, Wells,' he said, other ideas coming to him. 'Get either side of Grant. Bring your blankets and lie down next to the bugger. Come on. Don't look at me like that. I'm not asking you to shag him! Warm the poor bastard. I'll put hot blankets over you.'

For a moment the seaman and the apprentice stared in disbelief at Dunbar. His face, cracked and puffy itself, was like a mask. But his eyes glittered contentiously; he was still the mate, a man who, though young, was used to giving orders. The old habit of obedience asserted itself. Wells felt the potency of Dunbar's glare more keenly than the freezing discomfort of his cramped body. Slowly, bracing himself against the lurch of the boat, he did as he was bid. Then Kingston followed him. Dunbar returned to his duty of warming portions of damp blanket round the lantern.

Dunbar never knew why it was that particular morning that he came out of his stupor, but in the late afternoon they were sighted by a north-bound steamer. The fourth officer of the SS *Clytemnestra*, a Blue Funnel liner bound from Brisbane to Liverpool, had been preparing to take star sights and, while dropping Venus to the horizon, had picked up a flash of the quadrilateral mainsail of the *Fort Mackinac*'s port boat in the optics of his sextant.

Called to the bridge, the *Clytemnestra*'s master, Captain Evans, ordered his ship's course altered. An hour later, having made a lee for the boat and got the survivors to drop their sail, one of his own lifeboats had run alongside and embarked the remainder of the *Fort Mackinac*'s crew.

Then Evans rang on full speed and the Blue Funnel liner sped away to northwards, leaving the empty boat bobbing in her wake.

'Sunk by a bloody cruiser, were you?' Evans enquired, examining his newly acquired passengers in the ship's hospital later on. 'Any idea of her name?'

'*Augsburg*, sir,' Andrews volunteered. 'I read it on their boat when they boarded and on the cap tallies of the seamen.'

'Well done. What direction did she leave in?'

'South and west, sir, as far as I remember,' volunteered Dunbar.

'Thank God for that then. And you were the barque's mate?'

'Yes.'

'And the master?'

'He was shot by the officer who boarded us, a man called von Ketlar.'

'Shot, you say? *Diawl*, the bastards!' Evans jotted the name down in his pocket book. 'And what was your master's name?'

'Captain Crawhall.'

Evans wrote that down too and shook his head. 'I didn't know him,' he said, as if he should have done. 'Murdered in cold blood, you say?'

'Yes, sir.'

'Well, we can talk about this when you are rested. The doctor here will see that you are all right. Lucky it was us that picked you up. Not every ship's got a doctor on board.'

'There's one other thing, sir,' Dunbar said.

'Yes, what's that?'

'Two boats left the ship, sir. I don't suppose you've heard anything of the second mate's?'

Captain Evans shook his head. 'No, I'm sorry, Mr Dunbar. When did you last see the other boat?'

'About ten days ago . . .'

'It was twelve, sir,' corrected Andrews. 'Mr Dunbar won't recall much of the first two because of his injuries.'

Evans nodded. 'Well, there's not much chance now. Perhaps they've already been picked up. I'll tell my officers to keep a lookout, of course, but we've troops on board and my orders are to proceed without delay.'

He left them with the guilty feeling that they should have made more effort to keep in touch with Nicholls's boat.

'How the devil did you know that Boche officer's name, Jim?' Andrews asked after a while.

'Long story,' replied Dunbar, suddenly feeling very tired. 'Tell you one day,' he said yawning.

CHAPTER SEVENTEEN

The Averroist

The *Clytemnestra* steamed north at fourteen knots, her decks swarming with soldiers of the First Australian Expeditionary Force. Among these khaki-clad men the tiny handful of survivors from the *Fort Mackinac* were an insignificant addition. Placed under the supervision of the ship's doctor, they found themselves briefly the cynosure of the bored battalion medical staff accompanying the fresh-faced, eager young men *en route* to do their bit for the Mother Country.

The young 'medics', dreaming of the professional challenges of battle-field surgery, viewed Grant's immersion-foot with only passing interest. The condition had yet to become epidemic and revoltingly familiar to them, changing its name in due course to 'trench-foot'. Grant's condition was not so severe as to produce a dramatic amputation, and they drifted away with a vague air of disappointment. He lost only three toes, further gangrene was averted and medical interest in him evaporated.

Such were the conditions on board the liner that, though weak and flaccid for several days, none of those rescued from the boat deteriorated further. Warm and dry, well fed and rested, their hard life under sail had fitted them for privation and their restoration to health was simply a matter of time.

Despite the omnipresent soldiery, the war seemed very distant and the might of so substantial a ship as the *Clytemnestra*, built as she was to the massive scantlings of her owner's own standard, seemed immune to its effects. A week later, as she steamed through the blue seas of the southern tropics, Dunbar and Andrews were lounging on Number 6 hatch. Apart from meal times, when Dunbar ate in the officers' saloon, such were the calls upon the crowded liner's accommodation that the difference in their ranks was eroded. They were simply survivors, technically known as Distressed British Seamen, and as such obliged Captain Evans to feed and house them until he could land them at a British port. Now they yarned as old shipmates, men who had suffered together and who viewed each other in the light of that experience.

'What on earth made you suddenly come to life that last morning?' Andrews asked as they lay basking in the sunshine. 'I was quite done in. I think if you had not roused yourself, none of us would have lasted the next night.'

Dunbar shrugged. 'I don't know. I suppose when you pulled me out of the water I myself was at the end of my tether. That bloody German had knocked me about so much, and I had had such difficulty getting out of the charthouse and over the side, that I wasn't any use for some days.' Dunbar paused. 'I reckon I just felt better. . .' He frowned, 'No, I remember I started to get angry. I started to recall what had happened. I decided I wasn't going to give up and die. That was too easy; it was what that bastard wanted, why he shut me in the charthouse.'

'He shut you in?'

Dunbar nodded. 'Yes, I think so. It seems to me now that he wanted me dead.'

'Because you knew his name and had witnessed what he did to Crawlie.'

'Yes. But probably more for the former than the latter.'

'He could have shot you too.'

'No, he couldn't quite bring himself to do that.'

'Because he knew you?'

'Yes.'

'How did he know you?'

'Oh, we met in London. We had friends in common. He was studying there,' Dunbar answered evasively, unwilling to have all the sordid truth dragged out of him. 'It was all so long ago that it hardly seems real now.'

'I know what you mean. I think you called this man Kepler, like the astronomer,' Andrews went on.

'No, Ketlar. Ernst von Ketlar . . .'

'Ernst Ketlar?' Andrews frowned, then added quickly, 'Ah, I understand. An Ernst Ketlar was an artist, wasn't he? Could it be the same man? I saw some of his work once. Nudes.' He paused, then said, 'I saw your exhibition too.'

Astonished, Dunbar sat up. 'You did what?'

Andrews smiled. 'I saw your exhibition. In Hampstead. It was very good. I was impressed, though not as impressed as the little dolly I took with me.'

'You outrageous bugger, Andrews,' Dunbar said amiably. 'You never told me. And who was this critic, Dolly?'

Andrews sighed. 'A little tart from Whitechapel. She'd been an artist's model herself, among other things. There was a group of Jewish artists there; she used to pose for them. One day she took me to see a painting of her done by this man Ketlar. I'm sure it was by him. It was very erotic.'

'It would be.' Dunbar frowned. 'But Ketlar wasn't exhibiting with the Jewish artists, was he?'

'Oh, yes.'

'And your Dolly . . .'

'Her name was Ida, an awful name, but it was a small price to pay.'

'What, for a guide to an exhibition of erotic art?' Dunbar asked with unconcealed, prurient interest.

'Yes; that and other things! She had rooms – you know, Jack ashore has to sleep somewhere.'

'You know, Bill, it has always been a mystery to me how you haven't died of the pox.'

'Simple. Always piss five minutes after a fuck. Guaranteed.'

'And pray for good luck . . ..'

'I'm surprised at you, after the last two weeks. How many good men died through doing nothing more evil than getting cold? I long ago concluded it's all a wild game of hazard.'

'All right. I'm not making judgements.' Dunbar looked at Andrews. 'You'll forgive me for saying this, but you aren't a typical able-seaman.' A look of passing irritation crossed Andrews's face. 'I'm sorry, I didn't mean to pry,' Dunbar said quickly.

'Of course you didn't,' Andrews replied with a brittle smile. 'I suppose it's a natural enough question. But I visited that exhibition not because I'm cultured, if that's what you're alluding to, but because I was taken there by Ida.'

'What about Hampstead?'

'I read about that in a newspaper. You were described as "a new talent in an old tradition" and your work was "vigorous, manly and what was to expected of one of our merchant seamen with a keen and observant eye".'

'I recognise the unfaltering style of Icarus Dacre,' laughed Dunbar. 'But what did *you* think of the pictures? There was one of you, I recall.'

'I've already told you I was impressed. Besides, you must remember, I had seen most of them, including my own likeness.' Andrews hesitated a moment and screwed his face up in an attractive grimace. 'I must admit, it was an odd sensation seeing myself there, along with that villain Grant.' Andrews laughed, adding in a serious tone, 'You are a very competent painter, Jim, but you aren't an artist. Not yet anyway.'

'Oh?'

'You lack a theme. That critic Dacre was right in so far as you have talent and energy, but you need a – I don't know – a message. I think that's the right word; or a polemic thesis. That's it, a polemic thesis. The portraits were good, they said "here we are", but I suspect the *cognoscenti* would retort "So bloody what?" Those Jewish blokes in Whitechapel issued a manifesto. I hasten to say I never read the bloody thing – it seemed too full of overblown and incomprehensible statements of intent that no painter could possibly achieve – but I suppose it gave them something to live by.' Andrews looked at Dunbar, who was staring at the horizon. 'Oh dear,' he added, 'I suppose *I've* put my foot in it now.'

Dunbar turned to his friend. 'No, not at all. I was just thinking about what you said. I guess you are right. I enjoyed painting, but I never *cared* about it, not deeply. Not like the others. Even that bastard Ketlar cared . . .'

'I suppose a degree of dedication doesn't necessarily develop a pleasing personality,' Andrews said, adding flippantly, 'in fact, being a dedicated artist might be excellent training for piracy. Ida used to say he treated his models with contempt.'

'Yes.' Dunbar thought of Maureen, then asked with a slow uncertainty, 'D'you think the sinking of the *Fort Mackinac*, the shooting of Crawhall and our subsequent ordeal in the boat would make a series of paintings?'

'Do you?' Andrews fired back.

Dunbar looked at his interlocutor and said slowly, 'Yes, yes, I think I do.'

'Well then. You don't need a credo or a bloody manifesto. Your anger will transform your work. Look what it did for us all that last day. Whatever that Boche bastard Ketlar has done, he may ultimately have done you a favour.'

'You mean,' responded Dunbar drily, 'that there is a danger that I might owe my transformation into an artist to Ketlar? My word, that *would* be an irony.'

'I think,' said Andrews slowly, 'in all seriousness, allowing of course for the fact that I am no judge of these matters, that you have an instinct for the thing. I just feel that you are capable of better, more committed work. It's difficult for me to explain. It's not something I think about much and I certainly don't articulate it more than once in a blue moon, because I gave up on the world a long time ago and don't really give a monkey's shit for it.'

'D'you mind my asking why?'

'No,' Andrews smiled, 'I don't mind you asking.' He paused a moment, then said, 'The reason, at least in its abstract sense, is that I'm a victim of despair. Your father would consider that highly reprehensible, though I have never quite understood why despair is regarded as a great sin. Perhaps,' Andrews sighed, 'our present personal circumstances underline the hopelessness of our situation as human beings. If you look at what your friend Ketlar and his bloody cruiser achieved, it was a completely uncivilised, irrational and pointlessly stupid act, unless you look at it within the framework of warfare. Then it has a horribly rational logic, for it was a consequence of what Ketlar and his bloodthirsty ilk would call patriotism. Didn't someone, Dr Johnson I think it was, say that patriotism was the last refuge of scoundrels? Well, he was right. Look at these young men aboard here, all about to be victims of patriotism. We should have learned about modern war from the South African business; and fifty years earlier there was the Crimea, all a ghastly mess.' Andrews paused for a moment, then went on with a change of tack, 'If I thought for one moment that the righting of wrongs was possible,

321

or that having righted them they would remain thus; if I thought the wisdom of one generation could, like the trunk of a tree, provide the basis for the wisdom of the next to graft itself upon and produce a steadily progressive growth, then perhaps you might persuade me to be one of your muscular Christians. But alas, it is the tragedy of mankind to have to constantly relearn the lessons of its forefathers.'

Andrews was staring out over the rail to where the sun was descending slowly towards a heavy cloud bank. The sea was a curious brilliant jade green, the sun a red-bronze globe in a scarlet sky, the clouds a fantastic, castellated landscape.

'The problem is compounded by scientific progress, which makes each relearning process increasingly difficult. Look at how the *Augsburg* dispatched our poor old ship with a few shells from her secondary armament. A couple of generations ago it was almost impossible to sink a ship. You could shoot away her top-hamper, set her on fire and massacre her crew, but now you can send her to the bottom with a brace or two of shells.' He paused and turned to Dunbar with a smile. 'There, d'you think your old dad would forgive me my despair?'

Dunbar grinned back. 'No, of course not. He would argue for constancy in the long struggle, that there might one day be an enlightened generation, when things have got so bad that there is some enormous change, like the Renaissance. He would also say that you are too much involved with this world, and too little concerned with the next.'

'And d'you believe in all that?'

Dunbar shrugged. 'Sometimes I wonder why it is necessary to have an opinion about everything. Sometimes I wonder why I can't just wonder.'

'Because it's so bloody unsatisfactory!'

'Well, who says we're supposed to be satisfied?'

'Our intellects yearn for it in the same way that our bodies do, and don't tell me *that's* just for procreation!'

'I wouldn't. I'm sure what you do with Ida has little to do with procreation,' Dunbar laughed.

'Absolutely. Quite the reverse.' Andrews paused, then asked, 'Have you ever loved a woman like that?'

Dunbar nodded. 'My first experience was in a brothel . . .'

'Ah,' Andrews broke in, 'a brothel is the only honest institution on earth.'

'But whereas I fell hopelessly in love with a beautiful young whore, she had eyes only for money and I was spurned. Most humiliating.'

Andrews shook his head in commiseration. 'A humiliation indeed, but proof of my contention of the probity of the inhabitants of brothels.'

'Instead,' Dunbar went on, ignoring Andrews's facetiousness, 'I became attached to an older woman. She was not a whore, but acted as madame and may well once have plied her trade, though she was not a slut. It's a long story, but while I never loved her in any true, enduring sense, there grew something between us. I painted her.'

'And doubtless did it very well,' Andrews said quietly in the silence that followed the end of Dunbar's reminiscence.

Dunbar shrugged. 'People seemed to think so.'

'And?'

'And what?'

'And is that all?'

'You're a persistent bugger. More or less. I formed a liaison with a young woman back in England. It came to nothing and she married. At least, I suppose her to be married by now. Anyway, I'm ashamed to say I rather ruthlessly used a most beautiful creature whom, I fear, I treated rather badly, whom I hurt and have not stopped thinking about since. Except perhaps in the boat. No, I don't recall thinking of her there.'

'Did you think of her when you were drowning, or thought you were drowning?'

Dunbar shook his head. 'No. I remember distinctly lying on the charthouse deck quite reconciled to dying. There seemed to be a great attraction in it. It must have been something to do with the injuries Ketlar had given me. No man feels himself after a kick in the bollocks. At that moment, death seemed to invite me into the wholeness of life. Does that make sense? I'm not sure it does to me, really, but that's the way I felt, that I would be returning to something huge, dark and awesome, some tremendous embrace, a kind of completeness, a great universal soul.'

'You sound like an averroist.'

'A *what*?'

'A follower of Averroës, a twelfth-century Arabian philosopher who thought that the individual soul died and returned to a central, universal and immortal soul, whence the spirits of the newly born were drawn.'

'I've never heard of him.'

'Well it's not an idea that's likely to catch on, is it?' They laughed, then Andrews added, 'But no lover appeared to you in these moments.'

'No. Oddly, she seems to have faded out of the picture. I'm not certain why, unless it was her essential unattainability.'

'Oh, come on. You said yourself you shagged her. You're expecting too much. What d'you want – undying and wonderful union? Read about it in books, for it doesn't exist in reality.'

'No, we shagged each other. I'm not ashamed of the act of coitus. It was afterwards . . .'

'You got rough with her?' Dunbar nodded. He felt the need to shrive himself of this unwholesome memory. There was no room for mitigating circumstances; they were irrelevant. Andrews shrugged. 'It happens. I don't know why. I think some women like it. It means they're not being taken for granted and, for all its nastiness, I think it derives from a fear that men have of women.'

'Fear?'

'No, not fear exactly, that's too simplistic. Rather, resentment at their need for them. A sort of irksome beholdenness, if you see what I mean.'

'Yes.'

The sun had disappeared behind the clouds. The fantastic, cumuloid coastline had vanished, though the sun's light radiated through the crenellated gaps in the rim of the cloud bank and gilded them for a few, fleeting moments.

'Did you paint her?'

'No.'

'D'you regret not doing so?'

'Yes. Yes, I suppose I do.'

'Then you must,' said Andrews briskly. He shivered and rose to his feet. 'It's getting cold. I don't like feeling chilly nowadays.'

As the *Clytemnestra* clove her way north unmolested by any enemy, their evening chats became habitual. Unaffected by the rituals of the military routine that piped the soldiers to their bunks, the *Fort Mackinac*'s survivors enjoyed the luxury of unemployed idleness. The pressure on the ship's accommodation meant that they all remained in the hospital, a small portion of the poop deckhouse, the larger part of which was the galley for the multitude of Chinese who kept running the complex machinery that constituted the *Clytemnestra*. Firemen, greasers, cooks and stewards lived in the poop, ruled over by their own headmen, the Number One Donkeyman and the Tiger. The seamen lived forward in the forecastle, under the Chinese bosun, whose remit ran with almost the same authority as Captain Evans's own in that farthest extremity of the ship.

Among the exotic smells of Cantonese cuisine, where the ship's company's dhobi was augmented with that taken in by the opportunistic Chinese stewards from the officers of four battalions of imperial infantry, and where, rustling like rushes, the corpses of several hundred patiently strung fish dried in the wind and sun, the refugees enjoyed the peaceful reconstruction of their lives. Only the vibration of the screws under the counter disturbed the tranquillity of their existence, if one discounted the daily inspection by Captain Evans, his senior officers and those of the embarked battalions.

Apart from eating in the saloon, the other privilege granted to Dunbar as an officer was the freedom of the bridge, where he was able to take an informed interest in the ship's progress and keep his hand in at the occasional sight with a borrowed sextant. His moments there, free of the overcrowding that elsewhere was endemic, were of great benefit to him. His position as a former chief officer conferred upon him a status exceeded only by the *Clytemnestra*'s own chief officer and Captain Evans, for the ship's company regarded the commissions of the military officers as of little account, relevant only in so far as regulating the soldiery was concerned. In all other cases, even the colonel who was acting as brigadier was regarded with that easy-going, tolerant contempt that seamen have for all those uninitiated into the arcane mysteries of their profession. Set against these bored, ubiquitous khaki-drab denizens of the lower decks, Dunbar enjoyed a clear advantage. Occupancy of the hallowed planking of the bridge was therefore a rare privilege, and one to be cherished.

Dunbar tried to draw parallels between the *Clytemnestra* and the old steam tramps of the South Wales Steam Navigation Company. But she was so obviously superior, so clearly owned by a company whose acumen enabled them to run their ships above the bare requirements of satisfying shareholders and squeezing profits, whose concern for the welfare of their crews would, Dunbar was almost persuaded in believing, have ameliorated those in their employment who suffered the misfortune of losing their livelihood by enemy action, that the idea of serving in a well-run liner company suddenly offered a stark contrast to the rough life under sail.

Such was the seduction in this ambience that, on the first evening that Grant ventured out on his crutches, Dunbar put this point to the able-seaman. It was a well-meant remark, designed to heal the rift between them, but Grant's response suggested that the ordeal in the boat had robbed him of more than his toes.

The sun had set, and Andrews and Dunbar were on the point of turning in when Grant appeared on deck.

'Well,' Dunbar said, looking up from the scrubbed hatch tarpaulin of Number 6, where he and Andrews sat yarning, 'what d'you think of steam ships now, Grant?'

'What should I think of the bloody things?' he responded.

'It was lucky this one came along when it did, wouldn't you say?'

'I wouldn't say fuck-all, Mr Dunbar. What would you say about it?' Grant asked with a heavy and menacing sarcasm. 'I mean, you should know. You know all about everything. I shouldn't wonder if you gave our position away, what with your knowing that German officer.'

'What the hell are you talking about?'

'You knew him, that Kraut. I heard Andrews there ask how you knew him. He must be as mystified as me, though I knew you stank of trouble, the first time I set eyes on you.'

'Are you suggesting that I had something to do with the sinking of the *Fort Mackinac*?' Dunbar asked incredulously. 'What in God's name gives you that idea?' The proposition seemed so preposterous to Dunbar that he had difficulty in grasping it. He looked at Andrews for some sort of explanation, as if he could interpret these wild and irrational accusations, but Andrews only shrugged.

'Bugger's gone loco,' he muttered.

'Loco? You think I'm crazy, do you?' Grant shouted, his senses heightened to an acute state. 'Well, that'd suit you just fine, wouldn't it? Poor bloody Grant gone plumb loco. Stop his pay and stop his mouth. What you going to do next, eh? Kill him?'

'Oh fuck off, Grant. You're talking through your arse.' Andrews dismissed his fellow-seaman.

Grant let go of one crutch and wagged a finger at Andrews. 'You're in this too, I know. You're too bloody friendly with the officers. You always were; you don't belong amongst decent seamen. You're a Judas.'

'I think, Grant,' said Dunbar reasonably, 'it would be a good idea if you turned in. It's nearly dark.'

Grant nodded his head. 'Oh yes, I'll turn in all right, but I won't sleep. You bastards are in it with the rest. How does a British mate know a German naval officer, except they've been friends, eh? Can't tell me, can you, because there's no other answer.'

Grant stumped off and Andrews expelled his breath. 'What in the name of all that's holy . . . ?'

'Has he been drinking?' Dunbar asked.

'No, I don't think so, and certainly not obviously.'

'Then the balance of his mind is seriously disturbed.'

'That's a bloody understatement. It's this business of our pay ceasing,' said Andrews with a sigh. 'To be fair, it *is* a terrible injustice.'

'I agree. It includes me, but I can't see that it's my fault.'

'No, of course not, Jim, but he can't disentangle the whole mess. I don't know what happened to us in that boat, but it may be that Grant suffered more than we realised.'

'I can hear you.' Both men looked up. Grant loomed at the forward poop rail, stationed midway between the steam winches for the after-derricks.

'You're the bastard that got us here, Dunbar.'

'Mr Dunbar saved your life, Grant. Go to bed and don't be such an ungrateful shit.'

'He saved his own skin more like.' Grant waved his fist and his crutch fell to the deck with a clatter. 'He'll sink this ship next, you mark my words. You can smell death on him! I'd keep away from him, Andrews, if I were you.'

'Well, fortunately you're not me, so fuck off!'

'Hey, you blokes, pipe down! I've men trying to sleep here.' The sharp drawl of an Australian sergeant cut through the near-total darkness. Grant recovered his crutch and sloped off as Andrews turned to Dunbar.

'He's off his head, you know, Jim. I don't like him running around making accusations like that.'

'Well, no-one is going to take him seriously, for heaven's sake.'

'I hope not.'

'Let's turn in.'

The enforced intimacy with Grant made things awkward at night. During the day it was easy to avoid the man, or at least not to seek or encourage his company too much. But at night he ranted increasingly, seeking an audience among the survivors. Most soon got bored and fed up with him, and apprentice Wells more than once remonstrated that Dunbar had saved Grant's life.

Unfortunately, Grant increasingly believed in some confused way that Dunbar had arranged the fatal rendezvous between the German raider and the four-masted barque. This was based on the two facts that Dunbar had said he had written down the *Fort Mackinac*'s position on a scrap of paper, and that he admitted to having known the boarding officer Ketlar in London before the war.

To Grant's paranoid mind this circumstantial fact clinched the matter. His suspicions towards James Dunbar had leaped out of the rut of the normal and skidded wildly about in the wilderness of derangement. His disputatious arguments, at first an embarrassment and afterwards an increasing disruption to the overcrowded hospital, created such disturbance that the *Clytemnestra*'s doctor prescribed sedatives. Dosed with tincture of morphine, Grant was reduced to a helpless state at night as the liner steamed north, across the equator and towards the great war in Europe.

CHAPTER EIGHTEEN

The Assault

The situation remained quiescent for several days. Grant's outbursts were unpleasant but the sedation minimised them, though the surgeon was unwilling to keep him under constant dosage, preferring to ensure a quiet night and tolerating a degree of disruption during the day. Once Grant's dementia had been accepted, his accusations were dismissed. In fact they tended to produce a contrary reaction and, in refuting them, Dunbar's timely revival was seen as so crucial to the survival of the remaining inhabitants of the port boat that his actions were now thought of as heroic.

The 'tween decks of the *Clytemnestra* were a sound breeding-ground for such bravado. The teeming mass of young men, subjected twice daily to the imperial ritual intended to maintain healthy minds by exercising healthy bodies, were excited by the prospects of battle and its concomitant glory. They all aspired to be heroes and now they had one in their midst. They could, as it were, study the form.

Dunbar's natural self-deprecation only added to the misperception. He seemed perfectly cast for the part; they all recognised him from the books and stories of their boyhoods, books and stories they had not long ago set aside. His innate modesty, his handsome yet nobly weathered looks, even the aura surrounding him as the sole surviving officer, for here poor apprentice Wells was set aside, all added to the eager adulation of the young, raw and unsophisticated Australian recruits. Nor did the whispered intelligence that Dunbar had known a German officer detract from this collective perception. On the contrary, it added lustre to his image. Depending upon which particular version of the 'truth' was being peddled, Dunbar was either a bold and worldly Englishman who had once fought a duel with the dastardly Boche in defence of a woman, or he had been a spy who had cheated the Boche of some naval secrets and been sent off in sail to lie low before the war started.

Had he heard these embellished rumours, Dunbar might have been alarmed or amused, for there was, if one took a certain journalistic licence and a large pinch of salt, just sufficient material fact in his recent life to provide a tiny seed of veracity for either version. Perhaps sadly, Dunbar was unaware of the details circulating about him. Sadly, because he was still bothered about Grant. While he did not like the man, he remained morally responsible for him, despite the fact that the articles binding them as officer and seaman were literally dissolved when the *Fort Mackinac* went down. Dunbar might have repudiated his father's God. Nevertheless, his father's deep sense of obligation was an ingrained and unexciseable part of him. Repudiation was therefore impossible.

One night, as the *Clytemnestra* passed Madeira, her deck lights dimmed as she slid through the phosphorescent waters of the Atlantic Ocean, Grant woke. That evening the doctor, in company with Captain Evans and a number of his senior staff, had been a guest of the battalion officers in their extemporised mess. The ship was passing into a more intense war zone, and the fine weather would soon be behind them. The picnic was being packed up in the face of a looming thunderstorm.

The dinner had been a jolly, carefree occasion untrammelled by thoughts of the future. It had, though, culminated with cigars, cognac and toasts of high imperial endeavour. So moving and so plentiful had these been that the doctor had forgotten to sedate Grant.

Shortly before dawn the able-seaman woke from a fitful sleep to find Dunbar's bed empty. It was Grant's habit, a habit driven by the regularity of obsession, to lay his eyes upon the object of his irrational hatred. It was quite possible now to see Dunbar's abandoned pillow, a white, dimpled rectangle, which lay beneath a porthole through which a large, gibbous moon shone obligingly.

Dunbar's absence did not surprise Grant; he had been waiting for some such justification for all his jeremiads. It was clear that his concerns were to be vindicated and there was work for him to do. Cautiously he slid from his own bed and drew on his checked trousers, securing his belt and its sheath knife. Then he padded silently out of the hospital on bare feet. The moon slid behind a cloud. Grant smiled with satisfaction.

Creeping forward in the gratifying obscurity, Grant quickly traversed the after-well-deck and climbed the ladder onto the centrecastle. At that hour the ship seemed deserted. Ascending by degrees to the boat deck, he loped forward towards the final ladder to the bridge. Looking ahead, his heart beat faster. He was right!

Grant knew Dunbar would conspire to have the *Clytemnestra* sunk with the same alacrity with which he had disposed of the *Fort Mackinac*. And what an achievement! The deaths of hundreds of young soldiers – the cream of Australia's manhood were to be drowned before they could earn their place in the annals of the British army by defeating the German swine! Now the evidence of Dunbar's treason was plain before him. Grant could see the pencil-thin beam of light flickering out from the starboard wing of the *Clytemnestra*'s bridge, the dots and dashes of the morse code, which were distantly responded to by the German raider on the horizon. Greatly excited, Grant broke into a run, bounded swiftly up the ladder and, gathering himself momentarily at its head to draw his seaman's knife, hurled himself upon the figure hunched at the bridge rail.

'Hey! What the devil . . . ?'

Mr John White, the *Clytemnestra*'s astonished fourth officer, turned at the assault, but Grant sprung towards him. The fourth officer dropped the signalling lamp as Grant jumped him and clung to him. Just then the cloud cleared off the face of the moon. Grant rode his victim piggy-back, his legs about the fourth officer's waist, his left arm about the young man's head, pulling it back to expose the neck at which he sawed with his deck knife.

The clatter of the signalling lamp falling to the deck and the young man's single brief cry alerted the other occupants of the bridge. The Chinese quartermaster at the wheel let out a shout as he saw from the wheelhouse what was happening out on the moonlit starboard bridge wing. On the port wing, the *Clytemnestra*'s chief officer was preparing to take morning stars. Alongside him stood Dunbar. Both men held sextants and were concentrating on locating the best stars for their observation, but they turned at the noisy intrusion.

Dunbar had an uninterrupted view straight through the wheelhouse. He knew instantly who the assailant was from the checked trousers that Grant habitually wore and which, in the stark light, stood out with a peculiar and memorable vividness. Still holding the sextant, Dunbar raced across the wheelhouse with a bellow of outrage.

At that moment the fourth officer fell and, as he did so, Grant jumped back to survey his handiwork, his chest heaving with exertion, the bloody knife dark in his right hand.

'What the hell have you done?' cried Dunbar in a voice that visibly shocked Grant, for Dunbar emerged from the wheelhouse door into the full light of the moon. Grant looked at the body twitching at his feet and for a second realised that he had assailed the wrong person. In Grant's eyes this did not invalidate the activity that he believed was taking place. What other explanation was there for Dunbar being on the bridge at this hour? And with a sextant in his hand! Clearly Dunbar's powers and the depths of his treasonable activities went far beyond Grant's suspicions. The man was the ring-leader of a whole faction of traitorous officers, steam-ship officers!

He squared up to Dunbar, his teeth bared in a snarl.

Dunbar looked from Grant to the dying young man. 'You bloody fool—' he began, but then Grant was lunging towards him and Dunbar caught the glint of moonlight on the blood-darkened steel of the knife. In self-defence he punched at Grant's face with all his strength, shouting his furious outrage as he did so in an instinctive reflex that added power to the blow. He drove the heavy brass sextant forward like a huge knuckle-duster, just as the knife hooked upwards.

The impact of the sextant arrested Grant's lunge. The seaman's knife flashed up close to Dunbar's face as Grant staggered backwards, his face lacerated by the sharp edges of the mirrors and shades. But the impetus of his blow carried Dunbar forwards and he tripped over the fourth officer's body.

Flung backwards, Grant's retreat was stopped by the bridge rail. He gasped for breath and, wiping his bloody face with his left hand, recovered. His teeth were still bared in a malicious snarl as he stared for a moment at Dunbar.

Dunbar was on one knee, looking up at Grant, both

faces stark in the moonlight. There was the briefest moment of indecision visible in both protagonists, then the *Clytemnestra*'s chief officer, emerging from the starboard wheelhouse door in Dunbar's wake, shouted, 'Put down that knife!'

The command seemed to galvanise the demented seaman and he thrust forward again, intent on killing Dunbar, even if it were to be his last act on earth. Dunbar was a traitor, an officer, a deceiver, a man no better than himself, but one whom the world had enriched. All the hatred of Grant's existence was coiled within his body, all the petty jealousies of his jaundiced outlook, the whole exacerbated by his paranoia, provided the energy for his renewed assault. He leaped with the desperate and terrifying ferocity of a cornered tiger and Dunbar drew in his breath with a sudden, sharp and fearful indraught.

At that moment a shot rang out. Grant was stopped and flung backwards, into the very corner of the bridge wing, as though plucked from his purpose by the divine will in which Dunbar had no faith.

The next instant the bridge seemed to Dunbar to be full of people. Captain Evans was there in his pyjamas, as was the third officer and, at the top of the starboard bridge ladder, stood an army officer in mess undress, a wisp of smoke still trailing from the muzzle of his service revolver.

'You should keep your men under better control, Mr Dunbar,' the major said with a superior, informed air. 'I should not have been put to the disagreeable necessity of shooting the bugger, if the discipline of the mercantile marine was not so feeble.'

'You misunderstand, Major,' Dunbar said sharply, looking round the group of men assembled in Captain Evans's day cabin. 'Discipline on a merchant ship is based on the consent of men putting themselves under the articles of agreement. These govern our lives on a daily basis. The articles confer on a ship's master and his officers the authority to give lawful orders for the safe prosecution of a commercial voyage. We are not military men, but civilians. Moreover in this case, the articles ceased the moment our ship was sunk. Our time in the boats, and indeed our time aboard here, is an unpaid excursion.' Dunbar was conscious of stealing the dead Grant's phrase, but its aptness was striking. 'Nothing binds these men to me beyond our common experience. Perhaps one wishes otherwise, but there it is. There are no King's Regulations to back up my authority. Even in the boats it was largely habit that kept the men obedient.'

'I'm afraid Mr Dunbar is correct, Major Grattan,' Captain Evans added in support. 'The rules of engagement under which we operate are rather different from what you men in the King's livery, and I dare say a sizeable proportion of the Empire's population, suppose.'

'I see. Yes, well, my actions were consequent upon seeing the man Grant going forward in a stealthy and suspicious manner,' the major blustered. 'I'd been enjoying a last cigar after our dinner and, well, observed the cove . . .'

'Yes, yes,' interrupted Evans, 'there is no question that you acted out of the best interests. The balance of Grant's mind was clearly disturbed, as the doctor has testified.'

Their attention was diverted from Major Grattan, whose motive for shooting Grant may have owed something to the quantity of cognac he had drunk. They ignored the fact that it was not customary for officers to carry their revolvers when in mess undress. Instead they all looked at the sheepish young surgeon, whose face was still burning from the humiliation of admitting he had forgotten to sedate Grant.

'Fortunately,' Evans went on, 'this is war-time and

both the Board of Trade and my owners are not unfamiliar with the circumstances of disturbed persons running amok. It is unusual among the white race, though the Malays and Chinese often succumb,' the captain added didactically. 'We have already lost Mr White, a promising young officer. That fact is enough to satisfy the demands of natural justice. Let us conclude matters with the consideration that there would have been greater carnage if Major Grattan had not taken matters into his own hands.'

'I prefer the phrase "used my initiative", Captain,' Grattan protested.

'So do I, Captain.' The hitherto silent brigadier who commanded the troops terminated the impromptu inquest.

'Very well,' Evans said, clapping his hands. The captain's 'Tiger', a sleek, handsome Chinese steward, appeared, his starched white patrol jacket impeccably buttoned to the neck, his feet silent in soft, black velvet slippers.

'Ah, Chang. Whisky sodas for everybody.'

Chang inclined his head and Grant's inquest concluded, to the relief of men conscious of having seen an unpleasant duty through to its termination. Captain Evans would have to write a report, which would have to be witnessed and supported by statements, but the death certificate was completed, as was the formal business of registering the death on board.

'Well, Mr Dunbar,' Evans said, 'a sad business after you saved him, but a lucky escape for you.'

'Perhaps, sir. But I'm not certain that I can rest easy with the knowledge that Mr White's death was the cost of my own life.'

'Providence, Mr Dunbar,' Evans said quietly. 'Perhaps you are to be saved for a worse fate. These are unlikely to be anything but unquiet times.'

Dunbar was afterwards to recall those words of Captain

338

Evans, rendered sage by the master's age and the mellif-
luous tones of his whisky-enriched Welsh accent.

Just at that moment, however, he vividly remembered
Grant's remark that he himself smelt of death. He shuddered involuntarily.

'Are you all right, Mr Dunbar?'

Dunbar nodded. 'A grey-goose, sir.'

'Ah,' smiled Evans sadly, adding lugubriously, 'We all
scent the grave from time to time.'

Yet it seemed to Dunbar that the death of Grant changed
the mood of the survivors. Grant's irrepressible moaning,
his constant, obsessive reminders of the injustice of their
lack of pay, had grown to be a burden so huge that only
its removal revealed the extent of its oppression.

Within twenty-four hours of the inquest and the consequent writing of formal reports, Dunbar had returned
to the *Clytemnestra*'s bridge, not to keep his hand in
by taking star sights, though he continued to do this
intermittently for the remainder of the voyage, but to beg
some cancelled charts from the liner's second officer.

The *Clytemnestra* carried a vast range of folios for the
entire world, and these yielded up a number of redundant
sheets. On the reverse sides Dunbar began a series of
sketches of the sinking of the *Fort Mackinac* and studies
of the men in the boats that, it was clear to the watching
Andrews, would prove excellent source material for some
inspired paintings at a later date.

Of this Andrews was quite confident, though he said
little. And, though the two of them still sat under the
stars after dinner as the *Clytemnestra* drove northwards,
their conversation grew less intense and was more likely
to comprise the reflective silence existing between old
friends. Nor did Dunbar seek Andrews's opinion. While
he made no secret of doing the drawings, it was clear that

he did not particularly wish to discuss them. There was something withdrawn about him and, Andrews excepted, the others saw him again as 'the mate', as though recognising that he sought refuge for his rank in his occupation of drawing as a means of erecting the old and congruous barriers that they found neither awkward nor incomprehensible. Mr Dunbar had been instrumental in saving them and the enforced intimacy of the boat was now over. It was as if, in the death of Grant, they all saw the ending of a phase of their joint existences. In a sense it was from that dark act that the dissolution of the *Fort Mackinac*'s crew actually took place; it was the concussion of Major Grattan's revolver, a lesser echo of the *Augsburg*'s thunderous guns, that finally split the barque's crew into its individual constituent parts. Grant had posthumously succeeded in achieving what for weeks he had been accusing the capitalist owners of doing.

CHAPTER NINETEEN

Aftermath

England seemed to be clogged with uniforms. At Southampton, where the *Clytemnestra* berthed, the streets were gaudy with flags and lined with pale but cheering faces as the sun-bronzed Australians swung along, on their way to the railway station. A band played 'Waltzing Matilda' under a cloudy sky, which alternated a thin, wintry sunshine with showers of rain.

Dunbar was less glamorously employed. It took him an entire morning to screw out of the agents of Bullard, Crowe and Company a set of travel warrants to enable the crew of the *Fort Mackinac* to go home on survivors' leave. By noon he was exhausted and disgusted by the prevarication he had met.

'My dear Mr Dunbar,' the senior agency clerk had remonstrated, 'surely you don't expect me to advance cash without surety. Your owners themselves will have to close the articles and reckon up the sums owing to your men by way of their individual pay-offs . . .'

'This is outrageous!' Dunbar ranted. 'These men earned every penny owing to them. They have *enjoyed* an unpaid excursion from which several have not returned, only to find that no-one could care less about them. On arriving destitute on their native shores, you, as the representatives of Bullard, Crowe, refuse to let them have the means of

341

even buying a cup of tea, when the town is turned out to shower largesse on a brigade of Australians . . .'

'Sir, sir.' The clerk held his hand up and Dunbar, aware that his logic had surrendered to his emotions, came to a spluttering halt. He had seldom felt so angry. 'You cannot expect me to confuse business with patriotic fervour,' the clerk said dismissively, with a thin, contemptuous smile. 'The two are quite inimical.'

'Listen!' Dunbar said, suddenly furious beyond measure, 'If you do not at least telegraph Mr Crowe, I shall return to the *Clytemnestra* and ask Captain Evans to cable his own owners, Alfred Holt of Liverpool. They will, I am certain, out of charity alone, provide us with a small advance against our wages. Indeed, I am persuaded that Captain Evans would do the thing out of his own pocket, if he knew the shameful necessity I am reduced to in thus begging it of you.'

In the end Dunbar prevailed. The telegram was sent not to Liverpool, but to London. Nevertheless, as he waited fulminating for a reply, he wondered if the thin-lipped clerk had all the time been playing with him, like a cat with a mouse. But at last, after the interminable delays for the midday break and excuses about military priorities on the public telegraph system, the clerk paid them out a pitifully few sovereigns. It was, alas, but a prelude to further humiliation. At Southampton station and again at Waterloo, pretty, cocksure and well-dressed women confronted them with white feathers.

'What's the meaning of these?' Dunbar asked, about to take one from the bold redhead who reminded him, with a sharp pain, of Julia. Before she could open her red mouth, Andrews had loomed beside him and slapped the thing out of his hand.

'The little madam's insinuating you're a coward.' And before the young woman could say anything, Andrews, with a fearsome look of utter contempt which he thrust in her face, added, 'We've just spent three weeks in a lifeboat after our ship was sunk in the South Atlantic. Now fuck off!'

The woman recoiled as though struck. Recovering his composure, Dunbar remarked, half-amused, half-shocked, 'That was no way to treat a lady, Bill.'

'That was no lady,' Andrews responded grimly. 'And certainly no mother of sons, or she'd not want to see all these young fellows marching off to war. Christ, this is nonsense! Come on.'

It was too late for them to get across London with the faintest chance of finding anyone at Bullard, Crowe's offices. They made instead for the Seamen's Rest in Whitechapel where, deprived of all status, Dunbar was pleased to collapse onto a hard mattress.

'England, home and fucking beauty,' Andrews toasted bitterly as they sank a beer before turning in.

'What are you going to do, Bill? Go back to your Ida?'

Andrews shrugged. 'I don't know. If not Ida, then Amy or Annie, or Sally or any other bint looking for a good time. Not that there'll be much of a good time to be had from me with only a few weeks' pay to blow.'

'Why don't you settle down?'

'You mean marry? Who the hell would marry me?'

'You don't have to marry,' Dunbar said, grinning. 'Just take life a little steadier.'

'There's a war on, Jim. No-one will be taking anything steady for a while.'

'There'll be a lot of jobs in the country,' Dunbar remonstrated, 'what with all the farm-boys flocking to join the colours. A steady bloke like you should be able to find something.' He paused, took a long draught of his ale and, thinking of old Colonel Scrope-Davies, added, 'I may be able to help you.'

'Leopards can't change their spots.'

'Maybe not; but they grow rheumaticky and grey . . .'

'Or die young,' retorted Andrews, finishing his beer and banging the glass down on the bar. 'Can we afford another?'

'Just one, I think.' As they scratched in their pockets and ordered, Dunbar asked, 'Look, Bill, why don't you come down to Suffolk with me for a few days. It'll keep you out of trouble here. There may be an opportunity for you to swallow the anchor.'

Andrews took up his refilled glass and, after a long draught, lowered it and looked at Dunbar. 'All right', he said.

The shambling remnant of the *Fort Mackinac*'s crew shuffled into the owners' office next morning. The charity of the *Clytemnestra*'s crew had generously rigged them out in a weird range of apparel, but they felt their destitution acutely. The clerk, not recognising Dunbar who had grown a beard on the final homeward leg of the Blue Funnel liner's passage, at first made to shoo them out, declaring that there were no jobs to be had at Bullard, Crowe's 'headquarters'.

'The military theme seems to have taken over the world,' Andrews muttered darkly as Dunbar explained their identity. The men were made to sit outside while Dunbar was ushered into the inner sanctum, where Mr Crowe sat behind his desk, giving Dunbar the impression that he had been there unmoving since their last meeting.

'Do sit down, Mr Dunbar. May I offer you a glass of sherry?'

The ship-owner's solicitude extended for the twenty minutes it took Dunbar to recount the events of the *Fort Mackinac*'s ill-fated voyage and to submit his written report.

He sat in silence while Crowe quickly scanned the neatly penned sheets of foolscap, which bore the house flag of Alfred Holt and the motto *Certum Pete Finem*. After a few questions and answers, Mr Crowe assured Dunbar that the men would be paid off according to the provisions of the articles. 'Young Wells, of course, excluded.' As an apprentice, Wells was paid out of the premium that his father had advanced to Bullard, Crowe and Company as the price of his apprenticeship. Crowe looked down the list of survivors with which Dunbar's report concluded.

'Is that the best that can be done, Mr Crowe?'

'What's that?' Crowe looked up sharply.

'I mean, sir, that the men were some time in the boats, enduring great privation and the loss of several lives. It seems a hardship of the meanest sort to stop their pay the day the *Mackinac* sank. Perhaps you could allow them a little latitude, at least until they were picked up by the *Clytemnestra*.'

Crowe's shocked expression was unfeigned. 'My dear Dunbar, don't be sentimental. We can do no such thing. This is a war. Imagine the precedent. Perish the thought!'

'But it is so little to ask, sir,'

'On the contrary! It is a very great deal. Such a thing would be exponential. Now you forget these socialistic notions. The world of commerce is built upon sound principles, not sentiment. Idealism has its place and your concern for your charges does you credit, but be pragmatic, my boy. Those that you have brought home are safe and well and can soon be found new berths.' Mr Crowe's voice resonated with reason and now he switched to enthusiasm, a gleam of animation kindling in his old eyes as he leaned forward. 'Yes, you emerge with great credit, Mr Dunbar. I shall be happy to find you another ship as soon as you wish. We have need of men with nerve. These are exciting, profitable times for us. The *Fort Mackinac* will turn in a profit from her war-risk insurance which will more than recompense us for her loss.'

It took a second for the incongruity of Crowe's remarks to appal Dunbar. Looking at the older man, he could see no sense of this in his interlocutor's expression. He remembered the lines of a hymn: *The rich man in his castle, the poor man at his gate, God made them, high or lowly, and order'd their estate.* Crowe would understand that; Dunbar could not. He rose.

'Thank you, Mr Crowe, for your time and trouble,' he said with ill-concealed irony. 'I shall collect my pay-off.'

'Oh do, do, Mr Dunbar, it's well deserved, believe me. And let us know the moment you are ready to return to sea. I may have a command for you. We have just purchased two steamers, you know . . .'

At the door Dunbar turned. 'Was there any news of the other boat? Mr Nicholl's boat?'

Crowe shook his head. 'No, you are the only survivors. A great pity, Mr Dunbar, a great pity.'

Thus did Mr Crowe express the extent of his regret for the loss of his ship.

'He tried to buy you off then,' Andrews remarked as they walked towards Liverpool Street Station that afternoon. They had seen the rest of the survivors off and, all thought of duty behind them, sought the train to East Anglia.

Dunbar nodded. 'Yes, with notions of promotion . . .'

'This side of the ocean,' quipped Andrews. They halted as a battalion of infantry marched past, their boots crunching in unison.

'Up from Colchester to entrain for Dover, I suppose,' Dunbar remarked as they waited for the road to clear.

'Poor bastards.'

'They look cheerful enough.'

'So would you if you believed in King, country, God and glory!'

'He accused me of socialism,' Dunbar remarked.

'Oh?' There was a sardonic cast in Andrews's eyes. 'That is something Grant would never have done,' he said.

'No. But I think perhaps Crowe was the more accurate.'

'What? That you're a socialist?' Andrews was almost scoffing.

'Why not?' Dunbar responded. 'I grew up between the twin pillars of Church and State. I certainly had little time for the former, and recent events leave me querying the equity of the latter.'

'You'll make an artist yet,' laughed Andrews.

They crossed Bishopsgate in the wake of the column and entered the station.

'I need a drink,' Andrews said suddenly, searching for the bar.

'We've half an hour,' remarked Dunbar, reading the departures board.

'That's long enough.'

They drank for a few moments in companionable silence, then Andrews said, 'So Nicholls's boat was lost.'

'So it seems. We were lucky.'

'Yes. I guess we were.' He paused, then added, 'It was you who saved us, you know, Jim.' Dunbar looked up with a frown. 'You did,' Andrews insisted. 'You kept us together the night we were all about to chuck it in. I'd had enough, then you decided in your perverse way to save Grant. Saving Grant saved us all.'

Dunbar shook his head. 'Don't be silly, Bill. I was useless for those first days when you kept the show on the road . . .'

'And it was therefore the greater achievement to pull us round when you did. We had abandoned all hope, you know.'

'Oh, that's bullshit.'

'No it's not. You're a born officer.'

'What the hell are you drinking?' Dunbar scoffed, embarrassed.

'And I'm a common sailor.'

'For God's sake, Bill, what the devil's got into you? I can take you maudlin in the evening when you've had a skinful, but not in the cold light of day.'

'I'm a common sailor,' Andrews repeated almost wistfully, 'that's the beginning and the end of it all.'

'You are manifestly a very uncommon man.'

'But you are different. Everything about you is different. Grant knew it and he could not live with the knowledge. I think he felt it an unbearable burden. He was as good an able-seaman as any of us, but you always seemed to have that edge.'

'What's remarkable about that? I trained as an officer. Perhaps it was unfair of me to expect Grant and some of the others to accept me in the fo'c'sle.'

'Perhaps.'

'Did *you* resent me?'

Andrews shook his head. 'Of course not.' He paused, then said, 'I chose to be there.'

For a moment Dunbar stood puzzled, his glass arrested halfway to his mouth as he regarded his friend. Andrews seemed suddenly downcast, as if introverted by their conversation. The man had always been an enigma to Dunbar, a round peg in a square hole, as their friendship testified, and while Andrews had been evasive before, it had never spawned this abrupt melancholy. Then Dunbar recalled something that he had quite forgotten.

'Did you ever know a Lady Fowey?'

Andrews did not look up; instead he sighed, like a child

glad of having been found guilty of some naughtiness and absolved the tedious duty of confession.

'Thelma, Lady Fowey, is my half-sister,' he admitted flatly. 'She has not seen me for twenty-seven years and would not recognise me if she fell over me drunk in the gutter. She thinks I am dead. Why do you ask?' Andrews's tone was curiously uninquisitive. He looked up, as though brought suddenly into the present. 'Do you know her?'

'I have met her. She came to my exhibition in Highgate. She thought she knew . . .'

'My portrait! My God, I never gave it a thought!'

'Does it bother you?'

Andrews sank back over his beer and shook his head. 'No. Not really.'

'You chucked it all up and ran away to sea?'

Andrews gave a short laugh. 'Yes, just that. I was thrown out of Rugby school, my step-father's *alma mater*. My mother was an army widow and married Thelma's dear papa. He was a widower and had two children by his first wife. We were not a happy family. I thus had a half-brother and a half-sister, Thelma. My new papa, having conferred upon me the ineffable privilege of an education at what he believed to be the finest school in the land, was enraged – a not unusual circumstance for him, I might add – when he was informed of my immorality by my house-master. Vengeance loomed and I ran away, quite literally, to Liverpool, where I joined a fast little tops'l schooner that ran down to Spain and Portugal for fruit, oranges mostly. In Vigo I did properly what my house-master had falsely accused me of doing with his wife.'

'Ah . . .'

'Don't say "ah" in that infuriatingly knowing way. My life was changed. I won't say ruined, because I'm not certain I was ever fitted for anything else. If "ah" means you comprehend my pitiful claim to an education, then you would be partly right; if your "ah" means you think you understand my immorality, you might have guessed a little. But what your "ah" cannot encompass is the desolation felt by a small and terrified boy who acts and feels under the impulses of manhood, while at the same time needing the solace of ordinary, family affection.'

Dunbar held his peace. He knew something of what Andrews had suffered, but saying so would do nothing to ameliorate the other's pain and would only appear to be some cheap attempt to equate himself with Andrews. Andrews's suffering was his own unique property, inviolable, incomparable.

'My immorality consisted of my helpless stimulation by my house-master's young wife. She was not particularly attractive, but enjoyed a measure of impropriety with some of the boys. It was my misfortune to be lured into the old trap and then, to my shame, to be caught. Which of the three of us was the most ridiculous I have often since wondered,' Andrews said with a sad smile, straightening up and tossing down his glass. 'But I at least have had the opportunity of consigning my behaviour to the midden of adolescent memory. God only knows how the other two faced each other thereafter.' Andrews paused to swig his beer while Dunbar remained tactfully silent. 'So now you know.'

'Yes,' Dunbar smiled.

'You are going to say it was more enjoyable wondering what it was that made me chuck up my way of life, than hearing my pitifully banal explanation.'

Dunbar shrugged. 'No, I don't think I was going to be that uncharitable. I think I can imagine something of what it must have been like at the time.'

'The beating approximated what Ketlar gave you,' Andrews said, adding with a wry smile, 'relatively speaking, that is.'

Dunbar finished his drink. 'Let's make a move,' he

began, but then a tall woman in a fox-fur wrap came up to them, her long, gloved fingers elegantly twirling a white feather.

'This seems to be epidemic in railway stations,' Dunbar muttered, turning away. Andrews had other ideas.

'And what is that?' he snarled as she raised the offensive object between the two men.

'It's a white feather, gentlemen.' Her voice was cool, her words insolently charming and well spoken.

'And what does it signify?'

'That you ought to be in uniform, serving King and country.'

'Does it now.' Andrews's face softened and he took the feather. 'I don't know about King and country, ma'am,' he said pleasantly. About them the other drinkers had fallen silent. He stretched out his hand and dropped the feather. 'But I know about fuc*king* and *cunt*!' and with that his arm shot about the woman's waist and he forced a kiss upon her. She struggled violently as the bar erupted with a roar of appreciation and the barman came over with a remonstrating, ''Ere, what's going on?'

Andrews let the woman go and she staggered backwards, white-faced, her hand to her hat. 'Nothing, mate,' he said stepping past her. I've just been blown up by a German cruiser, spent three weeks in an open boat and that's the first tart that offered me anything.'

The outraged and speechless woman was settling her hat, her face scarlet with humiliation. Amused, Dunbar could not resist a smile. 'You should be more careful, ma'am, and remember the commandment about bearing false witness. He affronted you no more than you did him.'

And, chuckling, Dunbar left the discomfited woman and followed Andrews out onto the concourse. He caught up with him at the barrier. Andrews turned and said, 'I'm sorry, Jim, but I'm not coming.'

'Why? What about your ticket?'

'It's nothing. Forget it.'

'But you'll enjoy a break in the country . . .'

'Maybe.' Andrews smiled. 'No more jokes about country, please.'

'That was wicked,' Dunbar laughed, whereupon Andrews held out his hand.

'Good luck, Jim.'

'It was that woman, wasn't it?' Dunbar said.

'Maybe,' Andrews repeated, still smiling. 'Go home and paint those pictures.'

Dunbar grinned back. 'You're incorrigible, but I hope we meet again.'

Andrews shrugged. 'Thanks for what you did.'

'I did nothing. It was you . . .'

'Bollocks. Goodbye.' And turning away with a grin, Andrews was lost in the crowd. Dunbar watched him for a moment, briefly saddened by Andrews's change of heart. Moments of such vast and irrevocable parting were part of the sailor's lot. For him it was an old feeling, and not so very terrible.

As Dunbar stood there a soldier, one of a quartet burdened with kit-bags, gave him a shove. The act was deliberate, an accusation, part of the military madness consuming the nation. The four squaddies looked back over their shoulders with withering contempt in their eyes.

Dunbar turned away and made towards the platform. He wondered whether any one of those four soldiers would enjoy more than one parting from those they cared for.

His homecoming was a return quite unlike the last. Too late to reach Clayton Dobbs that evening, Dunbar spent the night in Ipswich and the following morning made his way to the coast. He had almost no luggage beyond his roll of charts, and walked from the station. A thick hoar frost lay on the countryside and beyond, over the salt-marsh, lay a dense white mist. As he caught sight of the square church tower, it occurred to Dunbar that it wanted a week before Christmas.

He approached the rectory with some concern, uncertain of his welcome. He need not have worried; his knock at the door was answered by his brother David, now installed as rector. For a moment David did not recognise the bearded Dunbar.

'D'you have a fatted calf to kill for the return of the prodigal?' Dunbar asked.

'Good heavens, James, what a surprise! Come in, come in.' David waved him inside and called the news back into the house. His wife Caroline appeared from the kitchen, wiping her hands on her apron, and Dunbar remembered his mother doing the same thing. Somehow the sight was a reassurance of normality and continuity. Dunbar had not met the young woman before and, as David performed the introductions, he took stock of his new relative. She was pleasant-looking, with cool grey eyes that held his own in the level appraisal of an equal.

'I've heard a great deal about you, James,' she said in a low, yet confident voice.

'I hope not,' he jested awkwardly.

'We knew your ship had sunk,' she remarked, 'but after that we had no news.'

'The ship was reported missing, presumed lost,' David corrected.

'Well, it amounted to the same thing,' Dunbar said quickly, smiling at them both. 'We were rather a long time in a boat and were then picked up by a cargo-liner loaded with troops.'

'Ah yes, the war. It has reached us here, with half the young men running off to enlist in the Suffolks.'

'On the way home we were regularly presented with

white feathers,' Dunbar said with a wry grin. 'It was rather galling.'

'Oh, how awful,' responded Caroline. 'Poor David's experienced something similar.'

'Oh, what was that?'

'Oh, nothing really . . .'

'No, you should tell James. It really is an outrage.'

'Well? Come on, out with it,' Dunbar prompted.

'Oh, it's only the children in the village. They run about pointing and shouting about the country needing one's services.'

'Venomous little brutes!' Caroline exclaimed. 'Come through into the kitchen and we'll have some tea.'

Apart from visiting his mother in her cottage in Spur Lane, Dunbar had been home for two days before he ventured out. He did not want the manifold distractions of the village to erode the vividness of his experiences. Memory dimmed, elevating the pleasant and suppressing the unpleasant, and while certain moments would stand out in stark and terrible relief, much of the contiguous detail faded, leaving just a remnant image of the truth to form individual recollections. He wished to transmute his raw pencil sketches into something more durable as soon as possible.

Despite the bitter cold he had asked David and Caroline if he could use the attic as a temporary studio. Under the old eaves the wind moaned with a low and intimidating howl. Half-frozen, Dunbar stretched a canvas and began to block in a large painting of the survivors in the open boat.

Two days before Christmas Caroline crept upstairs and, with many apologies at interrupting him and a warming mug of tea, announced the arrival of a message for Dunbar.

'Word of your return has reached the Hall,' she said. 'The colonel has asked you up for dinner tonight. He says you're not to bother to dress. He's given it up during hostilities, whatever that means.'

'Are you invited?' Dunbar asked without stopping his work.

'No, I shouldn't think so.'

'D'you mind?'

'What, your going or my not going?' she asked, smiling.

'Well, both.'

'No on both counts. What would I want to go to an all-bachelor dinner for? Very dull. You'll be fighting Agincourt, or Waterloo, or something all over again. Besides, the colonel, bless him, does not think I am quite proper as the rector's wife.'

'Why on earth not?' Dunbar lowered palette and brush and turned to look at his sister-in-law.

'I am a woman of what he calls independent mind. I believe in female suffrage and am thus held to be somewhat scarlet in my politics.'

'Oh, is that all,' Dunbar laughed. 'For a moment I thought white feathers might reappear.'

'Not in any conversation I might be a party to,' Caroline said, peering at the painting and then at the sketch. 'I say, that is rather fine.' She paused, staring reflectively at first the drawings and then the canvas. 'It is rather terrible too. It must have been awful.'

'It was.' Dunbar said.

Colonel Scrope-Davies was not alone and the dinner was not a dull bachelor evening. Julia and Icarus Dacre had come down from town for Christmas. Dunbar was greeted by Dacre, who wore the uniform of an infantry subaltern.

355

'Good God, Icarus, what a surprise.' Dunbar's astonishment was ill-concealed as he accepted the glass that Dacre offered him.

'A number of people considered I should be a conchie . . .'

'A *what*?'

'A conchie, a conscientious objector . . .'

'But as an art critic it was said that he had no conscience,' broke in Julia, entering the room in a startling dress of yellow silk. She looked ravishingly lovely, but had about her a new-found brittleness and shot frequent, almost uncertain glances at her husband. Dunbar bent over her hand. 'Julia, how lovely. I apologise for my lack of sophistication,' he said, gesturing at his drab suit. 'It's as well the colonel didn't want me to dress. I had to borrow this from David. I lost everything when my ship was sunk and . . .'

'Your ship was sunk?' Dacre asked, his eyebrows shooting upwards.

'We had no idea!' Julia said.

'By the malice of the enemy or the elemental indifference of nature?' Dacre asked.

'Do tell us about it,' said Julia.

'No,' interrupted Dacre, 'the colonel will be with us any moment. Save your story for dinner, James. Are you still painting, or did you lose work in the wreck?'

'I lost a lot of drawings, but I'm back here to work on a large painting of the open boat in which a few of us survived.'

'How dramatic!' Julia said. 'Will you let me sell it for you when you have finished it?'

Dunbar had not considered the matter of selling. He shrugged. 'I suppose so, if I decide to sell it. How is the gallery?'

'Interest has waned dramatically since August, but I sold a rather fine military picture last week—'

Dacre interrupted his wife again, 'D'you think the old boy's all right, darling?' he broke in.

'I'd better go and see.' Julia slipped from the room with a swift and uncharacteristic acquiescence, Dunbar observed.

'I'm on embarkation leave, James,' Dacre explained the moment his wife had gone. 'Things are a bit strained. I join my regiment immediately after Christmas and the gallery's not doing too well. I wanted Julia to come down here for the duration, but,' he paused, 'well, you know Julia, she's an independent creature.'

'I see. I'm sorry. Does she approve of your enlisting?'

Dacre gave him a thin, nervous smile. 'No, not really. I'm very glad you're still painting.'

'Kind of you.' There was an awkward silence, then Dunbar, moved by a sudden concern, asked, 'Have you done much training, Icarus? I mean, you're going to lead troops in the field . . .'

'Well, OTC at school and university, of course, and we've had a course or two, you know. One doesn't forget those things.'

'Pardon me for saying so, Icarus, but you have never struck me as being the typical soldierly type. Will you manage?'

'Look here, I don't know . . .' Dacre's expression was crestfallen.

'I mean no offence,' Dunbar broke in hurriedly, putting out a temporising hand, 'but I had a man go off his head in the boat for no more reason than he became possessed of certain obsessive thoughts. This occurred to a man who was fearless aloft in a sailing ship, but fell apart under the strain of the abnormal experience he was subjected to as a result of war. In the end he ran amok and killed a completely innocent man . . .'

'Well, that's hardly applicable, is it? I mean, what are you suggesting?'

'I'm not sure, but my brief taste of action seemed to lead to complications I'd never have thought of in my wildest imagination.'

'You were actually under fire?'

'Somewhat,' Dunbar replied drily. 'The ship was sunk under my feet—'

'My boy!' They were interrupted by the entry of Colonel Scrope-Davies on Julia's arm. The warmth of his welcome surprised Dunbar. He recalled the distance that had once lain between them, both socially and materially, but also the intimacy established by the old man after the rector's funeral. 'Julia tells me you've been sunk. Been in action, then?'

They shook hands. 'Well, Colonel, I've been on the receiving end of a cruiser's guns, if that qualifies as a baptism of fire. We had nothing to retaliate with, of course.'

Colonel Scrope-Davies shook his head. 'Damn bad, that. If merchant ships are to be targets, they'll have to be armed.'

'We were given time to abandon the ship, but the boarding officer shot our captain in cold blood.'

'Oh, how appalling,' said Julia.

'These raiders are damned bad news,' the colonel said, shaking his head. 'I've advised the board,' he added, referring to his interests in the South Wales Steam Navigation Company, 'to lobby the Admiralty to introduce a convoy system, but there is a great deal of resistance.'

'I know,' Dunbar agreed, 'the owners' profits under their war-risks policies are huge if they lose their ships.'

'You mean the owners profit more from a ship that's sunk than if she completes her voyage?' Julia asked incredulously.

Dunbar nodded, 'Yes it's quite likely, particularly if they're in ballast or carrying a low-freight cargo. And the crew's pay stops the day their ship goes down.'

'But that's obscene!' Julia turned to her uncle, 'Does your company do that?'

'I didn't appreciate that,' the old man admitted apologetically.

'Well, we can't alter matters tonight,' Dunbar said soothingly, aware that the conversation was growing gloomy. 'How are you all? Colonel, you told me not to dress and here you are looking dashing . . .'

They went in to dinner, during which Dunbar was reluctantly compelled to reopen the subject and told them something of the *Augsburg*'s attack. As they digested the yarn, Dunbar dissembled. 'Icarus, what happened to Ketlar? I suppose when war broke out he was obliged to return to Germany?'

'No,' replied Dacre, dabbing his mouth with his napkin, 'he went back to Germany sometime before the outbreak of war in August.' Dacre frowned. 'I don't think I saw him at all again after you left.'

'I did,' put in Julia. 'Once. Soon afterwards. He came to the gallery to pick up some paintings. Then he left us all high and dry. In fact I have some money owing him and he failed to leave a forwarding address.'

'And Rollo Münck?'

'Oh, that was a sad business,' said Julia. 'He was interned. Anyone with a German name or German connections was the butt of public prejudice, even if their families had been here for generations. Poor Rollo was more or less arrested. We rather lost touch, didn't we, Icky?'

''Fraid so.'

'Don't know any of these people, do I?' Colonel Scrope-Davies asked.

'No, uncle, I don't think so.'

Dunbar forbore mentioning Maureen. He found himself fearful of what he might hear. He could enquire of Julia later perhaps. Instead he said quietly, 'It seems

359

I am the one who most recently met Graf von Ketlar then.'

'What d'you mean?' Dacre said, looking up sharply, his laden fork poised betwixt plate and mouth.

'He was the officer who boarded the *Fort Mackinac* from the *Augsburg*. It was Ernst Ketlar who shot Captain Crawhall.'

'What's that?' the colonel growled. 'You mean you knew the Boche who shot your master in cold blood?'

'Unfortunately I did,' Dunbar admitted ruefully. 'And I rather think he wanted to do the same to me. Anyway, he left me in no doubt that he hoped I would not survive the sinking.'

'Damned outrageous.' Scrope-Davies shook his head again. 'Did you hear they were promising the war would be over by Christmas? No? Well, they said the same thing of the South African business and look how long that went on. It was interminable. This trouble with the Boche is much worse than taking on a few Boers. The Boers had no navy, for a start.'

'I'm sorry to have dominated matters this evening,' Dunbar said in a gallant, if belated, attempt to lighten the mood again.

'One can't get away from the war,' Julia said sadly, and Dunbar saw her eyes wander to Icarus, incongruous in his khaki tunic crossed by his Sam Browne belt.

'And what of Eric Retyn? Did you sell his "Macaw" paintings?'

'Oh yes,' Julia said, 'both of them. As for Eric, he became a conscientious objector. He took to speaking publicly against the war. He was arrested. He's in prison somewhere.'

'Richmond Castle,' said Dacre, 'in Yorkshire.'

'Things'll not be the same afterwards,' grumbled the colonel, then adroitly diverted the conversation to news of the Dunbar family. Dunbar learned that his sister-in-law was expecting a child in four months.

'I had no idea,' Dunbar said, laughing, 'though I've been lodging with her.'

'I don't suppose you looked,' Julia said, smiling at him and shaking her head in a general exasperation at the self-centred nature of men.

'She seems a pleasant enough young woman,' Scrope-Davies conceded, 'even if her head is full of this suffrage nonsense.'

'Uncle doesn't approve of women thinking for themselves,' Julia explained.

'I think Caroline knows that . . .'

'That's not true,' expostulated the colonel. 'Women should emphatically think for themselves. It's what they think *about* that concerns me. If they bother their pretty heads with matters that are properly the province of us men, who the deuce will worry about the things that should concern women? Are we supposed to do that now, eh? It'll be a bit difficult, damned if it won't.'

The conversation switched to politics until Julia, smiling half-apologetically, withdrew to leave the gentlemen to relax with their port and cigars.

After quarter of an hour Dacre announced his intention of following his wife and the colonel concurred. 'Of course, my boy. You don't have much time together.'

He watched Dacre leave, then turned back to Dunbar. For a moment he seemed about to refer to Dacre, then said, 'So you've met the bloody Boche then, James.'

'Yes, sir.'

'And you begin to know what it's all about.'

'Yes, a little. I tried to warn Icarus, but, I don't know,' Dunbar shook his head, 'he seems to think, like the whole country, that it's all a great game.'

'You'd have thought they'd have learned otherwise the last time. We waved them off to South Africa in the same lunatic way.' Scrope-Davies ground out his cigar and nodded at the door, indicating Dacre. 'He's not fit for it, you know; not properly prepared.' The colonel raised his hand and tapped his head, then blew a plume of smoke at the ceiling. 'He's an art critic, for God's sake, a dilettante, not an infantry officer. I don't much care for him, but what about all those young men who trust him and think he's one of God's bloody annointed, eh? What d'you think of that? You've been an officer, you know what the burdens are, don't you? I tell you,' the colonel went on, not waiting for Dunbar, 'it'll be Duffer's bloody Drift all over again.' There was a pause, then the colonel asked, 'D'you think Julia's happy, James?'

'I don't get that impression, sir. She seems nervous, less confident. I assume Dacre's imminent departure has something to do with her mood.'

Scrope-Davies shook his head. 'I'm not sure, but I'm an old fool and can't be sure of anything these days.' The colonel paused, then added, 'Keep an eye on her when I'm gone, James, will you? I don't think Dacre's the stuff that heroes are made of.' He paused to sip his port. 'Nor husbands, either.'

CHAPTER TWENTY

The Assignation

It was almost like old times in the rectory after Christmas matins during which, despite himself, Dunbar had thundered out the old carols with nostalgic and shameful enthusiasm. Behind him he sensed the great vermilion ensign rustling its folds in sinister mockery at his hypocrisy. But his mother deserved at least the formalities of faith and she was clearly happy to have a family around her again.

'I wanted her to move back in with us,' Caroline told Dunbar in an aside as they walked back to the rectory for lunch. 'There is plenty of room in this place.' She gestured at the old house. 'But she insisted on staying put in her cottage.'

'I suppose,' Dunbar replied, 'it would be difficult for her to move back into a house in which her word was once law. You would find it difficult too.'

They sat down to a huge spread and Anne Dunbar remarked it a pity that Jenny Broom was not with them.

'How is Jenny Slater, Mama?' Dunbar asked, smiling, aware of the irony of his correction, an irony that quite escaped his mother.

Anne Dunbar shook her head. 'She is not well, my dear, not well at all. I ought to visit her tomorrow.

Would you come with me, James? The ice in the lanes is so treacherous, I would like some support.'

'Yes, of course. I ought to see her too. I should hate her to think I'd forgotten her.'

His mother was right, the puddles in the lanes were frozen solid and she hung onto his arm and squealed like a girl, terrified that she would slip and break her leg. But she was light as a bird, shrinking with age and, Dunbar thought uncharitably, seemed happier in her widowhood.

The Slaters' cottage was at the end of a terrace of five. Smoke coiled into the still air from all the chimneys, and ash had been emptied on the paths so that their approach crunched the clinker underfoot. Their knock was answered by Albert Slater, Jenny's husband. He seemed fazed by their presence and Dunbar sensed that he would have kept them out, but his mother had a way of entering the houses of others and was used to the obstruction of men who did not wish the rector's wife to see their womenfolk. Such habits never died, nor did the deference of Slater, who stood reluctantly aside and let her in. Dunbar was mildly puzzled by Slater's attitude, unaware that the man in any way resented his wife's long connection with the rectory and with his family.

'Master James,' Slater said, greeting Dunbar and shutting the door behind them.

'Is anything the matter, Mr Slater?' Dunbar asked, allowing his mother to go ahead and to disappear into the rear room, which was both kitchen and living room. Slater stood awkwardly, unable to articulate his thoughts without a struggle. In the back room Dunbar could hear the noises of greeting and surprise and could see the shadow of his mother thrown on the wall as she took off her coat.

'Aye, happen things are difficult.'

'Is it Jenny? I heard she was not well. I hope it isn't serious.'

'Depends what you mean by serious, Master James.'

'If you want me to leave, I'll . . .'

'No, no. You come through. To tell the truth, I'd welcome another man's opinion on the way matters stand just now.'

And with this unresolved and mysterious introduction, Dunbar followed Slater through the cottage.

Jenny sat beside the range wrapped in rugs and blankets. Her appearance shocked him, for her face was sallow and more lined than he remembered, her hair untidily and hastily arranged.

'Oh, Master James! My, what a fine strapping young man!'

Dunbar was aware of another woman standing half-obscured behind his mother. He bent forward, kissed Jenny's cheek and felt her hand press his face to hers.

'Oh, Master James, how lovely to see you.'

'They tell me you've been in the wars, Jenny,' he said, using an old and familiar phrase as he straightened up.

'Oh, I'm on the mend, though it didn't make for a very happy Christmas with me laid low and the dinner to cook.' There was a brave falsity about her reply.

'Lucky we had help,' Slater's voice cut in and Dunbar looked up, past his mother, straight into the beautiful face of Maureen Fletcher.

'But you knew her!' his mother said as they walked home in the gathering darkness. 'How did you know her?'

The intensity of his mother's questions after the shock of recognition was as disquieting as the experience itself. It had proved impossible to pretend otherwise and, though both Maureen and Dunbar recovered their composure, a woman as astute as Mrs Dunbar could see that the pair of them were not strangers to each other.

As for poor Slater, Dunbar was conscious of not having rendered the assistance that was clearly expected of him. They had sat down to tea in an atmosphere of excruciating awkwardness, and Anne Dunbar had dominated the conversation with such a pointed monopoly that Dunbar had found the following forty-five minutes physically painful. Unable to lay his eyes upon Maureen, he was conscious of her presence as if pierced by Grant's knife.

It was only now being revealed that his mother too had been dissembling.

'What is so dreadful about knowing Miss Fletcher, Mother?'

'Because,' Anne Dunbar hesitated, then plunged on – her eldest son was no longer a child – 'she is . . . Oh, poor Albert. Poor Jenny . . .'

'Mother!'

His mother sighed. 'How do you know her?'

'We met in London,' Dunbar admitted, exasperated. 'She and Julia shared lodgings in Pimlico.'

'Of course. I quite forgot, quite forgot. How very stupid of me. Your father found her that place. I should have guessed Julia would know about her.'

'Father? I don't understand! What had Father to do with it? Or Julia?'

'That young woman,' Anne Dunbar explained, as though Maureen herself bore some reprehensible burden in her very existence, 'was Hugh Scrope-Davies's bastard!' She paused to allow the outrageous news to sink in and, it seemed to Dunbar in that strained moment, to chide him for his apparently disgraceful familiarity with the girl. 'Your father arranged first for her to be adopted and later for her to have lodgings in London, well away from Ipswich.'

Dunbar had a dim recollection of Julia making obscure

366

remarks about living in London with a relative, that distant Sunday when she had come to dine at the rectory, when he had shown her his early pictures. He remembered, too, how she had deflected his parents' probing interrogation.

'Good Lord!'

And the colonel had remarked about a love-child of Hugh's and the rector's help in avoiding a scandal.

'So Fletcher is the name . . .'

'Of the people who adopted her in Ipswich.'

'And I did see her at Liverpool Street Station that day I later ran into Jenny. Had they met? They must have,' Dunbar muttered, some light dawning on his recollections.

'Pardon?'

'Nothing, mother. I'm talking to myself. Then who is *her* mother?' But Dunbar already knew the answer and he almost echoed his mother as she admitted, 'Jenny.'

And he remembered now how, in his childhood, Jenny Broom had been accorded the courtesy title of 'Mrs' and how, after his father had long ago ranted against harlotry from the pulpit, he had received a bloody nose defending Jenny's good name when certain of the knowing village lads had called his parents' cook a harlot.

Suddenly Slater's dilemma struck Dunbar. Whether or not Alfred knew of his wife's teenage immorality, the poor man would not know what to make of having the squire's heir's bastard revealed as his own step-daughter! It was almost laughable, if it were not tinged with such utter sadness.

Nor, he thought with a tug of conscience, was he entirely unconnected with all this. He buried the thought as his mother, released now from the bindings of secrecy, let forth more details of the affair.

'The colonel knows all about her. He paid for her rooms. As for her foster parents, Mr Fletcher died some years ago, and his widow is a very old and infirm woman now. They were not young, you know, even then, but a good, kind childless couple; church people. It was an open secret that Maureen came from a good family.'

'How on earth did Father know about them – the Fletchers, I mean?'

'Oh, there was more to your father than met the eye. The duties of a parish priest are often less congenial or predictable than one might suppose. Such things are sadly not that unusual.' Anne Dunbar sighed. 'And she is such a very beautiful young woman.'

Dunbar held his tongue and his mother observed the telling silence unhappily.

It was quite dark when he dropped his mother off at her cottage. He spent a few moments with her and then made his excuses.

'You'll be going straight back to the rectory then?' she asked.

'Where else?'

His mother sniffed, quite unaware that her well-meant interference acted like a catalyst upon Dunbar.

The mist had rolled in again from the salt-marsh and the cold was so intense that the frost lay almost as thick as a snowfall. He would have to see her. The only questions were when and how? He turned out of Spur Lane and headed up towards the rectory. A few yards took him to the turning towards Clayton Wick, along which the Slaters' cottage stood. He turned the corner and, for the second time that afternoon, knocked on the door. Again Albert Slater opened it. His face was dark with puzzlement.

'I should like to speak to Maureen, Mr Slater. You see,' Dunbar said awkwardly, 'I know who she is and we were friends in London.'

For a moment Dunbar thought this admission had so astonished Slater that this further complication to his life would result in the door being slammed. But then it seemed that something of the weight of uncertainty and inexperience lifted from Slater and the man stood back.

'Come you in.'

They moved through into the kitchen, where Maureen stood at the sink bare-armed and washing up. There was no sign of Jenny.

'Someone to see you,' Slater said shortly and Maureen turned.

Dunbar cleared his throat. 'Maureen, I . . . I wished to speak to you . . .'

She shook her head. 'No, I don't think . . .'

'Please,' he pleaded. 'Please. Not now, but tomorrow, perhaps.' He saw her vacillate and look at Slater. 'May I call for you at two? Please, Maureen.' He was conscious of Slater's presence, but did not take his eyes off Maureen. She had stood an oil lamp on the windowsill and the soft, yellow light lit her face from below.

She nodded and Dunbar turned. 'Thank you, Mr Slater.'

As he was shown out Slater said, 'Jenny's bad, Mr Dunbar, but we haven't let it be known in the village.'

Dunbar paused and looked at Slater. He was worn with fatigue and in the half-light his eyes glittered with tears. 'Jenny's a good woman, Mr Dunbar, why . . . ?'

'What is it, Albert?' Dunbar asked softly.

'The doctor says it's a cancer. She asked for . . . asked to see her little girl again. I didn't know about her . . .'

'It makes little difference in the end, Albert. Has she long?'

Slater shrugged. 'Doctor can't be sure. Maybe a month or two. She's in terrible pain, though she insisted on

369

coming downstairs for Christmas. Seeing you and your mother was too much for her, though I mean no offence.'

'There's none taken, I assure you.'

'Your mother was always so good to her, and—' Slater broke off.

'When did you last have the doctor here?' Dunbar asked shrewdly.

'Before Christmas.'

'How long before Christmas?'

'A sennight, may be ten days.'

Or longer, Dunbar guessed. 'Call him in tomorrow.'

'But I can't . . .'

'Call him, Albert. I'll pay.'

Within a hundred yards of the Slaters' front door the mist engulfed them. They walked slowly towards Clayton Wick in a world of their own, divorced from everything, untouching and separate.

For a few moments they were silent, then Dunbar spoke of Jenny and what Slater had told him. 'Did the doctor call this morning?'

'No. But he was expected this afternoon.'

'Did you want to stay?' he asked quickly.

'No. It is better that she and Albert are alone at this time. I am a stranger. More so than you.'

'It must be very difficult for you.'

She looked up at him and the banality of his words fell far short of the intensity of his feeling. For a moment he was speechless in the face of her silence, full of his own inadequacy; then he threw aside the restraint of convention.

'Maureen, I am ashamed of the way I behaved towards you the last time we were together. I have been full of remorse ever since. It was unforgivable and yet I am desperate that you forgive me.'

She was silent for a moment, then Dunbar felt her hand take his. 'I forgive you then, if that is what you want.'

He stopped, turning her towards him and looking at her. He was almost choking with emotion. 'I want only what you want. If I want anything, it is the opportunity to know you better.'

She said nothing but turned and walked on, still holding his hand. The gesture heartened and encouraged him. He thought for one terrible moment of the intimacy Ketlar had established with her.

'I,' he began, and she thought his voice sounded strangled as he stopped as abruptly as he had started. 'Have you ever noticed,' he began again, 'how difficult we find it to say,' and here he gave a choked, bitter, monosyllabic laugh, 'exactly what we want to.'

There was another pause and she, in anticipation of his saying more, held her peace and thought, as she had thought before, of all the selfishness wrought in the world.

'I mean,' Dunbar blundered on, hesitating again so that she noticed he had reverted to the use of the personal pronoun. Her sudden understanding of his remark as a mere prologue caused a weakening towards him, a strange and sympathetic desire to comprehend him, for it was clear now to Maureen that he was trying desperately to communicate something of intense importance to himself.

'I mean, when it comes down to it, when we really want to be ourselves – our real, true selves – it becomes impossible. We employ artifice, we are so inhibited.'

She felt disappointed by the inner certainty that he had again ducked the issue. The personal pronoun had been but a decoy, a substitution. She stared up at Dunbar, willing him to speak, to sound out the depths of her unfortunate understanding and wipe out the shameful admission of Ketlar. She needed the honesty he was struggling so hard to find. Then a terrible distraction occurred to her: that he might not exist at all; that the whole scene, devoid of any material reference in the mist, was as insubstantial as a dream.

'What is it, James?'

They had stopped again. Her voice was low and gentle; like her dark eyes, it seemed to him that it was evidence of her seemingly infinite capacity for insight and sympathetic comprehension. Was this perception of his accurate? And, if so, would the powers of inhibition rob him of this touching of so much more than their hands?

He had no way of knowing how painfully her heart hammered in her breast. His own blood was less honourable; he was almost shuddering from the emotional power raging within him.

'Maureen,' he breathed in a dreadful tone that staked everything against a rebuff. 'I want you, but I want more than just your body. I want something else too.' She neither moved nor responded. He had had her mere body. He was rushing headlong now, as if having broken through the barrier of reticence and inhibition, he desperately needed to maintain the momentum of his courage.

'I want you to know everything about me and I want to know everything about you, as though we were in a perpetual state of intimate fucking.' He stood stock-still, with a curious immobility, as if keeping a distance between them until he had disencumbered himself of this catalogue of half-strangled desire. Then he sighed. 'Do I shock or upset you?'

She felt him deflate, his courage exhausted. She wanted to hold him, to show him the warm, welcoming wetness that his propinquity had produced, but this was how she had submitted herself to Ketlar, this was how her mother had been betrayed and how she herself had been conceived.

'We are only ourselves in childhood,' she said at last and Dunbar, not sensing her own misery, clutched eagerly at her remark.

'And what I am trying to say is that I wish . . . no, no, I want us to keep between us that childhoodness of our beings.'

'But it is too late!'

'No . . .'

'You are a vicar's son,' Maureen said with sudden assertion, 'you are bound to have such ideas, but I, I am a bastard . . .'

'My God, Maureen,' Dunbar interrupted ferociously, taking her face in his hands, 'it is because you are a bastard that I can talk to you so frankly!' He shook his head in fear of being misunderstood at this last confession. 'I do not mean to sound condescending or patronising. I am not descending in any sense, believe me! Please understand that I mean exactly what I say. That is why it is so difficult to say it! It has cost me a lot to lose my parentage, to stand alone. I cannot conceive of being myself, or of any value in the world, if these moments amount to nothing.'

'And your love for me is because you see me as one who stands alone?' There were tears filling her eyes. The desolation of Dunbar's previous departure seemed miraculously redeemed. She could not guess then what time and experience had wrought in him, only that the change was immense.

But she had misjudged before, and caution swayed her. That sweetness, that great yearning, that infinitude of insatiable desire had all but wrecked her once. What was there in this man to prove his steadfastness, his honour, his goodness?

'Maureen . . . ?' He relinquished her face and stood back in almost pathetic defeat, as though her forehead was branded with her misgivings and unhappiness. He was utterly drained, his eyes still haunted by the enormity of his self-revelation. If she spurned him now he would never, could never, return. And she would know a desolation more terrible than anything she had previously known.

'Kiss me,' she said.

WATERFRONT

Richard Woodman

Brought up amid the twin certainties of church and state in Edwardian Britain, young James Dubar goes to sea in search of romantic adventure. Even when he falls in love with a waterfront prostitute named Conchita, he continues to believe that the purity of his emotion can rescue her from the Hotel Paradiso, the notorious brothel of Puerto San Martin.

But Puerto San Martin is a place of commercial trafficking, and commerce, of one sort or another, is what makes it tick – it's no place for the innocent or the romantic. What Dunbar learns about his shipmates and the local inhabitants has a profound effect upon him. His meeting with the mysteriously veiled owner of the Hotel Paradiso reveals an event of terrifying brutality and makes him the agent of retribution; his encounter with the brothel's Madame confronts him with the demands of his own lust and these events not only alter his perception of life, but lead him to discover in himself a powerful artistic talent.

AN EYE OF THE FLEET

Richard Woodman

Dramatic action off the coast of Spain in Admiral Rodney's
famous Moonlight Battle . . . The capture of the
Santa Teresa . . . A nasty business below deck . . . A
commendation from Kempenfelt . . . Pursuing renegade
American privateers . . . Rebellion on board a prize ship . . .
Playing cat and mouse with *La Creole* . . . A perilous
expedition into the Carolina swamps.

An Eye of the Fleet is the first of the chronicles which chart
Nathaniel Drinkwater's stirring career in the Royal Navy – a
story rich in drama and incident, impeccable in historical
detail, the work of a master storyteller with salt-water in
his veins.

'Dare one muse that he is better than C.S. Forester!'
Irish Times

Other best selling Warner titles available by mail:

☐	Waterfront	Richard Woodman	£5.99
☐	An Eye of the Fleet	Richard Woodman	£5.99
☐	A King's Cutter	Richard Woodman	£5.99
☐	A Brig of War	Richard Woodman	£5.99
☐	The Bomb Vessel	Richard Woodman	£5.99
☐	Ebb Tide	Richard Woodman	£5.99

The prices shown above are correct at time of going to press. However the publishers reserve the right to increase prices on covers from those previously advertised, without further notice.